Praise for David J. Williams

"David J. Williams writes on the finest edge of science fiction. The Autumn Rain novels are driving and relentless, full of rock 'em sock 'em cyber warfare, space commandos, cutthroat politics and one stunning reversal after another. Strap yourself in. These books start fast and never let up."
—JEFF CARLSON, author of *Plague War*

Praise for
THE MIRRORED HEAVENS

"Williams's first novel delivers a powerful, rapid-fire SF adventure/intrigue story with echoes of cyberpunk. This stellar hard SF debut with hopes of sequels belongs in most SF collections."
—*Library Journal*

"Slam-bang action and realpolitik speculations."
—*Sci Fi Weekly*

"A crackling cyberthriller. This is Tom Clancy interfacing Bruce Sterling. David Williams has hacked into the future."
—STEPHEN BAXTER, author of the Manifold series

"*The Mirrored Heavens* is a complex view of global politics in time of crisis. Williams understands that future wars will be fought as much on-line as off. It's also rousing adventure with breathless, non-stop action—Tom Clancy on speed. And you will *not* be able to guess the ending." —NANCY KRESS, author of the Probability trilogy

"Explodes out the gate like a sonic boom and never stops. Adrenaline bleeds from Williams's fingers with every word he hammers into the keyboard. The razors of *The Mirrored Heavens* would eat cyberpunk's old-guard hackers and cowboys as a light snack."
—PETER WATTS, Hugo-nominated author of *Blindsight*

Praise for
THE BURNING SKIES

"[Williams] is standing toe to toe with Richard Morgan at his best."
—Rescued By Nerds

"I loved it! . . . *The Burning Skies* is a great blend of military science fiction and cyberthriller that should appeal to fans of Richard Morgan." —Pat's Fantasy Hotlist, 8 out of 10

"About as perfect of a middle book as you could ask for. . . . [The] perfect mix of physics, technology, and action." —MentatJack

"If any Hollywood producer is reading this please do take up this series and think of it as a cross between *The Matrix*, *Star Wars* and *The Spy Game*. David J. Williams is a terrific writer and his vision is definitely one which is vastly different from what is being currently offered on the SF market scene. His books are the kinds which are truly made for the big screen . . . and with the dramatic ending in *The Burning Skies* . . . you'll be shaking with anticipation for the third book to see how it all ends." —Fantasy Book Critic

BY DAVID J. WILLIAMS

THE AUTUMN RAIN TRILOGY
THE MIRRORED HEAVENS
THE BURNING SKIES
THE MACHINERY OF LIGHT

THE MACHINERY OF LIGHT

THE
MACHINERY
OF LIGHT

DAVID J.
WILLIAMS

 BALLANTINE BOOKS TRADE PAPERBACKS

NEW YORK

The Machinery of Light is a work of fiction. Names, characters, places, and incidents either are the product of the author's imagination or are used fictitiously. Any resemblance to actual persons, living or dead, events, or locales is entirely coincidental.

A Spectra Trade Paperback Original
Copyright © 2010 by David J. Williams

Published in the United States by Spectra, an imprint of The Random House Publishing Group, a division of Random House, Inc., New York.

SPECTRA and the portrayal of a boxed "s" are trademarks of Random House, Inc.

LIBRARY OF CONGRESS CATALOGING-IN-PUBLICATION DATA
Williams, David J.
The machinery of light / David J. Williams.
p. cm.
ISBN 978-0-553-38543-4
1. International relations—Fiction. I. Title.
PS3623.I556495M33 2010
813'.6—dc22
2010010097

Printed in the United States of America

www.ballantinebooks.com

1   2   3   4   5   6   7   8   9

Book design by Carol Malcolm Russo

To the Muses
For carrying me through

CONTENTS

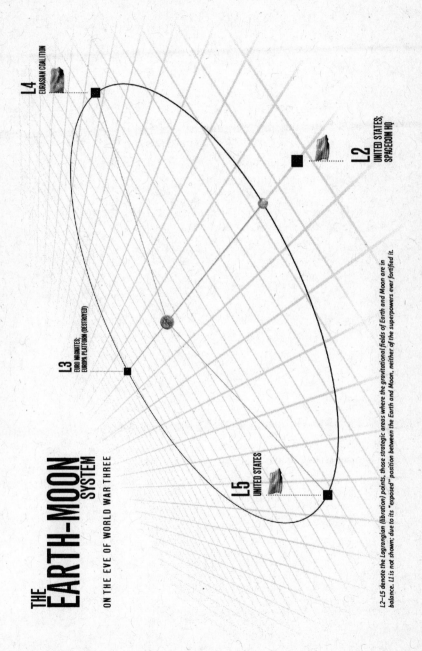

THE EARTH-MOON SYSTEM
ON THE EVE OF WORLD WAR THREE

L4 — EURASIAN COALITION

L2 — UNITED STATES; SPACECOM HQ

L3 — EURO MAGNATES; EUROPA PLATFORM (DESTROYED)

L5 — UNITED STATES

L2–L5 denote the Lagrangian (libration) points, those strategic areas where the gravitational fields of Earth and Moon are in balance. L1 is not shown; due to its "exposed" position between the Earth and Moon, neither of the superpowers ever fortified it.

SKETCHES OF THE AFTER

How then to do justice to such sketches? Start by saying that they were imperfect representations of imperfect things. They were flesh that wants to live reduced to ink or keystrokes—or just to memory ground beneath the mill of time. Yet those images, they might survive that flesh . . . that memory may yet evade the oblivion of eons, become instead the foundation for the tales that flow from old to young to ancient in endless migration across the chains of generation all the way to when the arks of the third planet scatter before the ravaging sun, when the descendants of apes watch the very concept of the years melt in flame behind them. Phrase the words just so, write them just right, and maybe they'll make it that far. Maybe they'll do justice to what really went down: the two twenty-second-century superpowers that watched each other across endless steppes and ocean—that feared and hated each other, that built arsenals that spanned the globe and more, looking down upon our planet from on high in space. *Space*. For even as the radio signals from the first Cold War echoed on the fringes of the Milky Way and sped toward the galaxy's heart—even as the transmissions from Sputnik and Soyuz raced out into the endless parsecs to join forever with those of Gemini and Apollo . . . the spark of conflict that set those vessels in motion flared anew in an hour when our race's promise *and* our race's tragedy surged together in a collision that shattered across the shards of time, leaving in its wake only this poor substitute for the real thing, babbled by a madman long gone on the sheerest midnight, riding astride that which might comprise the story of Autumn Rain, tales of pandemonium and glory, sketches of the after to end all others, liquid words flung down from the sky, absorbing all tears, frozen in the ground for all of winter, yet pregnant with the possibility of coming forth one day someday into eternal spring . . .

THE MACHINERY
OF LIGHT

InfoCom
INTELLIGENCE

22:05 GMT 10.01.2110
FROM: CONTROL
TO: ALL SENIOR HANDLERS
CC: PRESIDENT STEPHANIE MONTROSE

FLASH PRIORITY FLASH PRIORITY FLASH PRIORITY

> **PRESIDENT HARRISON IS DEAD**

> **PRESIDENT MONTROSE HAS ASSUMED COMMAND OF ALL U.S. FORCES**

> **PREEMPTIVE STRIKE AGAINST EURASIAN COALITION UNDERWAY**

While we have every confidence that the integrity of our zone/net infrastructure will be maintained intact during the destruction of the Coalition's military capability, each of you must be prepared to operate in isolation should the eventuality arise. It is therefore necessary to familiarize you with the overall contours of our calculations. Three factors are paramount.

1 *The Eurasian Coalition*: We anticipate that our DE/KE strikes will combine with our superior zone capabilities to deliver rapid and overwhelming advantage against the East. Establishing control of the Moon early will be critical, along with all libration points. In addition, the Coalition itself is just that: a coalition, and this can be turned to our advantage, as substantial fault lines exist between the Russian and Chinese nets, along with much mutual suspicion.

2 *SpaceCom*: The partnership between InfoCom and SpaceCom has been instrumental in Montrose's securing of the presidency/the zone's executive node. That said, we must regard this alliance as temporary at best. All SpaceCom agents within your respective purviews should be monitored in anticipation of eventual termination; orders for this could come at any time, possibly before the cessation of combat with the Eurasians.

3 *Autumn Rain*: As of a few hours ago, the core of this commando group was intact; while their individual situations vary (see attached ANNEX), all should be regarded as highly dangerous. They should be used if possible, but ultimately they must be disposed of. Information on any member of the Rain should immediately be reported to me, pursuant to further instructions. The Rain's spymaster/creator, *Matthew Sinclair*, remains imprisoned at L5, and our agents are currently taking custody of him. However, it is believed that various documents of Sinclair's remain at large; regaining such files is a task of utmost urgency.

RAIN TRIAD (PROTOTYPE):

Carson, Strom (RAZOR-MECH): Now working directly for President Montrose and responsible for recovering the rogue supercomputer *Manilishi*, which has escaped into the Congreve sub-basements beneath the lunar farside. Members of Montrose's own bodyguard corps are accompanying Carson, and if necessary will ensure his liquidation subsequent to the Manilishi's recapture. (It should be noted that Carson was one of the Manilishi's trainers ten years ago, and as such, undoubtedly maintains considerable emotional sway over her.)

Sarmax, Leo (MECH): Partnered with InfoCom razor *Lyle Spencer* to terminate fugitive U.S. handler *Alek Jarvin* and then investigate a Eurasian black-ops base beneath the Himalayas. Nothing has been heard from either Sarmax or Spencer since crossing into Eurasian territory some hours ago. Though Carson is the ostensible "leader" of the Carson-Sarmax-Lynx triad, Sarmax held that role in the years after the unit's initial formulation *(SEE FILE LG-340038AZ)*, when all three men held senior ranks in Praetorian intelligence. Sarmax retired soon after the non-prototype triads went rogue, when his lover—Rain agent *Indigo Velasquez*—joined the rebel Rain units. (We have reports that Velasquez was executed by Sarmax himself, which might explain the isolation/retirement from which he has only now emerged.)

Lynx, Stefan (RAZOR): Led ex-SpaceCom mech *Seb Linehan* in an attempted as-sassination run on SpaceCom commander *Jharek Szilard* at the orders of the now-deceased President Harrison. Since Szilard remains alive, Lynx and Linehan must be presumed dead. The SpaceCom flagship *Montana* is still in lockdown, and no further reports have been received. Whether Szilard is still using that ship as his actual base remains unclear, and we are working to ascertain his exact location.

RAIN TRIADS (NON-PROTOTYPE):

Subsequent to the surgically altered prototype triad, at least ten more triads were developed via genetic acceleration. A significant portion of the Rain perished during their attempted insurrection. The remainder went underground and only recently resurfaced, destroying the Phoenix Elevator and setting in motion the current crisis. It is believed that all remaining members of all remaining triads are now deceased, subsequent to their defeat at the Europa Platform *(SEE FILE LG-340489AZ)*, but we have yet to confirm this.

MANILISHI:

Haskell, Claire (RAZOR): Supercomputer/cyborg capable of running superluminal hacks *(SEE FILE LG-340527AZ)*. Haskell was originally handled/run by Sinclair's handler *Morat*, and maintained a romantic liaison with Rain agent *Jason Marlowe*. Both Morat and Marlowe are believed to be deceased at the hands of Haskell herself, and this history could be exploited when we take custody of the Manilishi. Acquiring control of her is our top priority.

MESSAGE TERMINATES MESSAGE TERMINATES MESSAGE TERMINATES

PART I
INCANDESCE

A woman listens to the world burn.

It's hard to miss. It's on every channel. Reports rendered in toneless staccato, attack sequences confirmed by unseen machines, horrified civilian newscasts that suddenly go silent . . . the woman's jaw hangs loose while her mind surfs the signals reaching the room in which she's riding out the storm, as far away from this craft's hull as possible. Vibrations pound through the walls as energy smashes into the ship from the vacuum beyond. The woman hears shouts as the soldiers in the corridors around her react to the blast-barriers starting to slide shut. She hears the muffled *boom* of each one closing, growing ever closer, the succession of walls parading past her and echoing in the distance.

She's locked into one of the modular sections now, along with ten other guards—and the prisoner in the high-security cell they're guarding. She looks just like the rest of those sentinels, though really she's nothing of the kind. She's not sealed in either; she may be confined behind these doors, but she's still in touch on zone, her razor awareness reaching out to the rest of the ship. Nearly half a klick long, the *Lincoln* sits at the heart of the L5 fleet's defenses, on the libration point itself. The whole fleet turns around it. Beyond that is a sight like nothing ever seen . . .

World War Three began ten seconds ago, with a sudden U.S. attack on the Eurasian Coalition's forces across the Earth-Moon system. A cacophony of light hit the East—and within a second the East hit back with everything it had left. A myriad of guns keep on flaring like there's no tomorrow. For many millions, there won't be. The war to end all wars is underway in style. Way behind the speed-of-light weapons come the kinetics: hundreds of thousands of hypersonic missiles, projectiles, railgun-flung rocks—all of it swimming through space and streaking through atmosphere. And right now most of it's way too slow in the face of massed particle beams and lasers: directed-energy batteries that flail against incoming targets even as they triangulate on one another. On the screens, the woman can see the Earth glowing as portions of the outer atmosphere reach temperatures they really shouldn't. Chunks are coming off the Moon's surface. The room in which she's sitting starts to shake even harder. She hears one of the guards praying—his words audible only inside his helmet, but she's hacked into that helmet, getting off on every fucking word— and every word is just one among so many . . . because now she's honing in on Earth, sifting through the traffic that's getting through the swathe of energy that's bathing the planet. It's so bad she has to take one of the mainline routes in; riding on the command frequencies, she plunges through air that's shimmering with heat, drops deep beneath the Rocky Mountains and into the command bunker within which America's planetside generals are monitoring events.

Those generals are exclusively InfoCom and SpaceCom. All the other ranking officers have been purged, or have sworn to obey the new order. The death of the president has been announced to the armed forces, along with the order to take revenge upon the Eurasian foe whose assassins struck him down in his hour of triumph. There's a new president now, and everyone's getting in line fast. They're too busy dealing with the blizzard of death blazing through the sky to do anything else. But so far the cities in both East and West are being left untargeted. Neither side can afford to bother with them. Both sides are bringing every resource they can to bear upon the challenge of breaking down the def-grids of the other, def-grids largely consisting of DE cannon arrayed in strategic perimeters, shooting at the waves of projectiles heading in toward them. It looks to be the mother of all free-for-alls.

It's anything but. The woman can detect an initial pattern already. The American preemptive strike has drawn blood. The Eurasians are reeling. She's studying the planetside portion of the Eurasian zone now, watching the webwork of nodes that stretch from Romania to Vladivostok, from the wastes of Siberia to the Indian Ocean. She takes in the Eastern def-grids as they struggle to adjust to the onslaught. She's looking for an opening, following the routes she's been instructed to take. Moving beneath the American firewall and through a back door into the neutral territories—into a data warehouse in London, from there to Finland and across the Arctic Circle and through long-lost phone lines beneath the tundra, straight into the Eastern zone . . . straight into Russia. She's never worked the zone like this before. She's running codes that make her virtually unstoppable, swooping in across the steppes, closing upon a target.

The target's a man. He's sitting in the sixth car of a Russian train, several hundred klicks east of the Caspian Sea, going at several thousand klicks an hour: full-out supersonic maglev, heading southeast. The train just went below the surface, and there's palpable relief aboard at getting underground before the rail got pulverized. It looks to be a normal transit train—the last ten cars of the train are packed with equipment, the first ten cars with specialists and staff officers, bound for various bases and various locales. There's nothing aboard that's even remotely atypical.

Except for the man the woman's tracking.

He's one of the staff officers, sitting in a compartment all his own, staring at the wall that's rushing past the window. She can see him quite clearly on the train's vid, but somehow she can't seem to get near him on zone. His codes are too good. She can trace the route they've taken, though. Doesn't surprise her in the slightest that he's come from the very center of Moscow, from cellars deep beneath the Kremlin itself.

And yet he's undercover. No one else aboard this train has the slightest clue he's anything but what his ID says he is: a medium-range gunnery officer, attached to somebody's staff in Burma. But the woman has been told this man is key—has been told she has to watch him closely. She expects she'll find out what that's all about soon enough. In the meantime, she's tracing some signals he's sending—riding alongside them as they flick out ahead of the train, along the rails and through a maze of tunnels, heading beneath the Himalayas, diving down toward the root of the mountains—

Down here there's nothing to see. Nothing to hear. Nothing going on at all. It's just the two of them now, waiting in this room. The lights of zone went off fifteen minutes ago.

"Too long," says Sarmax.

As he speaks, the mech triggers a light in his helmet. His face is two-day stubble and half a century's worth of lines. The only warmth his grey eyes hold is some kind of distant amusement.

"I don't think so," says Spencer.

"Who cares what you think? It's already begun."

"Probably."

"Definitely."

"So why haven't they switched this thing on?"

"I presume," says Sarmax, "that they're waiting for their moment."

THE MACHINERY OF LIGHT   13

Spencer nods. He figures that moment will come soon enough. The two men are deep inside something that was separated from the exterior zone to begin with, machinery that's situated in a mammoth cave beneath several klicks of rock, cut off from the rest of this black base, with all systems shut off as an additional precaution. Because you can never be too careful.

"Failsafe after failsafe," mutters Spencer.

"Hostile razors could be inside already," says Sarmax.

"Imagine that."

"We'll need to keep a close read on the politics when it all lights up."

And that's putting it mildly. The Eurasian Coalition is like two bodies sewn together. There's a reason its zone felt so jury-rigged— why it was so difficult to line up all the operational hierarchies. Spencer's wishing he had paid more attention to them on the way in, before they left the zone behind and reached this compartmentalized microzone deeper in the Earth than he's ever been before. Parts of it were opaque to him even then—the inner enclaves, presumably, but now the entire thing's been turned off, and he's blind. He doesn't like it.

Apparently Sarmax likes it even less. The mech's blind by definition, and it wasn't hard for Spencer to get him to agree to stay here until things clarify. So they've remained in this chamber for the last quarter-hour—just them and the unholy amount of nuclear warheads that line the walls around them.

"What do you think the total count is?" says Sarmax.

"About fifty thousand."

"Gotta be more than that—"

"I'm talking about the ones we've seen," says Spencer.

"I'm asking you to guess about the ones we haven't."

"We're more than a klick deep into this bitch," says Spencer. "How the fuck am I supposed to guess—"

But that's when he feels something clutch at his mind—

• • •

And retract. Sitting here at L5, she can't reach that deep. She knows someone's down there, though. Right now that's all she needs to know. She hauls her mind back to the borders of the zone—lets herself slot through that zone, out of the Himalayas, out beneath China—and back into the U.S. zone, back out into space. Earth is getting closed off to her now anyway. The carpet of directed energy has become too thick. It's all interference now—all satellites spitting light and plasma at one another in a web that's starting to look almost solid. Earth's upper atmosphere blooms incandescent. The lower orbits are a chaos of wreckage.

It's only slightly cleaner higher up. There's more space, though, and so far both sides are maintaining the integrity of their positions. The woman routes her signal through the American flagship *Roosevelt*, in the center of the perimeters at the American geosynchronous orbits. From their ramparts, she looks back upon the Earth . . . and either the air down near the surface is shimmering too, or else the oceans are starting to boil. Maybe both. But the overall picture in the *Roosevelt*'s battle-management computers is clear: the terrestrial Eurasian grids can't withstand much more of the battering they're taking. The woman sets various codes to work aboard the *Roosevelt*; she shrinks the Earth in her purview, and collapses back upon the *Lincoln* and her own body in the room somewhere near its center, her mind taking in the duel that's raging between the American fleet at L5 and the larger Eurasian one at L4. They're going at each other hammer and tongs, feeding in all reserve power, generators cranking and solar panels sucking in every drop of the Sun that washes across them so they can surge that much more energy into their guns. The shaking in the room the woman's in has gotten so bad it's like she's in the throes of an earthquake. Her visor's vibrating right in front of her. But she's not worried. She won't die. That's what the prisoner told her. He explained to her the reasons why, and they were utterly persuasive. She's staring at him now, on a screen that looks in on a room scarcely ten meters away, separated from her by still more locks. She's the nearest human being to that room.

Or she would be, were she human.

She certainly looks it. Same way she *looks* like a guard. She's more of a guardian, and she worships the man who's not really a man and certainly not a prisoner—worships him with all her heart. Nor is her worship based on something so narrow as faith. It's based on what he's told her—on what he's shown her. Before he was arrested as a traitor and taken to this place he's in now; before she even knew the full extent of where this was all going— back when he told her that she'd come to a room someday and sit there and watch him take in the universe, both of them hiding in plain sight at the heart of all networks, observing everything un-fold. The war's almost a minute old, and it's looking better by the second for the Americans—and almost perfect for their positions arrayed around the Moon. The extreme flanks of the L2 fleet are starting to scramble from their positions behind that rock, com-mencing runs that are clearly intended to get the drop on the Eurasian lunar positions. They're flinging out directed energy while they're at it, bouncing beams off the mirror-sats strung in orbit around the Moon for just this purpose, impacting the Eurasian ground-to-space artillery dug in along the nearside.

Which surprises the woman. She would have thought that the L2 fleet would have joined with L5's guns to catch the Eurasian L4 fortresses in a crossfire. But it looks like the American high com-mand has elected to allow the duel between L4 and L5 to continue to play out. It's not what the prisoner told her he expected. She wonders at that, wonders if he was deliberately misleading her, wonders if he's engaged in unseen battles of his own. But she sees the logic in the American move. They're gambling that they can shut down the Eurasian forces on the Moon before the L4 guns break through L5's defenses. So now she focuses on the Moon; her vantage point at L5 gives her a partial look at the farside—but she needs more than that. She routes herself through to the farside's center—Congreve, the main American base there—whips past its dome, drops through the city and into its basements and on into the sub-basements. The traffic is thinning out along with the

wires, but she keeps on threading deeper all the same, honing in on
the activity that she's detecting. Some kind of chase is in progress.
She's almost at the limits of the sub-basements now, at the edge of
the natural tunnels that honeycomb so much of the Moon—lava
tubes that bubbled through ancient magma, some of them rigged
with zone and used for mining, so many left unexplored even to
this day. The woman drops in around the pursuers. An elite
InfoCom squad . . . and she can't see what it's pursuing. She
doesn't need to. All she needs to do is hack in and do what she does
best.

Listen.

Somewhere deeper down, Claire Haskell is listening too.
Not that it's doing her much good. The team that's
hunting her is composed of experienced trackers. They're
locked into a tightbeam mesh less than half a klick back, trailing in
her zone-wake via some machination of the one who's leading
them. Haskell can practically *feel* that man who's pulling the
strings—his mental signature a blend of detachment and anticipation that makes her shudder. She feels like she should shut down
all her ties with zone, but knows that if she did, they'd be on her
even quicker. So she's just trying to go that much faster, her suit's
camos working overtime as she drops through shafts, races down
stairways, trying to calibrate her position against the maps she's
got—trying to put distance between her and the surface where
Armageddon keeps on raging. Zone's camera-images flare on her
screens; she takes stock of the carnage as she probes for the
American command nodes. High above her, in the L2 fleet, she can
see that a portion of the zone within the flagship *Montana* has been
shut down—presumably to keep out pesky razors—she flits from
there back down to Montrose's command center beneath Korolev
crater, west of Congreve. She can't get in there either, but she can
see the commands blasting out from within. The American attack

intensifies across the Earth-Moon system, probing relentlessly for Eurasian weakness while Haskell keeps on racing deeper into rock.

O n screens within his head, a man orchestrates the pursuit. The Operative is several levels up, but he's got the target right where he wants her. The target he's been pursuing all his life, though he's only just waking up to that fact. She isn't going to escape, though he knows damn well that's not going to stop her from trying. That's why she's the Manilishi— the foremost razor in existence, off-the-charts battle management capabilities merely the tip of the iceberg. That's why he needs her—to get her involved in the showdown with the East.

But first he has to catch her.

"Sir?"

The Operative looks at the bodyguard.

"Sir, the president wants an update."

And for just the briefest of moments the Operative thinks the bodyguard's talking about Andrew Harrison. The man who ruled the United States for more than twenty years before he was shot dead by the Operative about twenty minutes ago. There's a brand-new boss now—the one who orchestrated the death of the old one and blamed the whole thing on the Eurasians. She's on the line, and the Operative can guess what she wants to talk about.

"Put her through," he says.

"Carson." The voice of Stephanie Montrose is clipped, terse. There's a lot of background noise. Her image is fuzzy. She's clearly looking into a live feed rather than using a cranial implant. The Operative clears his throat.

"Madam President," he says.

Static. Then: "Carson. Can you hear me?"

"I can."

"Do you have her?"

"Not yet."

"What's taking so long?"

"What's taking so long is that she's hell on wheels."

Montrose says nothing. "How's it looking up there?" the Operative adds.

"We're winning."

"But not yet won."

"Is that sarcasm?"

"Just the facts," says the Operative.

"Spare me," snaps Montrose. "Their def-grids are collapsing. Their cities lie helpless before us."

"I don't believe in counting chickens."

"What the hell is that supposed to mean?"

"The Eurasians may have some tricks up their sleeves."

Her hawklike face looks at him almost curiously. "Do you know that for a fact?"

"Not even vaguely."

"So leave the contingency planning to me." Montrose shifts her head; the Operative gets a glimpse of the war room behind her: rows of screens and consoles, analysts pacing through narrow passages between them. "What the East is facing is the heaviest zone-attack ever mounted. Whatever last-ditch games they want to play can't matter. I'll rule the Earth-Moon system within the hour."

"You and Szilard."

"Again, I detect sarcasm."

"And again, I plead innocence."

"Szilard doesn't have the executive node software," says Montrose. "He's the junior partner."

"And what am I?"

"If you deliver Haskell, you're whatever you want to be."

"I want Mars," says the Operative.

"You'll have it," replies Montrose.

"Roll it up as a U.S. protectorate, make me protector?"

"Done upon the peace. Now bring the Manilishi back to me—alive *or* dead."

He stares at her.

"Believe me," she says, "I'd love to plug the bitch into my battle-management grid just to watch the sparks fly. But it's no longer a requirement. Our forces are carrying all before them. All I need's her body—one way or another."

"Understood."

"Report in as soon as possible."

The Operative cuts off the comlink. He looks at the three body-guards that Montrose has assigned to be in his presence at all times. Their visors stare back at him impassively. He knows they've been assigned to kill him under certain conditions. He'd love to know precisely which ones. He lets screens snap on within him that show him the next two klicks of underground chambers—show him, too, the cloud of probabilities that denote the best guess as to Haskell's position, now slashing out past the left flank of the trackers. The InfoCom razors recalibrate. The mechs move onto the outer boundary of Haskell's position.

Montrose's eyes flick away from the screen, return to flitting through a hundred others. Battle readouts parade in rapid-fire fashion before her, but they're just the summaries of summaries. The war room around her is processing more information per second than the entire twentieth century produced. Most of the actual targeting is being handled by computers; at a tactical level, the situation's moving far too quickly for humans to get involved, though razors are continually optimizing the targeting sequences and making overrides as necessary to the prioritization algorithms. But most of the human involvement is occurring at more strategic levels, some of it at the most strategic level of all—and now a new light's flashing. Montrose's aide-de-camp coughs discreetly as he steps up behind her.

"Admiral Szilard," he whispers.

"Put him through," says Montrose as she wipes the annoyed

expression from her face. The face of the SpaceCom commander appears on a screen before her, looking nothing if not sardonic.

"Stephanie," he says.

For a moment she's tempted to insist he call her *Madam President*. But she's come too far in life to get tripped up by formalities. Particularly when the man she's facing is one of the few factors she doesn't have full control of in a situation that's otherwise going her way.

"Jharek," she says smoothly. "What's the situation?"

"Funny," he says, "that's why I was calling you."

She knows they don't need such preliminaries. But somehow they're still playing this game. Same one they've been playing since they were both pretending to be loyal servants of Andrew Harrison. Same indirectness as always, born of dealing through back-channels and intermediaries. Didn't stop her and Szilard from mapping this whole thing out—from figuring out that the only way to deal with the president was to combine their strength and take him from both directions: lure him into concentrating on SpaceCom, lull him into thinking InfoCom was something he could trust. Or rather, use—and in reality Montrose was the one using him. She seduced the president, and she did it in more ways than one. Because Stephanie Montrose isn't wired like most people are. She thinks at angles to everybody. That's how she climbed to the top of Information Command by the age of thirty-eight. Now she's forty-nine, one of the youngest presidents in American history, and she thinks she might just have found a way to rule forever. She stares at the head of Space Command—the man they call the Lizard—looks into his eyes and smiles her most winning smile.

"We're winning," she says.

"I noticed," he replies.

There's no way he couldn't have. Not with the fattest wireless pipeline ever configured linking her base with his flagship. Behind Szilard she can see the bridge of the *Montana*—an HQ that looks to be every bit as extensive as her own. She takes in the screens that are visible, isn't surprised to see that the SpaceCom camera that's capturing the feed is systematically blurring the images of the readouts. She knows full well that what she's got with Szilard is an uneasy partnership. She wonders for how long it's going to be sustainable. She's knows a lot of that depends on what they're talking about now.

"The Manilishi," he says.

"Ah," she says.

"Do you have her?"

"Didn't I tell you I'd call you when I did?"

"I figured it couldn't hurt to know the exact status."

"We're working on it."

"Where is she?"

"We've got her cornered in the Congreve sub-basements."

"I heard she's gotten a little farther than that."

Which isn't what she wants to hear. Szilard shouldn't have access to that kind of data. Then again, he's had years to put his agents all over Congreve and everything beneath it. The farside may be the only thing that's out of the direct line of sight of the largest Eurasian guns, but it's also SpaceCom territory. And Congreve is even more so. That's why she's several hundred kilometers away, in a bunker whose construction she supervised covertly for years and which has only just been switched on. Nobody save InfoCom personnel are getting anywhere near her. Still, she can't help but feel that Szilard is way too close right now.

"She'll be in custody shortly," she says.

"And then?"

"We've already discussed that."

"And I've been thinking some more about it."

"Think all you like. She remains with me."

"You've already got the executive node."

"Because I'm president."

"And I need to remain admiral of the fleet."

"You can do that without the Manilishi."

"Sure, but—"

"What are you proposing, Jharek?"

"Joint control."

"Out of the question."

"Or bring her up to the *Montana*."

"The *where?*"

"You heard me. My flagship."

"You must be joking."

"I have trouble doing that," says Szilard. "Look, the farside's not safe."

"It's as safe as anything we've got."

"The East is *right there*, Stephanie. They're still holding out at Tsiolkovskiy crater—"

"Not exactly next door, Jharek"—her voice raised enough that nearby analysts dart covert looks her way. "And how is taking her to the *Montana* in any way consonant with joint control?"

"Doesn't have to be the *Montana*," he says evenly.

"Doesn't have to be anywhere in the L2 fleet," she says. "Haskell's a bona fide superweapon. Why the hell would we put her on a spaceship while combat's underway?"

"You think my position up here is exposed?"

She doesn't answer. She knows what's really going on here. They're winning so quickly that Szilard has already started trying to define the postwar order. Meaning she might just have to start moving up her plans. Szilard clears his throat.

"Let me try to put you at ease," he says. "SpaceCom's built on the reversal of appearance. What might look like vulnerable tin cans are actually the high ground. There couldn't be a more secure place to keep Haskell—"

"So why not L5?"

"Pardon?"

"We both know L2's yours. L5's a little more *even*. Once the war is over, we can move her there."

"To where Sinclair's in custody? I'm not sure putting her anywhere near her former boss is—"

"Interrogating them together may be the best way to crack them both."

"He may not be crackable. Harrison failed to—"

"So he failed," she says. "No reason we have to."

"So you'll move Haskell?"

"How about you let me catch her first?"

On the outside trying to get in: and just out of reach—Lynx can see the main data conduit that's been set up between the InfoCom and SpaceCom leadership—can see it, but can't get in. Which is too bad, because if he could crack the inner enclave, he might be able to figure a way out of this fucking place. He's still stuck in the shafts of the *Montana*. He's been crawling through Szilard's flagship in the wake of his disastrous attempt on Szilard's life, running low-grade hacks to keep the local wildlife in check, but unable to get much of a vantage point beyond that . . . until he got a break, stumbling upon a nest of wires that turns out to be the backup lines for some of the systems on the bridge. He's been in those wires for the last five minutes, using them to finally broaden his scope beyond this slice of the *Montana*. The Earth-Moon system is in chaos. He's relishing the sight.

The fact that SpaceCom marines are closing in on his position is a different story. He's got a glimpse into the views maintained by the *Montana*'s garrison—can see they've blocked off all the entrances to the shaft-complex he's in and set up checkpoints, all facing toward him. A move that makes no sense unless it's accompanied by another. Even though he can't see it, he knows it beyond a shadow of a doubt: the hunters have entered this section of the shafts. He can practically feel the hands reaching out for his neck.

But he stays where he is, uploading for the next thirty seconds, siphoning as much information from the comps as he can. He figures he's going to need it—figures you never know what might come in useful, knows he'll have only a few minutes to find a way to put it to use. He feels data fill him, rise up within him until he's brimming with practically nothing else. He gets ready to start running.

The Earth shakes as they streak beneath it. It's clearly only a matter of time before the tunnel collapses around them. They're way too close to the surface. Presumably that's why this train's engineers are pouring on the speed, racing for the junctions that will get them to the one place they need to be.

Deeper.

The man eyes the car around him. Nobody is above the rank of colonel. The man's only a major, but he's got pull that goes a little beyond that. Yet right now he's in the same boat as the rest of them—just Russian officers trying to make their luck go a little further, just soldiers all too glad they got assigned to this train and not the one behind it. There's nothing back there now. The def-grids are crumbling. American hypersonic missiles are starting to smack into bases in the steppe above them. The train accelerates still further.

Is something wrong?" says Sarmax.

"I'm fine," says Spencer.

"No you're not."

"No?"

"You just felt something grab at your mind, right?"

Spencer blinks. "You too, huh?"

"How much did you feel?" asks Sarmax.

"Just the hint of something."

"Could you see who?"

"No idea."

Not that he has much experience with stuff this weird. He was hooked up to the Manilishi during the run-in, via some kind of telepathy that was enabled surgically and had something to do with his zone interfaces. He has no idea as to the exact procedure—has no idea as to what this is really all about. Which is why he's getting so desperate for some answers.

"You and Lynx and Carson," he says.

"What about us?" replies Sarmax.

"You guys could only *sense* one another. You couldn't read one anothers' thoughts."

"Is that a statement or a question?"

"Just answer it."

"Told you already: only ones who could do that were the *real* Rain. Not us pipsqueak prototypes. The three of us were just modi-fied flesh, Spencer—just the goddamn *precursors*. The main team, they were the ones who had it all together."

"Except they didn't," says Spencer.

"Not without the Manilishi, no."

"She was supposed to be the linchpin of the whole thing."

"She still *is* the linchpin."

"Even though the Rain are finished?"

"You really think so?"

"I thought Haskell wiped them all—"

"All, *nothing*. Riddle me this, moron: if the Rain are finished, what the fuck was that yanking on our goddamn brains?"

"I was assuming it was Haskell."

Sarmax looks at him strangely. "Could you tell if it was fe-male?"

"No," says Spencer.

"You couldn't tell anything at all?"

"What are you getting at?"

"I'm trying to figure out who it was."

Spencer regards Sarmax curiously. "Right. I keep forgetting you *knew* them."

"Trained them, sure." Sarmax shifts the subject. "Look, there's more than meets the eye here. I was a wet-ops specialist of twenty years when they put me out for forty-eight hours and woke me up with the news that I was the new breed. I asked what the fuck that meant. They said, you'll see. And they were right. You just *act*. You make all the right choices, and you know that the other members of the team are making theirs—you just *know* it. And when you strike, you don't hesitate. And *everybody* hesitates. Even if they don't know it. Even for a fraction of a second. But not when you're Rain. You get the shot off quicker, and you never miss. You—"

"Carson told me something—"

"Carson told *you* something?"

"On the way back to Earth. He said the Rain are more than just killers. They're takeover artists."

"Sure. Would have thought that was obvious by now."

"He said it was an instinct for them."

"Sure. We were taught to seek heights. We *sense* heights."

"What the fuck is that supposed to mean?"

"Not sure I can explain. Call it intuition."

"Lot of it running around these days," says Spencer.

"If you're talking about the Manilishi, you can forget it. She's on a whole different level, man. She hacks the light fantastic so hard she's forced them to invent whole new classifications of razor ability. I've got a feeling that if she'd ever been plugged into the rest of the Rain, we'd be dealing with a lot more than mind reading." Sarmax pauses. "Where are you going with all this anyway?"

"Trying to get a line on the handler's file," says Spencer.

"The book."

"Yeah, the book."

"Any luck?"

"Not with the part that counts."

The thing that's been turning in Spencer's head contains three. The first is the location of the base they've penetrated. The second is the nature of the Eurasian secret weapon they're inside. Both of those have now been cracked. Neither holds a candle to the third part: the final section of the pages scrawled in languages the last American agent in Hong Kong invented for the sole purpose of better hiding the secrets that had driven him mad. Secrets he committed to the most archaic medium of them all, the only one that's safe from zone . . . paper. A whole book's worth, and now it's been burned, but not before it was photographed and uploaded by the men who killed him—Spencer and Sarmax—who were even more desperate than the handler was, and who can't afford to take the precautions he'd been taking. Spencer mulls it all over once again. He exhales slowly.

"It's definitely what we're after," he says.

"Rain," says Sarmax.

"Yeah. I've been able to suss out the section headings, made some inroads on the rest of it. I've figured out its source."

"Its *source?*"

"Its author."

"You mean the handler? Jarvin?"

"I mean who he stole it from."

"Oh."

"Oh. We're talking about the *key files,* Leo. Precise records of the Autumn Rain experiments, right? Sinclair had to keep track of it somehow. And somehow his onetime handler went and got himself a copy."

"An *alleged* copy."

"Sure. May be a fake. But I doubt it."

"Because?"

"Because I think it really *did* do something to his mind."

Sarmax starts to reply—and stops as a faint noise filters in from several rooms above . . . followed by an unmistakable *creak* as a hatch swings open. There's the sound of boots coming down a ladder.

"The access shafts," says Spencer.

"We need to make ourselves scarce."

Claire Haskell keeps on running, pursuit hot on her trail, and she's ever more certain that Carson's leading that pursuit—that Montrose hasn't had him liquidated for failing to capture her. Or just liquidated on general principles: because Haskell knows damn well what Carson is doing working for Stephanie Montrose. She wonders if Montrose knows too—wonders if Montrose has used her possession of the executive node to build up some means to protect herself from the world's most dangerous assassin.

But mostly Haskell's wondering about the door she's about to reach. It leads to a shaft she'd really like to get to. One she's pretty sure isn't known to Montrose. She wonders if it's known to Carson. It's barely known to her—even with her maps, it's not easy to find. That's because it's hidden in the bottom of an empty water pipe, looking like part of the wall within. She traces her hand along the frame—finds a switch and hits it.

Nothing happens.

The door's not opening. She hits it again. Same result.

She tries to hack the systems of the door, but she can't even find a zone beyond it. She's getting frantic now. Because she can feel the pursuit coming in behind her, moving in to cut her off.

And suddenly she gets it—a flash of insight or just some leering thought of his flung through rock for her reception: Carson knows about this door for sure—knows it's a way to the *really* deep shafts—and that's why she's just managed to get herself trapped against it. He knows damn well that she can't get through it. The codes she has are wrong. Or maybe they just got changed. Doesn't matter. All that matters is that she can't get through. And that the hunters are approaching along vectors that leave her with no way to get beyond them, back into the base's larger sprawl. She turns away from the door—

And looks longingly back. For one moment, it's as though Jason Marlowe himself is on the other side. Her dead lover—she wants to get through that badly. She contemplates using explosives against the portal, but figures that this door was designed to withstand anything up to a nuke. So she tears herself away, turns around, and starts climbing up the side of pipe, back into a passageway, taking stock all the while of the noose that's tightening around her.

The Operative watches his readouts as they show the margin of error vanishing. It's all over. Haskell's officially fucked, regardless of which zone-signature she's hiding behind. The probabilities are dwindling to the point where all her potential routes intersect with one of his formation's flanks. And those flanks are sweeping together like jaws . . .

He figured she'd take the route she did. It was predictable enough. He knows how Haskell thinks. After all, he was there when she started thinking. He intends to be there at the end too. Which can't be far away. He hopes it will be quick. He lets the contours of the war that's blazing overhead waft through him as he moves forward, bodyguards closing up behind him, following in the wake of his suit's thrusters.

Find the traitor.
   Find the fucking traitor and rip out his fucking heart. Tear his flesh to bits. Gobble his flesh right off the floor. Fucking *eat* him.
   Find the traitor.
   But other than that, there's not much in the way of thought. There's just a set of nerve-reflexes honed to professional levels and looking for a target. Because somewhere in this spaceship there's a traitor. And loyal SpaceCom soldiers are looking for that traitor. Loyal soldiers just like—
   "Linehan."
   Linehan looks around. But there's no one there. Just more of

this shaft that he's been crawling through, more of the endless innards of the *Montana*. The sights of his suit's guns triangulate on
the walls up ahead, but they're not picking up anything that even
passes for a target . . .

"Linehan."

It sounds like it's right inside his skull. It sounds familiar—like
someone Linehan used to know. Someone who knows more about
Linehan than maybe even he himself does. Someone who's become a trait—

"Show yourself," says Linehan.

"Why?"

"So I can kill you."

"I don't think so," says Stefan Lynx.

"You're marked for execution."

"So I've heard."

"You've betrayed Admiral Szilard."

"I didn't *betray* anybody, jackass."

"You were—"

"Trying to get control of his whole fleet."

"Because you're Autumn Rain."

"The original, baby."

"You tried to use me to kill the admiral but your buddy Carson
backstabbed you."

"Maybe."

"Definitely. You're a traitor."

"Whatever," says Lynx. "I know what you're thinking."

"Yeah?"

"That if you can keep me talking long enough your armor can
trace me."

"So far it's working."

"But here's the thing you should be wondering: why the hell
haven't you informed the SpaceCom razor you've been paired with
that you've been chatting with me?"

"What?"

"The SpaceCom razor. The guy who Szilard said go run point in the jungle for. Few score meters back in the shaft behind you, right? I'm sure that guy's at least a captain. Must be some hotshot razor."

"He's tracking you—"

"And he hasn't found me. So why the hell haven't you told him that the traitor's on the line?"

"You're . . . fucking with my zone-signal . . . my software—"

"Sure I am. But tell me why you haven't even *tried* to get him on the fucking line!"

"I . . . don't know. I—"

"I'll tell you why. Because you're dickless. Because I'm the fucking Cheshire cat and I've sent you my smile to tell you to wake the fuck up. Szilard's already sold you out."

"I—what are you talking about?"

"Jesus Christ! Do you leave your brain at the door when you check into Hotel SpaceCom? Did Szilard take out your fucking batteries? Come on, man: the Lizard's gonna purge you tonight."

"Prove it."

"Watch this."

A bruptly, the train starts slowing. Rocky walls outside the windows become visible as more than just something flickering by. The train keeps on braking, slows even further, hisses to a halt.

But it's clear all hell is still breaking loose outside. Vibrations keep on rocking through the floor. Apparently the Americans are pressing home their advantage. Everyone's looking at one another—except the major who's looking at nothing in particular, save for the readouts in his own head, affording him a vantage that's more advantaged than anyone else in the car. He exhales slowly—stands up, straightens out his uniform, and starts heading toward the door to the next car.

"The rats are leaving the ship," says someone.

"We're supposed to stay *here*," says someone else.

"So stay," says the major. The car door opens and he goes through as it slides shut behind him. He triggers override codes, locks it shut. He's in a freight car now—he makes his way through the narrow passage between the metal crates. He moves into the next freight car, and then the next.

Two more cars, and he's arrived at a door that's different than the ones he's been through. It looks to be a great deal thicker. It's still no match for his codes. It slides open, and he walks on through into the train's cockpit. The driver and engineer whirl toward him, their expressions just short of priceless.

Spencer and Sarmax get busy getting moving, through the trapdoor in the floor and down into the rooms beneath them. Those rooms are just as packed with nukes as the ones they left. They contain trapdoors that lead to shafts that lead to—

"Fuck," says Sarmax.

"We really shouldn't go in there," says Spencer.

"Not unless we're feeling lucky."

Or just really stupid. The shafts below this point aren't intended for humans. Just nukes, getting slotted through at high speed. Meaning that—

"We're trapped."

"Maybe," says Spencer.

"How many routes are there out of here?"

Depends how you count. The zone's still down, but Spencer got enough of a glimpse of this area before the lights went out to be able to map it out: a series of interlocking rooms, all of them packed with the fissile material that's both cargo and fuel. Spencer's trying to calibrate these rooms against the larger superstructure of the thing they're in, trying to make some calculations that are really just educated guesses. He's got no time for anything else.

"This way," he says, and starts moving through doors that lead to yet more of these rooms that are starting to drive him crazy. He wonders why the Eurasians didn't just build one big storage chamber. He knows the answer even as he thinks the question, that it's a matter of contingencies. The nukes themselves are failsafed. But if one of the warheads went off in here anyway, no precaution would matter. Yet the hi-ex trigger mechanism that's fastened to each warhead is a different story. If those started to detonate accidentally, they could do some serious chain-reaction damage unless they were contained. So each room is the equivalent of a bunker. And he and Sarmax have reached the one they've been making for.

"This is it," says Spencer.

"This is what?"

"Where we get off."

"What?"

"Well, these nukes weren't just carried down ladders."

"Ah," says Sarmax.

Because the truth is that these rooms don't add up. Stack them up against one another, and there's some empty space that runs through the center of them: space around which they're all clustered.

"The *spine*," says Sarmax.

"Now we just need to get in there," says Spencer.

"Easy enough," says Sarmax, turning to the wall—

Haskell's thinking that the best way out of this one is to play it cool. She's ghosting the passages, coasting past the sentinels, watching the back doors of her own mind. She knows that Carson has the keys to at least one of them. She's hoping she's got the keys to turn those keys against him. She heads up a ladder, through a doorway that opens without even knowing it's been opened. She's getting in behind the foremost of the InfoCom razors, letting them move ahead of her, running down one of her decoys. She's tempted to go for Carson himself. But she decides not to press her luck. Particularly as maybe Carson's luring her in toward him. She crawls on past . . .

And fires her suit-jets. Now it's a sprint. Her zone-bombs detonate behind her; two of the InfoCom razors go down writhing— her mind darts on through the gap they've left, and then her body follows. Power-suited mechs are firing in all directions, causing chaos. She feels Carson move to shore things up, but she's not sticking around to see the results; she ducks into a freight-chute, hurtles upward. Moments later, she's emerging—a quarter-klick farther away. She's broken through Carson's perimeter, doubling back toward Congreve.

Only to find another InfoCom force bearing down on her.

Too late, she sees the nature of the real trap. The luxury of numbers: Carson has had a second team of razors and mechs out there, sitting lights-out and waiting for just this kind of breakout. Even so, she's faster than they thought. But now they're hot on her heels. She blasts through storage chambers, moves past some of the directed-energy power generators. Wiring connects them to the guns spitting on the surface—and Haskell's just stealing past them, through a maintenance shaft, dropping into the chamber she's been headed toward.

The train that stretches through the room sits on rails that are part of the deep-grids: the sublunar rail network that connects the U.S. farside bases and that extends all the way to the lunar nearside. But all Haskell wants to do now is stay ahead of the InfoCom forces that are scarcely half a klick back. She steps inside the train's first car. There are seven others. All bear the moon-and-eagle SpaceCom standard. All look empty, but she's not about to make any assumptions. Doors hiss shut behind her. She places herself against a seat as the train accelerates. Walls rush by, so fast they look like they're buckling.

She starts. They *are* buckling. She's being hit by seismic tremors. The train's coming off the rails. She's applying the brakes, even though she knows that's not going to matter—because somewhere behind her a mammoth explosion's in the process of smashing the tunnel ceiling into the floor. She decouples the first car, fires its emergency rockets, runs them through sequences that her mind's improvising against the fractal edge of raw moment. She's crashing all the same. The cars behind hers disintegrate as she decelerates. Her own car's ceiling folds away from her as she grinds toward a halt. Car walls tear away on either side of her.

She looks around, tests her limbs, tests her mind. Her suit's still intact. So is she. She leaps out, starts scanning.

The tunnel's definitely collapsed farther back. If the blast was on the surface, then it was nothing short of colossal. She wonders if the tide just turned against the United States. But the tunnel up ahead still looks clear.

So she turns, hits her suit's thrusters even as she intensifies her hack on the train's line. Rail whips past her as she reaches out to the U.S. zone somewhere ahead of her. She can't find it.

And then she realizes why.

I need full data," snarls the Operative. "Triangulate, give me readings."

He's managed to restore some order to his squad. The InfoCom mechs take up defensive positions as the surviving razors mesh, triangulate. Data foams back toward the Operative.

"Fuck," he says.

There are way too many variables to determine the exact nature of the blast that just shook this area. But the Operative can figure out enough on his own. He no longer has a link to the surface—or even back to Congreve's basements. Something nasty has almost certainly happened to the largest American farside base. Calculations race through his head. One of the razors comes on the line.

"Sir, we're narrowing down the blast. Epicenter at"—he rattles off coordinates.

One of the screens that's surging static suddenly coalesces. The face of Stephanie Montrose regards him. For the first time, it shows concern.

"Carson. You're still alive. Thank God—"

"Looks like you're doing okay yourself."

"We've got a Eurasian incursion into the Congreve vicinity."

"Where?"

"Northwest sector ZJ-3."

"That's right on top of me."

"That's why I'm calling."

"How the hell did they get in? Their nearest base is—"

"Apparently they've been doing some digging. In anticipation of war. Like the North Koreans used to do back in their DMZ before the entire peninsula—"

"They might just have bagged the Manilishi."

"I was afraid you were going to say that," says Montrose.

"Got any heavy equipment I can use?"

"I'm scrambling everything now."

"Great."

"Get in there, Carson. This is your moment. Your time. Not just Mars. Everything beyond that."

"Over and out," he says.

His visor's right up against his face, and on the other side of that plastic are the walls of the shafts of the SpaceCom flagship *Montana*. But it's something even closer that's at stake now. Right inside Linehan's head, where another voice has just joined in.

"Line of sight," says that voice, and then Linehan sees it, at the intersection up ahead—the suit of the SpaceCom razor who's got his mind on the leash around his neck. He's informing Linehan that he's now passing into the mech's visual field. A standard protocol.

But what's not so standard are the shots that Linehan is getting off: two quick minibursts, one slicing through the razor's wireless antennae, the other perforating his armor with heated rounds. Pieces of bone and suit fly.

Just as another suit leaps down next to Linehan. And through the visor he can see that face: silver hair and ebony skin and a mouth that just can't stop laughing—

"Hiya," says Lynx.

"You fucking *bastard*," says Linehan.

"Is that how you thank the man who's reversed the conditioning Szilard skullfucked you with?"

"*That* is," says Linehan, gesticulating at the mess drifting farther down the corridor.

"Nice work," says Lynx.

"So now I work for you?"

"I wish I could do that kind of conditioning on the fly." Lynx grins. "Actually now you're working for *you*."

"Say what?"

"Man's been so long in the cage he can't even recognize the light of freedom! Better get out there and grab it before—"

"So I could just kill you right now?"

"You could try," says Lynx. "But I don't think you want—"

"I'm going to rip your suit apart."

"Do you realize how many times I've heard that?"

"This'll be the last," says Linehan—grabs Lynx, shoves him against the wall even as Lynx keeps talking:

"But don't you want to hear what I was about to tell you about Szilard fucking you over?"

Linehan pauses. Lynx laughs.

"You forgot all about that, didn't you?"

"I—uh—how come?"

"Because you were having too much fun killing that razor?"

"You *are* controlling me."

"And it'd be a lot easier if you stopped fighting it. Look, man, Szilard's got you marked. Think about it. Because even by today's standards, your history's pretty checkered."

Linehan lets go of Lynx. Confusion swirls through his head . . .

"So let me see if I've got it straight," continues Lynx. "You started out as SpaceCom and then got tracked by Autumn Rain and drenched in old-school drugs and turned by InfoCom, after which you got suborned to the president and then I took you over as part of the rump committee of Autumn Rain and brought you into a hit on Szilard in an attempt to take over the entire—"

He stops. Linehan's staring at him blankly.

"Do you remember *any* of this?"

"I—uh—some of it—but—"

"But here's the thing you've got to ask yourself: even if Szilard has found a temporary use for you while he's busy winning World War Three, do you really think he plans to keep you around?"

"I'll cross that bridge when I come to it."

"Well, let me be the first to welcome you to it: he's about to blow the whole *Montana*."

"This *ship*?"

"No, the fucking state. Big Sky Country's gonna get it *good*." Lynx slaps Linehan's visor. "Yeah, dumb-ass, this fucking ship!"

"To get at *me*?"

"Don't be so full of yourself."

"But what about Szilard?" asks Linehan.

"What about him?"

"Isn't he on this ship too?"

"Only if you jump to conclusions."

Russian trains have names. This one's called *Mother Volga*. Its cab is a tight fit under the best of circumstances. Which these most certainly aren't.

"What the hell are you doing here?" asks the engineer.

"Giving the orders," says the major, drawing a gun.

"Works for us," says the driver.

They clearly aren't looking for trouble. They've managed to find it anyway. They're obviously going to do whatever he tells them. Some things might cause them to hesitate. But not enough to try anybody's patience.

"I need you to get us moving again."

"The line's blocked up ahead," says the driver.

"Congestion," says the engineer. "It's sheer chaos. Everyone and their dog are trying to get the hell—"

"They'll clear the line," says the man.

"They will?"

"When you transmit these codes."

Sarmax activates his suit's laser and starts burning his way through the wall.

"Are you nuts?" asks Spencer.

"What's your problem?"

"They'll be able to see we were here."

"If they end up in this room, sure."

"Look, Leo, there's obviously a door here somewhere."

"Sure, but we don't have time to find it."

"How about giving me a chance to look?"

"How about getting the hell out of my way?"

Sarmax intensifies the beam, lets metal liquefy as he traces an incandescent line along the wall. Spencer watches anxiously. He's realized that the door out of here is actually the entire wall. If there's a manual release, it's on the other side anyway. Sarmax kicks in what's left of the softened metal and peers through.

"Bingo," he says.

Spencer takes a look.

"Shit," he says.

They're near the bottom of the elevator-shaft complex that runs up the spine. Below them's only about fifty meters, but above them he can see what must be at least half a klick of shaft before it's lost in darkness. Other shafts are dimly visible through gaps in the interior walls.

"Our new bolthole," says Sarmax. Spencer nods—and suddenly his mind reels as the ship's zone comes to life—

"Damn," he says.

Data pours across him, and he's poring over it. And processing the implications—

"What?" says Sarmax. "What the hell's the matter with you?"

"The external doors," says Spencer.

All along the vast metal hull of this thing they're in, all in one fell swoop in his mind—

"*Yeah?*"

"They just opened."

The tunnel up ahead is blocked by Eurasian commandos. She starts to hit the brakes, but it's too late: they're already firing a torrent of electromagnetic pulse straight at her. Her armor's flaring out around her, crashing against the rails, skittering to a stop as she kicks and screams inside her shell. The Eurasians blast down the tunnel toward her. She wonders how the hell she's going to get out of this—wonders for a moment if she should self-destruct. She ponders that for a moment too long—

Because now they reach her. Mongolian faces stare into her own. They pick her up, hustle her down the tunnel while more tremors shudder through the rock around them.

The Operative signals his team, gets them moving in new directions. They're charging into a new set of tunnels, well beyond Congreve's outskirts, dating from the end of the last century. The Operative can feel a whole sector of Congreve scrambling into action behind him. But he's not waiting—just streaking forward into the areas where the sentinels have stopped reporting.

And all the while he's thinking furiously. About what the fuck *Eurasians* are doing in the most important American base on the entire farside. Assuming they even *are* Eurasians. Assuming that Montrose isn't fucking with him. He's been expecting her to try—just not this early. So he has to assume he's dealing with the East—has to assume, too, that if they've managed to get in, it's due to either treason or a first-rate infiltration squad. Or both—

"Contact," says a voice.

It's one of the mechs on point. Data floods the Operative's skull as he coordinates the assault on the enemy that's blocking the corridors up ahead. It's basically an exercise in firepower: Montrose is feeding him reserves as fast as she can—and as fast as he can get them, they're being fed into the fray that's raging up ahead. Walls are getting torn up by hi-ex; suits spray one another at point-blank range. The Operative is giving up trying to keep his original force intact. He's just using it as the centerpiece of a club to break through the resistance as quickly as possible. He's succeeding—rocketing into the heart of the combat now, firing with all his suit's guns, getting in hand-to-hand with a Eurasian commando, dispatching him and gunning down the ones behind him.

Even though he knows he's lost. This Eurasian raid is clearly over. What he's facing is a rearguard, charged with buying the main force time while it retreats along tunnels that must have been dug awhile back. Tunnels that apparently link up with the U.S. deep-grid lines, hollowed out in preparation for this day. Meaning that presumably there are many others. The Operative's guessing this particular operation's based out of Tsiolkovskiy crater, the closest Eurasian farside territory to Congreve. Though he can't believe that place is still holding out.

Unless . . .

Even as he breaks through what's left of the rearguard and hits his jets, the Operative's working the hotline with Montrose's HQ, accessing and downloading the latest data for this section of the farside front. Turns out Tsiolkovskiy's the only place the East's got that's still intact on this side of rock. And there's no sign of Eurasian forces attacking Congreve from any other direction. Meaning what could have been the war-winning move under other circumstances is just a last desperate gamble.

Which is precisely what the Operative's dreading. He knows all about rearguards—knows, too, all about the word *expendable*. He's flooring his motors now, hoping to get past what he knows damn well is about to happen. He can practically feel the blasts start to rip the tunnel apart. It seems his whole life is going up in smoke before him . . .

But he's still breathing. Still moving—streaking out of the older tunnels and into newer ones. And as those all-too-recently hewn walls blur past him he starts to see something else. Something that's inside him—surfacing right inside his fucking head, coming out of nowhere. It's Haskell herself. Sounding as though she would rather say anything besides what she's saying now:

Help me.

The Eurasian charges start to detonate around him.

This place could go up any moment," says Lynx. Linehan stares at him. "And Szilard really isn't here?"

"He left the *Montana* ten minutes ago."

"Going where?"

"Great question."

"And why the hell would he blow up his own flagship in the middle of the ultimate smackdown?"

"Because we're kicking Eurasian ass. So he can afford to write it off."

Linehan shakes his head. "Fuck," he says.

"Textbook power play," says Lynx. "Szilard's luring everyone in his suspect file aboard this crate—all those other SpaceCom factions and anybody else who even *might* be trying to plot against him. All of them got assigned aboard the *Montana*. Seven out of nine of his generals, all the key prisoners, several of his less-reliable wet-ops squads: everyone's gonna get it good. Gotta admit, Linehan, we really got outplayed by him. Though he still would have gotten fucked if—"

"—you and Carson had managed to stick together."

"Yeah. Exactly. Look, we need to get off this ship."

"There's still a way?"

Lynx nods. "And it ain't even by way of heaven."

The codes get transferred; the authorization gets transmitted. The train starts up again, accelerating down the tunnels. Walls flick past as two men struggle to figure out how to deal with a third.

"So what happens to us?" asks the engineer.

"Nothing."

"You're going to kill us," says the driver.

"Keep driving and you'll keep living."

"You're an American agent," says the engineer.

"What gives you that idea?"

"Why else would you have that gun out?"

"I could be Chinese."

"He could be Chinese," says the engineer.

"Doesn't look it," says the driver.

"Doesn't matter," says the man. "Not these days. Anyone could be anyone."

The seismic tremors are starting up again, with renewed intensity. The major glances at the controls.

"And now I need you to ditch this train," he adds.

"You mean get off it?" asks the driver.

"No," says the man, "sever our link to the rest of it."

The driver stares at him. "But it'll stop—it's not authorized—"

"I don't feel like arguing."

Neither does the driver. There's a bump, then a lurch. The car accelerates markedly as the cars behind them go into automatic shutoff, disappearing in the rearview. The engineer pulls himself to his feet, stares at the major.

We just dumped twenty fucking cars, he says.

"And I'll dump you if you breathe another word," says the major. "Now floor it."

"That was our freight," mutters the driver.

"*I'm* your freight," says the man.

The driver nods, doesn't take his eye from the rail ahead of him. It lances out, not bending for at least the next twenty kilometers. The train builds speed toward the supersonic. The driver exhales slowly.

"So who are you?" he whispers.

"I'm here to make sure we win this war."

"How?"

"The Americans are killing us," says the driver.

"Just proceed along the following routes." The major hands the driver a sheet of paper.

"This is paper."

"Indeed. Now tell your engineer to sit the fuck down."

"Sit the"—but the engineer already has.

"And don't dwell on the baggage we just lost," says the man. "Tunnel control has already been notified of a breakdown. And no one's going to believe that the engine disappeared, so they'll just leave that out of their reports."

"Someone will think someone's mainlining vodka," says the engineer, laughing in a tone that's just a little too shrill.

"But this is taking us off the maps," says the driver suddenly.

"Your point being?"

"We should slow down. We're heading way beneath the Himalayas."

"Best place to be right now," says the man.

Hanging in a shaft in the machine to end all machines: Spencer lets his mind expand out into the world around him. Not that it gets very far—he's stopped at the confines of this vehicle within its microzone, completely shorn from any larger zone. But he can see everything he needs to all the same.

"What the hell's going on?" asks Sarmax.

"Boarding," says Spencer—and transmits pictures to the mech's helmet, letting him take in the shuffle of boots through corridors, the syncopated beat of marching suits. For over a half-kilometer above them, passages are filling with Russian soldiers. The wider galleries beyond that are filling with treaded vehicles.

"Fourth Mountain Division," says Sarmax.

"You know them?"

"*Of* them, sure. They're special forces."

"They're just the half of it," says Spencer, sending more images—these from the half-kilometer of corridors above the Russians. Sarmax laughs mirthlessly, shaking his head.

"Chinese," he mutters. "Fifth Commando."

Looking like they're ready for the fight of their lives and then some. Their suits shuffle forward almost languidly, sit down and start strapping in while swarms of mechanics bolt their vehicles to the walls.

"Time to get this show on the road," says Sarmax.

"I'm working on it," says Spencer.

"Work faster," says Sarmax, as the elevators above them slide into motion.

Haskell becomes dimly aware of faint vibrations. She's lying on her back, strapped down. She opens her eyes, finds she's in yet another train. Soldiers stand around her, their guns on her as they make signs to ward off the evil eye. She's wishing she could find some way to live up to her reputation.

But the soldiers have something else to worry about. Someone more senior is entering the car—the soldiers are saluting, clearly ill at ease. Haskell can see the newcomer only by craning her head inside her helmet—which is abruptly yanked off her. Someone strikes her over the head. Someone puts a metal clamp on the back of her skull. It hurts.

"Fuck," she says.

"The Manilishi," says a voice.

She's looking up at the newcomer—a Chinese officer. His suit's insignia's that of colonel. His English is perfect.

"I'm Colonel Tsien," he says.

"Chinese Intelligence."

"Of course."

"And this whole incursion was for my benefit?"

"So to speak," he says.

"I'm useless to you."

"No need to be so modest."

"You know I'm not going to help you."

"I'm afraid that's not up to you to decide."

"Don't be so sure. A lot could happen between now and Tsiolkovskiy."

He smiles. "What makes you think we're going there?"

"Don't bullshit me. It's the closest base you've got."

"Tsiolkovskiy's getting overrun."

"Yeah?"

"It's true," he says. "We just got word. Your accursed Stars and Stripes will be raised over what's left of it within a quarter-hour. Something that even these soldiers around you don't know. See how I confide in you, Claire?"

"So where the hell *are* we going?"

"Somewhere we can hide."

"You mean somewhere you can interrogate me."

"I mean somewhere we can finish up."

"What?"

But Tsien just snaps his fingers—a soldier grabs her head while another slides a new helmet onto her. They lock it into place. She stares up at Tsien as his voice echoes inside her head.

"One chance," he says.

"Let's talk this over."

"We don't want to damage you."

"You'll have to take that risk."

"This will be painful."

"Like you care."

"Of course I care," he says—his smile increasing. "My people are fighting for their lives. You're a monstrosity built to destroy them. Such irony if you could be harnessed."

"Do your worst."

He does.

The Operative watches on his rear screens as the tunnel behind him collapses. So much for the rest of his force. He's on his own now. At this point, it's the way he prefers it. Because there's nothing left to fight him. The Eurasian rearguard is shattered. Their main force has bugged out, leaving cameras and sensors in their wake. But the Operative's all over them, hacking them with abandon, snipping off the sensors, getting in there and replacing his image with shots of still more tunnel. He sets course toward Tsiolkovskiy. The tunnel that he's in merges with others tunnels; those tunnels contain more rails. The Operative knows that if the Eurasians have tossed Haskell onto a train, he's never going to catch her. But hacking into maglev is the work of a moment: his suit's insulation protects him as he extends a tendril onto the rail, his view telescoping all the way to Tsiolkovskiy base.

But he can't see any trains.

The Operative runs the sequence again. Nothing doing. There's nothing on that line. His mind races, considering all the angles. He's scanning the last battle management reports he received from Montrose. His side has probably already overrun Tsiolkovskiy. Meaning the East would have been idiots to take Haskell there.

And maybe they have been. People do stupid things in war. But none of what the Operative has seen so far looks stupid. The Operative's guessing the original idea in digging all these tunnels was simply to disrupt Congreve in the event of conflict. But presumably the Eurasians received intel that gave them a far more specific target. And they must have received that intel recently, because this war's less than an hour old. Meaning Montrose's operation has at least one leak. Probably more.

But that's not the Operative's main concern right now. The Eurasians will be planning to break Haskell, and they'll need to break her quickly. The Operative traces along that line again—his mind flashes back and forth to Tsiolkovskiy several thousand times. He starts hacking at the codes that control the line—the data that might reveal what's happened along it in the last several minutes. He starts feeding in all the other data he's got on this section of the moon—triangulates from all sides, makes the only connection he can.

His thrusters flare, and he's closing on a point several klicks ahead, where a number of old mining veins come suspiciously close to this tunnel—veins that are neither American nor Eurasian, that were mined out when the Moon was just another venue for prospectors and cash-hungry combines. The Operative's noticed that the area where those veins converge is the same place where he's detecting traces of what *might* be a zone-bubble designed to maximize stealth. Rendering whatever's inside almost in-visible to detection.

But not quite. Because now the Operative's hacking into a spe-cial set of sensors that have clearly been set up to keep an eye on this part of the tunnel. Their presence confirms what he's suspect-ing. By the time he rounds the bend in the tunnel and sees the opening in the wall a short distance ahead, he's already got a good idea of what he's going to be facing. No rails lead into that opening. Had he hurtled past at full speed he would have missed it. But it's positioned in such a way that a railcar equipped with rockets could easily move within.

So the Operative does, too: turns off his motors and steps in-side, straight through beams that are intended to act as tripwires—but his suit's already got the drop on them as he maneuvers through and into a cave beyond. The tripwires are convinced noth-ing's tripping them. There seems to be activity up ahead. He's in full-stealth mode now. Nothing can see him. And—as his sensors adjust—he can see all he needs to . . .

The razor locks in the mech, and they're off, traversing the maintenance shafts of the *Montana* once again. Only now they've got a different objective.

"The forward docks," says Lynx.

"What about them?"

"That's where the cleanup crew's basing."

"Cleanup crew?"

"Can't put all your enemies in a box and leave no one minding the store, can you? Wouldn't be very prudent, would it? Someone's got to make sure it's all going to go to hell the way the master chef wants it, and—"

"Speak English, for fuck's sake."

Lynx laughs. "Szilard sent in some picked marines to ferry in the last of the riff-raff. Not to mention making sure the charges are rigged and that no one else gets off."

"And we're heading to where they've docked."

"Sounds almost simple, doesn't it?"

There's some sort of barrier up ahead," says the driver.

"That's why I've been having you slow down," says the major.

And now they're coming to a stop. Eurasian soldiers stand in front of the blast-barrier that's blocking the tunnel. They've got their weapons out. The major looks at the driver.

"Open this train's door," he says.

The driver's complying. The door slides open as the train comes to a halt. A power-suited officer looks up into the cab.

"You're a long way off course," he says on the one-on-one, his words crackling in the major's head.

"I need admittance," says the major.

"I'm sure."

"Careful how you speak to me."

"Because you're under arrest?"

"Because I'm an agent of the Praesidium."

The officer stares as the major transmits codes. Even though everything seems to be falling apart for the rulers of the Eurasian Coalition, the Praesidium is still the most feared thing this continent's seen since Mao and Stalin. The special agents who report directly to them are the stuff of legend. No one wants to meet one. Nor does anyone want to prolong any such encounter they might have.

"Sir, a thousand apologies. You're cleared. But the two men you've got with you aren't autho—"

"I'll take care of them," says the man.

"Sir," says the officer—switches off the one-on-one. The blast-barrier starts to slide open.

The elevators are in motion now, and so are they. They're hanging onto the cables, moving up the shafts, then shifting onto other cables, descending. They're camouflaged acrobats, busy doing the one thing all good performers know how to do.

Buy time.

"Got it," says Spencer.

"Let's have it," says Sarmax.

Spencer beams the data over. He hasn't totally cracked the vehicle's microzone, but he's made some serious inroads. He's figured out where all the places worth cracking *are*. There's one in particular that's looming large on all his screens, more than a kilometer above them.

"That's it," he says. "The cockpit."

"How well defended?"

"So well I can't even see how to get in."

"I don't think we *want* to get in yet anyway."

Spencer nods. Sarmax is right. There's no reason to fuck with the flow. This thing's taking off, and they're going with it. Intervention can come later. Spencer takes in the position of the craft's cockpit and its defenses—marvels at how suspicious the Russians and the Chinese are of each other. The multileveled cockpit's nestled in just above the forward vehicle-hangars, all approaches scrupulously divided between the soldiers of the two nations. Same with the cockpit personnel. There are two captains, both of them strapped down, along with everybody else. Spencer turns to Sarmax.

"They're getting ready to hit it."

"Let's get in closer before they do."

She's plunging downward into herself. Darkness swirls in from all around. She can feel Tsien somewhere out there—circling her like a predator, hungry for what she contains. Fear billows up, threatening to choke her like thick smoke. She knows damn well what her captors are trying to do: turn her into something they can use.

And if they can't do that, they're going to destroy her. And since they're on the brink of utter defeat, they don't have much time. They'll have to cut some corners. She can feel them going at it too—coming in from all sides, trying to unravel her to find out what the hell she really is. It's tough when she doesn't even know herself. She wants to help them—she really does. She'd do anything to avoid the pressure that's now gripping her brain. But she can't see a way past it. She can't evade it: it's all starting to come apart and so is she. Darkness starts to shimmer. Shapes start to form within it—a face emerges from out of the blackness. A voice sounds in her ear.

"Claire."

"Fuck you."

"You've got to wake up."

"Fuck *you*," she repeats.

"Fuck *this*," says the voice—and then it's fire flashing through her, causing her heart to kick into overdrive, and she comes awake in a single instant. She gasps in pain, opens her eyes—finds herself staring into the eyes of Strom Carson.

"Shit," she says.

Blood's everywhere. So are shattered suits. What's left of Colonel Tsien's seems to have been mashed against the wall.

"You killed them all," she mutters.

"No one fucks with you and gets away with it."

"Except for you."

"You'll see the light soon enough."

Lynx steps it up, making the zone think they're something they're not, making the sentinels past whom
they're creeping think they're having just another boring
moment. The two men slide on through the makeshift perimeter
that's been thrown up around this portion of the *Montana*'s docks.
They're starting to pick up a lot of static.

"Jamming," says Linehan.

"Not exactly," says Lynx.

They crawl between steel girders, emerging onto the ceiling of
one of the medium-sized hangars. Two corvettes dominate the
floor. They look like they're in the final stages of boarding.
SpaceCom marines are positioned at the hangar's interior door-
ways. The larger exterior door is shut.

"Looks like we're on time," says Linehan.

"Just barely," replies Lynx.

According to his calculations, pushback's only a few minutes
away. He starts leading Linehan along the latticed ceiling, toward
the *Montana*'s hull. They climb up another level and find themselves in a crawlspace. Unearthly light shimmers from some opening up ahead.

"I don't like the looks of this," says Linehan.

"Set your visor for maximum shielding."

The two men creep to the opening, peer out. The fleet beyond is
visible—along with so much else.

"Oh my fucking God," says Linehan.

"God's dead," says Lynx. "And that's the fucking proof."

The railcar's accelerating once again, down tunnels whose in-
cline has steepened noticeably. Lights flash past, playing upon
the faces of the men within the car.

"What'd you say to that guy?" asks the driver.

"What needed to be said," says the man.

"Which was?"

"We're about to reach the end of maglev."

Not an answer, just more instructions. It's what the crew needs. They work the controls, seamlessly transitioning the train as maglev gives out and wheels extend. The train rolls on into the darkness of the tunnels beneath the Himalayas. Only about a fifth of the Eurasian rail fleet is capable of traveling on legacy track. That's one of the reasons the man chose this train. As for the others—

"Are you hunting traitors?" asks the engineer.

The major laughs. "What would give you that idea?"

"You're some kind of top-secret agent, right?"

"I am?"

"I saw the way that guy looked at you. You're trying to move so that you're invisible, and this is a black base and—"

"Will you *shut up?*" snarls the driver.

"What's your problem—"

"Now he's going to have to kill us—"

"He already knows we know more than we should!"

"Both of you relax," says the man. "You're loyal servants of Eurasia. That's all that matters."

The downward grade steepens even further. Now that they've gone beyond maglev, the engineer's having to apply the brakes. The train sways from side to side, rattles slightly. Up ahead a pin-prick of light is visible. The man seems to relax slightly.

"What the hell is that?" asks the driver.

The man just holds a finger to his lips. The light keeps on growing closer. The engineer crosses himself.

"You're taking us to Hades," whispers the engineer.

The man shrugs. The train rushes out into an impossibly mammoth cavern—rumbles out over a bridge that spans that cavern, moving in toward the gigantic object that's the center of more than a thousand searchlights.

"Saints preserve us," says the engineer—and hits the brakes. The train slides to a halt on one of the adjoining platforms. The driver glances back at the major—isn't surprised to see what's in his hand. He holds up his own hands with an expression of what might be resignation.

"You deserved to see it," says the man.

And fires twice.

T his is going to be bumpy," says Spencer.

"I realize that," says Sarmax.

They've done what they can. Each man has wedged himself into a corner of this particular part of the shaft, three levels down from the cockpit. Their armor's magnetic clamps are on. But they don't have the backup straps that the soldiers upstairs do. So they're just going to have to see what happens next.

Which turns out to be a countdown.

"Three minutes," says Spencer.

"Roger that," says Sarmax.

Spencer nods—watches the ship's zone as all systems sync with the countdown. All the exterior doors slide shut.

Except for one.

J esus Christ," says Haskell.

"Thought you might say that," says Carson.

Fun and games beneath the Moon: He's propped her up in one of the driver's seats of the railcar—has strapped her suit in. Through the windows she can see a large cave. The railcar's sitting on a trestle bridge in the middle of it. Tunnels in the floor lead farther downward.

"What the hell was the East doing?" she asks.

"Not *was*," says Carson. "*Is*. I only killed the ones up here. The rest are down there digging."

"For what?"

"A way in."

She stares at him. "How the hell do they know about *that*?"

"Maybe you told them."

"Just now? They've been set up here for a while."

"But not for much longer. My charges are about to go off. We need to get the fuck out of here pronto."

He hits the gas. She feels the vehicle lurch into life as its retro-rockets fire. It starts reversing. She watches through the window as cave gives way to tunnel. The Operative works the controls, and the train does a smooth 180-degree turn—and then accelerates forward . . .

"We're heading to Tsiolkovskiy," she says.

"Yeah."

"Is the East still holding out there?"

"Who knows?"

"Then why the hell are we going that way?"

"No one's going to see us coming."

The view is almost overwhelming. The Moon's just backdrop to frenzied space warfare. Ships are strewn all around, firing at will. The L2 fleet is locked in combat with an unseen foe. The DE isn't on the visible spectrum. It's lighting up their screens all the same, a barrage of every type of energy weapon imaginable.

"Any idea how it's going?" says Linehan.

"We're destroying 'em," replies Lynx.

Though the East is clearly putting up a fight. Parts of some of the larger ships look like plastic when it's hit by a blowtorch. A lot of the smaller ships just aren't there anymore. Clouds of missiles start emanating from a nearby dreadnaught—firing motors, they streak off into space.

"Probably aimed at incoming Eurasian ones," says Lynx.

There's a flash: an entire section of another dreadnaught suddenly gets pummeled by long-range laser. Debris and bodies pour from the ship's interior. As quickly as it began, the flow stops.

"Sealed," says Linehan. "They've cauterized what's left."

"Heads up," says Lynx.

The hangar doors beside them are sliding open.

What the hell . . . ?"

"What's your problem?" asks Sarmax.

"Someone else just got aboard," says Spencer.

"What difference does it make? We've got a few thousand assholes on this crate already."

"Seems a little strange to be so last minute."

Sarmax shrugs. He seems lost in his own thoughts. Spencer's running zone on the last man aboard this ship—the last door having slid shut right as he got in. An exterior camera shows a train's engine car reversing away along a bridge. The countdown moves under ninety seconds, and Spencer can't find anything on the newcomer.

At all.

"This doesn't add up," says Spencer.

"So get some hard data," says Sarmax.

A tremor ripples through the room they're in. The platforms and catwalks nestled up against the largest spaceship ever built peel away in a single fluid motion.

"Here we go," says Spencer.

They go supersonic in one easy burst, motoring down the tunnel toward Tsiolkovskiy. It's going to take them all of twenty seconds—assuming the lines aren't blocked. On the zone it looks good. But there's a lot of interference around their destination . . .

"I'm going to need your help here," says Carson.

"To enslave me?"

"To live through the next two minutes," he says, firing a bracket of missiles ahead of them. She watches those missiles go hypersonic, streak into the distance. She knows he's got a point— knows, too, that he's got her right where he wants her: siphoning off the requisite processing power, filtering it through his own software. She tries to turn it around, but he knows what he's doing. Especially with the help of the restraints the Eurasians placed upon her. The cage of his mind closes around hers. The missiles ahead of them start exploding. What's left of the maglev rails starts to disintegrate as Carson detaches the car they're in and fires its rockets. They roar toward Tsiolkovskiy's cellars.

"Shouldn't we be slowing down?" she asks.

"Yeah right," he says.

They're making their move as the first of the corvettes slides out. Their suits' thrusters flare gently, floating them down onto the hull of that corvette even as Lynx takes the hacks he's been running to the next level. A hatch opens in the side of the ship, and they drop within. It's that easy. Though . . .

"Something just occurred to me," says Linehan.

"Hold on a second," says Lynx.

The hatch slides shut and the airlock chamber pressurizes. Lynx looks around at the tiny room, then extends razorwire from his suit and plugs into the wall, tightening his grip on the ship's computers as that craft draws away from the *Montana*.

"Look," says Linehan, "there's something we should be—"

"I'm sure there is, but will you shut up—"

"*Think* about it, Lynx."

"Jesus Christ! Think about *what?*"

"This isn't just a matter of getting off the *Montana*. Szilard won't just have rigged his flagship. He'll have these corvettes rigged too."

Lynx raises an eyebrow. Linehan starts cursing: "Fuck's sake man! Otherwise, some of the assholes he's trying to nail might sneak aboard and—why are you laughing?"

"Because I'm way ahead of you."

Ø "Whoever he is, he's got some kind of special clearance," says Spencer.

"We're inside the Eurasian secret weapon, man. What the hell does *special clearance* mean now?"

"It means I can't crack him!"

"Because?"

"He's got some kind of souped-up zone-shield . . . " But Spencer's voice trails off as he becomes aware of something else. Something that's echoing through the ship. With under a minute to go, the countdown's been patched through onto the loudspeakers. Both men can hear the chanting of the soldiers all around them as they join in. Sarmax nods his head in time with the rhythm.

"This is going to be *fun*," he says.

◐ Rocket-powered railcar. Way too fast.

They roar through Tsiolkovskiy's maglev station and into wider passages. Carson engages the ship's guns, slinging shots out ahead of them. Haskell feels him shove her mind even farther out than that as the grids above them click into place. She can see that most of the Eurasians they're killing are dying because they're looking the other way—fighting desperately against the American commandos who have occupied the base's upper levels and are now pushing deeper. The train's coming in behind a set of last-ditch defenses. Carson's trying to coordinate with the Americans above. It doesn't look like he's succeeding. The Yanks aren't taking any calls. Up ahead, she can see the rearmost Eurasians turning to face them. Some of them are shoving a makeshift barrier into place. Looks like it's some kind of wrecked crawler, blocking the tunnel up ahead.

"Fuck," she says.

"I see it," he replies—accelerates still further.

"We're gonna crash," she yells.

"And how," he grins.

Szilard's stacked the whole game," says Linehan. He's starting to feel like the walls of this little chamber are closing in—like the man who's crammed up against him is enjoying this way too much.

"That's how he plays," says Lynx.

"So how come you don't seem concerned?"

"Because I've thought of it all already. *Of course* Szilard would rig this ship. Standard tactic—and it doesn't matter. It's still the only possible way off the *Montana*. Which, by the way, is about to go up like a fucking roman candle."

"After which we do the fucking same, huh?"

"Charges are rigged just aft of the corvette's cockpit. They'll get detonated by wireless transmission."

"Can you stop 'em?"

"Sure as fuck can *try*."

The countdown's reaching its final seconds. The chanting of the soldiers has reached a fever pitch. The noise is deafening. Spencer adjusts his magnetic-clamps one last time. He takes in the zone around him—the whole expanse of it crammed into this craft that's about to vault toward the heavens. The last man to get aboard remains impervious to all attempts to breach his barricades. It's the same with the cockpit. It's going to be difficult to do much about that until more systems come online. Which presumably is going to happen once things get moving. Spencer glances at the man next to him.

"We're about to find out how deep this goes."

"And how high it'll reach," replies Sarmax.

The screens hit zero.

Shit," says Haskell.

"Believe it," replies Carson; he seizes her with both hands, firing his suit's jets and bursting through the train window, out into the tunnel as their vehicle blasts past them and into the Eurasian position up ahead. There's a blinding flash—but Carson's already crashing through a side door and out into a labyrinth of industrial plants. Haskell feels her body shift as he twists and turns at breakneck speed. He's obviously trying to steer clear of the bulk of the fighting. She's doing what she can to oblige.

Lynx has hacked into this corvette's computers. He's got them covered. He's having a little more difficulty with the charges rigged right beneath the pilots' asses. And he's running out of time. Because now white light's permeating the pilots' view, blossoming across the windows.

"*Fuck,*" says Lynx.

"What's up?" asks Linehan.

What's up is that the SpaceCom flagship just blew to kingdom fuck. A series of microtacticals, rigged at judicious intervals: a gaping hole's opened at the very center of the L2 fleet. Lynx can see the way the charges have been rigged to minimize the debris—can see the firing patterns of the fleet adjust automatically to take into account the fact that one of their capitol ships is no longer available. But all of that's secondary to the more immediate problem. The two corvettes have now traversed more than half the distance to the ship they're making for. Only they're not going to get there—

"I just thought of something else," says Linehan.

"Shut up," says Lynx.

"Even if you defuse the charges, surely the rest of the fleet can just—"

"I said shut *up*," snarls Lynx.

The other corvette detonates.

The noise is overwhelming. The floor beneath them's shoving upward. The G-forces are going to town. The ship's rising out of the root of the mountain while door after door opens above it. Kilometers of rock are surging past.

"Looking good," says Sarmax.

Spencer's barely listening. He's just probing on the zone, pressing in at the entryways to the ship's cockpit, calibrating the communications going on all around. He's gaining more room to maneuver as the weaponry systems come online—all too many bomb-racks, far too many guns. But the real weapon is the ship itself, the name of which rises into view on its own zone like something glimmering within oceanic depths . . .

"*Hammer of the Skies*," says Spencer.

"Catchy," says Sarmax.

The last door swings open above them.

They rise through a series of ventilation shafts, coming out into one of the auxiliary hangars. It's just been overrun by American forces. But Carson and Haskell are no longer trying to talk to them. They're hacking them instead, splicing additional orders into the ones that the soldiers have just received, establishing the two of them as high-value assets that need to be removed from the premises immediately. The hangar doors open as an unmanned SpaceCom drop-pod descends into the chamber. Hatches on the pod slide back. The Operative shoves Haskell in, following right behind her. Engines roar as the hangar drops away, followed by all of Tsiolkovskiy base. Haskell gets a glimpse of American assault troops and ships pressing in upon it from every side. She feels the drop-pod accelerate. Moon streaks by below.

But she's detecting something else above.

"The hinge of fate," says Carson softly.

"Is that all?" she replies.

Snipping off the loose ends. It's what Jharek Szilard is good at. It's why he's now second-in-command to the president herself. And why a lot of people aboard the surviving corvette are suddenly realizing they've just become something they never planned on being.

Expendable.

Lynx is doing all he can to salvage the situation. He knows the whole thing was a longshot to begin with. He knew all along that should the charges aboard the corvettes not go off, Szilard would have backup guns ready to take out those ships, along with announcements to the rest of the fleet about how the corvettes contained the Eurasian saboteurs who just blew the *Montana*. Lynx has managed to hack the wireless conduits on the hi-ex, not to mention fucking with the guns that the nearby dreadnaughts have trained on them. He thought he'd done it in such a way that everyone would think the orders were to let the corvettes land—that he could run interference on Szilard's personal supervision. But now more guns are swinging onto the corvette. He's giving contrary instructions; his mind races out into the L2 fleet—out in too many directions. He's getting overextended. He can't keep up. He knows he's dead. The screens around him start to flare.

Pressurized armor offers only so much protection. Spencer's getting knocked black and blue. Yet even with all the specs in his head, he's having difficulty processing what he's seeing on the screens. *Hammer of the Skies* is more than two klicks high, more than half a klick wide. It shits out one nuclear bomb every second, channeling that detonation against the massive pusher plate layered up against its foundation as the ship climbs a column of atomic fire out of the Himalayas. Nuclear contamination rains down beneath it. But when you're fighting the war to end all wars the last thing you're worried about is environmental impact statements.

"Holy *shit*," says Spencer.

"For sure," says Sarmax.

The screens show it plainly—that the thing they're in is merely the pride of the massive fleet it's leading. The Eurasian Coalition has committed its main reserves from bases hidden deep beneath the Earth. The scale of the force now entering the fray beggars description. The sky above western China is turning black with ships and flame. And now those ships open fire on everything above them.

⬤ It's unmistakable. A new factor's entered the equation. Something's bringing long-range fire to bear upon the L2 fleet above them. And from the look of the emissions now lacerating the vacuum, those shots are coming all the way from—

"Earth," says Haskell.

The shit going on overhead is invisible to the naked eye. But no one uses those anymore anyway—it's all enhanced vision and extended wavelengths now. The sky is almost caked with fire. Shots slam against L2's dreadnaughts even as they return the favor.

"The East is bouncing DE off our nearside mirrors," says Haskell.

"Of course," says Carson. She's propped up next to him in the cockpit. He's injected her with something that makes it tough to feel her flesh. Everything's gone all fuzzy. But her mind's working on overdrive all the same.

"We need to talk," she says.

⬤ Lynx isn't one to miss an opportunity—his mind shoulders the pilots aside, seizes key software nodes in the cockpit, and sets the controls to send the corvette skimming past the nearest dreadnaught and straight at the converted colony ship that's just beyond it. Both those ships have other shit to worry about right now—like the fact that they're being shelled from the other side of the Earth-Moon system. Disorder hits the L2 fleet as it struggles to react to the new threat. The corvette plunges in toward the colony ship, which fills the screens as the pilots struggle desperately to regain control. Lynx hasn't the slightest intention of letting them do so.

"Clearing ten thousand meters," says Spencer.

"Roger that," says Sarmax.

The coast of Asia is passing beneath them. The vid-feeds show the chaos that's gripped the Chinese cities across the last hour. The American attack has punctured the Eastern def-grids in multiple places and left the population centers helpless.

"They're still intact," breathes Spencer.

"Exactly," says Sarmax.

The logic's plain enough. Why wipe out cities when you can tip them into anarchy instead? The electric grids are gone. The zone's fucked. Spencer and Sarmax gaze on pure pandemonium in the streets of New Shanghai and all its brethren. The occasional DE blast from the American satellites overhead has only added to the madness.

"Not gonna distract the East that much," says Spencer.

"But every little bit helps."

Meaning that every military resource the Coalition had in its megacities has been totally preoccupied. Meaning there's been that much more that the East's command structure has had to worry about. But now the tide is turning. The fleet that's just over a minute into its ascent is spreading out around all sides of the *Hammer*, all ships careful not to stray within the fiery clouds of the behemoth's exhaust. Yet Spencer can see that he hasn't been thinking big enough all the same . . .

"Fuck," he says.

"Hello," says Sarmax.

Off to the north: *Hammer of the Skies* has a twin. With its own fleet spread out around it. Combined, the carpet of Eurasian ships extends for several hundred klicks in all directions. An armada the likes of which the world has never seen—and Spencer can only imagine what it must look like from the American positions in low-orbit.

B lotting out the fucking planet," she mutters.

"I see it," he says.

The camera-feeds they're hacking into go out. Haskell can't tell whether they got destroyed or whether she's just lost zone-contact with what's going on closer to the Earth. There's enough shit going down that the answer could be both. Though the lunar portion of it still seems to be holding up. Congreve sprawls on the horizon, drifting ever closer. It looks almost serene from up here.

Haskell's mind is anything but. She turns toward Carson—is surprised to find she can move her neck far enough to do so. He glances at her while he works the craft's controls.

"Don't say it," he says.

"How do you know what I'm about to say?"

"Because you never could fool me."

"You're saying you can read minds too?"

"I'm saying we have a connection."

She almost smiles at that, shakes her head.

"Why did you join with Sinclair?"

"You asked me that already."

"He's going to eat you alive."

"He'll choke if he tries that."

T he corvette veers and yaws, partially the result of the struggle for control within its systems, but also a function of the evasive maneuvers that Lynx is putting it through. But the colony ship is almost on them; Lynx reaches out, commandeering that ship's emergency docking procedures. Hangar doors open on the colony ship as the corvette streaks into the outer hangars—plowing through into the inner hangars—

They're way out over ocean now, gaining height on a trajectory that will cross the coast of North America within the minute. Spencer feels himself shaken ever harder as the *Hammer* accelerates, spitting out incrementally larger bombs that send it streaking over the eastern Pacific. Directed energy is striking the hull from every direction, though it doesn't stand much chance of getting through several layers of tungsten hull.

"They can't touch this," says Sarmax.

Not by a long shot. Spencer can see that the *Hammer*'s twin is keeping pace, a hundred klicks north and slightly higher. He zeroes in on it while Sarmax watches over his virtual shoulder.

"We got a name on that thing?"

"*Righteous Fire-Dragon*," says Spencer.

"What kind of a name is *that?*"

"I'm guessing it sounds better in Chinese."

"Wonder if it's exclusively theirs."

"Probably divvied up the same as this one."

"Doesn't matter as long as they get to beat up on the Yanks."

"Speaking of—"

Sarmax nods. The coast of California sweeps toward them.

Two people in a room that comprises their whole ship. There's so much history between them it threatens to swamp the here and now. But that just seems to amuse Carson. Which pisses off Haskell even more. Especially when they're talking about the one man who no one's seen for far too long.

"Sinclair had me train you for a reason," says Carson.

"Did he arrange for you to fuck me too?"

"Who's to say I can't have ideas of my own?"

"Don't start that again," she snaps. "I was in *love* with Jason."

"Only because you could no longer have me."

Haskell turns to look back out the window. Congreve's filling most of it now. Most of the dome's dark. But lights blink throughout the spaceport that sits atop it. She turns back toward Carson.

"If I wanted you, it was only because I was rigged that way."

"But what about now?"

"Why does it matter?"

"For me, it was the only thing that did."

"You are *such* a fucking liar."

He looks at her for a moment like she's never seen him look. "That'd make all this a lot easier."

"You're even more cold-blooded than Sinclair."

"Not so cold as to not see that we're two of a kind."

"You and Sinclair?"

"You and me."

"Give me a *break*."

"Already did."

"What?"

"I trained you for ten years. Watched you grow up. C'mon, Claire. How could I *not* have fallen for you just a little along the way?"

"This is bullshit."

"Fine. It's bullshit."

"You murdered Andrew Harrison."

"I've murdered a lot of people."

She raises an eyebrow. He laughs, but it's not really laughter. "And I had to make it look like I was being played by Montrose. Had to say what she needed to hear."

"You were about to deliver me into her hands."

"I was going to break you out later."

"That is *so* much shit."

"Is it? How can I afford to let anyone else possess—"

"Exactly. That word."

"I didn't mean it."

"You've fucking injected me with a paralyzing—"

"It's worn off."

"What?"

"Try it."

And she does. She's moving. In the zone as well: the shackles are starting to fall from her mind. She runs sequences as Carson brings the craft down toward a landing.

"I could crush you now," she says.

"I'm betting you won't."

Or has he rigged her to preclude that? Is this all part of his latest game? She starts checking over her systems as the craft touches down—which is when the InfoCom special-ops team that has been staking out this area of the spaceport switches on its lights. Blinding glare pervades the cockpit. The *ping* of sonic targeting echoes through the ship.

"Fuck," says Carson. "They're—"

"Off the zone," she snarls. "You *planned* this."

"I swear to God I didn't."

"Then let's get the fuck out of—"

"We've got to make it look like you're still my captive," says the Operative—and switches Haskell's zone-restraints back on.

She stares at him. "You sick little *fuck*—"

"Sorry, Claire," says Carson—hits another switch; Haskell convulses—just as the door to the pod gets yanked open by a man wearing a colonel's uniform. Carson stands up, pulling at Haskell.

"I need you to take us to Montrose," he says.

"You're no longer giving orders," says the colonel.

 N ow *that's* what I call a landing," says Linehan. "Shut *up*," says Lynx.

But neither man's pressing the point. They've already put what's left of the corvette behind them. They're both feeling lucky to be alive. Though Linehan has his doubts about how much longer that's going to last. Because surely any moment this whole ship will . . .

"He can't," says Lynx.

"What?"

"This ship. Szilard can't blow it."

"Why not?"

"It's one of the largest in his fleet."

"You're talking about the man who nuked his own flagship," says Linehan.

"Back when he was winning the fucking war."

Hammer of the Skies and *Righteous Fire-Dragon* synchro-nize their assaults. Doors open all along their hulls; both ships start laying down a carpet of bombs as they rise through the heart of the defenses above the American homeland, their accompanying fleets following them in swarms that stretch halfway back across the Pacific.

"Surprised they'd lead with explosives," says Spencer.

"They're just softening the joint up."

And then some. Most of the bombs are getting nailed by ground-based DE. But those that remain are detonating—

"Holy fuck," says Spencer.

"Xasers," mutters Sarmax.

The ultimate directed-energy weapon: warheads that channel the X rays of their nuclear explosions into a lethal rain of invisible fire that's wreaking utter havoc on the def-grids. The ships coming in behind start flinging down hails of nukes. The American cities are going dark.

"Fuck *me*," says Spencer.

"Those lights won't be coming on again," says Sarmax.

The fleets accelerate toward orbit.

PART II
APOGEE

The Operative's about as furious as he's ever been. He's being hustled through the Congreve spaceport, and his escorts are making sure nobody's getting near him. They're refusing to tell him where he's going. Montrose won't take his calls. The president has clearly decided that there's no compelling reason to have him anywhere near her HQ. He wonders if he's being hauled away to execution. He's looking for the moment to try something along the way.

But they enter another hangar before he can act. A shuttle sits in the center, prepping for launch. He's hustled in toward it. The pilots are standing on a ramp, conferring with mechanics. The Operative thinks there's something familiar about those pilots, but it's not until one of them turns toward him that he knows for sure.

Haskell's coming to her senses. They don't amount to much. Her head hurts. She's on her back, restrained, in another train moving down another track. The only difference is that the heavily armed soldiers standing along the walls are American. An InfoCom colonel stands next to her.

"Awake at last," he says. "Just in time to see the president—"

"—go fuck herself?"

"She'll want you to be more articulate than that."

"She can *want* all she likes."

"I'd be careful about pissing her off."

"Yeah? Why's that?"

"She's in a pretty bad mood right now."

"I can imagine."

"You don't need to *imagine* anything. We'll be there in less than five minutes."

She stares up at him. "What's your part in all this anyway?"

"I'm a loyal servant of the president."

"That's a role that's going out of fashion."

He shrugs, turns away.

Carson," says Riley.

"Been too long," says Maschler.

"Indeed," says the Operative. He's trying not to look surprised. Trying to make it look like he knew this was going to happen—like he knew he was going to run smack into the men who ferried him off Earth all those days ago when that Elevator blew and set this all in motion. "You guys been staying out of trouble?"

"We've been staying off Earth," says Maschler.

"And that's fine by us," adds Riley.

They look at one another.

"How soon do we leave?" asks the Operative.

"That'd be now," says one of the soldiers.

The train's slowing to a halt. Doors hiss open. Haskell's guards steer her gurney onto a platform, through more doors and into an elevator. She feels her stomach lurch as she drops at speed through the shaft. She's estimating she's now a couple of klicks beneath the level of the train, which was nowhere near the surface to begin with.

The doors open. Haskell's pushed out, down another corridor, up a ramp to a massive pair of blast doors. More InfoCom soldiers stand in front of them. Haskell's escorts halt.

"Now what?" she says.

"Now we leave you," says the colonel.

"You mean you don't make the cut?"

"I follow orders," he says in a tone that says *maybe it's time you started doing the same*. But Haskell says nothing. The colonel gestures to his soldiers and leads them back down the corridor while the blast-door guards scan Haskell. They wear the uniforms of Montrose's bodyguards.

"Can't be too careful," she says.

They ignore her, standing back as the doors swing open. Haskell watches as the space behind them becomes visible—

"Huh," she says.

She's looking down five more meters of corridor, at an even larger set of blast-doors. The bodyguards push her toward them, stop. As soon as the outer doors behind them close, the soldiers go to town, stripping Haskell down to her skin. Their eyes go wide as they see how that skin's been marred—covered with half-healed scars of endless intricacy.

"Who did this?" asks one of them.

"That'd be me," she says.

Back when she was trying to map out the vectors of Autumn Rain's zone attacks. Now she's got it all figured out. Though maybe it's too late anyway. The soldiers get busy lacing her with IVs, transferring her to another gurney and rigging her in yet another suit of specialized armor. They position the suit so that now she's upright.

"Thanks," she says.

The inner doors slide open.

Congreve's dropping away. The engines of the shuttle continue to throttle up. The Operative shakes his head.

"You're InfoCom agents," he says.

"Imagine that," says Riley.

"Reporting directly to Montrose?"

Maschler laughs. "And all the time the man thought we were slumming it."

"Because you do it so well," says the Operative.

"Easy now," says Riley. "It's all just business, right?"

"Going to tell me where we're going?" asks the Operative.

"L2."

The Operative furrows his brow. "SpaceCom territory."

"Sure," says Riley.

"And if I try anything?"

"Try anything you like," says Maschler. He smiles—arches one of those bushy eyebrows. "If this ship deviates in its course, it gets taken out."

"Thought you might say that."

"So you may as well make yourself comfortable," says Riley.

The Operative's got a little too much on his mind for that. He knows that Montrose is moving him as far away from the action as possible. L2's the last place he wants to be right now. That is, other than in a ship that might blow to hell at any moment . . .

"Relax," says Maschler. "If she were gonna do you, she would have just done it back at Congreve."

"Besides," says Riley, "you're too important."

"Yeah? How's that?"

"You've got a new mission."

"Which is?"

They don't take their eyes off him, but both men are laughing in a way that makes it clear they're both sharing the same joke. And now the Operative gets it too.

O The American command center is a series of rooms that open into one another. Screens line the walls. Equipment's everywhere. Haskell's guards wheel her forward, maneuvering her down narrow aisles lined with consoles and seated technicians. No one pays her any attention. Apparently they've got other things on their mind. The atmosphere's thick with tension. Haskell's feeling the same way herself. She's wheeled up a ramp and onto a raised area that presides over the lower levels beneath. More bodyguards eye her. Stephanie Montrose turns from a conversation she's having with a member of her staff and regards Haskell with cold curiosity.

"So this is the famous Manilishi," she says.

"And this is the woman who stole the presidency."

"This isn't about who's president," snaps Montrose. "It's about our country."

"What's left of it."

"Exactly. We're losing this war."

"And you're the one who had to go and start it."

⊕ You want me to bag Szilard," says the Operative. "Think of it as your greatest hit," says Riley.

Lunar horizon's dropping away from the window. The Operative exhales slowly, getting ready to move fast if he has to.

"So what happened to the real guys?" he asks.

"The real who?"

"The real Riley. The real Maschler."

"Don't know what you're talking about."

"Don't play stupid with—"

"Relax," says Riley. "They never knew what hit 'em."

Maschler scoffs. "And why are you asking such silly questions?"

"Was that you back at the Elevator, or was that them?"

"Us. They'd already been taken care of."

"You were riding shotgun on me that whole time."

"We were watching you strut your stuff," says Maschler.

"Did all the work for us and then some," adds Riley.

"*Fuck,*" says the Operative.

"It's all good," says Maschler. "We hung around the Moon and did some odd jobs these last few days."

"Prepping the ground for the chief whore?"

"Ain't no need to get snippy," says Riley.

"We just haul the mail," says Maschler.

"Then you'd better start looking at the big picture. The East is coming to bash your skulls out."

"We've got the high ground, Carson. Those barbarians are about to get blasted back down the well."

"They've won unless you can switch the Manilishi on."

"Well, see, that's all on the boss. She'll find a way."

"You really think so?"

"She's a clever one," says Maschler.

"Not so clever playing with the Lizard."

"She had to do the dance," says Riley.

"She'd better know when the music stops," says the Operative.

"That'd be when you reach L2," says Maschler.

Montrose gestures at one of the screens behind her. The screen splits in two. Each half shows one of the massive Eurasian ships.

"Take a look at those things," she says.

Haskell's looking. "How big are they?" she asks.

"Two klicks long. Tungsten armor. As well as—"

"Pulse-detonation engines," says Haskell. "Nuclear warheads as fuel."

Montrose nods. "You see what we're up against." She gestures at one of her staff, and the view on the screen expands to take in the larger perspective—a vast armada, rising out of the gravity well. Set against the shadow of the Earth, the ships of the East look almost like phosphorescence glimmering beneath the sea. And it's almost like Montrose's voice is a wave rolling in from those depths . . .

"Our lower orbit position is a total shambles," she says hollowly. "North America is shattered."

"And our defenses up in the geo?"

"Won't last long."

"So you've lost the planet."

"It's only a matter of time."

"I'm not sure I can help," says Haskell slowly.

Montrose gazes at her evenly. "I've already had the Praetorians purged. All the president's men and then some. More than ten thousand executed in the last two hours and you're welcome to join them."

"Cut the shit, Stephanie. We both know you're not going to do that."

A flicker of a smile. "Want to bet?"

"What's the point? You've bitten off more than you can chew, and you're not going to pass up any opportunity to get yourself off the hook. You're dreaming if you think I'm going to cozy up to you—"

"But you could do it," says Montrose, and buried deep in her voice Haskell can hear the faint stirrings of a plea. "Don't deny it. You could hack them, Claire. You could save our lunar forces—"

"Maybe. If the East's ships are even hackable. Have you been trying?"

"There's so much interference we can't get through."

"And you think I can?"

"I don't know *what* you can do, Claire. And I don't think you do either. But we can plug you into the systems and see."

"With your failsafes keeping an eye on me."

"You won't even notice them."

"Damn right I won't notice them. I've been down this road before and I know where it fucking leads. That's why I'm staying right where you've been keeping me. Right inside my skull. Because it sure as shit beats serving you."

"Goddammit," says Montrose. "I already told you, this isn't about *me*. This is about our nation's darkest hour—"

"Which happened *decades* ago when scum like you stuck a knife into the heart of America. Snuffed out what was left of the republic and sold our people down the fucking river—"

"Don't you dare talk about our *people*," snarls Montrose. "Not when you're willing to stand by while they're condemned to slavery—"

"They're slaves already. Slaves of you, slaves of the East— what's the fucking difference in the end?"

"Just because they couldn't govern themselves doesn't mean we weren't in the right to rule them. To save them. They're *dying*, Claire."

"Let them die," says Haskell. "All they wanted to do was watch war on the vid. Now war's hit them where it hurts. Ever hear of the chickens coming home to roost?"

"You're talking like a traitor."

"Said the woman who had the president butchered. It's all total *shit*, and you're all going to be swept away when I get out of here—"

"Enough," says Montrose. She signals to a technician. "We'll find the lever that moves you or we'll break you trying."

"Good luck with that," mutters Haskell.

The screens within her flare with unearthly light.

And then it's as though she's falling down some long dark tunnel, as though she's been falling all her life and then some, as though she's never going to be doing anything else, as though she never ever wanted to. Static surrounds her, assails her, beats against her. But up ahead a light's growing. She doesn't know what it is. She doesn't want to. She's praying to God that she won't reach it. She's cursing God for doing this to her—even though she knows she's the only one worth cursing. The light's growing all around her, shredding all the darkness. Thermal bloom blossoms toward the brightness of the sun.

But then static resolves into laughter that doesn't even sound unkind. She feels a presence close at hand. Even though she still can't see a thing.

"Show yourself," she demands.

"That would be tough," says a voice.

It's not a voice she's heard before. It sounds like it's right next to her. Sounds like it's amused. She's anything but.

"Goddammit," she says. *"Tell me who you are."*

"What would be a better question," says the voice.

"Shit," she mutters. "You're—"

"A creature of many names."

"Name one."

"We'll start with Control."

Moonscape keeps on falling away. Horizon curves past it. Lights keep on flaring out in space. The Operative stretches. He's doing his best to look more relaxed than he feels.

"So are you man enough to nail him?" asks Riley.

"A loaded question," says the Operative.

"You're the best assassin we've got," says Maschler.

"So what if I am?" says the Operative.

"So the boss can't relax with you prowling around the Moon."

"I've been loyal to—"

"Yourself," says Riley. "So cut the shit."

"Though it's not like we can blame you for playing your own angles," says Maschler. "Who would have thought a supercomputer would come in such a tasty little package? You could practically wrap a bow on her and—"

"Careful," says the Operative.

"Easy, Carson." Riley grins. "It's just us guys now."

"And we've got some time to kill," says Maschler.

"Interesting choice of words," says the Operative.

'I've been looking forward to meeting you, Claire."

Haskell can well believe it. She's heard about Control: the machine that's Stephanie Montrose's prime razor—and that had more than a little to do with the machinations that brought down Andrew Harrison. Because Control's specialty is intrigue.

And interrogation.

"I wish I could say the same," she says.

"Don't be so hard on yourself." Control's voice is smooth. "You've got every reason to hold your head high."

"I don't know what you're talking about."

"I've followed your career for a long time. Who would have thought you would execute it with such aplomb?"

"I'm not into rhetorical questions."

"You'll miss them when I get to the real ones."

She nods. She's thinking fast. Control has her in a zone-lock. If there are any ways out of here, he's got a hold on them. But she's not ready to have him turn her inside out. She's not going to go down without a fight—

"I expect you to," says Control.

"To what?"

"Fight."

"You can read my mind?"

"I'm inside it already, aren't I?"

"But not all of it."

"That's why we're having this conversation."

"So what if I don't resist?"

"Then I'll have you all the quicker. This isn't about resistance, Claire. This is about the puzzle that's your mind. Which my lady Montrose has charged me with unlocking."

"You're not the first to try."

"I'll settle for being the last. Shall we begin?"

"I thought we already had."

Laughter rises up to swamp her.

The shuttle's risen past the outermost of the Congreve traffic zones. Maschler's working the controls. The ship lurches as more engines fire. Suddenly the Moon's moving away at speed.

"Express haul," says the Operative.

"It's still going to take a few hours," says Riley.

"So let's cut to the chase," says Maschler. "Montrose knew what you were up to from the start."

"Did she really."

"For sure."

"How?"

"Fuck's sake man, you were too good to be true. Praetorian traitor willing to turn over the keys to Harrison's back door and bag the Manilishi while he was at it?"

"It *was* true."

"But not the whole story."

"Is it ever?"

"Look at him," says Riley. "Like the cat that ate the canary. I think he still thinks he can beat us."

"Is that true?" asks Maschler. "You still believe that, Carson?"

"I think you guys are getting ahead of yourselves."

"You're the one who's done that. By thinking that the fact that you're Autumn Rain makes you invincible."

"I'm not *exactly* Autumn Rain—"

"You're not exactly *anything*," says Riley.

"Neither fish nor fowl," says Maschler. "How does it feel to be a prototype, Carson?"

"Never had much to compare it to," says the Operative.

We'll start with some control questions."

"That's fitting," says Haskell.

Control ignores the barb. "With whom am I talking?"

"Claire Hask—" but as she says the words, pain boils up from within her, engulfs her in agony. She knows she should be screaming, but she can't. She can't even move her jaw. Can't close her eyes either—all she can do is stare transfixed at the featureless light shimmering around her as fire sears across her nerves.

And subsides.

"Wrong answer," says Control.

"Fucking bastard," she says.

"What I am is incidental. What matters is what *you* are."

"I'm Claire Hask—"

More pain. Control's voice seeps slowly through:

"We might agree to call you *Claire* for the sake of convenience. But what you really are is Manilishi."

She says nothing.

"Isn't that right?"

"Yes," she says slowly. "That's right."

"And what is Manilishi?"

"Isn't that the big question—"

"I'm not asking for the full answer," snaps Control. "You don't know. I realize that. That makes two of us. Just tell me what you *do* know."

"I'm a biocomputer able to perform hacks faster than the speed of light."

"And how do you do that?"

"I don't know."

Control says nothing.

"I don't *know*," she repeats. "I've tried—"

"So what would you guess?"

"I'd guess retrocausality."

"I'd say we can do more than guess."

"Signals from the future," she mutters.

"Could there be another explanation?"

"It's not much of a fucking *explanation*."

"Then perhaps we should think of it as a start."

"So let's see if I've got this straight," says Riley. "You and Sarmax and Lynx were the first out of the gate, but—"

"What is this, true confessions?"

"Call it what you like," says Maschler.

"You're beaming everything I say back to Montrose."

"So what if we are?"

"Let me speak to her."

Maschler laughs. "I think you overestimate the smoothness of your tongue."

"Not to mention our ability to get her on the line," adds Riley.

"She's too busy losing the final war, huh?"

"Take it like a man," says Maschler. "Can't talk to the judge after she's handed down the verdict, can you?"

"She's under no illusions," says Riley. "She took your measure, Carson. Overmighty subject plotting for the day when—"

"I'm not sure I'd agree with the word *subject*."

"And therein lies the problem," says Maschler. "No one who became the Rain ever did."

"Only three people ever *became* the Rain," says the Operative.

Riley shrugs. "An imprecise term," he says. "But I think we're on the same page. The danger of creating the ultimate hit team, eh? Three were *modified* and the rest were born to it—engineered from the very start—but all of them shared the same lust to dominate all else. And all of them went through a similar process. One that—"

"Linked minds," says the Operative.

"And how much do you know about the actual process?" asks Riley.

The Operative laughs. "Only one man knows what counts."

I t starts with Matthew Sinclair," says Haskell.

"Of course it does," replies Control.

"He set it all in motion."

"But what *was* all of it?"

She hesitates. "That's a control question?"

"I daresay we're starting to move beyond them."

She shrugs. The light around her seems to be shifting as though it's water—like waves rising and receding, but it's still as opaque as ever. She glances down at her hands and wonders what's happened to her real body—wonders if she's being operated on in a far more comprehensive fashion than Carson attempted. Perhaps her flesh has already been disposed of. Perhaps it was never that critical anyway. Maybe Montrose and her AI jackal have managed to figure out the part of her that really matters. Or maybe—

"Sinclair said something to me once."

"You sure it was him?"

She ignores this. "He told me that every cell of me computes."

"Are you asking if we've carved you up yet?"

"I guess so," she says.

"We're keeping our options open."

"Great."

"Though perhaps *your* options are foreclosed, no? With information from the future tossed into the mix, who knows what the ramifications upon the present are?"

"It's all tactical," she says. "Short-range. I've got maybe a second or so advantage when I'm running hacks and that's—"

"Still more than enough to allow you to lacerate any normal razor. And yet you protest too much, Claire. Your intuition extends out farther than your hacks, doesn't it? Glimpses, visions, premonitions—call them what you will. What's the mechanism in your mind that drives it? What's the conceptual paradigm behind it? Advanced Wheeler-Feynman waves? Sarfatti's back-action?"

"If I knew that, then I'd—"

"Nor can we just look at you in isolation," says Control, ignoring her. "We have to strive for an integrated framework, no? So take it from the top: Sinclair experiments with something that involves, among other things, retrocausality and telepathy. We don't know the extent to which the processes that underpin these phenomena are related, but you seem to be the primary focus for the former. As to the latter: he takes the three best Praetorian operatives and flatlines them—we don't know for how long or under what conditions—and then zaps them into life again. Only now they've got some kind of connection, albeit not a particularly refined one. They can only coordinate in the crudest of fashions—"

"It's still mind reading," she says.

"Of course it is. Even if Carson and Lynx and Sarmax can do little more than sense one anothers' presence, it's still mindreading. And yet still nothing compared to what the second batch could do. The core of Autumn Rain. Thirty men and women who were bred in the same vat and who came into the world fully linked. Except for—"

"Me and Marlowe."

"And now Marlowe's no longer a factor."

"Not that he ever really was," she says ruefully.

"Indeed. He was merely the device via which you were bound

to your brethren. Whereas you were the key to the whole situation."

"The intended linchpin of the Rain's group mind."

A momentary pause. "I didn't realize you knew that."

"Carson told me."

Control chuckles. "Not like him to speak the truth."

"We have to tread carefully," says Maschler.

"I'll say," says the Operative.

Most of the farside's now visible, spiderwebs of craters ringed by mountains. No fighting's in evidence down there. If any combat's taking place, it's confined to mop-up. The Operative looks out into space. Shakes his head.

"Why the hell is Montrose picking a fight with Szilard?"

"We were talking about Sinclair," says Maschler.

"We still are," snaps the Operative. "It's impossible not to. We're all caught up in his plan."

"Caught up? Or do you mean you're still trying to carry it out?"

"I'm not even sure there's a difference," says the Operative.

"You'd better start learning," says Riley.

"Same goes for Montrose," says the Operative.

"She knows what she's doing."

"Does she?"

"She's the president," says Maschler. "And it's her duty to ensure the integrity of the executive node—"

"Political theory's my favorite line of bullshit."

"Screw the theory," says Riley. "Let's talk about the practice. Ever seen a beast with two heads? It doesn't survive. Montrose and Szilard can't share power and they both know—"

"Nothing," snaps the Operative. "Neither of them knows a *goddamn thing*. If they did, they wouldn't be *losing the fucking war*. Sinclair's going to have the last laugh yet."

Riley coughs. "If the Eurasians win, how the fuck does that help Sinclair?"

"That's the part I'm still trying to figure out."

He's the most dangerous man alive," says Control. "Carson's a close second."

"Are they working together?"

"Each wants the other to believe that," she says. "But as to whether they really are—"

"Has Carson told you that he still loves you?"

"What?"

"I'm not talking about how he conned his way into your teenage pants. I'm talking about recently."

"He's implied it. It's still bullshit—"

"Hardly. He may well believe it."

"It still wouldn't matter."

"I'm glad you realize that. Insofar as he's capable of such emotion, he lives only to betray the objects of it."

"What does a machine know of such matters?"

Control laughs. "Am I making you anxious?"

"Are you trying to?"

"Naturally. Because now we're getting into the thick of it. *What does a machine know of such matters,* indeed. Perhaps I should put that question back to you."

"I'm flesh and blood."

"And software. All of it greater than the sum of its parts. Such a complex piece of work. Such a tough nut to crack. This is where it's going to get painful."

"Even more so when you have to tell Montrose you couldn't pull it off."

Control ignores her. "The key to the problem is memory," he says. He sounds like he's giving a lecture. But she's hanging on his every word. She feels a need to shake him, beg him to hurry up. She knows that's merely part of whatever it is he's doing—

"Memory," she repeats.

"Indeed," says Control. "And we need to unravel yours."

"But I remember all of it."

"Do you really?"

"I already made that breakthrough!"

"With Carson as midwife."

"With Carson as . . . " She trails off. "Fuck."

"You see? You're walking on quicksand. And even if he led you straight, he may not have led you deep enough."

"What the hell's that supposed to mean?"

"It means we have to take this all the way back, Claire. Your memory is the key to you in some manner that we don't fully understand. It wasn't just the means via which your would-be masters aimed to control you. It's bound up in the very essence of your powers."

"You're not making sense."

"It's very simple," says Control, and as he talks she can't help but notice the amorphous light around her is fading. "Your conscious callback accounts for only the merest fraction of what we're interested in. Your unconscious material is where the real secrets lurk."

"You're talking like a fucking shrink," she says.

"As does any good interrogator."

She tries to reply, but she's having difficulty forming words. It's like the fading light is taking the ground out beneath her—like the gathering dark is sapping her will to resist. She feels herself tossed through the canyons of her own mind and it's all she can do to hang on—

"Cat got your tongue?" asks Control. "Think, Claire, what a fragile reed even the truest of recollections are. So much seen and yet so little understood. So much that goes down before we even comprehend it. What was done to you back in the vat? Do you have any idea? What happened in those first few hours? *What happened in those first few minutes?"*

Darkness envelops her.

They've been stuck in the dark for a little too long now—crawling through narrow spaces while trying to ignore the clanking and creaking all around them. Generators whining, KE racks humming: this ship's clearly heavily involved in whatever combat's going on outside.

"How long has it been?" asks Linehan suddenly.

"Just under an hour," says Lynx.

"No kidding."

"Can't you tell time?"

"Not with any certainty."

He's been drugged and rebooted a few too many times for that. Now Linehan's living in something that approximates the eternal present. Past and future seem to be collapsing in upon him. He feels like he's been in these shafts forever. But there's something that's been growing on his mind—

"So where the fuck are we?"

"This is the *Redeemer*," says Lynx. "Registered with the Zurich Space Commission in 2108. Scheduled for the Martian orbits by the year 2115. State-of-the-art colony transport. But all the time she was shaping up to be one of the heaviest gunnery-platforms in the L2 fleet."

"That's what covert construction will get you."

"Sure," says Lynx. "And now she's giving all she's got against the East."

"How's she doing?"

"Haven't a clue. I can't access the ship's mainframes."

"You're cut off from zone?"

"The parts that count. That's one of the reasons we're staying mobile."

Linehan nods. Spencer had explained it to him once: the zone's like a series of hills. Different positions give different vantage points. Certain locations are inherent deathtraps. Others allow you to rain shit down upon your opponent. Or just act like you're not there.

"Do they know we're here?" asks Linehan.

"Of course they know we're here. We fucking crash-landed into their goddamn hangar bay."

"I meant are they on our trail?"

"Presumably."

"You don't know for sure?"

"Until I get the full zone picture—"

"I've heard this already." Linehan opens a trapdoor; they keep on crawling.

Ⱥ "Stabilized at last," says Spencer.

"And it's about time too," says Sarmax.

It's taken long enough. They've been in this elevator shaft doing nothing but hold on while the ship's been shaking like it's on the point of falling apart, even as it pulverizes the opposition. The American geo positions were speed bumps and nothing more. The ship's starting to put the Earth behind it.

"Not a pretty sight," says Spencer.

It never is when a side of planet gets hit by everything and then some. The atmosphere is still burning. The Eurasian reserves have swarmed through the lower orbits. The only resistance they've left is underground, and most of that can be safely bypassed. Doesn't matter how many American forces are down there as long as their ground-to-space weapons have been eliminated.

"All that counts now is the high ground," says Sarmax.

And that's clearly the next stop. *Hammer of the Skies* and *Righteous Fire-Dragon* have left the rest of their fleets in the dust. Except for—

"Take a look at *that*," says Spencer.

"Ballsy," says Sarmax.

The rear camera feeds aboard this megaship are positioned to capture images between each of the nuclear blasts that keep on propelling the ship ever farther out into space. When those blasts are detonating, armored shutters ensure instrument integrity. And when those blasts aren't—

"Someone's getting danger pay," says Spencer.

Rigid tethers lashed to the sides of both behemoths are splayed out for scores of kilometers into space. Each cable's towing several ships, which look to be modified corvettes. They've obviously received more radiation-shielding than usual. Even so, it looks like they're taking damage—

"It's worth it," says Sarmax.

"I'm sure," says Spencer.

"The summit of the Earth-Moon system," continues Sarmax, as though he's giving a briefing. "The East has nothing up there now. They've been cleaned out of their lunar positions and their fortress at L4 is a smoking ruin. But the Americans have fuck-all back on Earth. And now that their geo position has been rolled up they're reeling. They're outnumbered. And we're the mobile spearhead. These two dreadnaughts are getting out ahead of the main fleet so they can strike while the iron's hot. That's why we're towing so many fucking ships—they want to get up there as quick as possible with as big a force as possible."

"Probably."

"If you'd managed to hack the Eurasian net we wouldn't need to be guessing."

"Easier said than done," says Spencer.

"Apparently."

"Look, this is a *whole separate net*, okay? Totally cauterized from what's left of the East's original. Deliberately kept dumbed-down and crude. Oh, and by the way, all external signals reaching us are occuring between nuclear fucking detonations."

"You sound like you're making excuses."

"I like to think of them as reasons."

"And I don't like it."

"Tough shit, Leo. All I can hack is this ship."

"And not even all of that."

"Then how about you fuck off and let me get back to it."

"And the handler's file?"

"Has taken a backseat to cracking the ship's cockpit."

"Maybe it shouldn't."

"And you're being *such* a big help. Look, the file's insane. And I can't work miracles with the Eurasian zone, okay? Same way you wouldn't be able to take on the whole Eurasian army, all right? So you're going to have to deal with the fact that *so far* I haven't cracked the cockpit, and *so far* I still don't know what's up with the newcomer."

For a moment there's silence.

"What newcomer?" asks Sarmax.

"That guy who slipped aboard at the last moment."

"That guy?"

"Yeah, *that* guy. You didn't seem that concerned at the time."

"He didn't just head to the cockpit?"

"Why would you assume he'd head to the cockpit?"

"If he's impervious to hacking, he's obviously important."

"Doesn't mean he's in the cockpit."

"Even though it's basically impregnable?"

Spencer shrugs.

"So where the fuck is he?" asks Sarmax.

"In his quarters."

"Which are where?"

"Other side of the ship."

Sarmax looks thoughtful.

"Wait a second," says Spencer, "you're not thinking—"

"Why not? Let's go say hi."

You're playing a dangerous game," says the Operative.

"You're one to talk," says Maschler.

"The difference is I'm under no illusions,"

"Name a single one that governs InfoCom."

"Keeping Sinclair alive is a good idea."

For a moment there's silence.

"We already discussed why that's necessary," says Riley.

"Have we?"

"He's the only one who knows the formula that created Autumn Rain."

"You sure about that?" asks the Operative.

"Who else did you have in mind?" asks Maschler.

"There must have been scientists. Technicians. Lab records."

"Yeah?" asks Riley. "You seen any?"

The Operative shrugs. "I heard Sinclair had a file—"

"Which went AWOL," sneers Riley. "As you damn well know."

"News to me."

"I can't believe I'm even *listening* to this bullshit," says Maschler. "For all we know you were watching while Sinclair burnt everybody involved."

"For all we know you were the one who did it," adds Riley.

"I didn't have that kind of access," says the Operative mildly.

"I'd bet you'd like to."

"Is that an offer?" asks the Operative. "Does this mean you're turning off the goddamn tape and beaming Montrose back some dubbed bullshit while the three of us get down to business?"

"We've already gotten down to business, Carson."

"Then why don't you start acting serious, huh? Haven't you numb-nuts interrogated Sinclair already?"

"Harrison already tried," says Riley.

"Before you shot him," says Maschler. "As you well know. Christ, Sinclair's just fucking gone."

"Like nothing we've ever seen," snarls Riley. "Fucker taunts us and then he just seems to switch off. Even though he's still fucking breathing. Chemicals and pain and none of it matters. Not now. He's beyond our reach."

"As opposed to me?" asks the Operative.

"Ah, yes," says Maschler. "Riley, what do we think of what Carson told Montrose about what he'd done to his own mind?"

"I think we think it's bullshit," says Riley.

"Though give him points for trying," says Maschler. "But Carson, even if you really *did* rig yourself with death-switches to prevent your head from being skull-fucked, what makes you think we'd hesitate to put you to the question anyway?"

"Because it'd be the last question you'd get to ask."

"Is that a fact?"

"Or maybe you're just too chickenshit to take the chance and take me apart."

"Or else we'd rather have you take out Szilard instead."

The Operative yawns. The ship keeps on motoring toward L2.

She wandered in that desert for forty days and forty nights. The whole time she knew she was just moving through the wilderness of her own mind. It didn't matter—it was still as real as anything she'd ever seen. Or remembered: She trudged beneath two suns that scattered her shadow into long fragments across the sands—kept on stumbling through the desolation while evening draped around her and morning rose, and all the while she knew that scarcely seconds were going by, that the greatest war in history was still raging on outside, that she was still helpless in the depths of Montrose's command center with the creature called Control still crawling through her brain. She didn't dare go to sleep, not even for a moment. She knew as soon as that happened that Control would penetrate whatever was left of her: that he would rule her dreams and subjugate her to everything within her she'd feared and never understood. So she just wandered through those trekless dunes, fighting off that mount-

ing urge through sheer force of will. Her eyes remained open and
her spirit remained hers—and by night those suns gave way to
starless expanse in which was set a single moon that shimmered in
her heart and looked identical to the one that had swallowed her
back in the world she'd left so long ago. She felt that moon all
around her—felt it calling to her, telling her all the things she already knew and didn't want to hear. The fortieth dawn rose but
there was only one sun now. It wore a face.

They keep on crawling through the industrial plant of
the colony ship-turned-warship: an endless maze of
crawlspaces and narrow passages. If they're being pursued, Linehan hasn't seen a sign of it. Then again, he's figuring
that by the time he does, it'll be too late anyway. Meaning it's all
coming down to whatever's going on in Lynx's head. And Lynx is
even more close-mouthed than usual. His standard cock-of-the-
walk attitude seems to have faded a little. Linehan thinks about
this. He opens up the one-on-one.

"So when do you kill me?" he asks.

"What?" says Lynx.

"You heard me."

"Why would I want to kill you?"

"Same reason you're keeping me alive."

"I told you, you're making your own decisions—"

"Tell me what you're planning."

"I'm making things up as we go."

"But you must have *some* idea how we're getting off this ship."

"Who said we're getting off this ship?"

"We're just going to stay here?"

"Why shouldn't we?"

"Because we're in the middle of World War—"

"Sure we are," says Lynx, "but you're not thinking."

"Sometimes I have that problem."

"So let me spell it out for you. We got the drop on SpaceCom by getting onto this fucking ship, right?"

"Right," says Linehan. "Though it seemed more like luck than skill to me—why the fuck are you laughing?"

"Because luck's the best kind of skill," says Lynx.

Y ou really want to pay this guy a visit?" asks Spencer. "It's either that, or we have a crack at the cockpit."

"Which we eventually have to try. So why take unnecessary risks in the meantime?"

"Define *unnecessary*," says Sarmax.

Spencer shakes his head, ponders what he can see of zone and all the space that lies beyond. The ship's still running smooth, putting the Earth behind it at speeds that ought to be illegal as it continues to vector in toward the Moon, taking increasing amounts of fire. It doesn't seem to be troubled in the slightest.

"Look," adds Sarmax, "it's real simple. This guy looks important. And he also looks like he's a damn sight easier to get to than the cockpit."

"Which may be the point."

"Meaning?"

"Could be a trap."

"Yeah," says Sarmax, "I thought of that—"

"Well, keep thinking. Because I can't think of a better way to catch whatever assholes might be lurking in the woodwork—"

Sarmax laughs. "We've snuck into a secret weapon that's gone operational and you're still clucking about the *risks*?"

"I'm just trying to calibrate them."

"Doesn't change the basic picture. We need to get control of this ship before it hits the Moon, sure. But maybe that guy has part of the key to doing so. Maybe he's planning the same thing himself."

"Why the hell would he be doing *that*?"

"Because the Eurasians are like us, man: they're divided against themselves. Look at the way the ivans watch the chinks and the chinks keep an eye on the ivans. No one trusts anyone for shit. And with things looking ever worse for Uncle Sam, the tension's getting cranked up ever higher."

"You really think the East might succumb to civil war?"

"Let's just say they wouldn't be the first."

The ship keeps on throttling heavenward. The Moon's now a ball in the window, and the L2 fleet is looking like a starfield preparing to engulf them. The Operative laughs.

"This hasn't a chance of working," he says.

"It *working* and you *living* are two very different things," says Riley.

"Touché."

The most basic rule of assassinations: the shooter is expendable—or better still, marked for disposal. The Operative's pretty sure that's how this one is going to go down. Right after he's managed to kill the Lizard, he'll be gunned down by either Szilard's bodyguards or the men he's talking to right now. That's why Montrose has sent him up here in the first place. This is a one-way trip. Even so, he can't see how the hell Montrose is expecting him to take out Szilard. Unless—

"And here we were thinking that you're the expert in connnecting dots," says Riley.

"Sometimes I need a little nudge."

"That's for sure." Maschler looks like he's trying not to laugh. "Look, there are three ways to crack a fortress. You either blast your way in, you sneak on through, or else you . . . " His voice trails off.

The Operative stares. "Or what? You're telling me we've been *invited* to see Szilard?"

"Why not? We're all trying to stop the East, aren't we?"

"He'll be suspicious as all fuck."

"Of course he will be."

"So what's the angle?"

Riley and Maschler look at each other.

"Well?" repeats the Operative.

"Maybe it's time to show him the cargo," says Riley.

The sun's face is one she recognizes. Even though she doesn't want to. Even though she hasn't seen it in so long. She stands in the midst of her own desert, endless wastelands stretching out on all sides as she looks up at what's leering down upon her.

"Hello Claire," says Morat.

"That's not really you," she mutters.

"What makes you say that?"

"Because you're dead."

"Am I really?"

"I saw you destroyed."

"And yet I live on inside of you."

"Only in my memory."

"More than enough. Shall we begin?"

She says nothing. The light of his face is getting ever brighter. The sky beyond it is going black.

"What the hell's happening?" she mutters.

"Control is forcing its way ever farther inside you."

"And you're helping."

"Except for the fact that I don't exist."

"You're a part of my mind that's been set against me."

"I seem to recall I was on your side."

"You were my worst enemy," she says.

"Only after you betrayed yourself."

"I never—"

"Fooled yourself too. You know I speak the truth. You're Rain. Yet you denied them again and again. In that SeaMech beneath Pacific. At the Europa Platform. And then afterward, when you helped to snuff all your brethren. Thus were the Rain undone by the very weapon built to complete them. Thus was—"

"Not all of them."

"What?" asks Morat.

"I didn't kill all of them."

"Carson and Lynx and Sarmax aren't in the same league as—"

"I'm not talking about the original trio," she snarls. She feels she should shut up, but she can't. Not with Morat's disembodied head looking down at her like that. "There are still other members of the Rain left."

There's a pause. Morat flickers.

"How would you know that?" he asks.

"I've felt their minds."

Morat beams at her. "Oh good," he says.

"So *nobody's* getting off this ship," says Linehan.

"Give the man a hand," says Lynx.

They've come through into a wider set of passages. The lights are few and far between. All they can hear is the continued clanking of distant guns. They're deep in the interior now.

"And we're staying in the bowels of this thing."

"It seems like the prudent thing to do," says Lynx.

"Because there's no point in going near the hull."

"Given that nothing's leaving: no."

Linehan nods. He gets it, though it took him long enough. Szilard knows which ship they're on. It would have been hard to miss. But the commander of SpaceCom can't afford to blow any more dreadnaughts just to get at rogue elements. He's way past that luxury now. So all he can do is take precautions. Which is why nothing's getting off the colony ship. At least until—

"All debts will be settled when the war's over," Linehan mutters.

"And a lot of them long before," says Lynx.

Linehan nods. They keep on moving.

They leave behind the ledges where they rode out the launch and head out into the elevator shafts—riding cables, moving adroitly from one to the next. Spencer syncs up the zone with the topography that's all around them. Shafts extend down beyond his sight, electric light flickering in the distance. Elevator cars clank past, packed with soldiers. Machinery's everywhere. Spencer's view is shot through with the false color of augmented zone-vision. For a moment it seems to him like this ship has become the universe, like everything around him is just the gears of existence turning: the guns raining death out into the beyond; the armor taking fire from the massed batteries on the Moon and at L5; the endless conveyor belts upon which nukes are slotted through the bowels of the ship and spat out into the vacuum beyond. But he's leading Sarmax in the other direction, moving into the middle areas of the ship, getting extra stealthy.

"We're almost at the troop quarters," says Spencer.

"Roger that," says Sarmax.

Riley leads the way—the Operative follows him, and Maschler trails after. The Operative appreciates the way they move—like the professionals they are—and even though they're probably not expecting him to try anything, they're ready for anything he might. He wonders how he could

THE MACHINERY OF LIGHT 105

have let them fool him back at the Elevator. He's guessing it had more than a little to do with the fact that he had a lot on his mind.

He's got the same problem now. They descend a ladder into the ship's main cargo hold. Riley hits a switch; lights flicker dimly all around. Auxiliary holds sprout off from the main one. Containers are racked up everywhere, faint vibration washing through them from the engines directly below. The Operative wonders if he'll end up in one of those boxes. He can't deny it'd be fitting. He feels like his life has come full circle, that these two men may as well be the ferrymen taking him across the Styx.

"Is this the part where you try to off me?" he asks.

"Even better," says Riley.

"Right this way," says Maschler, heading in toward one of the auxiliary chambers.

A desert with a population of one. A woman with the feeling that the face that's leering down at her is getting a little too close for comfort.

"The Rain's out there," she says.

"Where?"

"At L5."

"With Sinclair?" asks Morat.

"They're guarding him."

"I would put it the other way around." One eyebrow raises. It looks obscene. "He shielded them from you when you were Harrison's servant. And he thinks we haven't figured it out since—"

"He's playing all the angles," she says. "You can't hope to beat him, Stephanie, please listen to me, you have to kill him *now*—"

"Spare me," snaps Morat. "The president can't hear you. She doesn't micromanage interrogations."

"She leaves that to something even colder than her."

"If you like," says Morat. He seems amused. "But I'm pleased to wear this face while I tear your skull apart."

"So now we see your real one."

"Oh," says Morat, "let's not get all literal here. I'm not *Control*. His mind's aware of what we're saying, but I really *am* part of you. That's the point, you see. You think you're whole, but you're really scattered piecemeal. Taking you apart is just a matter of putting it all together."

She says nothing. Wind brushes sand onto her face.

"Can you detect Sinclair?" he asks.

"No," she says.

"You're both blind to each other," says Morat. "As it should be."

"What's that supposed to mean?"

"Once posthumans get into the mix, the whole game changes, no? Especially if what makes them posthuman is mental. Especially if it can be replicated."

"Isn't that the big question? A man can be modified, but—"

"Can he beat that which is born into it? He might deceive himself that he could. Lynx and Carson and Sarmax certainly did. In the end they couldn't even keep their own team together. Who would have thought they would go out so early?"

"They're dead?" She manages to keep the edge from her voice, but it's as though Morat has heard it anyway.

"My condolences," he says. "Carson's fucked you over for the last time."

"How did he die?"

"He's going to kill Szilard for his president."

"*Going* to?"

"Or he'll fail in the attempt while our backup team finishes the job. Either way, he's dead. And there's no way off L2—"

"You're an idiot," she spits. "You're a fucking idiot. If you're going to kill Carson, then fucking *kill him*. Don't try to *use* him. Don't give him the slightest chance—"

"Sounds like you *want* him dead."

"I *do* want him dead. I want him to live forever. Whatever. He's far more of a threat to Montrose than Szilard ever could be."

"Abstract pronouncements. All of Montrose's enemies now live on borrowed time."

"As does Stephanie Montrose. The fucking Eurasian fleet's steaming in toward you, or haven't you noticed? And for all we know, Leo Sarmax is in control of it by now."

"Or else he's dead in the Himalayas," says Morat. "What does it matter? It's still the same hardware. Still the reason why Montrose needs to attain control of you—along with total possession of the L2 fleet. The last thing she needs with the East's spearhead coming straight at her is to not be able to trust her second-in-command—"

"I'm not sure that's how Szilard sees himself."

"You summarize the problem nicely."

"Your real problem's Sinclair. He's the one who's ten steps ahead of everyone else."

"More than that," says Morat.

"What are you saying?"

"You know exactly what I'm saying."

She stares up at that face.

"We both know what Sinclair is," he adds.

She shakes her head. "Carson said that Sinclair had mapped it all out."

"Go on."

"All the possibilities, every which way the game might break. Said he gave him a very specific set of instructions that allowed him to thread his way through the maze."

"More retrocausality," says Morat. "Somehow he can see what's coming—"

"Presumably. But . . . " Haskell hesitates.

"What is it?"

"I—went through something similar at the Europa Platform. Everything converged on the moment when the combat started."

"I suspect Sinclair has a slightly wider purview."

"The question is how far it extends."

"What do you mean?"

"He told Carson there was a moment coming up past which he couldn't see."

"Now we're getting somewhere," says Morat.

"I'll say," says the voice of Jason Marlowe.

They've come through into a new part of the ship. The ceilings are much higher now, the walls far wider.

"Waste of space," says Linehan.

"Not really," replies Lynx.

They're looking at a vast garage of vehicles. Most of them are crawlers. Rigged for some heavy terrain from the looks of their treads . . .

"Ready to tame the red planet," says Lynx.

"I thought this wasn't really a colony ship."

"It's not," says Lynx. "This is in case it needs to pacify the Moon or something."

"Or something?"

"Or land dropships on Earth. Give me a fucking break, man. I'm no strategist. I'd thought the sole point of this ship was to rig as many guns as they could fit on it." He gestures at the vehicles. "What they want with this shit, who the fuck knows. Maybe it was in case of inspections by the Eurasians under some fucking Zurich armaments limitation line-item—"

"Where exactly are we going, Lynx?"

"Told you already. We're getting away from the hull—"

"Stop bullshitting me. You know more than that."

"And trust me, you don't want to."

They've made their way into some high-ceilinged chambers positioned around the spine of the ship. Below them are hundreds of grav-couches. Each one contains a power-suited Russian soldier. Those soldiers have received orders to stay put. Unexpected accelerations could tear through this ship at any time. If that happens, Spencer's hoping he can hold onto his current perch. He can practically feel hundreds of eyes staring through him. He makes himself as one with the ceiling as possible, gets busy figuring out the next step—hesitates a moment, then leads the way into another duct.

Deja-vu: the auxiliary cargo chamber looks disconcertingly like the cargo hold in the Antares rocket that lifted the Operative from Earth several days back. For a moment, the Operative's brought up short, thinking about all that's transpired since—all that scrambling to stay alive, making sure all those others died. He follows Riley to a pressurized door set into the wall. Riley keys codes, breaks the seal—

"You sure you want to do that?" asks the Operative.

Riley says nothing. There's a hiss as the door slides aside. The room that's revealed is small. A raised platform is set into its center. Lying on that platform is something that looks like a cross between a suit of powered armor and a sarcophagus. Screens atop it show vital signs.

"Voilà," says Riley.

"You are shitting me," says the Operative.

"Not even vaguely," says Maschler. He's standing in the open door, his expression wary while Riley leans over the sarcophagus and keys in more codes. A visor slides back. The Operative recognizes the face behind it.

So you made it," says Haskell.

"Wouldn't miss it," says Marlowe.

"Lovers reunited," says Morat.

"That would be tricky," says Marlowe, "since I'm dead."

He looks even worse than that. Another disembodied head—a second sun burning in the leaden sky. But his face is the one she remembers from right before she killed him: that strange mixture of boyish wonder and unreflecting mind. He looks like he's genuinely pleased to see her. Like maybe he still loves her.

"You shouldn't have come," she says.

"I was here all along," replies Marlowe.

She nods. She feels that Control's probably almost at her center. Everything's shifting around her. Desert blooms in fast-forward, becoming jungle. She feels she's no longer alone—feels the eyes of all too many predators upon her body.

"I can hear them, Jason."

"Them?"

"The surviving members of the Rain. I can feel their minds."

"How many triads?"

"That's your first question?"

"That's the *only* question, Claire. What does Sinclair have left? What has he kept in reserve?"

"I can't tell."

"You can't *tell?*" asks Morat.

"It's fuzzy," she says. "There could be one. There could be many."

"Your powers are still in their infancy," says Marlowe. "You'll know soon enough."

"You'll be both searchlight and laser when we figure out how to *really* switch you on," says Morat. "The rest of the Rain won't stand a chance against you. And then we can neutralize Sinclair from a distance."

"But why not execute him right now?" she asks.

There's a flicker of hesitation up there. Around her, the jungle abruptly starts to wither. She shivers as the temperature plunges, watches as greenery shrivels.

"You can't, can you?" she asks.

"No," admits Morat.

"Montrose no longer controls the L5 flagship," she says.

"Montrose no longer controls the L5 *fleet*," says Marlowe.

The temperature keeps dropping. Snow's falling in sheets. Vast ice sculptures are visible in the middle distance. The suns above her are growing faint.

"Sinclair's taken over up there," she mutters.

"Apparently," says Morat.

"But the L5 ships are still fighting the East?"

"Oh yes," he says. "Still coordinating with the rest of the American fleet. Still firing on the oncoming Eurasians."

"Normal communication is being maintained," says Marlowe. "It's the higher-ups we can't get through to."

"Classic Rain takeover," she says.

"Probably," says Morat.

"You have to let me out of here."

"You have to help us," says Marlowe.

"We need you back in the game," says Morat.

"So release me."

"First we need you to allow us control."

"I don't know how to do that."

"You're about to find out. We've almost broken through."

She feels that's correct, like the final wall in her mind is paper-thin, about to be torn. She feels something bearing down upon her that she can't hope to avoid. The snow intensifies, swirls against her face. The ground starts to freeze beneath her feet.

"So now we move to the *real* question," says Morat.

"Why did you kill me?" says Marlowe.

"Don't you dare go there," she says.

But he already has. And it's already set something in motion that she knows she can't stop. Some kind of chain reaction going off within her as though she's nothing but thousands of tiny gears and pulleys now cranking into operation—ten million dominoes toppling in long lines across vast illuminated floors—and she's powerless to stop it. She's on the ground now, and it's all ice beneath her while she lies on her back and snow falls into her open mouth and eyes. Her innermost desires are exposed to the light—and the face of Jason Marlowe is streaking fire as it drops burning from the sky toward horizon . . .

"I didn't know what compulsions he'd been rigged with," she whispers.

"You don't know what compulsions *you've* been rigged with," says Morat. "Why didn't you shoot yourself too?"

"Maybe I should have."

"Carson might not like that."

"Who cares what he likes?"

"He thought to enslave you."

"It's me who's enslaved *him*."

"Given that he's the world's best actor—"

"You've got it all wrong," she says. "He's only fooling himself. He's spent his whole life running from his own emotions. If he faces me again, his mind will be in my power. Trust me on that—"

"I don't need to trust you ever again," says Morat. "That's the beauty of all this."

"That's what you think—"

"Your psychology is endlessly fascinating, Claire. The more cornered you get, the more arrogant you become. Even though that acrid odor you're smelling is the core of your own mind burning out."

She can't smell a thing. Still can't move either. She hears sharp cracking noises around her. Turns out that what she's sprawled on is really pack ice breaking up. She feels herself pulled in all too many directions. Everything beneath her is starting to go.

"It's been nice knowing you, Claire." Morat's voice morphs seamlessly into that of Control. "Take comfort in the fact that you're the most fascinating challenge I've ever faced."

"You're done?"

"In ten more seconds."

"Which is when—"

"You become the world's most intelligent automaton. A shame you won't be able to let me know how it feels."

"Fuck you to the gates of damnation—"

Frigid liquid closes in around her head.

They've entered the domain of gravity. Apparently this is the rotating part of the ship. They cross a bridge, and Linehan can't even see the bottom. Lynx isn't even looking. Linehan can only imagine how much wider of a purview that man must have. He always thought razors were sad, confined creatures who couldn't take the world and lived within themselves. Now he's realizing that they've got the only world worth having. Ayahuasca taught him that. That, and Spencer—who told him that for a razor, it was basically altered consciousness every time they jack in, that all life was just a shimmering of maya anyway— endless pixel fragments scattered down some endless well of dark. He can believe it. He's heard that back on Earth there are tribes that believe that by eating the bodies of their enemies they consume their souls. He feels like maybe that's what happened to his. He follows Lynx as that man leads the way into a vast chamber.

And then he sees what lines the walls.

"Oh dear God," he says.

"That's what they'll be calling me when this is all over," says Lynx.

One-third of the way to the Moon, *Hammer of the Skies* is drawing within range of lunar artillery. It's starting to take increasing amounts of fire. It's not bothering to return the favor.

"The whites of their eyes are a long way off," says Sarmax.

But getting closer. The ship is starting to speed up slightly. Spencer feels his magnetic clamps gripping just a little bit tighter against the wall of the shaft they're crawling through. They're getting ever nearer to the hull, approaching a small room set against it, identical rooms set around it. Officer quarters—and Spencer's looking through the cameras at one officer in particular. He wears a major's stripes. He's sitting cross-legged, smiling very faintly. His eyes scare Spencer shitless.

You fucking bastards," says the Operative.

"We're just the errand boys," says Riley.

The opaque visor has slid aside. Sightless eyes stare up at him. The face of Claire Haskell is without expression. Her mouth is slightly open. She's breathing slowly.

"It's not her," says the Operative.

"Believe it or not," says Riley, "it is."

She dwelt underwater way too long. But then one day all that sea boiled away in an instant. Leaving only a voice.

That of Matthew Sinclair.

"Claire," he says. "Can you hear me?"

"I can," she replies.

She can feel him, too. His mental presence is very clear, totally unmistakable. Her mind can suddenly see straight through the mainframe in which she's captive, out beyond Montrose's base—

out across the Cislunar, all the way to the L5 fleet and the ship that
sits at its center. Sinclair's brain burns before her with the intensity
of a firestorm, but all she can think of is a single question.

"Is this part of the interrogation, too?"

"A better word is by-product."

W hat the fuck is this?" asks Linehan.
        "What does it look like?" says Lynx.
        "I thought this wasn't a real colony ship."

"Guess it's got all the accessories."

Cryo-bays stretch around them. The sleepers are packed about
as tight as possible. Their eyes are open. Their vital signs are checking out. Lynx walks over to one of them, rips a socket out of the
wall. One set of vital signs flatlines.

"Let's get on with it," he says.

T hirty seconds," says Spencer. They're pulling them-
        selves through spaces barely wide enough to accomo-
        date their armor. They're within the duct-system of the
officer quarters now. The man's still sitting there, staring straight
ahead. Spencer's hoping that this isn't some image that's been put
there for his benefit. Even so, he's got a nasty feeling—

"This guy's Autumn Rain," he says.

"You know that for a fact?" says Sarmax.

"I'm asking *you*. I think you know—"

"I don't know *shit*," snarls Sarmax. "Except that we gotta be
ready for anything. Are my angles correct?"

He's referring to the laser mounted on his shoulder; it's just
swiveled, pointed downward at the wall ahead. But Spencer's the
one with the blueprint.

"Burn it," he says, and Sarmax does just that.

⊕ "What do you mean it's really her?" says the Operative.

"Now we got him excited," says Maschler.

"Now you got me wondering what kind of bullshit you're trying to fucking *pull*," mutters the Operative. "There's no way that Montrose is so stupid as to turn the Manilishi over to Szilard."

"Unless?" asks Riley.

"There's no unless. That's not the Manilishi—"

"Hold that thought," says Maschler.

The woman's eyes open.

◑ "I don't understand," says Haskell.

"You don't have to," says Sinclair.

His face is coming into view now—the one she remembers from four days ago. Its eyes are wide. Its lips are parted. She feels herself being pulled in as though by an undertow—feels like she's already gone under.

"You broke into the InfoCom systems," she says.

"On the contrary," he says. "You broke *out*."

◈ "Did you just kill that guy?" asks Linehan.

"He didn't feel a thing," says Lynx.

Linehan can believe it. None of the people around him seem to be aware of much. The corridor stretches away, sleepers racked every step of the way. Plastic medbeds, looking disconcertingly like trays, are stacked upon one another, ten per each two meters of corridor.

"Easier to think of them as meat," adds Lynx.

Sarmax vaults into the room; the camera-feed that Spencer's giving him merges seamlessly with what's actually sitting in the room, wearing the uniform of a major in Russian intelligence and the smile of a man who's way ahead of everything. Sarmax brings his guns to bear.

"Don't fucking move," he says.

"Glad you could make it," says the man.

Carson," says the woman.

The Operative stares at her. She sounds just like Haskell.

"Claire?" he says.

What the hell's going on?" says Haskell.

"Exactly what I planned," says Sinclair.

"We're all just your puppets?"

"More like all just part of the pattern."

Meet the Martians," says Lynx, as he starts running jacks into the wires he's ripped from the walls. Linehan keeps an eye on the corridor while he does so, trying not to think about all those staring eyes . . .

"What the fuck are you talking about?" he asks.

"That's where they thought they were going."

"What was the point of having them here on a warship, then—of lying to them?"

Lynx shrugs. "To make the overall lie that much more convincing?"

Spencer drops from the duct into the room, takes in the scene. There's a buzz as Sarmax opens up the one-on-one.

"Who the fuck is *this?*" he demands. But Spencer says nothing—

"You don't recognize me?" asks the man.

"Should I?" asks Sarmax.

"Here's a hint: you killed me once already."

It's very simple," says the woman.

"I'll bet," says the Operative.

"I'm Claire," she says dreamily.

"You're on drugs," says the Operative.

"Are those two things so incompatible?"

"You're a *clone,*" he says.

"Not quite," says Riley.

"You really want to discuss this in front of her?"

"Why not?" says the woman. "I'm at peace with it."

"With what?"

"Being God," she says.

Anything but that," says Haskell.

Sinclair laughs. "You think you're God?"

She's starting to wonder. Because all of a sudden her purview is stretching all the way to that shuttle in which Carson and Maschler and Riley are approaching Szilard's lair. The ship that contains the cargo that's made in her own image—the woman whose mind she's now inside. She can't control what that woman's saying. All she can do is watch.

Though she really doesn't want to.

"I think I'm going crazy," she tells Sinclair.

THE MACHINERY OF LIGHT 119

"Crazy enough to believe you're the one to judge the living and the dead?" He chuckles, and it's somehow almost obscene. "You're so much more than *that* bullshit."

"I just want to be a normal fucking human being."

"Your flesh is as close as you get to that."

"My *flesh* is locked into a tank while a bodyless machine goes to town on it—"

"Control? Let it keep on flailing away."

"But it's about to enslave me—"

"Again, you've got it backward."

L ynx has ripped out a panel of the wall. Wires link him to the electronics behind it. All the bodies around him are breathing except for one.

"So who was he?" asks Linehan.

"Who?"

"That guy you just killed."

"Luckless."

I 'm Alek Jarvin," says the man.

"*Fuck*," says Sarmax.

"Prove it," says Spencer.

"The same way you could prove you killed me?"

Spencer gets the dilemma. Nothing's certain these days. Not when faces are malleable. The man they shot to death in the floor of that safehouse back in Hong Kong, who looked exactly like a rogue CICom handler—he could have been a plant. Could have been hired to play the part—could have been *manufactured*—without knowing how the role was going to end. There's no way to know for sure.

Though it's possible to narrow down the options.

"You stole something from me," says the man.

"Which you stole from Matthew Sinclair," says Sarmax.

"Get your facts straight," says the man. "I stole files from him, which I then compiled into my *own*. How much progress have you made?"

Spencer coughs. "We're still working on—"

"We're asking the questions," snaps Sarmax. "Listen, asshole, even if you *are* Alek Jarvin, then what the fuck are you doing *here*?"

"Staying in the game," says the man mildly.

H ate to break it to you," says the Operative. "You're not God."

"But I will be soon," mumbles the woman.

"You're not even in your right mind."

"I'll be in *your* mind shortly."

"What's that supposed to mean?" asks the Operative. He feels stupid even getting into this conversation. He feels even dumber with Riley and Maschler watching the whole thing. He feels his emotions getting the better of him. It's not a feeling he's used to.

"You're being too hard on her," says Maschler.

"You guys need to level with me."

"We already tried doing that," says Riley. "You wouldn't listen."

"Listen to *what?*" demands the Operative.

"The last words Szilard will ever hear," says the woman.

S uch a thing as biting off more than you can chew," says Sinclair.

Haskell nods. She feels that's all she's ever done. She wonders if Sinclair's some cancer that took her over long ago. She can still feel Control rummaging around inside her—can sense Montrose somewhere beyond that, eagerly awaiting the results.

"Montrose made her bid too soon," says Sinclair. "Should have kept Harrison in the picture for just a while longer. Too many players out there still. Too great a chance of getting squeezed."

Haskell knows the feeling. She's starting to feel increasing amounts of pressure in her skull. Her awareness is expanding out on all sides. Her head seems to be encompassing so much more. She feels herself gaining in everything.

Save understanding.

"Matthew," she says.

"Claire," he replies.

"What do you *want?*"

"Nothing I don't already have."

Apparently the dead have their uses. Lynx has thrust wires into various parts of his head, has slotted more wires into the skull of the man he's killed. His eyes look like they're far away. He's smiling the smile of a man who's found the thing he's been seeking.

"Everything you see around you is SpaceCom property," Lynx says. "These schmucks signed up to go to Mars and here they are months later still stuck in the departure lounge."

"Sure," says Linehan, "but I'm still wondering what's the point of having them here in the first place?"

"I'm starting to think it might have something to do with a master needing servants."

"So *you've* been running *us*," says Sarmax.

"Indeed," says Jarvin.

Sarmax doesn't even bother to use the one-on-one: "What the hell's your *problem*, Spencer?"

Spencer shrugs. "How was I supposed to know he was this good?"

"How the hell else could I have stayed alive in HK?" asks Jarvin. He's smiling that smile again, and Spencer's doing his best to ignore it. "Once I cut loose from Sinclair, I was a free agent. In more ways than one."

"So what's to stop us from just killing you now?" says Spencer.

"I don't think you get it," says Jarvin. "I've got Spencer's whole zone-signature *covered*. Shoot me and there'll be nothing to stop the East from seeing you."

"You played us like a fiddle," says Spencer.

"Pretty much."

"You knew what we going to do the whole time."

Jarvin laughs. "After I fed the Praetorians some dirt on the East's secret weapon, it wasn't hard to guess what their next move would be. Straight onto my little square of the board. I let you in first, gentlemen. And I gotta say, you did a nice job running point."

"*Fuck*," says Spencer.

"That's right," says Jarvin. He looks around—like he's glancing through the walls of this vast ship. Spencer suspects that's probably exactly what he's doing. Eyes snap back to face them: "Move on me, and the Eurasians will detect you."

"Come on," says Sarmax, "we need more than that."

"What do you mean?"

"We're done with you calling the shots."

"I realize that. That's why I let you into this room."

"We need to team up," says Spencer suddenly.

"Late to the party as ever," says Jarvin.

Too late she sees the trap: Sinclair's claws are reaching for her mind, far beneath any surface that Control or Montrose can perceive. Too late—and yet she slides aside and dodges past, slamming a door she didn't even know she had. He gazes at her through its translucence.

"Claire," he says.

"Matthew," she replies.

"Open this door."

"I can't do that, Matthew."

"What you can't do is resist me. You're not capable—"

"I am now."

And for a moment she sees something in his face—utter animal rage—and she keeps her shields up. Even if she doesn't know what's shielding her. Even if this psionic power she has remains almost completely undefined, save for the fact that it has something to do with consciousness. Something to do with mind reading.

"And something to do with time," says a voice.

There's a blinding flash.

The woman's face suddenly spasms. Her eyes shut.

"She's flatlining," says the Operative.

"No," says Maschler, "she's not."

Eyes snap open. Haskell stares at the Operative.

"*Carson,*" she says.

"Claire," he mutters.

"The lady's joined us," says Riley.

"This isn't really *me,*" says Haskell. She's looking around the cramped room. She's looking like she's starting to panic.

"Easy," says the Operative.

"Can you hear me, Claire?" asks Maschler.

Haskell says nothing—her face contorts—

"*Can you hear me, Claire?*"

"Yes," says Haskell.

"Your real body is back on the Moon. We're putting your mind through its paces. Seeing what it's made of. Do exactly what we say, and you'll return to your own flesh safely."

"Who are you?"

"They're InfoCom agents," says the Operative.

"Assistants to your interrogation," says Riley.

"Great," says Haskell.

"I'm their prisoner," says the Operative.

"Whose body am I in?"

"It's yours now."

"Whose body *was* it?"

"No one's," says the Operative.

She frowns. "I'm wearing my own face, aren't I?"

The Operative can't say anything. He just nods. He can see she's trying not to cry. Then suddenly that face is all resolution.

"Let's get on with this," she says.

Master and servants," says Linehan.

"Yes," says Lynx.

"This is Szilard's ship."

"Exactly."

"That's why you steered us here."

"For sure. It's his new flagship."

"And his escape ship," says Linehan.

Pause. Lynx's smile cuts out.

"You're quick," he says slowly.

"If it all goes to shit—"

"Goes? Try *going*."

"Those megaships are still coming on?" asks Linehan.

"Like juggernauts, man. Their speeds are insane—"

"He'll send the L2 fleet out to do battle with them."

Lynx gestures. "And be ready to fire this thing's motors if that fleet gets shattered."

"They'll follow him to Mars," says Linehan.

"They'll have a lot to keep them busy in the meantime."

"But eventually—"

"What makes you think he'd stop at *Mars*? This thing's got some serious engines. He could go to ground in the rings of Saturn—or make a break for deep space, try to run this all the way out. At least lead them on a good chase."

"With a fuck-sized entourage keeping him company," says Linehan.

"And guess who gets to get in there and stop him."

W e need to take control of this ship," says Jarvin. "Precisely what we were thinking," says Sarmax.

"Sure," says Spencer, "but under what terms?"

Both men look at him. He shrugs.

"It's a fair question," he says. "Sarmax here is a member of Autumn Rain. And for all we know, you are, too—"

"I'm not," says Jarvin.

"You sure about that?"

"Anyone who's sure about anything is a fool. Same with all this *member* bullshit you're on about. Like everyone in the Rain went to the same country club. So Sarmax was part of the prototype. So what? Whose side are you on now, Leo?"

"Mine," says Sarmax.

"My kind of thinking," says Jarvin. "You guys up for a three-way partnership?"

"For sure," says Sarmax.

"So quick to agree." Jarvin looks amused. "You can always take me out when we've hit paydirt, huh?"

"I wasn't thinking—"

"Well, it's about time you started." Jarvin gestures at Spencer. "Maybe he and I will take *you* out."

Sarmax laughs. "Give me a break—"

"Why should I? It's not like your track record for team-ups is the best. You and Carson and Lynx sure ballsed up the reunion, huh?"

"That was Carson," says Spencer. "He pulled the plug—"

"Shut *up*," says Sarmax.

"I could have predicted that," says Jarvin. He turns to Sarmax: "You *should* have predicted that."

"I thought he'd at least wait until we'd won before going for the big backstab."

Jarvin laughs. "Carson's got a knack for devising schemes so complex you can't even figure out what his angle is."

"How do you know so much about us?"

"He's got the file, doesn't he?" says Spencer.

There's a pause.

"And the one we took from you was bullshit?" asks Sarmax.

Jarvin smiles.

"And you still have the—"

"Of course I still have the real one."

"And we've got the fake one," says Sarmax. *"Fuck."*

Spencer shakes his head. "But those schematics of the Himalayan black base were real!"

"Which ought to tell you something," says Jarvin.

"It tells me you gave us the real scoop on the Eurasian base and the fake scoop on the Rain—"

"No," says Jarvin.

They look at him.

"I held back nothing."

M aschler's drawn a sidearm.

"What's that for?" asks the Operative.

"To encourage you not to do anything stupid."

"Why would I do that?"

"You've been known to around Claire."

"Just stay calm," says Haskell. It hadn't occurred to the Operative to be anything else, but maybe everyone's way ahead of him. "Let them do what they're here for," she adds.

"What the hell's going *on*?"

"Easy," says Maschler—a smooth, reassuring cadence the Operative uses himself when he's about to kill someone. He's still in the doorway, about four meters from the Operative. Riley's on the other side of Haskell, punching buttons on a console. The Operative feels his head starting to spin. He feels like he's having a stroke. He goes down on one knee.

"Carson," says Haskell.

He drops. He's kissing metal. Everything's gone black. All he can hear is Haskell now. Though he's not even sure about that. Just a faint voice he remembers from so long ago:

"Carson," she says softly.

"Yeah," he replies.

"What are you seeing?"

The answer's nothing. Except—

"You," he says.

"Because I'm inside your head," says Haskell.

"But I'm not in yours."

"And that's just fine by me."

I don't like this," says Linehan.

"You don't have to like it," says Lynx.

"Talk about obsession. You're fucking crazy."

"What's crazy is thinking we can do anything else."

"We should be thinking about getting off this ship!"

"Got somewhere in mind?"

"Somewhere that's a little more solid than this fleet."

"Like the Moon?"

"We should never have left that fucking rock."

"Shoulda, coulda, woulda—*who the fuck cares?* We are where

we are. This place is in lockdown. Szilard knows we're aboard, right? So now it's set up like the *Montana* was. Nothing's getting off."

"Not even him?"

"Why would he want to leave?" asks Lynx.

"He knows rogue agents got aboard."

"So?"

"So why the hell hasn't he bailed? Rig a shuttle and scram?"

Lynx laughs. "Sums up why you're *taking* orders and I'm *giving* them. Christ almighty, Linehan. This is a *big ship*. It's not like Szilard's in the next room. He's camped out somewhere in the rear of this bitch, inside two heavily guarded perimeters, and you'd have him just shit in his pants and run for a *shuttle?*"

"So he can set up shop somewhere safe—"

"*Safe?* He knows damn well we'd be aboard that shuttle *waiting for him.*"

Linehan shakes his head. He looks around at all the sleepers—looks back at Lynx and the wires sprouting from his head.

"Two perimeters, huh."

"You know you want it."

Ø   "So you *didn't* crack the files," says Spencer.
    Jarvin looks at him strangely—as though he's just seeing him for the first time. He adjusts his major's insignia idly.

"Not the core of it," he says.

"All those goddamn languages," says Spencer.

Jarvin nods. "Sinclair's created a code that may be impossible to crack. Ironic, no? You've got what may be the master file on Autumn Rain right in front of your fucking *eyes*, and you're still none the wiser."

"But I know they're records of the experiments," says Spencer.

"Yeah? What else?"

"That's as far as I've got—"

"Spencer," says Sarmax, "shut *up*—"

"Interesting," says Jarvin, and he sounds like he means it. "I got deeper than you. And here I was hoping it'd be the other way around. That you could help me."

"Like we'd do that," says Sarmax.

"Then you can hardly blame me for not returning the favor."

"What else is in that goddamn book?" asks Sarmax. "Dammit, we need to know—"

"Nothing," says Jarvin. "For now. How about we table the rest of it until we've taken over the cockpit?"

"You're the boss," says Spencer.

"For now," says Sarmax.

"Nothing's forever," says Jarvin.

W hat the hell's going on?" says the Operative—and *says* nothing. His lips aren't moving. He can't even feel them. Nor can he feel anything else. He's out cold on the floor, aware only of Haskell's voice sounding in his head, a sound far more intimate than the wireless-enabled one-on-one:

"He's adjusting the controls on my console," she says.

She sends him the image, too: static, grainy. She's still flat on her back. Riley's got his gun trained on the prone figure of the Operative. Maschler's working the controls again.

The image cuts out. The Operative's back in black.

"What the hell's he doing?" asks the Operative.

"Allowing us to do what *we're* doing, I'm guessing."

Which is something he's never done before, even though he's lived with its latency all his life. Even after so recently realizing his true nature—when Sinclair restored his memories, reminding him that all his life he's had intimations of Lynx and Sarmax's mental patterns; all that time catching glimpses of those other minds—

and all of it was nothing compared to what he's seeing now: Haskell's burning in his brain. He can't help but draw back in pure astonishment.

"You're beautiful," he mutters.

"Shut the hell up," she says.

"I mean it."

"Said the boy who cried wolf and kept on crying. They're operating on my fucking mind *again*, and you're the one who started it."

"I—wanted to have you for myself."

"You never will."

"I get that now."

"Then you also get that you're not getting out of this one."

"I've heard that before."

"I don't believe this," she snarls. "You're out cold on that floor—Riley just prodded your face with his fucking *boot*—and you're still convinced you're walking out of here."

"Because they need me," says the Operative.

"For one last service," she replies.

And then he's history," says Maschler. "He'll walk into Szilard's ship while you fly shotgun via your amplifier."

"My what?" asks Haskell.

"Your *body*," says Riley, gesturing at her.

"You mean my new one."

"Yours all along," says Maschler. "It's got your DNA."

"Who grew it?"

"Montrose," says Riley.

"How did she get my specifications?"

"She got into Sinclair's files way back."

"You're kidding me."

"We're the lords of information. Why act so surprised?"

"Because you're fucking crazy," says Haskell. "You've only got whatever Sinclair wanted you to—"

"More theories," says Maschler.

"Said the man whose boss tried to build another Manilishi."

"Relax," says Riley. "All we have is you."

"Why I said *tried*."

"So how are we gonna do this?" says Linehan

"We're already halfway there, man."

"What the hell are you talking about?"

"Them," says Lynx—waves a languid hand at the sleepers all around.

"I'm not following."

"That's 'cause you're not listening. These guys thought they'd gotten the long ticket, but now they're our ticket to the real show."

"How's that?"

"Their life-support systems are run by this ship's mainframe."

"Oh."

"*Oh*," says Lynx. He fingers a wire almost lovingly. "From where I sidestep into the security databases."

"Nice one," says Linehan.

"Szilard will find it less enthralling," says Lynx.

"So how are we going to hit that cockpit?" asks Sarmax.

Jarvin looks at him. "How were *you* guys figuring on doing it?"

Sarmax looks at Spencer. "How *were* we figuring?"

"Fucked if I know. There's no way in."

Jarvin laughs. "That's why you had to come to me."

"All right, asshole," says Sarmax. "How *are* we getting in?"

"By staying in plain sight."

"They're going to have you just walk in there," she says.

"I realize that," he replies.

But what he hadn't realized was the path that InfoCom devised to thread the SpaceCom needle. He only got it just now. He's going to walk in there, all right. But he's not going to be alone.

"I'm coming with you," says Haskell.

"One last time," he replies.

It's all he can hope for, really. He's still out like a light, and her voice is the only contact he's got with anything outside the island of his own mind. But that voice keeps on wavering in clarity, like a radio signal shifting across frequencies. The Operative thinks of Maschler tuning the dials, thinks of the creature called Control messing with Haskell's brain.

"They're killing all their birds with one stone," he says.

"A page from your playbook," she replies.

Not that the Operative needs to be informed of that. Uncovering something's true capabilities means you have to push that thing to its limits. Which presumably is precisely what Stephanie Montrose is doing right now. Her servants are going to turn the Manilishi inside out while Haskell's mind rides shotgun on the run on Szilard.

"Along with this body," says Haskell.

"Exactly," says Maschler.

He's looking down at her the way a doctor might look on a particularly problematic patient. The furrows on his brow are making his eyebrows do strange things.

"You're Carson's ticket onto the *Redeemer*," he adds. "Szilard's new flagship."

"A step down from the *Montana*."

"Or a step up," says Maschler. "The *Redeemer*'s one of the Class V colony ships."

She mulls that over.

"One of the *fully loaded* colony ships," adds Riley.

"Damn," she says.

"Szilard's the man with the plan," says Maschler.

Riley snorts. "He could be Noah to his own little ark if he had to."

"Except he's not going to," she says.

"He won't need to," says Maschler. "Our best estimate is that the combined strength of lunar gunnery and the L2 fleet will take down those Eurasian megaships."

Riley coughs. "After which we'll just have to see how much we have left to deal with the rest of the Eastern forces coming up the gravity well behind them."

"None of which is Szilard's problem," says Maschler.

"Given that he'll be dead by then," says Riley.

Haskell looks puzzled. "So what's the story that Montrose has fed Szilard to get him to open up?"

"What do you mean?"

"Carson shows up on a flight from Congreve carrying the Manilishi, along with a little note from Montrose that she's managed to clone the most powerful weapon ever built and here it is and go knock yourself out?"

Maschler laughs. "Not quite."

Lynx pulls the wires away from his head in a single stroke. "Let's go," he says, gesturing at the panel he's slid from the wall.

"That looks like a tight fit," says Linehan.

"Less so for me," says Lynx, disappearing through the hole. Linehan pulls his way in after him—finds himself in a narrow space that seems to parallel the walls of the room they've just left. He follows Lynx, pushing through wires like they're undergrowth in a jungle.

"The support systems around the sleepers," says Lynx. "Try not to damage anything. We're trying to keep a low profile."

Linehan's hoping that Lynx has got any alarms covered. The razor's small enough to sidle through the narrow space. The mech's a different story. Wires are getting torn. Circuitry's getting shredded.

"Tell me we're getting somewhere," he mutters.

"*I* am," says Lynx. "But you'd better pick up the pace."

But that's tough when wires are all Linehan can see. He shoves through them, thinking back to some scene in some book some girl told him about a long time ago. Some children were wandering in a closet and came out into some other land. Linehan can relate. He feels like he's stepped into some other world himself these last few days. Seasoned wet-ops specialist, seen-and-done-it-all, wham-bam-thanks-man Linehan, the legend of the SpaceCom hard corps—and then suddenly he got launched against the Rain and propelled into a brand-new life. Linehan gets that lives like that don't last. Ayahuasca's afterglow reinforces the point, confirms it. Existence is moving toward some climax he won't survive. He's pretty sure he doesn't want to. And now he's emerging from the wires . . .

"Holy fuck," he says.

"It gets even better," says Lynx.

The special liaison of the Praesidium has left his quarters and is proceeding toward the cockpit of the *Hammer of the Skies*. He didn't have a bodyguard when he got on, but he's got two of them now. Zone is showing they were aboard already. Working undercover, all with the highest possible clearance: Jarvin, Spencer, and Sarmax have gone up three levels of ladders, taken an elevator up another ten floors. Now they're approaching the elevator banks that are one of only two routes leading to the cockpit. A mixture of Chinese and Russian soldiers cluster around those banks. They're obviously on high alert. They seem to be as busy watching one another as those who approach.

"Let me do the talking," says Jarvin.

W hat are they talking about now?" asks the Operative.

"Maschler and Riley?"

"Who else?"

It's not like there's anybody else that matters right now. Unless there are more voices in Haskell's head. He wouldn't put it past her. Her signal's all he's got—even louder than his internal monologue. He no longer knows what he wants.

"Yes you do," says Haskell.

"What?"

She says nothing—though it sounds like she's laughing at him. Or maybe it's his own mind cackling as it finally goes over the edge. He finds himself grasping at anything that's solid. He can think of only one thing.

"So what the hell's the plan?" he asks.

"You already know the plan," she replies. "Convince Szilard that you stole the Manilishi from Montrose."

"That's not the only possibility," says the Operative.

Haskell nods slowly. "*You* didn't steal me—"

"Maschler and Riley did."

"Right."

"They're SpaceCom agents."

"They're pretending to be."

"Christ, Claire, they probably *are*."

"I guess we're going to find out."

"How close to L2 are we?"

"Like they'd tell me."

"Ask them anyway."

She does. Maschler looks at her. "Getting warm," he says.

"And you're SpaceCom agents?"

Riley laughs. "Now what would give you that idea?"

"Just answer the question."

"I doubt we could do it convincingly," says Maschler.

"You are, aren't you?"

"Szilard thinks we are," says Maschler. "That's all that matters."

"You guys had better—"

Riley laughs. "Like we'd ever cross our lady. She sees everything."

"Knows it all," says Maschler.

"Bullshit."

"Yeah?"

"You guys don't *look* like you're crazy. If you're working for InfoCom, then you're about to die. Killing Szilard's a fucking suicide mission."

"Not if it succeeds," says Maschler.

"Even then the assassins will die—"

"That'd be Carson," says Riley. "He's the triggerman."

"Or at least the guy who gets close enough," says Maschler. "He's a goner."

"And you're not?"

"We draw danger pay for a reason," says Riley. "And we're going to torch everybody on the *Redeemer* who can link this back to Montrose."

"Me included?"

"Don't you worry your pretty little head," says Riley. "You won't feel a thing."

"Except for now," says Maschler.

W hat the hell is this?" says Linehan.
    "What does it look like?" asks Lynx.
    It looks like ice. Sheets of it stretch away on all sides.

"How big is this place?" Linehan asks. He pulls himself out of the last of the wires and crawls through the hatch that Lynx has opened.

"Couple hundred meters," says Lynx. "This is the core of the ship. And over there is frozen methane, so we've got fuel and water from a single locale, and also the backbone of the sleeper freezing units."

"And the route past the outer perimeter."

"You catch on fast," says Lynx.

They extend crampons, start to rappel out onto the slopes of freeze.

S ir," says a Russian sergeant, "your codes."
    "Here," says Jarvin—sends them over. At least, that's what Spencer is forced to presume. But now the Chinese sergeant steps forward.

"Your codes," he says. "Sir."

"Again?"

"I must insist."

"Don't you trust your colleague?" says Jarvin, indicating the Russian sergeant.

"I trust my orders."

"In other words, no." Sarmax's voice is coming through loud and clear on the one-on-one in Spencer's head. "Things must be getting tense in that fucking cockpit."

"They've probably got the balance just so." Spencer's thinking fast. "Three more Russians may throw things out of whack."

"But the Praesidium is supreme authority across the whole Coalition. So they have to let—"

"They don't have to do *shit*," says Sarmax—but the Chinese sergeant nods. The Russian sergeant clears his throat.

"You're cleared, sirs," he says. "They're sending an elevator down now."

"Very good," says Jarvin—and now that voice echoes in Spencer's helmet: "This whole place is in lockdown mode. God only knows what it's like up there."

"We'd better be ready for anything," says Sarmax.

"We've got the highest clearance," says Jarvin. "Theoretically, we can confront the captains and take command of the ship."

"*Theoretically*," says Spencer.

An elevator door opens. Jarvin starts toward it—just as the ship suddenly changes course without warning. Spencer's hurled toward the wall—along with everyone else.

⊕ *F*uck," she says.
"What?"
But there's no answer. He gets a quick glimpse of what might be Haskell's face, falling away from him as though it's tumbling through some endless space. And suddenly he's back in the real one—opening his eyes. A boot is prodding against him.

"Wakey wakey," says Maschler.

◐ *S*he's coming 'round," says a voice.
It's news to Haskell. She feels like a freight train just ran through her skull. She senses something fading that might be vertigo, but in reverse—as though she's already hit the ground and is still getting used to that fact. Awareness starts to crystallize all around her—as if all existence is a grid, and she's sitting at the very center.

She opens her eyes.

"Welcome back," says Stephanie Montrose.

They're creeping along sheets of ice. Sensors are everywhere. Linehan can only hope Lynx is dealing with them. He normally doesn't worry about stuff he can't control, but this place is giving him the creeps. As extensive as it is, it's also intensely claustrophobic. The sheets of ice are only a few meters apart at points. Linehan feels like the whole thing could fold up at any moment—like he's about to end up in a glacier sandwich.

"How much more of this?" he says.

"Carson told me nothing rattled you," says Lynx.

They crawl over a slope and along its other side. They seem to have left the central portions of the ice behind. The space they're in is getting even narrower—so cramped now that Linehan can brace himself against both walls. Soon it's just a tunnel in the ice. He follows Lynx along it, sees the razor opening another hatch. He follows him through.

And finds himself in a small chamber. Looks like some kind of storage space. There's only one other way out—yet another hatch. But Lynx scarcely spares it a glance. Instead, he sits down in a corner. Linehan looks at him.

"What the hell do you think you're doing?"

"Shut up and take a seat," says Lynx.

Hammer of the Skies is changing its trajectory. The fact that it's doing so without warning is causing no little inconvenience for many of those within. Spencer can hear the intercom ringing in his ears, instructing everybody to assume the brace position, but the position he's already assumed has very little to do with anything he had a chance to brace for. He's spread-eagled against the wall. So is everyone else. He hears the voice of Sarmax ringing inside his head.

"Must be evasive action."

"No shit," says Spencer.

"Wrong," says Jarvin. "We just got a new destination."

Haskell struggles to focus. She's still on that souped-up gurney, back in the InfoCom HQ. The place looks like it's cranked up to even more frenetic levels of activity. She can see screens showing the megaships. Only they're no longer heading for the Moon.

"Next stop L5," says Control. The voice is coming from one of the consoles. She suddenly realizes that's the console her mind's held in—that she's actually in that console too, watching her body watch her, feeling Control's zone-presence hovering around her. As her zone-view coalesces, so do the InfoCom battle management systems, spread out across hundreds of thousands of kilometers of vacuum. Earth's a lost cause—entirely Eastern now, along with the rest of the near-Earth orbits. Most of the Eurasian ships are consolidating at the geo. Yet most of the zone-focus is on the East's advance team—the two megaships. They've climbed about half of the distance to the Moon and have just veered off at a sharp angle, attaining even greater speeds as they race toward L5. Haskell can see the lunar batteries flailing away, can see the smaller fleet at the libration point raining fire down upon the approaching dread-naughts and the ships they're towing. The battle management computers don't seem to think it's looking good.

"Sinclair's about to get taken off the board," says Control.

"Don't jump to conclusions," Haskell mutters.

"You'd be advised to avoid them as well," says Montrose—and as she speaks, Haskell feels something tighten around her in the zone—like a vise that's constricting all around her, cutting off her energy, starting to suffocate her . . .

"*Fuck*," she says.

"Let's get some things straight," says the president.

G et up," says Maschler. The Operative staggers to his feet, pain gripping his head as he looks around.

"Same as you left it," says Riley.

And all too familiar. That cargo chamber, the two InfoCom agents, that sarcophagus-suit—and the woman within it. Unconscious again now.

"So who is she, really?" he asks.

"No one," says Maschler.

"A temporary receptacle," says Riley.

"Sure, but what the hell's the receptacle?"

"Cloned body," says Maschler. "Implanted with an artificial personality construct. A primitive one."

"But effective," says Riley.

"Enough to get us near Szilard?" says the Operative.

"We're about to find out."

S o when do we start the run?" asks Linehan. "Earth to Linehan: we already did."

Yet for now they're staying put. They've been marking time for a few minutes now. Linehan's starting to get antsy. All the more so as he gets that Lynx has taken him in tow for muscle—and that the razor must be badly in need of that muscle to try to leverage *him*.

Or else there's another angle to all this.

"You've been using me," says Linehan.

"Of course I've been using you."

"That's not what I meant."

"C'mon, Linehan. You're the mech—"

"Who used to work for SpaceCom."

"Who got rigged with a compulsion by them," says Lynx.

"Which you reverse-engineered."

"Which is why I showed myself to you back on the *Montana*. Right. But—"

"But I'm also your back door into the SpaceCom mainframes," says Linehan.

Lynx grins. "One among many."

The megaship's continuing to accelerate, but now its route has straightened out. Soldiers are pulling themselves off the wall, taking up positions again around the elevator-bank. Spencer steadies himself while Jarvin moves back toward the elevator-banks.

"We can't let you up there," says the Chinese sergeant.

"We already had this conversation," says Jarvin. "Out of my—"

"Sir," says the Russian sergeant, *"we can't let you up there,"* Guns are out now.

"I already gave you my clearance."

"Sir, they just revoked it."

So now I'm your slave," says Haskell.

"You're alive. You're not in pain. Count your blessings."

Haskell studies Montrose from several angles. The president looks as if she's been under a lot of stress. Though now she seems to be perking up a little.

"You're the most powerful instrument in creation."

"Instrument," repeats Haskell.

"And someone has to wield you."

"I had myself in mind."

Montrose throws her head back and laughs—loud enough to make the visors of her nearest bodyguards turn. "Like you have the maturity for *that*."

"Fuck you—"

"You see? 'Fuck this' and 'fuck that'—you keep on ranting and all the while all you are is a mind so close to the edge of sanity that you're only fit to be the tool of the ones who really run the show. Jesus, Claire. I expected better from you."

"Would you rather I wasn't strapped to this table taking orders from you?"

"I'd rather you were a little nicer about it. Seeing as how we're going to have to get used to each other."

"And how we've got work to do," says Control.

She feels that leash brush up against her throat.

The Operative's climbing back into the main cargo bay. Maschler and Riley are both following him this time. Both men have their guns out now. The Operative's head hurts too much for him to even think about trying anything. He winces.

"Not to worry," says Riley.

"We'll dose you with some 'dorphs before we set you loose," says Maschler—snorts with laughter. But the Operative says nothing—just grabs a ladder, starts climbing back into the cockpit. He knows exactly what he's going to see in its windows. He hears the proximity alert starting up.

B ang on schedule," says Lynx.
    "What the hell are you talking about?" Linehan's
thinking Lynx's smile is starting to look ever more demented. But the razor just laughs.

"You didn't think we were going to do this alone, did you?"

"The way you keep talking, I don't know what to think."

"All good assassinations are done from all sides."

"Whatever you say, Lynx."

"JFK, for example. They—"

"Who?"

"Kennedy."

"You mean the spaceport?"

"I mean the president."

"Never heard of him."

"That's because you've got no education. Grassy knoll, book depository, Secret Service, open season: they got the bastard from every direction."

"Good for them."

"For us, you mean. We're going to do the same to Szilard."

"With me as expendable?"

"We're *all* expendable, Linehan. But if we manage to pull this off, we might yet get out of here in one piece."

"After which we go where?"

"First things first."

F ine," says Jarvin—turns, fires suit-jets to steady himself
    as he exits the foyer. The other two men follow him.
       "So what the hell do we do now?" asks Spencer.

"Figure out another way in," says Jarvin.

"How the fuck can they deny codes from the Praesidium?"

"Because someone in the cockpit told them to."

"God only knows who's in charge there now," says Sarmax.

"Could be the Rain themselves," says Jarvin.

"Was wondering that myself," says Spencer. "Or they could just be taking no chances."

"Whoever it is," says Sarmax, "they certainly don't want any competition."

Jarvin laughs. "Now that we're about to hit L5, who would?"

A s I anticipated," says Control.

Haskell can hardly fault that machine for sounding so conceited. Especially now that she's his humble servant—she's been slotted in, given access to the full range of his battle-management calculations. Apparently he's been predicting this move for some hours now—had anticipated that the megaships' drive on the Moon was a feint, that their real target was L5. There's decidedly less hardware there than at the Moon, meaning that the megaships have a far better chance of taking the libration point by themselves than they would have of destroying all of the American lunar forces—

"If they take L5, the Moon will be next," says Montrose.

"Of course," says Control, "but they'll need to bring up the rest of their fleet from the Earth orbits. That'll give us some breathing room."

But Haskell is barely listening. She's too busy getting cranked up to new heights. She doesn't want to go there, but she's being rushed toward them by Control's implacable grip. She feels herself opening out toward the universe. Other minds glimmer here and there: Carson in the shuttle that's almost docked; another mind deeper within Szilard's flagship. Still other minds seem to be present at L5, but they're more opaque—as though they're being shielded. She can guess by what. Even if she can't *see* it anymore, she can still feel that monstrous presence lurking out there, practically screaming at her intuition. The heart of L5: and she wonders how Matthew Sinclair plans to deal with millions of tons of Eurasian steel—wonders, too, who's really in control of that steel now. She feels herself surging ever higher. The parameters for the run on Szilard click in around her, incandescent matrices flaring out toward infinity. She takes the whole thing in—draws back from what's being asked of her . . .

"Begin," says Montrose.

N ot bad," says the Operative.

"That's all you can say?" asks Maschler.

"Nothing rattles our Carson," says Riley.

The Operative shrugs. He's in this way too deep to waste time gawking at the sight in the windows, impressive though it may be: the *Redeemer* spans almost half a klick, gunnery flaring all along its length. Beyond them the Operative can see a swathe of ships, a blaze of fire—and yet all of it a mere fraction of the fleet that lies beyond.

"The ramparts of L2," says Maschler.

"For now," says the Operative—and takes in the aft-bay hangar toward which the shuttle's descending. Massive doors start to swing open. Light gleams from within.

"Good luck," says Maschler.

"Fuck you very much," says the Operative.

Y ou'd better give me data," says Linehan.

"What kind?" asks Lynx.

"I was thinking the blueprint of this ship."

Lynx looks at him. Linehan does what he can to meet the man's stare. Which is tough because Lynx's eyes keep shimmering. The walls of this tiny room keep getting closer to one another. Linehan's guessing that has a lot more to do with whatever's going on in his own head than with anything that passes for objective reality. One more reason why he's angling to get a better view . . . .

"Why the fuck would I want to give you that?" asks Lynx.

"We're about to move in on Szilard, right?"

"Fuck, you're quick."

"And you're fucking *not*," says Linehan. "Say we get separated? What then?"

"If we get separated, we're fucked anyway—"

"You mean *I'm* fucked."

"So?"

"So why make it easy for them? C'mon, man, you know I'm a one-man wrecking ball. And if the mission's going south, I gotta have as much data as possible so I can keep doing as much damage as possible. What's the downside to *that*?"

Lynx says nothing. Linehan warms to the point.

"At the very least, I'd be creating that much more havoc for you to pull some shit. Why let them trap me in a dead-end—"

"Fine," says Lynx, "you win."

"Cool," says Linehan—data starts pouring into his skull. He watches grids of elevators and passages and crawlspaces coalesce around him, watches as they keep on stacking in upon one another—along with his own position, halfway between the outer and inner perimeters that have been set up around the heart of Szilard's defenses in the core of the *Redeemer*. Linehan exhales slowly.

"So where exactly is the big cheese himself?" he asks.

"Patience," says Lynx.

Three men in one of two Eurasian megaships hurtling toward the libration point that has been an American possession for more than fifty years. They're moving through the ship's shafts, away from the elevators that lead to the cockpit, looking for some kind of backup plan, feeling themselves subjected to intense scrutiny. Partially because the only people moving during transit are those who have to. But also . . .

"I'm surprised the cockpit hasn't issued a warrant for our arrest," says Spencer.

"Actually," says Jarvin, "it just did."

"*Fuck*," says Sarmax.

"What did it say?" asks Spencer.

"That we were American spies."

"Yikes. You suppressed it?"

"On the zone, yeah. But I can't do so for much longer. They'll figure out what's happening and launch a manhunt."

"So where are we gonna hide?" asks Spencer.

"In the cockpit," says Jarvin.

Haskell takes it all in. She feels like a skier at the top of a vast hill—only one direction to go, and ready to maneuver as fast as possible. She feels everything closing in around her—feels reality collapsing in upon a single point. She observes Control moving in behind her—can see Montrose somewhere beyond that. Coordinates mesh as she moves toward the L2 fleet. The *Redeemer* clicks in around her, a vast cage of lights—

The Operative climbs back down to the cargo bay—moves through to the adjunct bay beyond that. The sarcophagus is closed, though all vital signs still check out, indicating the flesh within is functioning just fine. The Operative braces himself, feels the ship shudder as it docks, followed by a muffled clanking as the locks slide into place. The floor beneath him starts to sink. He holds himself steady, then keys the intercom to the cockpit.

"What about a suit?" he asks.

"What about it?" asks Maschler. There's the noise of laughter.

"I knew we were forgetting something," says Riley. "Now *where* did we put that battlesuit that Carson was gonna wear?"

"Gotta be around here somewhere," says Maschler—the Operative turns off the intercom—realizing he should have known better than to ask. It's not like Szilard would let him aboard in anything other than a normal uniform anyway. He's going to walk in with neither weapons nor armor. He'll die that much more quickly. That's the plan. He's gets it now—finally sees he's not even the triggerman. He wonders who is.

L ynx closes his eyes. Carson's shuttle has docked. The hangar's airlock has sealed. The doors of the shuttle are opening, meaning the doors of this tiny room are about to as well. Lynx can't wait to get busy punking Carson one last time. He can't wait to use Linehan as the cannon fodder that he was born to be—can't wait to feed Szilard his own entrails. This time it's going to work, especially now that InfoCom is on board. And he doesn't mind taking out the trash for Montrose either. He's going to screw her over too, once he gets back to the Moon and back into the real game. It's all going down any moment now. He looks at Linehan.

"Let's do this," he says.

T hey've made their way into one of the ship's storage areas: a multileveled warehouse of equipment of every type. No human presence is visible. There are cameras, but Spencer's guessing that Jarvin's jamming them. If not, they're about to have bigger problems anyway . . .

"How the fuck do we get to the cockpit from here?" says Spencer.

"We need some hardware," says Jarvin—and reaches out to hold on as the room suddenly shudders—

"We're taking fire," says Sarmax. "Ship's getting it *hard*."

"So what?" says Jarvin. "We're going to crush L5 to rubble."

"You still think we can take control of this ship?"

"I don't think it," says Jarvin. "I know." He moves toward one piece of hardware in particular. A vehicle. Sarmax and Spencer stare at it.

"You're shitting me," says Spencer.

"Wish I was," says Jarvin.

She's running sleek and perfect now, maneuvering through the data-grids of the *Redeemer*, her mind doubling back upon itself as she bypasses security codes and failsafes. She takes in the specs, marvels at the way it's been rigged for dual purposes: a fully equipped colony ship modified with all the capabilities of a Class A dreadnaught, rigged with DE and KE batteries capable of striking targets in the low Earth orbits. The ship contains several companies of SpaceCom marines—as well as ten thousand colonists. She checks that one again, confirms it. They've been in hibernation for months now. She's guessing there has to be more to that story. She sets her mind on the problem even as she triangulates on Szilard's location—even as she keeps on searching for some way out of the lock that Control's got on her.

The shuttle's cargo hatch swings open. Light pours in. As do suited SpaceCom marines. They shove the Operative against the wall and search him while others climb up toward the cockpit. Another moves to the cargo, begins scanning it.

"Easy," says the Operative. "The admiral wouldn't want that damaged."

"Shut the fuck up," says a sergeant, activating the controls on the sarcophagus. Wheels extend along the floor. The faceplate slides back. The woman inside is still out cold. The Operative's glad to see that. It's going to make this a little easier. The SpaceCom marines step away from him, and he turns around to face them.

"I'm here to—"

"We know why you're here," says the sergeant.

The Operative hopes that's not the case. He hopes that Maschler and Riley are holding their own in the cockpit. A SpaceCom lieutenant strides into the cargo bay. He's not wearing a suit—just a smile that looks all too fake.

"Strom Carson," he says. He holds out a hand, shakes the Operative's. "My name's Sullivan. Szilard's chief of public relations."

"Public relations?" asks the Operative.

"Why not?"

"Who the hell's the public?"

Sullivan shrugs, gestures at the cargo. "You'll be pleased to know everything checks out."

"Of course."

"He doesn't like to be kept waiting."

"I'm ready when you are," says the Operative.

The door opens. Lynx and Linehan head on out, finding themselves in a maze of passages. They head along them, turning left, right, left again. They climb up stairs.

"Notice something?" asks Lynx.

Linehan's noticing all sorts of things, but most of them are doing a magic-lantern act in his head. He's feeling like these corridors are merely part of some labyrinth within his own mind. Maybe Szilard shoved him into a virtual reality construct and all this is merely the SpaceCom admiral toying with him. He scans the corridor they've just turned into.

"This place is empty," he says.

Lynx chuckles. "It looks that way on the screens too."

The vehicle's a standard minicrawler, optimized for low-gravity assault by virtue of its magnetic treads. It's about four meters long. Jarvin is releasing the deadbolts that hold it in place.

"Get in," he says.

But Spencer and Sarmax are already doing so. It's a tight fit. It gets even more so when Jarvin joins them. He seals the craft, gestures at Sarmax.

"You'd better drive," he says.

"Why?"

"You're the better driver."

"Sure," says Sarmax, "but where?"

"We were talking about the cockpit," says Jarvin as part of the wall slides back.

There's no way out of this. She's checked that six billion times in the last second. The fact that she hasn't given up yet is more a matter of sheer stubborness than any rational consideration. Control's grip is ironclad. He's covering all the angles, using her like a battering ram now, propelling her forward in spite of herself. She's almost cracked the *Redeemer*'s inner enclave. She'd better finish the job quick, before Carson reaches his destination. She knows she's in denial that he's about to die, even though she feels that he may as well have bitten it all those years ago—that the man she thought was telling her all his secrets was actually holding out on her, maybe even on himself. He's become ensnared in the web of his own schemes, and he's going under. But she's got a feeling he's going to go down fighting, and she's going to have to watch it. Live with it, too, though she doubts she'll have to do so for much longer. Deep in the *Redeemer*'s zone, she watches on one camera in particular, one hangar bay among so many—

The Operative emerges from the shuttle, takes in the moon-and-eagle banners of SpaceCom emblazoned on the hangar walls. Marines are everywhere. Two of them trundle the faux Haskell down the ramp behind him. Her face remains exposed behind plastic. The Operative stares at it as it passes him.

"Everything okay?" asks Szilard's public relations officer.

The Operative turns back to him. "Of course."

"Then follow me." The faux Haskell is pushed along behind the Operative and Sullivan, through the hangar bays, and deeper into the *Redeemer*. At every intersection, the Operative catches glimpses of marines blocking off all other access to the route that he's being led upon. They reach an elevator bank containing several lifts. One of those doors slides open.

"After you," says Sullivan.

Hurry the fuck up," says Lynx. Linehan's doing his best, but it's tough when Lynx keeps changing the route. They've doubled back once already. Now they're doing it again.

"Can't you get this straight?" asks Linehan.

"They're taking another way in," says Lynx. "Now open this fucking door." He gestures at the blast-door they've stopped at, but Linehan's already on it. A flamer protrudes from his shoulder, swivels, starts up. Linehan glances over at Lynx.

"You've got the zone behind this door covered, right?"

"I will by the time you get there," says Lynx.

oly shit," says Spencer.

"Shut up," says Sarmax. He hits the gas and starts piloting the crawler into the *Hammer*'s hull. It's a real maze. There are several layers of armor. Even Jarvin's hacking at the failsafes can't open all the doors at once. Each one opens to admit them, then slides shut behind the crawler in succession as the craft moves on through. Finally bolts extrude, and the largest door of all slides back—

"Ah *fuck*," says Spencer.

"Hold on," says Sarmax.

losing," she says.

"Good," says Montrose.

Strange conversation: Haskell feels like some kind of underwater creature that's protruded an eye-stalk above the surface. Her mind swings in behind Lynx while she locks in on Carson, Control increasing the pressure as Montrose sits in her command chair and presides over it all. Haskell can see that face so clearly now—gritted teeth, aquiline nose, resolute eyes. She feels that under different circumstances, she might have even liked this woman. But given how it's all turned out—

"You're not going to pull this off," she says.

"No," says Montrose, "you're going to do it for me."

The Operative spares scarcely a glance at Sullivan and the two marines in the elevator with him. It's a tight fit, to say the least. Particularly with the contraption that's taking up most of the room.

"So how did you get your hands on her?" asks Sullivan.

"Long story," says the Operative.

The elevator stops going down, starts going sideways. It's all relative anyway. The ship's got several sections, some of them rotating, others in zero-G. The Operative maximizes the magnetism of his boots, braces himself in a corner, and leans back. Looks at Sullivan.

"So what do you do every day?" he asks.

"I'm sorry?"

"You said you were his PR man."

"Sure."

"So what do you do?"

"Manage his image."

The Operative snorts. "He keeps a pretty low profile."

"That's the idea," says Sullivan.

Linehan's flamer cuts out. The blast-door's still intact, but it's sporting a hole wide enough to crawl through.

"After you," says Lynx.

"Figures," says Linehan, but he scrambles through anyway, triple-scans the corridor on the other side. It's empty. It's becoming increasingly apparent to him how this is working. Szilard's cleared as large an area as possible inside his perimeters. Anything moving within them is a problem by definition. Though that logic falters if you lose your view and don't know it. Linehan assumes that Lynx has that one covered. He wonders when Lynx will decide he no longer needs a mech—resolves to be one step ahead of that moment.

It's like being on the surface of some demented comet. Space is all around them, sheets of stars wallpapering the sky. Energy is surging past: the DE fusillade that's aimed at the ship, the bombs that comprise the ship's own fuel. Spencer catches a glimpse of the Moon amidst a glimmering blackness. He can't help but notice that they've emerged on the side of the ship that's facing away from Earth. He's guessing that's quite deliberate, intended to reduce the likelihood that this little outing will be seen by Eastern eyes. Anything American *might* hesitate before shooting at them. Because there's no good reason why the Eurasians would be going walkabout on the wrong side of the thickest armor ever created. That armor's received so many hits now that it's like a pockmarked landscape. Sarmax keeps maneuvering the vehicle in and around craters that raw energy's scooped from the surface. Spencer can only imagine what contortions Jarvin's going through to keep the ship's sensors from picking up the vehicle that's sliding over them. His helmet keeps on adjusting as gunnery flares right next to them. His brain's too gone to think of anything save a single question.

"*So how the fuck do we get back inside?*" asks Sarmax.

"*I'm working on it,*" says Jarvin.

And after we take out Szilard?" asks Haskell.

"Win the war," says Montrose.

"How?"

"I'm sure you'll think of something."

Haskell shrugs. She gets it. The president's a practical politician. The next problem isn't nearly as important as the one right now. So Montrose is applying the same strategy to Szilard that she applied to the Eurasians.

"Get your blow in first," says Haskell. "That's what it's all about?"

THE MACHINERY OF LIGHT

"That's what it's *always* about," says Montrose. "That's why I need both you and Carson—"

"Did you have this kind of caper in mind all along? Or did things go off the rails with Szilard?"

"A little bit of both."

"Because he wants to be president."

"Because he was a little too interested in you."

"Seems like that's been going around—" And suddenly it's like she's shoved back underwater; Control's angling her in, plowing through Szilard's outer perimeter, keeping pace with the men on the scene—

The elevator doors open. Sullivan leads the way out; the Operative follows, the two soldiers bringing up the rear, still pushing the thing that Montrose has sent Szilard—the thing that the Operative's supposed to have stolen. The Operative's starting to lose track of who's supposed to believe what. He regards that as a sure sign he's about to get dealt out of the game for good. But as they keep moving, he can't help but notice something.

"You guys fail to pay the rent or something?"

"What do you mean?"

"Where the hell is everybody?"

"There's a war on," says Sullivan. "Didn't you notice?"

"Must be getting down to the wire," says the Operative.

Same with the overhead lighting. The Operative assumes if he asked Sullivan about that, the man would say that everything was being channeled toward the DE batteries. Which might even be true. But the effect's a little eerie nonetheless. The lights are turning on only in the sections of the corridor they're in, are remaining illuminated only in the five meters ahead and behind them. Everything else is darkness. The Operative snorts, trying to sound more confident than he feels.

"This is how you guys set up perimeters?"

"I'm not in charge of security," says Sullivan.

"I'd like to meet the guy who is."

"You're about to."

They turn the corner and come face to face with a mammoth blast-door.

"Now what?" says Linehan.

"Now we hold tight again," replies Lynx.

They're still crouched in darkness. Linehan just saw some light in the distance, but now it's gone. He thinks they're inside the inner perimeter, but he doesn't know for sure. He's starting to wonder if Szilard's really the target here. Maybe it's someone else. Or some*thing* else. He wonders where that hot bitch of a cyborg got to, wonders whether she's wrapped up in this somehow. He can't wait to get something tangible in his sights. He glances at Lynx, but only sees the expression of a man who's thinking furiously. Linehan starts doing the opposite—just gets ready to respond on reflex.

This may be the hull of the largest ship ever launched, but there's only so much room for a way-too-fast crawler to crawl. They're through onto the forward sections. And as they round a curve, close in upon the nose, they can see what the *Hammer of the Skies* is heading toward—

"We're running out of margin," says Sarmax.

"I get that," says Jarvin.

Spencer can see that Sarmax isn't kidding. The lights of L5 shimmer in the sky ahead like some kind of nebula. Their guns are firing full-on at the monster that's roaring in toward them. Spencer looks around for some way out—

"*There,*" says Jarvin—but Sarmax is already on it, swerving into an indentation, swiveling the craft, hitting the brakes. They shudder to a halt.

"This won't buy us much," says Spencer.

"Stop complaining," says Jarvin. "I need your help."

"*You* need *my* help?"

"Whatever you guys are going to do, do it quick," says Sarmax.

The inner perimeter," says Control.

"On it," she says—and she is, dodging left and right in a million directions with a million limbs. Szilard's new flagship is falling prey to a whole new bag of tricks. She's narrowing down his location, too, closing in on the place from which the SpaceCom reins are getting pulled. She can see all the false leads and dead-ends Szilard's configured. He's good—she has to give him that. There's a reason he's managed to stay alive for so long. But those defenses weren't designed for the likes of her. She's becoming acutely aware that Montrose and Control now know things about her that she doesn't—that they're operating from a larger playbook she can't see. They've got the strategy. She's been reduced to tactics. She's peeling back the *Redeemer*'s security like the layers of an onion. Everything's checking out. Running perfectly.

With one exception.

The blast-door swings back. The Operative follows Sullivan through into a room that contains several suited marines lined up in front of a second blast-door. He's being scanned once more, along with the cart that contains Haskell's simulacrum. He can't blame Szilard for all the precautions. He wonders if they'll be enough. The first blast-door closes. The second opens. Sullivan gestures at the doorway.

"It's all you," he says.

"I'm not sure I follow."

"Through there. He's waiting for you."

"You guys aren't coming with me?

"We're not allowed to."

"He doesn't trust you?"

"He doesn't trust anybody," says Sullivan.

"Fair point," says the Operative.

G ot it," says Lynx.
      As he knew he would. Like crosshairs sliding to-
gether in his mind, it's all coming into focus. He's got
Carson in his sights—Szilard, too. The SpaceCom defenses may as
well not be there for all the trouble they're causing him. He feels
the Manilishi's zone-presence slide in behind him, feels himself
glide forward.

S pencer's mind meshes on the zone with Jarvin's. He
      sees the problem immediately. The hull door they're
parked against is only meant to be opened from the other
side. It's rigged with several more failsafes than Jarvin was counting on. And the key to those failsafes is in the—

"Cockpit," says Jarvin.

"Roger that," says Spencer—but their minds are already racing along the wires on the other side of what was built to be the escape hatch for the ship's pilots. Directed energy blasts over their
position as the L5 gunners start up a new barrage. Another ten
meters forward, and they'd be melted. If the megaship changes
up its angle, that's going to happen anyway. But Spencer's giving scarcely a thought to that dilemma. He's just running secondary razor to Jarvin's primary, twisting in on the underbelly of the

cockpit, accessing the evacuation sequences without making them realize they're being run, telling them to initiate escape procedures—

"Got it," says Jarvin.

The hatch opens—

It's like something just swung shut within her mind, as unmistakable as it is strange. Everything else is checking out. The overall pattern remains intact. But there's one slight problem. It's within the margin of error—except for the fact that she doesn't make errors. Nor has Control seemed to notice it. She keeps an eye on the anomaly while she keeps on tightening the noose around Szilard's position—watching on the cameras as Carson walks down a corridor, pushing a cart that contains a woman who looks a little too familiar—

And it's all the Operative can do to not look at her face. He knows that if he's fucked, this woman's doubly so. Even if it's not Haskell, he's falling for her anyway. He's guessing that's the point. He wonders what happened to the man he used to be, the man who never gave a fuck about anyone, the man for whom Haskell was just one more *assignment*. But that was back when he thought he was going to outlast them all. Now that he's wised up it's way too late. The corridor bends left, then right, becomes a ramp that steepens to the point where the Operative's having to hit the brakes on the cart. Some kind of room is just ahead. It doesn't seem to be small. The woman's eyes open.

"Hello again," she says.

L ike a flock of birds alighting: Lynx feels something descend out of the zone and into his mind. It's Haskell—
not just on the zone, but full-on telepathy. He thought it
couldn't happen, but here she is anyway, and he hasn't the foggiest
idea how. And right now it doesn't matter, as she syncs with him
on both zone and mind. The final map of the inner enclave of
Jharek Szilard clicks into his head. He fires his suit-jets.

"You sure about this?" asks Linehan, as he does the same.

"Prime your weapons," snarls Lynx.

T hey're scrambling out of the crawler and into the shaft
as fast as they can. Radiation's still pouring over them
all the same. Their suits are getting soaked. Their flesh is
okay so far—they've got more immediate problems to contend
with.

"Close this goddamn *hatch*," snarls Sarmax.

"We're working on it," says Spencer.

They're having to do some serious multitasking. Spencer and
Jarvin are damping the sensors along the shaft while they simultaneously check out the approaches to the cockpit and—

"Get rid of it," snarls Jarvin. Spencer's already on it, hacking
the controls of the crawler they've just left, releasing the brakes.
The crawler slides past the opening, tumbles off into space.
Hopefully it'll just be written off as one more piece of metal
knocked loose from the surface, annihilated in the bomb-blasts
that keep flaring beyond the rear-shielding. It's out of their hands
now. The hatch swings shut. The cockpit schematics expand in
Spencer's head.

"About time," says Jarvin.

She arrives at the core of the *Redeemer*'s inner enclave. She's got all their numbers now. Except for that anomaly, which keeps on sprouting new tendrils, keeps on growing, encompassing her while she continues on with the mission. Nothing tangible seems to be affected. She's still running smooth. She wonders if this is something that Control is doing to gain a more complete mastery of her—the formula through which Montrose unlocks her still further. Maybe she isn't supposed to have noticed it. Maybe the fact that she has will give her some margin. But suddenly it's as if she's being drawn on a string, hauled across vacuum—

Here we are," says the woman who wears the face of Claire Haskell.

The Operative looks around. The room is as large as it is empty. All it contains is a dais in the center. The walls are cut through three levels, a walkway circling the room halfway up. Several marines stand along that walkway. Several more ring the entrance in a semicircle. They wear the insignia of Szilard's bodyguard. Their guns are trained on the Operative and the conveyor. He raises his hands.

"I'm unarmed," he says.

But none of the marines say anything. And as the Operative stares at them, he realizes why.

"They're dead," says a voice.

Still rotting too, from the looks of the faces inside the visors. But apparently their armor's working just fine. The suits immediately in front of the Operative step aside, gesture at him to move forward. A man's appeared on the dais, though he's flickering ever so slightly. A holograph.

"Admiral Szilard," says the Operative.

"Forgive me that it's not in the flesh," says Szilard.

W e've got him," says Lynx.
"So where the fuck is he?" says Linehan.

In one of about twenty rooms, according to the readouts—a complex on which Lynx and Linehan are now closing. Lynx's mind centers on the chamber where Carson is, traces back along the signal that's being projected to that room: the signal that shows the holograph of Szilard—the signal that's being sent from one of those twenty chambers—now narrowing down to fifteen . . . ten . . .

"You are *so* mine," says Lynx.

T he cockpit of *Hammer of the Skies* isn't small. It's divided into two areas—Chinese and Russian—each of which sweeps back from a central section where two captains monitor events. Pilots and navigators and gunnery specialists man consoles. Soldiers line the walls. There are only two ways in. One's the elevators. The other's the escape shaft in which three men are crouching.

"So what now?" says Spencer.
"Now we take over," says Jarvin.

S he's getting slotted into cranial matter that's not her own but that's all too familiar nonetheless. Her mind's turning in upon itself, wandering through the meat of someone else's brain while she wrestles with some kind of pattern that's threatening to overwhelm her. She's trying to hold steady, but it's no use. Everything's collapsing in upon her, and it's all she can do to keep from getting buried. But in the cacophony that's sounding all around her she's starting to get glimpses of what she's been missing. She opens her eyes—

"So this is the Manilishi," says Szilard.

The Operative can see why people call this man the Lizard behind his back. He's as tall as he is thin. His tongue keeps on flickering out in a disquieting manner. There's a scar down the right side of his face that looks fresh. The woman in the cart clears her throat, coughs—

"I've come to make you an offer," she says.

"Are you really in a position to do that?" replies Szilard.

"Do you want to be president or not?"

"Maybe you should let me speak to the man who stole you."

"Maybe you should both shut up," says the Operative.

They look at him—her face staring up from her cart, his face blinking as though he's just been slapped. He knows he'd better talk fast. He can think of only one thing to say.

"There's a plot against you."

"Just one?" says Szilard.

"Instigated by Montrose."

"Oh," says Szilard, in a tone that says *is that all.*

"This man's lying," says the woman.

"Who cares what you think?" says the Operative.

"Sounds like you two need to get your story straight," says Szilard.

The Operative laughs. "*I'm* the one who stole *her.*"

"My fucking heart, you mean."

He glances at her. He suddenly realizes she really *is* Haskell now. That's when he hears her voice inside his head too.

"You're doing great," it says.

"What's the nature of this plot?" asks Szilard.

"What happened to your bodyguards?" asks Haskell.

"Only people I can trust are those who are already dead."

"And either you or Montrose are about to join them," says the Operative.

"Tell me something I don't know," says Szilard.

"The president's one step ahead of you," says Haskell.

"What do you mean?"

"The only way to get inside your perimeter. Hand you something you have to have."

"That cuts both ways," says the admiral.

The Operative nods. He examines that image, examines the lifeless visors of the bodyguards—gets ready to move fast. Szilard laughs.

"You think I don't know what this is all about? That I don't know who you are?"

"He's Strom Carson," says Haskell. "We know you know it."

"The leader of the original Rain triad," says Szilard.

"*Leader*'s not exactly how I'd put it," says the Operative.

"So how the hell does Montrose think you're going to nail me?"

"She doesn't," says the Operative.

"You sure?"

"In case you haven't noticed, I'm a captive."

"But whose captive?" adds Haskell.

"Ah yes." Szilard's tongue flashes out again. Another holograph materializes in midair beside him: a camera-view of the interior hangar, looking out along the line of sight of a KE gatling, aimed down on the shuttle that the Operative rode to L2.

"Jon Maschler and Nik Riley," says Jharek Szilard. "I get it. Really, I do. The idea was to make me think *they'd* stolen the Manilishi."

"A story only a fool would buy," says the Operative.

"Right," says Szilard. "Because if they *really* stole the most valuable object in the fucking solar system, *why the hell would they bring it to me?*"

"Because they're SpaceCom agents," says Haskell.

"Of course they're SpaceCom agents," says Szilard. "Treacherous ones, too."

"Doesn't mean they can't be useful," says Haskell.

Szilard shrugs. "How else was I to get my hands on the original Rain operative?"

"And the Manilishi," says the Operative.

"Stop patronizing me," says Szilard, "I know damn well—even if she's speaking through it—*that's* not the Manilishi."

"But it was intended to be," says the Operative.

"More bullshit," says Szilard. "Lies within lies. Montrose wanted me to believe she'd created a duplicate Manilishi."

"She almost did," says the Operative.

"And if she had, she could have switched it on at your very doorstep," says Haskell. "Checkmated you at point-blank range."

"Too bad she failed," says Szilard.

"You don't know the half of it," says Haskell.

"But I do," says Szilard. "Montrose almost ran off the rails completely. In creating a link between you and your would-be doppleganger, she opened the door to Sinclair."

"You *saw* that?" asks Haskell.

"Don't count me out of the game yet," says Szilard.

L ynx frowns. "Shit," he mutters.
    "What's up?" says Linehan. Lynx doesn't even look at him.

"I said—"

"I heard what you said."

"You can't admit something's wrong?"

"I'll admit to anything if you'll shut the fuck up."

R *un the fucking sequences,*" says Sarmax.
    Jarvin's already doing just that. And it's all Spencer can do to keep up with him; his mind's getting swept up in Jarvin's, up along the wires that lead into the cockpit, into the main consoles that contain the executive software for the ship. There are two such consoles. One's Chinese. One's Russian.

Jarvin's going for both of them simultaneously, and Spencer's running backup. He's starting to get a sense of just how good a razor Alek Jarvin is—how easily that man's been running rings around him. Now that they're within the main cockpit firewall, Jarvin's taking those databases apart—running a blizzard of sequences while Spencer triple-checks them, processes the patterns, scans the implications. The codes necessary to take control of the entire ship are coming into focus. Until—

"Shit," says Jarvin.

The screens go crazy.

I'm not even Montrose's biggest problem," says Szilard. "Sinclair is—"

"—about to get two megaships up his ass," says the Operative.

"Or else Sarmax is going to hand the Eurasian fleet over to him," says Haskell.

"Give me a break," says the SpaceCom admiral. "Sarmax is out of the picture by now—"

"As opposed to you," says the Operative. "Machinery to register mental emissions? Tracing Haskell's telepathic signature? Not bad. And yet—"

"Not enough to get in on any conversations," says Szilard.

"Though that might change if you got your hands on the rest of Sinclair's files," says the Operative.

"Are you trying to make a deal?"

"He might if he actually had those files," says Haskell.

"I hate it when people play stupid," says Szilard.

Data blurs in Lynx's mind. He's bringing all his zone-prowess to bear, triangulating across the decks of the *Redeemer*. But the static that's engulfed Szilard's signal seems to be intensifying. It occurs to Lynx that maybe *he's* the one who's getting punked—that maybe the SpaceCom marines are closing in on his position even now. He wonders if he should just have Linehan charge on in. He scans back over the *Redeemer* one last time.

Fuck," says Jarvin.
"What?" asks Sarmax.
"EMP," snarls Spencer.
"L5's guns must have nailed the cockpit," says Jarvin.
Meaning they've all got the same problem. The ship's circuitry just went haywire. Backup comps are coming on, but the hack that Jarvin was running on the cockpit has been lost. The three men crouch in that access-shaft while a backup zone flickers on and Spencer and Jarvin try to get things back on track. Only to find that—
"No gunnery breakthroughs on the forward armor," says Spencer.
"What?" says Sarmax.
"That EMP," says Jarvin. "It came from *inside* the ship."

Not sure I follow," says the Operative. "I don't have—"
"You don't *need* Sinclair's files," says Szilard. "You fucking *wrote* half of them anyway."
"Or you were there while the recorders took dictation," says Haskell.
"If you want to know what's driving the retrocausality, you can forget it," says the Operative. "I don't know, and the only way to find out is—"

"To take me apart," says Haskell. "Which Montrose is doing her best to do."

"Even as you use that amplifier of yours to ransack the *Redeemer*'s systems," says Szilard. "Turning me inside out, eh?"

"I already finished," says Haskell. "Your ship's mine. And you're—"

"Full of surprises," says Szilard.

A massive explosion rocks the ship.

W hat the hell was that?" yells Linehan.
"All part of the plan," says Lynx.

Though he's a lot less confident than he sounds. Nothing was supposed to happen until they reached Szilard. The plan may just have gone belly-up. Or maybe he never understood the plan in the first place. He hopes he's not getting sold down the river again. He hears something else—close at hand—gunfire—

"Someone's lighting this place *up*," says Linehan.

I *nside* the ship?" says Sarmax.
"Definitely," says Spencer.

"Maybe a malfunction," says Jarvin. "Or maybe—"

"We got combat ten decks down," says Spencer.

K ill him," says Szilard—but the Operative's already moving, leaping at one of the bodyguards, vaulting over its shoulder and landing on its back while Haskell hacks the bodyguard's armor, handing control off to the Operative—who grasps it with his neural software on wireless, starts riddling the other bodyguards even as they start getting their own shots off. Projectiles are flying everywhere. Szilard's image has disappeared. An explosion tears away part of the ceiling—

—along with part of the wall. Lynx and Linehan blast through from different directions, add their guns to that of Carson, catching Szilard's bodyguards in a crossfire. Linehan dodges a micromissile, smashes into one of the remaining bodyguards, rips its helmet off with jet-enhanced fists—rips off the head as well, screaming obscenities all the while. Haskell starts screaming too.

"What the fuck's up with *her?*" yells Lynx.

"It's not her," says Carson.

Not anymore. She's falling away from all of them—tumbling back from L2 as though she's being hauled back toward the Moon on a tether. Space and time reel before her, reveal that her mind's back in that tank again. She's struggling to get her bearings.

Apparently everybody else is too.

"What the hell's wrong?" asks Montrose.

"We're still processing," says Control. For the first time, Haskell hears emotion grip that voice—or more precisely, tension. Same with Montrose:

"Hurry it *up,*" she snaps.

"The Manilishi's back online," says Control. Haskell feels everything stabilize around her—a kind of equilibrium. It'll have to do.

"Can you hear me, Claire?" asks Montrose.

"I can," says Haskell. She takes in the confusion that's starting to grip the war-room. The battle-management computers are still functioning, but not much else is. There's something wrong. Some kind of—

Anomaly.

"Fuck," says Haskell.

"We're under attack," says Control.

 Fighting underway outside the cockpit," says Jarvin. Spencer wonders whether that's too fine a distinction. The cameras show that chaos is breaking loose throughout the *Hammer of the Skies*. Explosions are going off. Firefights are everywhere. It's total pandemonium. And it looks like commandos are trying to force their way up the elevator to reach the cockpit—

"Americans," says Sarmax. "Must be."

"Not a chance," says Spencer.

He knows there's no way—not in the numbers that are now wreaking havoc aboard this ship. This involves the ship's soldiers and crew. And the only Americans aboard are in this shaft.

As far as they know.

"It's Autumn Rain," says Jarvin.

"Shit," says Sarmax.

The last of the lifeless bodyguards collapses against the wall, shredded, busy being deceased again. The woman who's neither dead nor living keeps on screaming.

"You've lost," she howls. "You've fucking *lost* and your souls are forfeit and Satan's going to fuck you in the *ass*—"

"Shut *up*," yells Lynx—and puts a bullet through her head, sends chunks of brain flying. The Operative whirls on him.

"Goddamn you—"

"You've got bigger problems," says Lynx.

The Operative can see he's not kidding. Lynx's powered armor looks virtually undamaged. The Operative's got fuck-all. He stares as his erstwhile razor's guns line him up.

"You were saying?" asks Lynx.

"We need to work together," says the Operative.

"Feel like I've heard that one before."

"He's right," says Linehan. "We need to join—"

"*I'm* making the decisions," says Lynx.

"Sure you are," says the Operative, "but where the fuck's Szilard?"

"*I'm asking the questions!*" yells Lynx.

"*You've lost him, haven't you?*"

They hear more gunfire in the distance.

"W e've got shooting outside the bunker," says Control. "What the *hell?*" mutters Montrose.

The bunker's emergency blast-doors slide shut. Montrose's bodyguards take up positions around her, help her into her suit. Haskell notices the command bunker's been systematically cut off from the zone. She has no idea how that's happening. She wonders what she's missing.

"You," screams a voice.

It's Montrose. She's in her armor now. She strides over to Haskell and starts shaking her.

"*What the hell are you seeing?*" she demands.

"Why don't you release my fucking bindings and let me fucking find out!"

Montrose shakes her all the harder. "Don't think you can fucking trick me that easy!"

"Fuck you and your paranoia!" yells Haskell. "I lost the fix on Szilard. I got booted from my amplifier. I—*get your fucking hands off me!*"

Montrose slaps her across the face—hard enough to turn Haskell's head, nearly hard enough to snap her neck. Her bodyguards move in as though they're about to restrain their boss.

"We can still salvage this," says Control.

One of the blast-doors suddenly bursts inward.

L5's outer perimeter is breached. The American flanks are turned. The megaships swoop past L5, curve back in toward the libration point. It's going to be over within minutes. Data on the collapsing defenses keeps on flashing across the screens of the cockpit, and the crew keeps on holding course—

Even as they try to deal with more immediate problems. The automated guns that protect the shafts that lead to the cockpit are getting taken out. On the camera feeds, Spencer catches glimpses of power-suited infantry through a blizzard of static. The two captains are doing their utmost to raise the rest of the ship. They're not succeeding. That's when one of them draws a pistol and shoots the other through the head.

"*Goddamn,*" says Spencer.

"Should have guessed," mutters Jarvin.

Give me one good reason I shouldn't just pull this fucking trigger," says Lynx.

"That's your reason right there," says the Operative, gesturing in the direction of the gunfire.

"You already backstabbed me once!"

"For a chance to win it all, you'd have done the same."

"And look where it got you," says Lynx. "Standing here with my guns aimed at your head—"

"And nothing in yours," snarls the Operative. "The Manilishi's approaching activation. Sinclair's still at L5. He may have a full triad with him. He may have *more*. And meanwhile your scam to nail Szilard has gone so far off the rails you can't even see the fucking *tracks*—"

Another blast shakes the room. Much closer now. Linehan looks at Lynx—

"Shit or get off the pot," he says.

"Let's get the man a suit," says Lynx.

Power-suited infantry are storming into the InfoCom command bunker, firing at everything in sight. Explosions start ripping apart consoles. Smoke's everywhere. It's pandemonium.

"Get the president out of here!" screams Control.

But the bodyguards are already moving. One of them releases the restraints on Haskell, slides a helmet on her, seals her suit, and pulls her from her berth. Her neck hurts like hell. She flops over the shoulder of the bodyguard while he starts scrambling after the others—vaulting over more consoles toward the emergency exit that's opening in the wall. She gets a glimpse of oncoming shock troops—sees the insignia on their suits.

"*SpaceCom,*" she says.

"I noticed," mutters the bodyguard.

Along with everybody else. Virtually all of the bunker staff are suitless. They're trying to surrender. They're being given no quarter. It's a total massacre. Montrose's bodyguards charge into the escape passage. Haskell can see the consoles that house Control getting shredded.

The elite of the Chinese Fifth Commando kick down the elevator door and start shooting. Blood and bodies fly. It looks to be totally out of control.

Though really it's quite targeted.

"So much for the Russians," says Spencer.

"Bet you this is going on across the fleet," says Sarmax.

"Try throughout the Coalition," says Jarvin.

Certainly throughout this ship. The view's becoming a lot clearer as the Chinese zone dissolves its Russian counterpart. The EMP surge from earlier was just an opening salvo. Camera-feeds show suited Russian soldiers getting zapped in their armor, suitless technicians getting exposed to vacuum as airlocks open.

"So much for the great partnership," says Sarmax.

"Had to end sometime," says Spencer.

And no better time than now. With the East on the brink of winning the war, China's chosen to get its blow in first. It's obviously been planned that way. Across the vast fleet in Earth orbit, Russian soldiers and pilots are being purged en masse. A bombardment of the Russian homeland is in progress.

"How's your Mandarin?" says Sarmax.

They're moving out of Szilard's audience chamber at speed. The Operative is wearing one of the less-damaged suits of the bodyguard. The smell of rotting flesh assails his nostrils. He considers himself fortunate that his own isn't going the same way. He meshes his zone-capabilities with Lynx and they start devising strategies while their suits kill everything that moves.

"Why the hell aren't we heading for the hangars?" yells Linehan.

"Shut up and keep shooting," yells Lynx.

The Operative nods. They've got enough to do without Linehan demanding to be kept in the loop. Every ship in the

Redeemer's hangar is forfeit. The shuttle the Operative rode in on was the first to get blasted. So now they're closing in on a very different objective. The Operative's not surprised that the combat they're hearing nearby is tracking in the same direction.

"They're not stupid," says Lynx.

"We'll take them all the same," replies the Operative.

Back out in vacuum: the bunker escape hatch slams shut behind Montrose and her escorts. Haskell's got a feeling it'll be opening again soon enough. She's still slung over the bodyguard's shoulder—still watching the flames of the suit-thrusters of the man as he holds formation with the rest of them. She has no idea what Montrose intends to do next. She wonders if Montrose knows either. The walls of the passage widen as they come out into a larger chamber—a subrail station. The bodyguards hustle Montrose into the first car of the train that sits in the center of the grooved floor. The bodyguard holding Haskell straps her into one of the seats. For a moment she's face to face with Montrose.

"You really fucked this up," says Haskell.

"It's not over yet," says Montrose.

The train slides out of the station.

The screens show L5's inner perimeter crumbling. *Hammer of the Skies* moves in toward its quarry. The Russians in the cockpit who've surrendered are being summarily executed. Vacuum-pumps have been turned on to drain the blood from the zero-G. Chinese soldiers are mopping up.

"They'll be coming down here next," says Spencer.

"Not if we convince their bosses they already did," replies Jarvin.

The garrison of the *Redeemer* is trying to defend against the incursions now cutting through it, but it's tough going. All the more so as the attacks are along angles that the original defenders didn't anticipate—straight out of the off-limits high-security area along its axis. Alarms are sounding throughout the ship. Reserves are scrambling into their suits, all too many of which are getting hacked.

"They're fucking reeling," says Lynx.

"It may not matter," says the Operative.

"What's that supposed to mean?" says Linehan.

"Szilard might blow this ship at any moment."

"Why the hell would he do that if he's on it?"

"Don't you love it when you answer your own question?"

"This whole thing was a *trick?*"

Neither Lynx nor the Operative bothers to reply. Of course the whole thing was a trick. It's the only possibility that makes sense now. But as to what the Lizard's game is . . . they're still working on it. And right now they've got more tactical concerns. Marines block the way ahead—Lynx fucks their suits while the Operative springs open the triple-locked doors behind them. The three men blast on through. The Operative looks around at the room they've just reached.

"Made it," he says.

"Not so fast," says a voice.

The train abruptly slows, slides to a halt.

"What the hell's going on?" demands Montrose.

"Not sure," says a bodyguard.

"Then get out there and find out!" snarls Montrose.

But the bodyguards are already opening the doors of the train, heading out into the tunnel. Lasers and explosions start flaring. One of the bodyguards gets blasted back into the car. The SpaceCom marine who just shot him leaps in, followed by several others.

"President Montrose," says one.

"You're under arrest," says another.

Ø   *Hammer of the Skies* and *Righteous Fire-Dragon* pour fire onto the L5 fortress at point-blank range. They've suppressed enough of the defensive fire to start deploying troops: clouds of power-suits billowing across the gigantic central station and its attendant war-sats.

"Impressive," says Sarmax.

Neither Spencer nor Jarvin reply. They're too busy trying to keep up with the shifting Eastern zone within this megaship. The Chinese zone continues to consolidate, taking control. But as it does, Jarvin's mind slides in behind it, Spencer riding shotgun in a maneuver as quick as it is elegant—

"Got it," says Jarvin.

The last of L5's guns cease firing.

The room is almost empty. It contains only a single console—and a door, through which Maschler and Riley have just entered, their guns still smoking.

"Figured I'd find you guys here," says the Operative.

"You always were quick," says Riley.

"A little too much so," says Maschler.

"And guess who's holding your zone-leashes?" says Lynx.

"You're kidding," says Riley.

"Try us and see," says the Operative.

Though he knows they're figuring it out for themselves. He and Lynx snipped their link back to Montrose all too easily. Whatever shit's hitting the fan back at the president's HQ made that move even easier. Meaning that the two men who held his reins the whole way up just got co-opted. And they're going to find it very difficult to do anything that Lynx and Carson don't want them to.

Though right now everybody's got the same objective.

"We've been trying to figure out the sequence," says Riley.

"We're one step ahead of you," says Lynx as the Operative starts keying commands into the console.

The SpaceCom soldiers keep their guns trained on Montrose and Haskell while the train reverses back along the tunnel. Montrose is offering them riches beyond their imagination if they'll let her go. They're not saying anything in reply. They just let her plead while they keep an eye out of the windows on either side. The train pulls back into the station. Montrose and Haskell are hustled out.

A man's waiting for them on the platform. He's so tall his suit's obviously custom built. His smile's clearly visible through his visor. He looks down as Montrose and Haskell are thrown at his feet.

"Hi there," says Jharek Szilard.

The sack of L5 is in full force. There's a lot of it to bust up. The main structure is a kilometer across. Sections of the *Lincoln* have melted in the DE bombardment like wax in an oven. The thousands of Chinese soldiers storming through what's left are meeting with little resistance. Feeds from the suit-cams of the assault troops churn through Spencer's head as the soldiers close on one section in particular.

The prisons.

"What the hell's going on?" asks Sarmax.

"We've got control of this ship's net," says Jarvin.

"Sure," says Sarmax, "but what about Sinclair?"

"We'll know in less than thirty seconds," says Spencer.

The *Redeemer*'s disaggregation sequence is an absolute last resort. The fact that it needs to be triggered manually is one of several failsafes that keep it from getting activated accidentally. But the Operative and Lynx have already hacked through all the precautions. They've won through to this backup control room and killed almost everyone in the vicinity.

And Maschler and Riley were thoughtful enough to take care of the rest. They didn't know they were working in coordination with the Operative and Lynx. They didn't need to. All anyone needs to do now is hold on—

"*Do it*," hisses Lynx.

The Operative hits the last command. Sirens wail. Airlocks slam shut. Explosive charges throughout the ship detonate.

"On to the next round," says the Operative.

"Goddamn," says Maschler.

The *Redeemer* is breaking into twenty modular pieces. Designed for emergencies that might befall the mother-ship in Mars orbit or beyond, each is a spaceship in its own right. Each starts maneuvering into the L2 fleet on routes already established by the Operative and Lynx. Some of the L2 guns begin firing at the anomaly that's sprouting in their midst, but most of them hold off in the absence of orders—even as the *Redeemer*'s fragments close in on them—even as one fragment in particular closes in on—

"That one there," says Lynx.

"Everybody brace yourself," yells the Operative.

Still don't think it's over?" asks Haskell.

"*Shut the fuck up*," says Montrose. "Jharek, this is an *outrage*. You shoot your way into my headquarters and—"

"Please, Stephanie." Szilard raises a hand. "No need to make this embarrassing. We both know the game we've been playing."

"I've been trying to win this war—"

"And trying to win the war against me while you were at it. Yes. And now you see why you couldn't. I'm never where anyone expects me to be."

"You're a traitor," says Montrose.

"I asked you not to make this embarrassing."

"Spare me and I'll put the InfoCom net at your disposal."

"It already *is* at my disposal," says Szilard. "Except for one thing."

He gestures at two of his men, who grab Montrose's suit—she kicks against them, but they ignore her as they rip away the suit's safety seals. Montrose starts screaming. They haul off her helmet—hold her suit upright while she convulses in the vacuum. It's over quick—and when it's done, they drop her back onto the ground in front of Szilard. He turns to Haskell.

"So nice to finally meet you," he says.

PART III
LODESTONE'S VIGIL

M y fellow Americans."
It's two days later. The U.S. president is on the screen. The latest one, at any rate. It's been getting increasingly hard to keep up. Particularly when it seems to matter less and less each time a new one takes over.

"I come before you at a critical hour. Since I last addressed you, the situation has grown graver. All our peace overtures to the Eurasian Coalition have been rejected out of hand. It is now clear that the only peace the Coalition envisions is one that involves our complete submission. As long as I am president, that will never happen.

"But I must be candid regarding the magnitude of what has befallen us. We have heard nothing from our forces planetside. All we know is what we can see: that the Coalition has occupied North America, and has begun what I can only term the enslavement of our population. To the extent resistance continues, it is confined deep below the surface, and has no military impact that we can discern. The East's control of Earth's orbits is now total, and the buildup of their fleets at L4 and L5 has continued without abatement. All of our forces at L5 are either dead or prisoners of war. I wish I could offer you assurances that they are receiving the treatment that the laws of war demand, but I am unable to do so. The East was always capable of anything; now that they are on the brink of domination, we at last see their true colors.

"We are the only thing remaining in their way. When I addressed you two days back it was to tell you of the sad news of my predecessor's death. But it was also to inform you that President Montrose met the same hero's end as our beloved Andrew Harrison: at the head of our forces, fighting for the liberty of all of us. And with her last breath she bequeathed the presidency to me and charged me with the leadership of our nation. I accepted this sacred trust, and with that trust, I swore to be true to the American people.

"Nor can there be any doubt now as to what we face next. We are confined to the Moon and the immediate lunar orbits. And we still have our fleet at L2. But the Eurasian Coalition controls all else. Once their fleets at L4 and L5 have reached critical mass, they will strike at us from two sides with a combined force far larger than our own. They will seek to crush all resistance and trample the last American flags beneath their boots. They will seek to place us in bondage and rule humanity forever. We are all that stands in defense of freedom.

"And we have no choice but to be worthy of that task. My admirals and I are formulating plans that will take advantage of the overwhelming overconfidence that the Eurasians now display. They think that they have already won. We are going to show them just how wrong they are. We shall deploy new weapons, about which I can provide no details lest we play into the hands of our enemies. To say we have not yet begun to fight is mere understatement.

"I know these last few days have tried us all to our very depths. The hours to come will try us still further. Our hope is to destroy the Eurasian ships before they reach the Moon, but this may not be possible in all cases—some enemy units may attain the Moon before our countermeasures take full effect. They may even force their way into the lunar cities. Should this happen, we will fight them every step of the way. We will battle them in the streets and in the tunnels, because there can be no surrender. Because Americans have no place in the dark new order the Coalition is bent on establishing—no place at all, save that of slaves.

"We did not choose this war. We offered the Coalition an honorable peace, and instead they struck down the greatest of our leaders. The Eurasians have waged this war without mercy, and we will defeat them utterly. We will hurl the East from the orbits, and we will retake our homeland. May God aid us in this sacred task. May God defend the United States of America—"

The screen beside the window goes blank. Presumably the rest of the screens across this ship have done the same. Lynx chuckles.

"He's fucked."

"Not necessarily," replies the Operative.

"You believe all that shit about secret weapons?"

"He's already got at least one," says the Operative.

"*If* he can figure out how to harness her."

"I'm sure he's working on it."

"Why would he succeed where you and Montrose both failed?"

"It's funny. Everyone keeps underestimating Szilard. Yet here he is, still in the game."

"Not for much longer," says Lynx.

"Think about it, man. He's already had more chance to crack Haskell than Montrose got."

"He's certainly done a better job of keeping hold of the reins than she did."

"The man's an expert at keeping out of sight."

"So where is he now?"

"Nowhere near us," says the Operative.

"Can't disagree with that."

They gaze out the window. A swathe of the L2 fleet is clearly visible, stretching away from them like a bridge of lights. The far side of the Moon lies beyond.

"He's still down there," says Lynx.

"Leaving us in a real fucking bind."

Lynx sighs. "Surely there are *some* exceptions being made?"

"In theory, sure."

"But not in practice."

"You've seen the data," says the Operative. "If you spot anything I've missed, name it. Nothing's left this fleet. Nothing's gone back to the Moon. Nothing will."

"Funny how our minions don't seem to get it."

"They'll figure it out sooner or later."

"Linehan was trying to strut his stuff in front of the dynamic duo. Telling them that Szilard's keeping the fleet out here makes no strategic sense."

"He may not be wrong."

"Bullshit."

"Relax," says the Operative. "Feed the current situation into ten battle-management computers and—"

"They'd just laugh in your face. Tell us we're screwed."

"Sure. But the question is how to play a shit hand. I'll bet you it'd be a split jury, and at least a couple of those comps would say what Linehan just said—oh yeah, get those ships close in behind the Moon *pronto*—and the others might say hold back here and engage from long range. Who knows? We're in uncharted waters now. But none of this relates to the *real* reason the fleet's staying put out here—"

"Us."

"Yeah," says the Operative. There's a moment's pause. "Nice to be wanted, huh?"

"Two of the three members of the first Rain triad, still on the loose, with the *Redeemer* blown all over the rest of the L2 fleet. At least fifteen sections docked in different places. You and I could be anywhere by now."

"But still on the goddamn fleet. Pinned down."

"It's stalemate," says Lynx. "We can't get at him and he can't get at us."

"So let's talk about what we *can* get."

They can't get their hands on anything that matters. To say they've been outmaneuvered is putting it mildly. They've been trapped on this stupid ship for two days now. These last forty-eight hours have seemed like years. Long enough to cut their way through to some of the main shafts, not that it's done them any good. All the places worth getting to involve leaving this ship.

And that's impossible. Everyone's staying put. The crew's been confined to the ship, as have all remaining soldiers. Spencer wonders if that means someone's wise to their presence. Jarvin explained it's just a precaution. Same reason the search parties are combing this ship. The Chinese know full well there are rats hiding within the walls. It's just that every rat they've caught so far is Russian. On-the-spot executions are getting meted out like they're going out of style. Though Spencer's got a feeling they'll always be in fashion.

Particularly now that the Eurasian Coalition's under new management. All traces of the Russian zone have vanished completely. China's making its bid for domination of all existence. Some of the Russian ships have been destroyed. Most just got taken over—repurposed with skeleton crews. Spencer's got a ringside seat into the fleet that's building up around the *Hammer of the Skies*. The size of it is way beyond unprecedented. It's like nothing that Spencer's ever seen—a colossal armada, and beyond it are still more ships: the endless reinforcements, long lines of convoys chugging up the gravity-well from Earth. A similar scene is going on at L4. The Coalition's forces at the libration points already outnumber the American ships behind the Moon by two to one. Meaning things could kick off any time.

And that would really suck. Because it turns out that Spencer and Sarmax and Jarvin are on the wrong megaship. The one that counts is *Righteous Fire-Dragon*. That's where Matthew Sinclair got taken as soon as he was placed in custody, along with all the other high-security prisoners. He's still there now, because no one's left this whole time. Not that Spencer sees where within the *Righteous Fire-Dragon* Sinclair's being held: he's got a clear enough view into the rest of the fleet, but not that megaship. It's the same with Jarvin.

At least that's what the man claims. Spencer doesn't trust him for shit, of course. He's spent a lot of the last forty-eight hours trying to devise a way to protect himself from whatever Jarvin might pull. Anyone who rose to head up CICom operations in HK is going to be a master manipulator by definition. Jarvin's faking of Praesidium credentials was the icing on the cake. It was just too bad that he picked the wrong side of the impending civil war. They're working on getting at one with the Chinese way of thought now. Jarvin gave them the Mandarin downloads. The Chinese zone's harder to navigate than the Russian. But they're managing so far. They've got new suits, stolen from one of the armories. They've got new identities. But nothing's got clearance to get off this fucking ship.

Leaving Spencer's software plenty of time to sort through zone permutations while his mind sorts through everything else. Memories pour over him . . . the lights beneath the Atlantic . . . the smile of a woman he used to know back in Minneapolis. He knows she's dead. He wonders what it was like when the def-grids broke and the rain of fire poured in. He can't believe the United States has been wiped off the map. He looks at the Moon, and he can't believe what's left. He knows this game is closing on its end. He knows that ultimately Jarvin and Sarmax are the competition—figures that's the only sensible way to view things. Jarvin's all analysis, no weakness. But Sarmax is getting ever more volatile—progressively more dangerous as his mood gets worse and worse. Spencer wonders what's bugging him—guesses that whatever it is, it's not what would be getting to the typical mech in this situation. The typical mech would be driven crazy by inaction—would be going out of his mind sitting there and waiting for the razors to come up with a solution. But Sarmax seems to be a man who's used to dwelling within himself. Whatever's eating him is something deeper. Particularly since he's showing the same signs he was showing back when this run was first beginning—back when he and Spencer were hiding out in Hong Kong. Some demon's eating at Leo Sarmax. Spencer wonders if it's the same thing that dragged him back into the game after all those years on the lunar South Pole—maybe even the reason why he went AWOL in the first place.

But all of it is mere background to the main event that's going down in Spencer's head. His primary focus across the hours has been dealing with the thing that's plagued him for so long. All those files within his head, compiled by the man whose suit is attached like a limpet a little farther down this shaft—and who stole those files from the man held captive in the other megaship. And the deeper he gets into those files, the more Spencer finds that it's all starting to blur together—the men around him, the ship about him, the clouds of lights beyond—all of it coalescing while Spencer paces through the canyons of his mind, thinking along angles he's never thought before. The files are giving way before him. Twenty-four hours, and he's making progress by pure process of elimination. Twelve more, and finally he's cracking some codes. All those letters from all those faux alphabets—he's at last seeing a rhythm to their seeming randomness. Something's coming into view before him. Vast realms of data, and he really doesn't want to believe what it's telling him. The audacity of it all floors him. The fact that this is simply the tip of the iceberg scares him shitless. But it also offers a new way to approach the current situation. He keys the conduit to the other two men.

"I got an idea," he says.

The president's convoy has been on the move inside the Moon for two days now. Two days in which Haskell's lived many lifetimes over within herself. She keeps on thinking of the face of Strom Carson. She can't believe he's dead. She wonders if he really *had* turned a corner—if he glimpsed something larger than his own ambition in the moments before he died. She wonders if he died well. She's wondering who did it—speculating whether she could have pulled the trigger if it had ever come to it. She's glad it never will. The endless trek through the Moon seems like some kind of relentless dream. President Szilard doesn't intend to make the same mistake as his predecessor. He believes in mobility. It seems to be working so far—no coups have come close to succeeding. He's still running things, even if they're falling down around his ears. Haskell's been in and out of more maglev trains than she can count. And a lot of crawlers too—moving down long tunnels bereft of rail, en route to the next railhead, shifting through the seemingly endless labyrinth of tunnels dug across the century of man's occupation of the Moon.

Now they're in a shuttle of some kind. She can't believe that Szilard's risking a move above the surface, but presumably he has his reasons. His marines have continued to show her every courtesy. She figured they'd be keeping her in a crate. But instead they've allotted her comfortable quarters aboard every vehicle. Maybe Szilard's trying to win her over. Or soften her up.

But what he *hasn't* tried to do is interrogate her. He hasn't attempted to do what everyone else has—take her apart and find out what makes her tick. She knows he's going to have to try. Particularly when what's in her brain might be his only hope of staving off the East. But he's been holding off. Doesn't take a genius to figure out why. She's a Pandora's box. Her mind's a maelstrom stretching out beyond time. She can't even begin to get a grip on what she's becoming. Despite the fact that Szilard's cut her off from zone, she's somehow eavesdropping on the universe. Static pours across her naked brain, most of it unintelligible, but shot through that cacophony are thoughts, emotions . . . other minds . . . she catches images of refugees pouring south into Mexico, of the mass graves the Eurasians are digging up and down the U.S. eastern seaboard. She feels the agony of the planet itself as though the biosphere was a living thing—as though it was flesh from which great chunks had been torn. She figures she's going insane. She can't wait to get all the way there. The expressions of the marines who bring her food and water tell her just how far gone she is. They're all too conscious of the designs scratched upon her body. They won't even look at her—they're terrified of her. She knows the feeling.

But eventually the moment that she's been waiting for arrives. It's just a moment like any other. Yet somehow she sees it rolling in toward her anyway—sees the door slide open.

Szilard enters the room.

"Figured you'd come eventually," she says.

A rec room aboard the American cruiser *Spartacus*: a lot of off-duty personnel here, biding time between shifts. Everyone's looking pretty tense. Those who aren't might be suspected of downing a little bootleg booze. The MPs keep on busting up the stills hidden all over the ship, but they can be certain they're failing to find them all.

The Operative and Lynx have a whole different set of fish to fry. They enter the room and head over to where three men are playing gin rummy.

"Can we interest you in a game of Shuk?" says Lynx.

"Why not," Maschler shrugs.

"You guys have been gone for half an hour," says Linehan.

"So?"

"So where the fuck were you?"

"Eating out your mom," says Lynx.

"Everybody relax," says the Operative.

Riley starts dishing out the cards. "They've been scoping out the next move, of course."

"Of course," says Lynx.

"Namely?"

"The next shuttle out of here."

Maschler checks the schedule. "The 22:10?"

"That's the one."

"But what's the *plan?*" says Riley.

The Operative laughs. "You're all still alive, aren't you? Still under our zone protection, right?"

"For now," says Maschler.

"For as long as it suits them," says Linehan, and flicks a card onto the table. "Look, no offense, but I'm *sick* of this. We've been bouncing around this goddamn fleet like a goddamn Ping-Pong ball for *two days now,* and the two of you haven't given us a *clue* as to what's really going down."

"You know exactly what's going down," says Lynx.

"*We* are," says the Operative. "Trying to get to the Moon."

"So why haven't we done it yet?"

"These things take time. We're in a war—or didn't you notice?"

"Oh, we noticed," says Maschler.

"Caught the president's speech," says Riley. "Good stuff."

"You're talking about the man who fed your last boss to the sharks," says Linehan.

"Gotta stay flexible if you want to stay afloat," says Riley.

This I can't wait to hear," says Sarmax.

"I've got a way off this ship," says Spencer.

"There *is* no way off," says Jarvin.

"All crew are confined," says Sarmax.

Spencer looks at the two men—looks at all the designs unfolding in his head. He feels almost reluctant to tell them what he's about to, feels like he might be saying too much. He's tempted to just steal away in these shafts and go for it himself. But he's figuring he still needs these men. He's all too aware of the delicate balance. As soon as one of the three gets killed, that'll leave the second utterly in the power of the third. Spencer's already gone through the scenarios: if he gets taken off the board, Sarmax will be at the mercy of Jarvin—and the mech will be in a similar position vis-a-vis Spencer if Jarvin bites it. Yet Sarmax is also the only counter Spencer has to Jarvin himself. It's complex enough to make one's head spin. But together, the three of them might be able to take on whatever's going on in the next megaship. Spencer knows that once they start moving again, the stakes get raised even higher. But he also knows they're running out of time. That he should have thought of all this half a day back. That it's just too bad he wasn't quicker.

"Well," he says, "it's like this."

"Where are we now?" she asks.

"Heading for the South Pole," says Szilard.

"You don't need to go aboveground to do that."

"Somewhere nearby, then."

"Prime real estate, huh?"

Jharek Szilard laughs. Unexpectedly, he sits down on the floor in front of her, folds his lanky body up in a movement that's almost sinuous. He gazes up at her.

"You're quite a woman," he says.

She looks at him without expression.

"Oh don't worry. My tastes don't run that way. Doesn't mean I can't express admiration for the girl around whom it's all spinning. Especially with all that *art* you've adorned yourself with—"

"Let's cut the bullshit," she says.

"Who said it was bullshit?"

"To you I'm just a *tool*."

"Wrong. That's the mistake that Montrose made."

"Among others," says Haskell.

"And I took advantage of most of them."

"Do you have a back door to me?"

"No."

"Then how did you beat Montrose?"

"Never ask a magician to reveal his secrets."

"Control was your creature, wasn't he?"

"I suppose that's one possibility," says Szilard.

"There are others?"

"Stephanie started something she couldn't finish."

"Me."

"Exactly. She couldn't figure you out."

Haskell makes a face. "I've got the same problem."

"That's the way Sinclair set it up."

"And you *really* think you can beat him?"

"Do I need to? If he's still alive, the Chinese have him."

"If that's so, that's only because he wants it that way."

"You think he's *that* good?"

"I think you need to stop thinking of him as human."

Szilard sighs. "Look, Claire, I get it. Okay? This war is mere veneer on the real war that's raging. And to seriously answer your question: I can't be sure of beating him unless I've got you. Will you help?"

"My answer makes no difference."

"Of course it does."

"You can't afford to let me go—ever. Nor can you afford to venture into my mind without the proper key."

"Let me get back to you on that," says Szilard.

"Time to go," says the Operative.

"Just when I was winning," says Linehan.

They troop out of the rec room. They're all dressed as SpaceCom marines—as is virtually everyone else they pass in the halls. They start climbing ladders down to the shuttle bays.

"These guys are fucking with us," says Riley.

"You've said that already," says Linehan.

"Nothing wrong with restating the facts," says Maschler.

The three men are on their own wireless channel, with their own codes—ones that Spencer gave Linehan back in the day. He knows that there's a chance Carson or Lynx might have hacked the line. He wonders if they're using him to keep an eye on the other two. He scarcely cares. He feels that his grip on reality has been getting ever more tenuous these last two days. But that doesn't mean he's not up to playing a role.

"The facts are that neither of you guys is a razor."

"You ain't either," says Maschler.

"Which is why we're getting buttfucked by two men who are."

"Mechs are worth less and less every day," says Riley.

Linehan snorts. "So why the hell *did* Montrose detail two mechs to keep an eye on Carson?"

"What should she have done?"

"Use a fucking razor!"

"She did," says Maschler.

"The Manilishi was riding shotgun," says Riley.

"That didn't seem to work as well as your boss hoped."

"That's why she's not our boss anymore."

"And Carson is."

"Or Lynx," says Maschler. "No telling who's got the upper hand."

"I'd bet on Carson," says Linehan.

"You do that," says Riley. "We won't get in your way."

"Not when we've seen the man in action," says Maschler. "He was hell on bloody wheels when that Elevator blew."

"You already told me," says Linehan wearily.

"It bears repeating," says Riley. "He's a fucking Houdini, and no mistake. We were fresh out of options and he found a way to get us high and dry."

"You think he'll be able to get us off this fleet?" asks Linehan.

Maschler laugh. "*Himself* off, sure."

"Even when there's *literally* no way to do that?"

"That's when the man's at his best," says Riley.

That is *so* much bullshit," says Sarmax.

"I wish it was," says Spencer.

"It's the craziest thing I've ever heard."

"I daresay you'll hear crazier before it's all over."

But while he replies to Sarmax, Spencer's keeping an eye on Jarvin. That's the reaction he's really interested in. He watches that man's face behind that visor, watches him mull over possibilities—watches his lips form the words—

"What's your angle on this?" asks Jarvin.

"My angle's getting us off this ship."

"But this—what you're saying—it's *insane*—"

"Does it hurt that I've gotten ahead of you on these files?"

Jarvin says nothing. Spencer decides that it probably does. He decides to rub it in.

"Take a look at what you're missing," he says, beaming data to Jarvin and Sarmax. Not all of it, of course. Just enough to make the point. He waits—counts to just shy of thirty seconds—

"You got this from the *files?*" says Sarmax.

"No," says Spencer, "I used the files to get this."

"What kind of yarn are you spinning?"

"The best kind," says Jarvin. "He's right."

"You're convinced?" says Spencer.

"Doesn't mean I have to like it."

The shuttle's been pitching and yawing for some time, as though it's maneuvering through rugged terrain. Not being able to see where it's going makes for a disquieting experience. Haskell's relieved when the craft finally touches down. She feels vibration roll beneath her as whatever platform the shuttle's just landed on starts lowering. Ten seconds later, all motion stops.

Five seconds after that, there's a knock on her door. She doesn't know why they bother, but Szilard seems determined to keep up appearances. So far he's been the only one to show up unannounced. She figures she may as well humor them.

"Come in," she says.

The door opens. The marine who stands there won't meet her eyes.

"We need you to put on a suit, ma'am," he says.

"To go where?"

Hesitation—"The president awaits you."

The auxiliary hangar of the *Spartacus* has several shuttles docked, several bays empty. There are a lot of mechanics and technicians. Lot of soldiers, too. Looks like someone's making last-minute rearrangements of the fleet's garrisons. There are five men in particular who aren't complaining.

"Let's go," says the Operative. He moves toward the shuttle door; the other four follow him. They give their IDs—a commando squad getting reassigned. They get on board. The shuttle pushes back. The hull of the *Spartacus* falls past, giving way to a spectacular view: the L2 fleet stretching away, ships slowly rotating in the sun. The Operative gets on the one-on-one with Linehan.

"Was wondering if you had time for a quick chat," he says.

"Why not," replies Linehan.

They maneuver stealthily past more Chinese soldiers. There's still a lot of cleanup going on. Blood's literally getting mopped off the walls. They're well into the rear of the craft now. Spencer's mind billows out around him, gathering the whole ship under its sway. A hatch swings open.

"Let's go," he says.

She's in a suit that contains just the basics, being led along passages of a place that could be virtually any lunar base. A few more minutes, and her escorts usher her through into a much larger room—possibly a quarter-kilometer across. It's a dome.

And what it contains used to be a garden.

"Jesus," she says.

It's been burnt all to hell. Ash is everywhere. The skeletal remains of what might have been a forest jut here and there. Pieces of the ceiling hang like icicles, casting eerie shadows in the floodlights that have been set up by the marines standing sentry all around. Haskell's escorts lead her through a path in the ash. It seems like maybe it might have been a stream once, but there's no sign of water now. Up another hill of ash, and they reach what's left of a gazebo . . .

Jharek Szilard stands within. Haskell's escorts stop just short, motion her forward.

Linehan stares out the window at the flickering lights. They look all too familiar. L2's the closest thing to home he's ever known. That's why he's always wanted to see it burn. He's glad he came back here to see it happen. Now he can barely wait.

"What's up, boss?" he says.

"You've been talking with Maschler and Riley?" Carson asks.

"Sure," says Linehan.

"What'd they say?"

"You don't know?"

"Pretend I don't."

"Just low-grade bitching, boss."

"Define 'low-grade.' "

"The kind that's only a problem when it stops."

"Has Lynx talked to you?"

Linehan says nothing.

"Well?" demands Carson.

"No."

"Why do I not quite believe that?"

"What do you want me to do if he does?"

"Hear him out. Laugh at his retarded jokes."

"That might be tough."

"What'll be tough is if you cross me."

"What's in it for me?"

"Other than the fact that otherwise you're dead?"

"I understand sticks just fine," says Linehan. "But I like carrot too. What are you and Lynx looking for anyway?"

"Who says we're looking for something?"

"I'm not stupid, Carson."

"Then you'll appreciate the importance of finding a way off this goddamn fleet."

"Sure, but you guys are running some other agenda. All this beetling back and forth to different parts of the fleet—you're searching for something."

"An interesting theory. What do you think we're after?"

"Beats me."

"Good," says Carson. "Look, being kept in the dark is frustrating. But trust me, you don't want to *know* the big picture."

"How about letting me be the judge of that?"

202 **DAVID J. WILLIAMS**

"How about letting me worry about the shit that's above your pay grade? Point is that when the moment comes, you're going to have to make a choice."

"Between you and Lynx."

"Maschler and Riley are only along for the ride because we're going to need all the muscle we can get for the stunts we're about to pull. I know you won't give anything they say a second thought. But Lynx is nothing if not persuasive. He's got a way of getting inside one's head with his twists of what he'll try to convince you passes for logic. But he won't forget the fact that you already fucked him over."

"*Szilard* fucked him over. Using me."

"You think that matters to him?"

"Probably not."

"What matters is that you never crossed *me*. And you saved us all at the Europa Platform. Stay on my side, and you'll have anything you want, Linehan. Anything. Freedom from all this bullshit, no bosses, dominion over whatever—doesn't matter. Fuck, you can have *Mars* if you want it."

"That's what Harrison offered me. A place up there—"

"I'm offering you the whole planet."

Pause. "You're not serious."

"Why not?" says the Operative. "Not like I want the dump. Look man, the one thing I'm loyal to is loyalty. And I'm going to need it when the shit hits the mother of all fans."

"And that'd be when?"

"Hate to say it, but probably before we're ready."

"You're running behind schedule?"

"Now we'll see if you can keep a secret."

The shuttle initiates docking sequence.

They head from the maintenance shafts to auxiliary shafts to elevator shafts. They reach the spine of the ship in short order and start making haste along it. There's a clanking noise below them. Cable starts to reel past them.

"Grab it," says Sarmax.

They do—it starts to haul them out of the forward levels of the ship. The elevator car whips past them, heading in the direction they've come from as they drop into the middle layers.

"Let's change it up," says Spencer.

"Agreed," says Jarvin.

Spencer finds that annoying. It doesn't matter what Jarvin thinks or says, now that Spencer has the data in his head—the vantage point on Eastern zone he's been seeking, which in turn provides perspective on so much else. He steps from the cable onto the wall of the shaft, his magnetic grips clinging while his camo cranks away. The others follow him through a crawlspace that leads into one of the parallel shafts. This one's much narrower. The elevators that run through it are intended purely for personnel. They grab another cable, alight on an elevator car that's moving fast toward the rear of the ship—they enter via the ceiling into the empty car.

"Let's hope your confidence is justified," says Jarvin.

"Not my fault you couldn't translate what you stole," says Spencer.

"You really broke through on *everything?*"

"Not all of it, no."

"But enough of it to—"

"It's their zone tactics," says Spencer. "Their strategy."

"Autumn Rain's."

"Like nothing I've ever seen. Precise guidelines—a fucking *manual*—for how to use the legacy zones to creep up and around the current ones."

"Like they did in South America."

"And at the Europa Platform. And everywhere else. *And* how to remain undetected while they were doing it. I took a tour through

yesterday's Russia, climbed out into today's Moscow, and got in behind the Praesidium's firewall."

"Penetrated it altogether?" Jarvin sounds skeptical.

"The next best thing. Managed to move a few files outside of it.
Got the blueprints for what we're heading toward—not to mention
the real lowdown on the fleet logistics."

"Which are?"

"They're about to green-light the final assault," says Spencer.
He works a sequence on the zone; the elevator slows, slides to a
halt.

"What the hell's going on?" says Sarmax.

"We're between floors," says Jarvin.

The doors are opening anyway—

Haskell walks up to the president. He looks down at her,
floodlights reflected in his visor. The blighted garden
stretches all around them. Szilard's bodyguards stand
close at hand.

"Quite a place," she says.

"It used to look a little more impressive."

"I'll bet."

"What happened here?" he asks.

She shrugs. "Some Rain operatives had a dustup."

"Fighting among themselves?"

"A habit of theirs."

"Sarmax and Carson, right?"

She nods.

"Who won?"

"Does it look like anyone won?"

"And you know all this because—?"

"Carson told me."

"He told you? Or can you *sense* it?"

"I'm not that good."

"Not yet," he says.

There's a pause. "So how much *do* you know?" she asks.

"A lot more than I did."

"These last forty-eight hours—where have we been?"

"All over," Szilard replies. "Some backup mainframes beneath Agrippa. Some bombed-out tunnels beneath what used to be Eurasian territory. A storage locker in Congreve. Not to mention—"

"Nansen Station?"

Szilard shakes his head. "I delegated that one. Didn't think it would be prudent to go there myself."

"Too predictable?"

" 'Predictable' is a word I rarely use," he says. "If something's predictable enough, then only a fool would do it, meaning no one expects you to do it, meaning more often than not you can pull it off. The possibility for double- and triple-fakes is endless, especially if you're dealing with Rain. And God only knows how many would-be pretenders are trying to do to me what I did to Montrose. I've stranded most of the problem cases up at the L2 fleet, but the Moon's crawling with collateral fallout from the last few days: surviving Praetorians, rogue InfoCom agents, everyone who's been dispossessed by the constant regime changes—"

"But this isn't just about your staying out of the crosshairs of those who would take your place."

Szilard says nothing.

"It's also about getting ready for the next phase," adds Haskell. "And thus your scavenger hunt."

Szilard nods.

"Found much?" she asks.

He shrugs. "I've found enough. Old files of Harrison's, captured Eurasian intel briefings, interrogation transcripts—it's strange how much got scattered across more than twenty years. You've got something you want hidden, you put it out of reach, and yet that doesn't mean it gets passed over forever. These days your data often has a longer lifespan than you do."

"Sarmax's hasn't outlived him yet."

"No," says Szilard. He looks thoughtful. "And yet I think that man died inside many years back."

"Because of Indigo Velasquez?"

"Indeed."

"She's still alive."

"You assert that with such confidence."

"Because I saw her."

"Along with who else?"

"She's part of Sinclair's team up at L5."

"And what about Sinclair's team down here?"

Pause. "I've seen nothing."

"You hesitate."

"I was thinking it over," she says.

"I think you're only seeing what he wants you to see."

"Possibly."

"That's his M.O., isn't it? All the way from the start, right? He put you and Marlowe alongside each other to keep you preoccupied, keep you distracted while—"

"He's not invincible. Look at how Morat played him—"

"And now Morat's dead."

"Maybe."

Szilard cocks his head. "What's that supposed to mean?"

"Morat appeared to me when Montrose was interrogating me." Pause. "Montrose was using his image."

"I'm not so sure," she says. "His presence felt . . . real."

"Well, of course it would—"

"And Sinclair appeared soon after, and he *was* real. That tank Montrose was holding me in had leaks. Maybe more than one. For all I know, Morat's out there playing his own game. Or is back in the saddle with Sinclair—"

"But I thought *you* were the one to kill Morat."

"I killed a robot. The original might have been elsewhere. Or somebody might have created more."

"Well," says Szilard, "one more reason for me to take my precautions."

"It won't save you."

Szilard grins ruefully. "I doubt anyone thought I'd be the one to harness you either. Sinclair and Harrison cut me out of the loop from the start. They thought I was just one more nonentity. Harrison tried to take me out, and I took him instead. The Rain tried to play me, and I spaced their hit squad. Montrose tried to make me second fiddle, and now she's a frozen husk. Because I do my homework, just like I've done with you. Everyone else just rushed in and got what they deserved. You're something you don't fuck with. You mind envelops anything that tries to control it. Your brain uses whatever tries to use you—you escalate automatically beyond the ability of any interrogator to reach. Montrose thought she'd cracked you, and all she'd done was undermine her own defenses."

"What about Carson?"

"What about him?"

"Back on Harrison's ship. He knew what he was doing—"

"*Thought* he did, sure. He had Sinclair's backing, but Sinclair gave him only part of the data. The old man wasn't stupid enough to allow your full powers into the hands of any of his minions. 'Cause suddenly the minion starts thinking they can be the master, right?"

"Just like you're doing now."

"And I'm not going into the lion's den without some serious hardware. These last two days have been quite the journey, Claire. Quite the haul. The sequencing on your incubation. The diagrams of your mind's metaprocesses, the way you run zone—I've got them now. I'll be able to get past the hurdles that tripped up Montrose. All that's left is one more step."

"Assuming Sarmax comes through for you."

"Let's find out, shall we?"

Two marines step into the gazebo with them. The floor begins to descend.

A shudder passes through the shuttle as it docks with the dreadnaught *Lexington*. Exterior hatches swing open. Everybody gets up and starts heading for the exit—or nearly everybody, anyway. Five people stay behind. Maschler and Riley look befuddled. Everyone else looks amused. The pilot appears in the cockpit doorway.

"End of the line," he says.

"Not for us," says the Operative.

"What's your problem?"

"Check your schedule," says Lynx.

"I already did," says the pilot.

"So check it again," says the Operative. There's something in his tone that makes the pilot do just that—accessing screens within his head—looking bemused—

"I don't understand," he says.

"Last-minute update," says Lynx.

"You guys intel or something?"

"Something," says the Operative.

"And we haven't got all day," says Linehan, getting out of his seat. He's twice the size of the pilot. The pilot re-enters the cockpit, the door to that chamber starts to slide shut—

"You can leave that open," says Lynx.

The door slides back open. The pilot works the controls. Exterior hatches shut; engines rumble into life as the shuttle pushes back once more. The Operative hears the one-on-one start up within his head.

"You'd better be right about this," says Lynx.

"Shut the hell up," says the Operative.

Ø "We're between floors," says Sarmax, echoing Jarvin.
"Let's go," says Spencer.

They move through a series of passages that aren't on any of the ship's blueprints they'd had access to previously. They see no other sign of life, no sign that anything's been here since it got built. There's that much dust. It reminds Spencer of all that nanotech back on the Europa Platform. He hopes he hasn't signed on for a repeat performance. They reach a door that looks to be quite strong.

"You got the key?" asks Jarvin.

"I'd better," says Spencer.

Turns out he does. They go through more, each one thicker than the last. Each time he finds he's got the right access codes. Turns out the cockpit wasn't the most secure area on the ship, because everyone knew where it was. But this—

"Everyone stand back," says Spencer.

The last door slides open.

◐ The gazebo floor-turned-elevator trundles downward. Shaft walls slide by. Szilard's two bodyguards eye Haskell. Haskell eyes Szilard.

"Where are we going?" she asks.

"Don't you know?"

"Pretend I don't."

"Can't you see the future?"

"It's a very clouded view."

"That's about to change."

They descend through the ceiling of a room unlike any Haskell's ever seen.

Way out near the edge of the L2 fleet is a medium-grade war-sat that was obsolete as of ten years ago. It's nothing special. It sees very little traffic.

That's the point.

"We don't even have clearance," says the pilot.

"You will in a second," says the Operative. He and Lynx are doing their damndest to make sure of that. None of this was easy to find. Sometimes the best place to hide secrets is right out in the open. Sometimes all you need to do is knock . . .

"Got it," says the pilot.

"Told you," says the Operative.

A battered hangar opens to receive them.

Three men pile into a room. The door slides shut behind them. There are no other doors visible.

"Jesus Christ," says Sarmax.

Dust is everywhere. The place looks like it's never been used. The walls are made of a strange kind of metal. Each wall has a suit-sized alcove cut in its center. Each such alcove looks as if it's meant to be stood in.

"Well," says Spencer, "here we are."

"And no one else on this ship knows about this?" Sarmax looks skeptical.

"If they do," says Spencer, "they're not talking."

"They don't," says Jarvin. "This was the trump card of the Eurasian leadership. In case their ships slipped the leash."

"They didn't count on us, though."

"Maybe they did," says Sarmax.

"Let's find out," says Spencer.

Picture a square turned forty-five degrees. That's what this room's like—it's set at angles. There's no floor, just vast walls slanting down along diagonals to meet in a V-shape: a metal-lined groove that runs along the bottom of the room. There's another such groove at the highest point of the room too—and a hole in the wall that rises up to meet that groove. The elevator-gazebo has just dropped through that hole, trundling along vertical rails down to the catwalks that crisscross here and there. A pillar is at the very center of the room, running from floor to ceiling.

"Quite a place," says Haskell.

"Wait till we turn it on," says Szilard.

They don't waste time. Lynx switches the shuttle's zone classification to *undergoing maintenance*; the Operative switches the war-sat's maintenance schedule to ensure that they won't be getting to the shuttle anytime soon.

"And what about me?" asks the pilot.

Linehan shoots him through the head. "Are we ready?" he asks.

"I think we are, " says the Operative.

The shuttle door opens.

Spencer's sending out wireless signals at point-blank range. A panel unfolds from the wall, revealing a console.

"Aha," says Sarmax

"What order are we going to try this in?" says Jarvin.

"All at once," says Spencer.

This is the place Sarmax hid from Carson," says Haskell. "He hoped to use it again someday."

"How'd you find out about it?"

"Would you believe he told me?"

The elevator stops. They've gone as far down as they can go. One of the marines leads the way onto the catwalk; the other follows Szilard and Haskell as they move toward the intersection of catwalks at the center.

"Actually," says Haskell, "I would."

If Sarmax thought it could be used as a tool against Carson, anything's possible. And if this place does what she suspects it's about to—

They move out into a deserted hangar. Equipment's everywhere but nothing looks flyable. Or even useful, for that matter. This stuff is from a bygone era.

"We're off the beaten track," says Maschler.

"We're going even farther," says Lynx. "You ready, Strom?"

"Assuming Maschler and Riley are ready to run point," says the Operative.

Maschler and Riley look at him. "Sure," says Riley.

"What route?" says Maschler.

"We'll tell you as we go," says Lynx.

How does this work?" says Sarmax.

"You get in one of these alcoves," says Spencer.

"You first."

"There's something I need to do first," says Spencer—starts working the console. The fact that it's totally unintuitive matters not in the slightest when he's already hacked the instruction manual—the manual that sat at the heart of the Kremlin for all

THE MACHINERY OF LIGHT   213

that time, the one that Jarvin almost found. But not quite—and now Spencer's the one who's calling the shots. He keys in the last of the sequence. There's a low rumbling hum. The alcoves light up, shimmer with a strange energy.

"Well don't just stand there," he says.

The pillar at the center of the room is a strange kind of metal Haskell can't identify, without evidence of grooves or bolts. It looks more organic than mechanic. She's got a funny feeling it's made of the same substance as the rails that run along the floor and ceiling. She walks up to it.

"Don't touch it," says Szilard.

"You don't know what the fuck you're doing," she says.

They head through corridors that look like they could use some maintenance. It's mostly dark, save for their own sensors. They're seeing no one. Maschler's voice comes through on the group channel:

"What are you expecting?" he asks.

"Surprises," says Lynx.

The men on point get the message. They shut up. For now, at any rate. They keep on cautiously leading the way, Lynx and Carson following, Linehan walking backward, bringing up the rear. He figures that if anything was following them, it probably would have made its move by now. But he doesn't know for sure. He watches the passageway recede, hears Riley's voice echo in his head:

"Lights. Up ahead."

Spencer walks calmly into one of the flickering alcoves. Jarvin does the same. Sarmax simply stands there.

"*Move*," says Jarvin.

"Why?" says Sarmax.

"What the hell's your problem?"

"You guys really think you're going to pull this off?"

"Got an alternative?" says Spencer.

"Take over this ship," replies Sarmax. "Drive it into deep space."

"And do what?" asks Jarvin.

"Live in splendid isolation."

"Without your precious Indigo?" says Spencer.

Sarmax stares at him.

"She's still alive," adds Spencer.

"How the fuck do you know that?"

"Better hurry if you want to find out."

Sarmax walks into an alcove. There's a blinding flash.

You do *not* want to turn this thing on," says Haskell.

"It's not a question of what I *want*," says Szilard.

Haskell can see the president isn't wasting any time. While he's talking, he's operating controls via wireless—she feels a low hum pass through her suit. Far overhead, the ceiling-rail starts flickering, along with the rail below. But nothing seems to be happening to the pillar. The humming intensifies.

"I'm begging you," she says.

"You think I'm walking into Sarmax's trap?"

"Try Sinclair's."

They've come through into an area of the war-sat that looks to be a lot better maintained. The lighting's a lot more reliable. There's an open door up ahead. Emanating from within is a noise that sounds a lot like someone's fingers hitting a keyboard.

"Hmmm," says Lynx.

"No shooting unless I say otherwise," says the Operative.

"Now he tells us," says Riley—gestures. Maschler moves through the doorway, guns at the ready.

The flash dies away. Spencer blinks, adjusts his vision. Looks at the alcove he's in—at the room beyond that. It looks exactly the same as it did before. He feels like a jet engine just went through his head. Dust is everywhere. A lot of it looks like it just got blasted from the alcoves.

"What do you mean she's still alive?" says Sarmax.

"I don't think this worked," says Jarvin.

Sinclair *wants* you to switch this on," says Haskell. "I'll find a way to surprise him anyway."

"You've got the coordinates?"

"Absolutely."

"He's way ahead of you, Jharek. Turn that on and God knows what will happen."

"You know what they say about desperate times, Claire."

The pillar's starting to glow in a very weird way: some sort of greenish-blue. It starts to pervade the place, shadows running up and down over the walls. The two marines move in closer to Szilard.

They take the room like any good commando squad: those on point going through, moving out into the room in different directions, the rearguard suddenly charging past the guys in the middle and in after the point and—

"All clear," says Linehan.

The Operative and Lynx move through. The room looks like any normal office. Fancy, though: wood panels along the walls and door opposite. Nice carpet underfoot. A well-appointed desk takes up most of one corner. A very attractive woman sits at it. She regards them calmly.

"Can I help you gentlemen?" she asks.

She's not in armor—just civilian clothing. She looks so good she's got to be genetically engineered. But it's not her looks that are making the Operative nervous.

"We're here to see Dr. Sorensen," says the Operative.

"Are you nuts?" says Lynx, and shoots the woman in the chest.

They step out of the alcoves.

"You'd better answer my question," says Sarmax, moving toward Spencer. Jarvin cuts in between them.

"Easy," he says.

"You guys have been talking behind my back," says Sarmax.

"Better get used to it," says Spencer. "We're the razors."

"Where the hell's my Indigo?"

"Where she's always been," says Jarvin.

"At Sinclair's side," says Spencer.

H e's counting on you doing this," says Haskell. "Just not so soon," replies Szilard. The pillar is now blazing so bright they're having to adjust the shades on their visors. Haskell's watching everything get just a little darker. She realizes the equipment has reached activation frequency.

"It's too early," she says.

"You mean this doesn't appear in any of your visions?"

She nods. He laughs. "Such a shame," he says. "So sorry to disappoint you. But in truth, nothing's written."

There's a blinding flash.

T he woman's blown backward out of her chair. She drops behind the desk.

"Suck it," says Lynx.

"What the fuck's your problem?" says the Operative.

"Let's go see the doctor—*shit!*"

The woman's coming up from behind the desk with a carbine, spraying explosive rounds. Lynx fires his suit-jets, leaps to one side and unloads on full-auto, unleashing in tandem with the four other men. Now the woman's taking damage. Bullets slice through her flesh, starting to reveal the metal chassis underneath. The Operative tosses a grenade at the woman's feet. It detonates, taking half the room with it.

H ow am I supposed to reach her?" says Sarmax. "She's within a klick of us," says Spencer.

"But like Jarvin said—this didn't *work*," says Sarmax.

"I've changed my mind," says Jarvin.

The flash subsides. The room looks the same as it did before. Szilard looks puzzled.

"We haven't moved," he says.

"We weren't supposed to," says Haskell.

"This didn't *work?*"

"Depends what you mean by 'work,' " says a voice.

The room's a shambles. So is the secretary-android. Smoke's everywhere. The opposite door's been blown down. Lynx is already moving through it. The Operative turns to the other three men.

"You guys stay here," he says. "Set up a perimeter."

"Perimeter?" asks Linehan.

"This room is the only way to reach what lies beyond it."

"How long will you be?"

"Depends on how many questions you've got."

Linehan mock-salutes. The Operative moves after Lynx.

You're saying we just—?" asks Sarmax.

"More than just saying," says Spencer.

"Welcome to the *Righteous Fire-Dragon*," says Jarvin.

"Jesus," says Sarmax. He checks his suit readouts—they all check out. "Is this *me?*"

"Who else would it be?" asks Jarvin.

"Say hi to the new you," says Spencer.

"What happened to the old one?"

"Nothing good."

"*Fuck,*" says Sarmax.

"And you might have lost a thing or two along the way."

"What the hell do you mean?"

"No such thing as quantum cloning," says Spencer. "Something always gets lost in the shuffle."

"You're saying we should check our memories?" says Sarmax. "Like they weren't suspect enough—"

"He's saying don't be surprised if you start bleeding out," says Jarvin. "We're just going to have to see how this plays out, huh."

Spencer nods. "Terra incognita for sure."

"Teleportation's *real*," mutters Sarmax.

"Real question is who else knows it," says Jarvin.

She's been thinking in that direction for a while now. After all, Sinclair's been fucking with the space-time continuum. Once you've sent messages back from the future, bypassing space isn't so far beyond the pale. But now she's face to face with it. Because everyone in this chamber's whirling. Standing on one end of the catwalk is a figure wearing what looks to be a seriously sophisticated suit of powered-armor.

"Who the hell are you?" asks Szilard.

"The person who's going to kick your ass," says the figure—right before it starts firing.

The Operative and Lynx move through into what looks to be a standard office complex, though all the offices on either side are empty. Their sensors are cranked—they're looking for anything with a heat source.

"You really think he's here?" asks Lynx.

"Bastard never goes anywhere without that bitch of his."

They start getting ready to move out. Spencer does a quick scan on the zone around him. Sarmax keeps going on about teleportation.

"I'm still trying to get my head around this," says Sarmax. "The amount of computational power needed—the amount of *energy*—you're talking about something that's—"

"Off the charts," says Spencer. "But just so we're all on the same page, spare us all and stop playing stupid."

"Who says I'm playing stupid?"

"You know all about these fucking devices."

"I don't know if I'd go that far."

"*Heard* about them, then."

"Okay," says Sarmax, "so I've heard about them—"

"In your goddamn basement," says Jarvin.

Flame streaks across the room. Szilard's two bodyguards leap in front of him, taking the shots. One of them takes a few too many. His suit starts burning. Szilard's grabbing at Haskell—but she's leapt from the catwalk, finds herself tumbling down in low-gravity toward the rail beneath. The figure advances on Szilard's remaining bodyguard, who closes rapidly, firing all his weapons. Szilard comes to a quick decision—he ignites his suit-jets and blasts upward toward the elevator shaft.

They've left the offices behind and have come to what looks more like a lab-complex. Equipment's everywhere, gleaming like it's seen recent use. Standing in one corner is a man who looks at them like he expected this all along.

So I had one in my cellars," says Sarmax. "So what? Didn't mean I ever switched the fucking thing on. Problem with having a teleporter is—"

"Not enough to have just *one*," says Jarvin.

"Got to know the location of the others," mutters Spencer.

"If you don't, having only one is worse than useless," says Sarmax. "Never know when something just fucking *manifests*—"

"That's what the Praesidium intended to do if rogue elements got ahold of these megaships," says Jarvin. "They could just beam in commandos and—"

"So could the Rain," says Spencer.

Jarvin laughs. "The Coalition's has been played. If they have these devices, it's only because the Rain wanted it that way."

Spencer looks at Sarmax. "Who installed yours?"

"That'd be Sinclair," says Sarmax.

"Let's trash this place," says Jarvin.

Szilard shoots into the shaft and disappears from sight. His second bodyguard fights on for about two more seconds before getting torn apart. The newcomer vaults over the catwalk, fires its jets, speeds down toward Haskell. She's still falling, picking up speed. The figure catches up to her just before she hits the bottom.

You're well off the beaten path," says the man.

He looks pretty old. His beard's gone almost white. His face is wizened, but his eyes are bright. He smiles like he's trying to cover up how scared he is.

"Where the fuck is it?" demands Lynx.

estroying the teleportation chamber isn't a no-brainer. Once it's done, they can no longer get out. But the only place they can escape to is the ship they came from. And the risks of anyone else catching up with them using the same technology is just too great. A few silenced rounds of ammo and some good old-fashioned battering with their fists, and the room may as well have just been bombed.

"Nothing like burning bridges," says Jarvin.

"Let's go," says Spencer.

The ship's zone clicks in around him.

askell feels herself seized by gloved fists; she watches walls rush by as the suited figure fires its jets, hauls her back up, and dumps her unceremoniously onto the catwalk. The shattered bodies of Szilard's bodyguards lie nearby. The president's nowhere to be seen.

"He'll be back any moment," says the interloper.

here's what?" asks the old man. "Where the fuck is the telepor—"

"Let me handle this," the Operative says to Lynx on the one-on-one. He opens up the channel again: "You're Dr. Arthur Sorenson."

"Is that a question?" says the man.

"More like confirmation," says Lynx. "We've already got your résumé."

Sorenson looks at him a little strangely. "Which résumé?"

"That'd be the real one."

They leave the wrecked equipment behind, head out through passages that look familiar. An identical set of doors as on the *Hammer of the Skies*, only this time they're going the other way. Spencer feels like he's retracing his footsteps. It's strange to think he isn't. In short order they reach the elevator shaft—between floors, same as before. An elevator car's just arriving for them.

ho the fuck are you?" says Haskell.
    "A secret admirer."
    "With access to the teleport machines—"
"Narrows it down, doesn't it?"
"Goddammit, who—"
"First things first."

t all happened so long ago," says Sorenson.
    "May as well have been yesterday," says Lynx.
    "At least tell me which ones you are."
"Originals," says the Operative.
Sorenson's eyes narrow. "Where's the third?"
"We're asking the questions," says Lynx.
"So how about you give us a guided tour," says the Operative.

he elevator hurtles toward the rear of the ship.
    "Which is where Sinclair is," says Sarmax.
    "You got it," says Jarvin.
"And Indigo's a prisoner too?"
"They may not be prisoners," says Spencer.

The figure leans forward, unlocks the restraints on Haskell's suit in one fluid motion, and beams her data. Haskell realizes they're coordinates—that the figure is giving her directions. Only—

"These aren't for the portal," she says.

"Because it doesn't lead to where you need to go."

"Szilard thought it led to the—"

"He was wrong. Use the map I just gave you; Sarmax's own back door. Eighty klicks south to Shackleton. To the South Pole." A pause. "You know about the South Pole?"

"I've known all along."

"Then you know what lies beyond it."

"South of every south," says Haskell.

They look at each other.

"And you?" she adds.

"I'm going back the way I came. To run some more errands. Which starts with blowing this equipment behind me." The figure tosses plastique, starts to turn—

"Are you Matthew Sinclair?" asks Haskell.

The figure says nothing, just starts up the machinery, surging jets and heading in toward it. Haskell's eyes narrow.

"Morat?"

A laugh: "Not even vaguely."

You want me to show you around?" asks Sorenson.

"Don't make me ask twice," says the Operative.

"No need. But there's no teleportation device here."

Lynx laughs. "Do you want to die, old man?"

"I dream of it every day," says Sorenson.

They may be running a takeover sequence," says Jarvin
"They may be running this place already," says
Spencer.

"Only one way to find out," says Sarmax.

The elevator comes to a halt. The doors open.

Haskell watches a door slide open in the pillar, watches
the figure step toward it—and turn back toward her
one more time. She hears the voice echo in her helmet.

"*Go,*" it says.

She fires her suit-jets.

They follow Sorenson back into the rest of his labs.
The Operative's keeping him in his crosshairs the
whole way. He's got no idea what the guy might try. All
he knows is that this is a man who's been on the run for a long
time—who knows all the tricks. That's how he was able to seclude
himself in the backwaters of SpaceCom—just another weapons
laboratory among so many, this one producing something on paper and somehow never quite being called upon to produce it for
real. None of which mattered when the funding kept on arriving
and all inquiries got led down false trails. But every reckoning
comes eventually.

They move through more corridors. Spencer's checking
out zone-grids. *Righteous Fire-Dragon* turns out to be a
very different proposition from its sister ship. It's a lot more
complex. The cockpit's even better defended than on *Hammer of
the Skies*. The ship's executive node is far more formidable. But

Spencer's mind is sifting through it all the same. His new zone techniques put the old ones to shame. He and Jarvin triangulate on the area of the ship that's been turned into a prison. They're plotting their route in. But that route includes one preliminary stop—one they've almost reached. They prime their weapons.

She's roaring through more tunnels, and her mind's awhirl with a million thoughts. She's got a very narrow window on the zone now, too—the microzone contained within this tunnel. She can see the pursuit boiling in behind her. Szilard's marshaling the rest of his force. He's coming after her with the most elite marines SpaceCom can muster. He knows if he doesn't take her back he's meat. She feels the rock around her shake as though a large explosive just detonated. She can guess what just blew. She wonders how the hell Sarmax acquired it in the first place—wonders if he even knew it was there. Her thoughts are racing—Szilard didn't seem to realize what he was dealing with, thought this was the gateway to Sinclair's true fortress—that he could get there before the old man himself showed up. But he ended up getting punked. Haskell's wondering whether maybe she did, too. She's still doing analysis on the nature of the device she was just face to face with—the radiations it emitted, the energies it was accessing. She reaches the end of a tunnel, drops through a trapdoor—sees what she's been told was there, starts its motors before she's even reached it.

They come through into the rear areas of the lab and reach another door. It's got several seals on it.

"We need to put on special suits to proceed," says Sorenson.

"We're dressed just fine," says the Operative.

Sorenson glances back at the Operative's armor. "At least let me—"

"Fat chance," says Lynx. He rips off the seals, yanks open the door and—

"Shit," he says.

They're into some of the more restricted areas aboard the *Righteous Fire-Dragon*. They're still seeing no one. They transition from passageways to shafts, quickly crawl down them, smash through a grille—and drop down into a room.

That room contains three Chinese soldiers in powered armor. They're still alive, but only just. Their armor's malfunctioning about as badly as Spencer's been intending it. Same as it ever was: once you get the high ground on the zone you can wreak havoc on everything below it. Spencer and Jarvin mesh minds and catch what's left of their targets in a death grip. The suits go haywire, electrocuting the men within them.

Sarmax climbs into the room and stares at the bodies.

"What have we here?" he asks.

"The key to Sinclair's cell," says Spencer.

More like a missile than a vehicle: it's a state-of-the-art maglev minicar, already starting to sling itself down the tracks toward the tunnel at the far end of the room. Haskell adjusts her thrusters, matches speeds—drops down into the single seat, straps herself in as the canopy lowers and the car accelerates. She catches a glimpse of suits pouring into the room behind her, but then rounds a bend in the tunnel.

S hould have guessed it," says the Operative.
         The room contains twenty transluscent cryo-units.
Each one's occupied. Half are male, half are female.

"And none of them are human," says Lynx.

"They're Rain," says the Operative.

Sorenson says nothing.

"Never mind the Rain," says Lynx on the one-on-one. *"We need to find his goddamn teleporter."*

"He told you already," says the Operative. "He ain't got one."

"And you believe him?"

"It was always a longshot. His expertise never extended to that kind of stuff anyway."

"So how the fuck are we getting off this fucking fleet?"

"The old-fashioned way," says the Operative.

W ho the fuck were these guys?" asks Sarmax.
         "Us," says Spencer.
"You mean now we're them."

"I always was," says Jarvin.

Sarmax frowns. "What the fuck are you on about?"

Jarvin kicks one of the Chinese soldiers with his boot. Sarmax can't help but notice the major's insignia on the shoulder of the dead man's armor. And suddenly it all clicks—

"My counterpart," says Jarvin.

"Oh," says Sarmax.

"Yeah."

"You were sent by the Praesidium as one of the two interrogators of Matthew Sinclair. Took the place of the Russian one—"

"Who would have died anyway when the Chinese purged them," says Spencer.

"Maybe," says Jarvin. "Maybe not. Who cares? The point is, now he's dead. And so is this one. And we've got their codes."

"So let's go say hi to the head of CICom," says Spencer.

Haskell accelerates, pouring on the speed. But she still can't get access to the larger zone—just a mere fraction of it, a tiny thread that represents this rail line. Obstensibly, this particular tunnel is a component of Sarmax's ice-processing operation, eighty klicks north of Shackleton. Only now it's more like sixty klicks. Haskell's feeling okay about keeping the pursuit behind her for the next few minutes. It's what's in front of her that's got her worried.

So what exactly was your plan?" asks the Operative.

Sorenson laughs. "Who says I had a *plan*?"

"This flesh," says Lynx, gesturing at the cryo-tanks.

Though right now that flesh isn't saying much of anything. It's just sitting there, all life systems reduced to an absolute minimum. The Operative can't read anything in those faces. But he can see a thing or two in Lynx's. He opens up the one-on-one again.

"What the hell's on your mind?" he says.

"The colony ships," Lynx replies.

"What about them?"

"They're *full* of sleepers."

"That's why they call them colony ships, Lynx."

"The ships are a subterfuge. Why not the cargo?"

The Operative addresses Sorenson: "What about the colony ships?"

"Mostly just colonists."

"But not exclusively."

"There are a few anomalies here and there."

"Made by who?"—but even as he asks the question, the Operative realizes its absurdity. Everyone's been trying to duplicate the Autumn Rain batch ever since it came out of the vat. Every player's got their own breed of posthuman in the mix. Szilard's undoubtedly been working his own angles. But no one's ever been able to attain the breakthroughs that Matthew Sinclair made two decades back. Nobody's come close to replicating them. Partially that's because he executed all the scientists.

Except for one.

"I never had the big picture," mutters Sorenson.

"Who the hell did?" says the Operative.

"That'd be *you*," says Lynx.

Flanked by his escorts, the man who's been charged by the Praesidium with interrogating the most important asset to ever fall into the Coalition's hands is approaching the section of the *Righteous Fire-Dragon* that's been designated as maximum security. All prisoners taken from the L5 fortress have been moved there. There weren't that many. Most of the garrison was killed subsequent to surrender. But there were a few exceptions . . .

"He's in there, alright," says Spencer.

"At least officially," says Jarvin.

"And where the hell's Indigo?" asks Sarmax.

"Right here," says Spencer—beams the map over to him, showing the holding cells and their denizens. There are only five: Sinclair, and four of the soldiers who were guarding him. And Spencer's fairly sure not all of those soldiers are who they seem to be.

"When they took the libration point, the Eurasians killed *everybody*," says Spencer. "A total massacre. They knew what they were up against. They knew that Sinclair wasn't an ordinary prisoner, that the Rain might have *infected* L5. That's why they took no chances—why the only exceptions were quarantined and put into lockdown—why the only ones getting into this cell-block are—"

"Us," says Sarmax.

They turn a corner. Guards block the way ahead.

Y ou're barking up the wrong tree," says the Operative. "Sinclair kept the whole thing compartmentalized. And only he had insight into the specifics of the core quantum processes—"

"Along with the physicists," says Sorenson.

"Who were the first to go," says the Operative.

"Because you killed them," says Lynx.

"On Sinclair's orders."

"But not before you made them talk."

"Let me assure you that Sinclair had already deprived them of that ability."

"I was a fucking *biogeneticist*," says Sorenson. "I'd heard the stories, sure—of what was really going on at the center of his fucking Manhattan Project. Of tapping into nonlocalized consciousness to tune the mind as a neurotransmitter. Of—"

"Telepathy," says Lynx.

"—leveraging quantum entanglement to enable remote duplication of matter."

"Teleportation," says the Operative.

He and Sorenson look at each other.

"And?" asks the Operative.

Sorenson looks as if he's about to weep. Lynx looks at the Operative.

"What do you mean, *and?*"

"You know what I mean," says the Operative to Sorenson. Sorenson closes his eyes.

"Say it," says the Operative.

"Something to do with time," whispers Sorenson.

Careening through a hollow tube beneath the lunar mountains: Haskell's halfway to Shackleton, and she can only imagine what she's going to find when she gets there. She feels the South Pole beckoning beyond it—feels it with an intensity that makes the antipodes at the Europa Platform look like the artificial constructs they were. Her awareness is cranking up to new heights. And all the while she's doing her utmost to dissect the nature of the machinery fading behind her.

Sinclair could see the future," says Lynx.

"So could the Manilishi," says Sorenson.

"Only Sinclair's ability trumped Haskell's," says the Operative. "She just had it in flashes. Sinclair's view was a little more *comprehensive*, wasn't it?"

Sorenson shrugs. "But the Manilishi was able to deploy hacks—"

"Don't play the retard," snaps the Operative. *"This isn't just about precognition, is it?"*

"No," whispers Sorenson.

For a moment there's silence. Lynx whistles.

"Fuck," he says, "if Sinclair can violate causality wholesale—"

"Then we'd know it," says the Operative. "We'd have already lost."

"And if one of those teleporters wasn't *really* a teleporter," says Lynx. "And if it got switched on—"

"Like I said," says the Operative, "we'd know it."

Running scans, checking readouts: it's somehow only just beginning to dawn on her that she really *is* on the Moon—that she's reached the object that she and Jason set out for so long ago. She feels like she's stabbed him in the back by arriving up here without him—feels like she's betrayed him repeatedly ever since. And somehow *feels* him too, like he's somewhere out there even now. As if anything's possible. She watches walls streak past. Shackleton's drawing ever closer.

Time machines," says Sorenson. "He was trying to develop time mach—"

"*Is,*" mutters Lynx. "We need to move—"

"I get that," says the Operative. He shoves his guns up against Sorenson's face. "Too bad this goddamn hunk of metal where you and that blowup-bitch of yours have been holed up contains not a single portal of any use whatsoever."

"God help me it's true," says Sorenson. He's cowering like he knows he's about to get it any moment—

"And you don't even know the details of the fucking recipe to cook up some Rain," says Lynx. "*So what the fuck have you been growing here?*"

"My best effort," snaps Sorenson.

"And you were going to activate them *when?*"

"I figured to use them as a bargaining chip instead."

"You've signed your own death warrant, old man."

"That happened long ago."

"You may yet avoid it," says the Operative.

Sorenson looks at him. "What do you want me to do?"

"Wake them up, of course."

◎ Visors can be deceptive. Sometimes the screens that they project can face the other way. These three show Han Chinese faces. But on the inside it's a different story . . .

"Special agent Zhou Tang," says the man who's not. "Here to interrogate the prisoner, at the express instruction of the Praesidium."

IDs flow up and down the ladders of command. The word comes back. A sentry signals. The door opens—to reveal a second barricade. More sentries step forward.

⊕ You can't be serious," says Sorenson.
"I never joke," says the Operative.
He and Lynx have already gotten busy siphoning off all the data—the schematics on this particular batch of would-be superwarriors; the records Sorenson's kept of his long stealth burn through the glacial layers of the SpaceCom bureaucracy; the tantalizing fragments from all the years before that. He snatches at files with timestamps from the 2080s. Data fills him up till he feels like he could burst. He looks at Sorenson.

"So fire it up," he says.

Sorenson starts warming up the brain-farm.

◐ She's coming in on Shackleton like a bomb now, and she still can't break through to the larger zone beyond. It's just not happening. She almost wonders if she's been damaged irreparably by everything that's gone down. But her mind feels anything but damaged. It feels like it's burning out in all directions. She's bringing new insight to the situation at hand. She's now almost certain that machine was a teleporter—and only that. None of her readouts show a trace of tachyons. Meaning that figure *wasn't* from the future. Whoever it was is from the present. Maybe even from somewhere else on the Moon. But within the zone itself, Haskell's still confined to this tunnel, blocked off at both ends—and even that perspective's shrinking as someone pulls the plug on the maglev. She wonders why they didn't do it earlier— maybe they figured there's no point, because now she's switching to rockets—she barrels forward toward her destination—

Cryo-machines hum. Life-support systems chirp. Flesh is waking up.

"How much longer?" says the Operative.

"Only a couple more minutes," says Sorenson.

"And how soon will they be ready for combat?"

"Within the hour."

"Might need to cut some corners," says the Operative.

The guards of the second perimeter put them through the paces. Codes, backup codes, failsafes, voice recognition . . . but Spencer is sufficiently high up in the Eurasian zone that he's got all the answers. Or at least he's able to make like he does—he still can't penetrate the Praesidium itself, but he can fool it into thinking he's carrying out the orders. The second set of doors slide away—reveal the third and last dead ahead.

She's heading into the outskirts of Shackleton, and she still can't reach the zone. She can only assume that's because there's no direct link to it from this tunnel she's in—a tunnel that's suddenly starting to widen, joining up with other tunnels. Sarmax's infrastructure is giving way to the infrastructure of the whole city. It spreads out before her.

Almost there," says Lynx.
   The Operative says nothing. He's lost in the faces of the waking sleepers. They look so familiar. There's one woman in particular that he feels like he's seen before. Probably because the face isn't dissimilar to Claire's. He can only imagine where she is now. He wonders just how good this batch will be. Not quite up to the stuff of the originals, but maybe that's just as well. He watches the seconds slide by, gets ready to start giving orders.

The codes are running. The sentries who guard the last door are waiting for the results. Spencer feels like he's reached the threshold. Sarmax's suit-monitors show his pulse accelerating to dangerous levels. Spencer wonders whether he's going to give them all away. It's just a few more meters to the man who tried to turn this whole game inside out—the man who may yet be running the whole thing. He feels that power's within his grasp. He lets the zone-bubble he's created slide in around them. The doors open—

Like slalom on acid: Haskell starts weaving her way into the tunnel-network around Shackleton. She's dodging past other trains, stations, freight. Sirens are sounding. Klaxons are howling. Apparently the garrison is finally waking up. But she's still detecting no zone presence.

And suddenly she gets it: they've switched it off altogether. Contingency planning—faced with the likes of her, they've gone to communicating purely by analog line and loudspeaker. But mobilizing under those kind of conditions is anything but easy. She's eating up the klicks, rising through levels, closing on the heart of the city. Even as she feels something closing in on her . . .

"We're going to need to get them some weapons," says Lynx.

"*They're* the weapons," says the Operative.

And equipping them will be the least of his problems. This war-sat contains enough shit to blow up a small asteroid anyway. Redundancy has its advantages. Same with these twenty men and women. They'll be the firepower needed to initiate the next phase—the ticket back to the Moon. Sorenson's files are going to be helpful, too. The Operative glances at the scientist and wonders if there might actually be some use in keeping him alive. The eyelids of some of the sleepers are starting to flicker.

A repurposed storage chamber: the walls look like they've been seriously reinforced. The center is dominated by a squat structure that stretches almost to the ceiling.

"Huh," says Spencer.

It's a box—a room all its own. It's been custom built for a single purpose. A single door's visible, along with a window next to it.

The three men move forward as the hatches through which they've entered slide shut behind them.

She rockets through the basements of Shackleton. All the maglev is out, as is the rest of the electricity. It's all a scorched-earth strategy to slow her down. The Space-Com garrison is taking up positions. She can't *see* it, but she can *sense* it—and the fact that nearly all of their defense sequences were prepped to deal with attacks from without makes it difficult to scramble to meet an incursion from within. Particularly since all Haskell's really concerned about is getting out herself. She swerves back onto a set of passenger rails. Raw contingency hits her like a wave. A face starts boiling up inside her mind.

The Operative wills himself to remain calm. The last thing he wants is to sit here and wait while these things wake up. Particularly when everything around him is coming to a head. The Eurasians might start their final attack at any moment. The endgame could kick off anytime. The eyes of the sleeper nearest to him open.

Spencer looks in the window. Sitting cross-legged against the wall opposite them is Matthew Sinclair. Unsuited, his eyes closed. Four people are chained adjacent to him. They wear Praetorian colors. Three are very clearly dead. Blood's dripping from their ears and noses.

The fifth looks fine. Her face isn't one that Spencer recognizes. But it seems like Sarmax does. He's obviously struggling to control himself.

"Steady," says Spencer.

Sinclair's eyes open.

She's transfixed—can't turn away. The old man's surging into her head like some tide she can't withstand. She's not sure why she ever wanted to. Her mind collapses in upon itself like some kind of sinkhole, yet the deeper it goes the more acute her insight gets. Tunnel blasts past her while she maneuvers through the Com forces with near-perfect precision. They're still hoping to trap her and take her alive—and she's only got a few more seconds before they realize that's just not going to be possible. But anything can happen in those seconds. Particularly inside the endless reaches of her head. The jaws of Sinclair open to receive her.

The Operative can't take his eyes off that woman— the one who resembles Claire. It isn't her, of course. It's not even a clone. But he can barely look away. It's like watching someone being born. He feels the eyes of the others upon him now—feels himself caught up in a vortex of his own making. He wonders what happened to the old Carson—the one who never made mistakes, who always forced others to pay for theirs. He wonders what his motives for all this really are. The woman's mouth is forming soundless words.

Spencer's trying to keep his mind focused. The eyes of Sinclair are like pits into which he's tumbling. He's fighting to pull himself away. He's conscious of almost nothing else.

Except for Sarmax.

"Easy," Spencer says again.

"Shit," says Jarvin—but Sarmax is already igniting his lasknife, slashing through the seals on the cell door.

The SpaceCom forces are giving up on trying to capture her. They're opening fire—but she's firing first, unleashing a rack of torpedoes, then calibrating her own route to steer in amidst the blasts detonating throughout the labyrinth of Shackleton. And Sinclair's riding her mind as she rides the tunnels—she shoots out through one of the larger caves—gets a quick glimpse of buildings all around—and then she's back into the narrower passages as she closes in on the far side of the city. The very edge—she's roaring in toward it as Sinclair forges in toward the center of her awareness. He seems to be looking for something. She's terrified he's about to find it. She pivots within herself—

Carson," whispers the woman.

The Operative isn't surprised. It's as though he's been here before. It's as though all this is memory in reverse. He tries to speak—succeeds—

"I'm here," he says.

The roar of autofire suddenly fills the room.

As Sarmax practically rips the door from its hinges, Spencer realizes that the man has shut down the zone-conduits for his armor.

"Stop him," yells Jarvin.

But Sarmax is already firing.

She's wrestling with the old man for what's left of her sanity—all the while racing out of the transport-tunnels and into corridors intended for personnel, rushing in through the last streets of the city toward the city-wall. She's almost there. The SpaceCom forces are falling back before her, waiting for her to slow down—waiting for her to turn. It doesn't seem to occur to them that she's not going to. She fires her last rack of torpedoes.

Lead's flying everywhere, along with thousands of fléchette rounds. It's all light stuff. It's all bouncing off Lynx and the Operative as they whirl to face the shooter who's standing in the doorway. Sorenson hits the deck, but the sleepers are getting diced. Flesh sprays the walls.

Sarmax opens up with his suit's flamer, spraying liquid fire over all those within the room. Flame engulfs the chamber, surging back over him like some fiery tide.

Explosions half blind her, but Haskell's firing the craft's afterburners anyway, crashing through the SpaceCom barricades, blasting through the hole in the city-wall that her torpedoes just carved, shredding through the face of Matthew Sinclair as she shoots out into open space—

Linehan ceases firing. Smoke's everywhere.

"Fuck you *both*," he says.

"You're dead," says the Operative.

"And you're fucking crazy!" yells Linehan. "Where the *fuck* do you get off on waking up minions who will try to turn you into *fucking meat?* You want to bring more *Rain* into the mix? You have fucking *lost it*, man, and you can—"

"He's right," says Lynx.

It's inferno. It's all Spencer can do to sever the smoke alarms and shut down the fire detection system—but he lets the sprinklers go into action, hurling water everywhere. Smoke belches in gouts from the cell-chamber. Jarvin grabs Sarmax—who seizes him in turn. But before either can strike the first blow—

"We've got bigger problems," says Spencer.

And it doesn't get any bigger than this. Shackleton is on the slopes of the South Pole basin—one of the largest impact craters in the solar system, more than ten klicks deep, a massive complex of sloping walls and cliffs and darkness. Haskell cuts the afterburners, damps the rockets, and lets the craft arc down like it's a particle of light drawn into some black hole. She sees mountains towering above her—catches a glimpse of Malapert's fiery peak presiding over all of it. But that view is nothing compared to the zone. Now that she's gotten past sublunar Shackleton's shut-down networks, she's got access to wireless; it pours over her like a million waterfalls, giving her the leverage she needs to sweep away the last fragments of Sinclair as she plunges in toward nadir.

The Operative takes it all in—the shredded bodies, the acrid smoke, Sorenson huddled weeping in a corner. Linehan pulls off his helmet.

"I'll make it easy for you," he sneers.

"Put that back on," says Lynx—and on the one-on-one to Carson: "This is the part where you get a grip."

"He killed them."

"He did us a favor."

"You really believe that."

"Who knows what compulsions those things were saddled with?"

"By Sorenson? He's nothing—"

"By Sinclair."

That wasn't her," says Spencer. "Wasn't him—"

"That's why I killed them," says Sarmax.

"That's why you're crazy."

"Not at all," says Sarmax. "That was one of Sinclair's *amplifiers*—"

"We need to get out of here," Jarvin says.

She's picking up speed now—just missing a rocky over-hang—tumbling past walls of cliffs while her mind ascends through the lunar satellites and out into the American zone, paralyzing all weaponry that's aimed at her. She's like a thousand-eyed insect now, seeing everything, in every direction—the lunar defenses ready for anything, the L2 fleet standing by behind the Moon, the vast Eurasian armadas gathered at L4 and L5. She feels at one with all of it; adjusting her rockets, she drops in toward the very center of the South Pole's maw.

You don't know that for sure," says the Operative.

"That's the point," says Lynx. "The man just delivered us from temptation—"

"And how the fuck are we getting off this goddamn fleet *now?* Without that firepower—"

"By making do with what we have."

"Meaning we have to let the motherfucker *live.*"

Lynx nods. "But if you got to have an outlet—"

"Thanks," says the Operative—smashes an armored first through Sorenson's skull.

Full triad," confirms Spencer. "Closing."

"What the hell's going on?" says Sarmax.

"This was a Rain trap," says Jarvin, tossing a shape-charge against the entryway hatch.

A whole world plunges past her. Mining installations sprout off from cliffs like limpet growths; bulldozers parked on the edge of nothing; ramps that lead down to nowhere. She's dropping below the level of the sun, dropping into darkness, though the contours of the crater echo loud and clear within her head—she sees the view from the satellites overhead, triangulates along a grid as she keeps on falling . . .

What's left of Sorenson's head slides down the wall, the rest of his body crumpling with it. The Operative looks at Linehan.

"Should have been *you*," he says.

"So work on your aim."

The Operative opens his mouth to reply—and closes it again as sirens begin wailing at full volume.

The hatch disappears in a sheet of flame—the three men charge through, firing while the microbombs they'd planted back at the second and first doors detonate. Sentries go flying. Those who aren't are facing the wrong way anyway—the three men gun them down as they roar through, desperate to get out of the cul-de-sac and gain some maneuvering room in the face of an onrushing Rain triad.

"Almost there," says Spencer.

The engines of the Eurasian fleet ignite.

Like a myriad of fireflies: Haskell takes in the sprawling clusters of heat-signatures out at L5 and L4, as the Eurasian guns start laying down the mother of all bombardments. Suddenly DE is blanketing vacuum—intensifying even further as the American forces return fire. There's so much energy out there that Haskell's losing her wireless links with the U.S. zone. It's like her fingers are getting pried away from some edge. But right now it doesn't matter. She fires her vehicle's retrorockets, powers into the caves within.

Alarms are howling. Klaxons are wailing. Suddenly three men are feeling way too exposed.

"They've found us," says Linehan.

"Worse," says Lynx. "That's the general fleet alert."

"The East is on its way," says the Operative.

A quick glance on the zone confirms it. And the American fleet behind the Moon is going into ultra-lockdown mode—

"We need to get out of here," says Linehan.

"Thanks for the newsflash," says the Operative. He opens up the one-on-one with Lynx.

"Is this for real? Looks like they just—"

"Sealed all ships," says Lynx. "Yeah."

Meaning it's no longer just a matter of nothing being allowed to leave this fleet. Now the same rule's being applied to each individual ship. Total paranoia is in ascendancy. All intrafleet transport is at an end. Which means that—

"We're fucked," says Lynx.

"Not at all," says the Operative.

"We're *fucked*," repeats Lynx, "and it's all *thanks to you*. This whole Sorenson bullshit was a bridge too far. We'd already gotten all we needed these last two days—"

"We thought he might have a teleporter, remember?"

"So what the fuck are we gonna do now?"

"Show everybody why we're the best in the business."

*R*ighteous *Fire-Dragon* is accelerating at a disturbing rate, moving well out ahead of the rest of the fleet, taking heavy fire from the American lunar positions. But all of that is mere background to what's front and center on Spencer's screen: only a few corridors away, the Rain triad is less than fifty meters ahead, steaming straight at them, operating on some kind of zone that's in a class of its own. Spencer's only detecting it because he's using Rain protocols. But as to staying competitive with it—

"We can't fight this," says Jarvin.

"We're not going to," says Spencer. He meshes his mind with Jarvin, gets his zone-shields up just in time to repel an incoming blow that would have fried the mind of any normal razor. As he does so, he lets the blueprints of this part of the ship whip through his head. Looking for—

"Anything," hisses Jarvin. "No time for perfection."

"Then you're gonna love this," snarls Spencer.

PART IV
ETERNITY'S ASHES

The caves and tunnels beneath the South Pole are even more tangled than the craters that surround them. Haskell lets her lights shine out ahead of her as she makes hairpin turns. She hasn't detected any pursuit yet. But she's under no illusions—it's underway. If Szilard wants to be a player in the endgame, he's going to have to get his hands on her brain. He'll be mobilizing all forces in order to do so. She rockets ever deeper.

A trashed antechamber that contains the shredded remains of the android-bodyguard-secretary of a man who no longer needs any of those services. Maschler and Riley look up as Carson, Lynx, and Linehan storm into the room.

"What's up?" asks Maschler.

"Everything," says Lynx as he sweeps past. Maschler and Riley get the hint—charge after the other three as they rush out of the room, firing their suit-jets. Maschler keys the one-on-one with Linehan.

"Do you know where we're going?" he asks.

"You wouldn't believe me," mutters Linehan.

"T̶his way," yells Spencer, firing his jets and letting Jarvin and Sarmax trail after him while he hurls zone-decoys out in every direction. The Rain triad adjusts slightly; the wings spread out as they vector in on their quarry's changing position. But Spencer's relying more on speed than stealth. He and the other two blast toward the rearmost portions of the ship, flying through into one of the bomb storage chambers, moving away from the main elevator—

"Wrong way!" yells Sarmax.

"Wrong," says Spencer.

H̶askell drops through some of the active mining areas. She's exposing herself, but it's the most direct route. She's fucking with the zone something fierce while she blasts through caverns filled with equipment. Miners stare agape as she burns past like a fever dream.

T̶he five men careen out of the R&D areas and into the adjacent wing of the war-sat. It sports most of the ship's weaponry.

"This isn't the right way," yells Riley. "The hangars are—"

"Go for it," says the Operative. "You'll win the record for most guns to ever target a shuttle at once."

Though he knows it's unlikely to be anywhere near that dramatic. The bulk of the American guns are staying silent—not exposing themselves as they wait for the Eurasian armada to draw closer. But that leaves a lot of weaponry still in the game, firing away at the largest force ever assembled by the hand of man. The writing's on the wall. The Americans don't stand a chance. But right now the Operative has more immediate issues. The five men reach a chamber at the far end of the weapons wing—a dead end.

Spencer opens fire—lets shots streak past the thousands of nukes and along the conveyor belts, taking out the hatches to which the belts lead. The doors spin aside and he leads the way into the backup bomb shafts. They're not in use right now, but that could change at any moment. In which case it won't be pretty: bombs are slung through the shafts at railgun velocities. The three men reach the far end. Another hatch bars the way. Beyond it's vacuum. Not to mention nuclear explosions.

"You do *not* want to open that," says Jarvin.

She's leaving the upper-level mines behind, dropping through shafts that haven't seen use in a long time. There are a number of active mines still beneath her, but she's hoping to steer clear of them. The fewer witnesses she has, the better. Even if she butchered them all—reached in and fucked them via their zone-interfaces—the corpses would still be clues to her trail. And mass executions aren't her style anyway.

But running zone is. And she's never done it at this level before. Everything else has just been a precursor. Which makes it all the harder to take a route that will ultimately lead her beyond the reach of zone. She's considered the other options. She could head for Agrippa or Congreve, infiltrate their mainframes, and try to wrest control of the U.S. forces from Szilard.

But even if she succeeded, it would still leave the Eurasians to deal with. And the East is nearly invulnerable to her hacks. They got burned so badly by the U.S. zone assault in the opening moments of the war that their remaining forces have switched off all wireless interface save a few point-to-point communications within the fleet. So even if Haskell was in control of everything America has left, she doubts it would matter. There's only one thing that does. She plans on getting to it as fast as she can.

"Here we are," says the Operative.

"Those are missiles," says Maschler.

"You're quick," says Lynx.

"Climb on," says the Operative.

Maschler and Riley look at each other, then look at the missiles racked along the wall, pointed at the ceiling. Each one's several meters long. They're standard space-to-spacers, with a range of several thousand kilometers. They're intended to defend against incoming missiles and ships . . .

"This is the dumbest idea I've ever heard of," says Riley.

"Not as dumb as yours," says Lynx.

"I didn't propose anything!"

"Meaning your plan is just *stay here and eat it*." Lynx meshes his mind with the Operative's, assists him in stripping out the guidance controls on five of the missiles and reprogramming them with their own sequences. While they're at it, they're climbing onto those missiles, adjusting their suits' magnetic clamps, and deploying their tethers for addded effect. It doesn't take long.

"Everybody ready?" asks the Operative.

"Oh sure," mutters Riley.

N ow what?" says Sarmax.
    "Now we burn a hole through to the next shaft,"
says Spencer. "Get through to the maintenance shafts beyond that."

"Right," says Jarvin, "but there *is* no next shaft."

"Yes there is," says Spencer. He glances again at the zone—
does a doubletake.

"Well?"

"There was ten seconds ago. On the zone—"

"And guess who's been fucking with it,"

"Fuck," says Spencer.

"You're a fucking idiot," says Jarvin.

All the more so as the Rain are now entering the bomb-bays
they just left. There's no escape. It's just a question of whether the
triad meets with any resistance worth the name. Spencer starts to
scramble back up the shaft—

T he U.S. zone is disappearing in the rearview. At least
    for now. Haskell passed the last conduits on this partic-
ular tunnel half a klick back. She's losing herself amidst
the moon, and silence reigns within her head once more. She's calibrating all the maps; that wilderness of man-made tunnels and
natural caves that make the area beneath the South Pole such an
intricate honeycomb. Yet as the zone drops away from her mind,
other things are coming into focus; now that her suit's no longer
locked, everything that Control stirred up within her is starting to
crystallize. Her mind expands outward like a balloon inflating. It's
the strangest thing she's ever felt—something she'd find impossible to explain. Her body's no longer the receptacle, just the focal
point for an expanded consciousness that she's now bringing to
bear upon the universe at large. She finds what she's looking for almost immediately.

The Operative keys the sequence. The hatches through which they've come swing shut. Airlock procedures initiate. The wall's sliding away . . .

"Oh *fuck*," says Maschler—but they're already being flung forward.

Twenty missiles total—and the five that count have had their accelerations adjusted to make the launch something less than lethal. But even with their suits cushioning the blow, it's still a wild ride. The view's making it even more so. They're right in the thick of the L2 fleet. They just miss a frigate's antennae, zip past another war-sat and between two dreadnaughts. Linehan watches lights whip by and wonders if he's died yet. He feels like he must have long ago. One ship in particular's rushing in toward him.

They've precisely calculated how much time they have before the fleet's defenses react—or rather, the backup defenses, since they're taking the precaution of hacking the main ones. Those defenses were designed for a lot of things, but being fired on from within the fleet wasn't on any of the automatic sequences. That gives the men now maneuvering through vacuum a tiny margin. It's still not enough to make it to their main objective. They're settling for the next best thing—

"Brace for impact," says Lynx.

They're about as fucked as it's possible to be. They're heading back up the shaft purely to sell their lives dearly. They've got essentially zero chance against a full triad. And in a few more seconds, that triad's about to pump this bomb-shaft full of grenades. Better to die meeting the enemy head on. Spencer adjusts his zone-shielding, takes in the Rain team's zone-signature as it enters the room that he and Sarmax and Jarvin just left. He can see them all too clearly.

And then he hears a voice.

pencer," says Haskell.

"*Jesus Christ,*" says Spencer.

Though of course he's not saying anything at all. It's all telepathy—the reactivation of her previous link with Spencer, the one that Harrison configured to expedite the run on the Eurasian secret weapon and that got shorn when everything went awry. But that time she was on the zone. Apparently she's come a long way in these last few hours. And she feels like she's still picking up steam. She keeps on dropping through the shafts of the Moon while she springs from Spencer's mind into the zone of the *Righteous Fire-Dragon.*

"Do exactly what I say," she says.

Missile strike: an explosion rips through the hull of the colony ship *Memphis.* Metal tears away space—but it could have been a lot worse, since only one warhead detonated. Somebody went and tampered with the rest—and that same somebody's now steering more missiles toward the just-created hole, dodging past the chunks of debris flying out it—

"*The brakes,*" hisses Lynx.

Five missiles do a 180-degree turn, use their engines as retro-rockets as they decelerate through the new opening, powering down the whole while. The Operative gets a quick glimpse of a corridor streaking past. He figures he won't feel much if the hi-ex aboard his missile ignites. He's trying his best to make sure that doesn't happen. An airlock door's closing up ahead as the computers of the *Memphis* attempt to seal off this section of the ship. But the missiles slide through the doorway, skid along the walls, and slow to a stop—even as the five men fire their suit-jets.

The backup door to the bomb-chamber suddenly swings shut. Looks like they're trapped in the shaft for real now—

"What the fuck?" says Jarvin.

"Back the other way," yells Spencer.

"There's no other way out of this—"

That's when the trapdoor that leads to vacuum opens—

Deep within the Moon, working the gears of the *Righteous Fire-Dragon* as it puts L5 in the rearview . . . that's easy. It's dealing with the Rain that's the problem. She sees them clearly on zone—even sees them for real now as she filters out the wavelengths on the bomb-bay's camera-feeds to reveal them as they truly are: three figures in custom battlesuits, each one painted in a riot of different colors. She figures that's their private joke. But the joke's on them now—she cannons against them in zone, almost breaks through entirely. The razor and the razor-mech within that triad merge to fend her off, stopping their pursuit of Spencer's team while they deal with a whole new enemy—

Something wrong here," says Lynx.

"No shit," says the Operative.

But as to what it is, he doesn't know. There's definitely something funky about this ship's zone, though. Especially when it's presenting to the rest of the L2 fleet as normal. Not that the L2 mainframes are looking too closely. All they care about right now is that the gunnery of the *Memphis* is working. But as for the crew—

"What the *hell*," says the Operative.

"Doesn't change a thing," says Lynx.

Spencer hits his jets—feels the ship lurch as he hurtles back down that last shaft—Sarmax and Jarvin following him even though it's plain suicide. Because out there is nothing but the ship's bombs detonating—

But now there's not even that—

Righteous Fire-Dragon's acceleration slows ever so slightly as the bomb-feed halts and three men head out into space. She's buying them time. It may be all she can give them. The Rain are resurging against her, forming a zone-shield that's meeting her halfway, pressing back on her onslaught. She's tempted to go for broke trying to finish them. But for all she knows, this is yet another of their traps. Nor can she rule out the possibility that there's another triad in these tunnels with her. She has to play it safe, can't overextend herself. Especially given what she's now detecting—

W hat the hell's going on?" says Linehan.
"Shut up," says the Operative.
The five of them are streaking through one of the *Memphis*'s main conduits—part of the axis that runs from end to end. There are a lot of bodies. Dead SpaceCom personnel are floating everywhere. Nothing living. Nothing moving. But with his ayahuasca-soaked senses, Linehan's somehow *sensing* something all around.

"This is fucked up," says Maschler.

"This is the least of it," says Lynx.

T hey're right where they shouldn't be—smack in the zone of maximum lethality. The surface of the pusher-plate stretches around them on all sides—a surface that could be shoved right up against the sun and still survive. The bombs that spit from the bays blast energy against it that sends the ship forward. But right now there aren't any bombs. There's just these three suits, making haste across a landscape no one's ever seen under these conditions, clinging to it so as not to be left behind. The Eurasian fleet spreads out before them, churning in their wake. Another trapdoor on that pusher-plate opens—

—1ike something sliding aside in her mind. There's a new peril, close at hand. The SpaceCom dropships now plunging into the South Pole badlands are so real it's as if she's seeing them on camera-feeds. And she can't even reach their zone—it may be switched off altogether. She sees them anyway, though, but that's all she can do—other than increase her pace as she continues to duel with that Rain triad tens of thousands of kilometers away. They're falling back now, deeper into the megaship, and she's moving after them, springboarding off Spencer's mind, increasing the pressure on theirs—

The Operative's mind is racing. All this butchery just happened. It's still fresh. The five men blast through what remains of it. Blood splatters against their visors. Most of the corpses have been torn from their suits, ripped apart.

"Those look like *bite marks*," says Riley.

"One guess as to why," says the Operative.

They head through the second trapdoor, back up a new shaft. Spencer feels like a herd of elephants are trampling on his grave. The Manilishi's using his mind to battle the Rain, and it's giving him one nasty headache. He's struggling to focus. He's half expecting more bombs to come flying down this new shaft at him. Instead, a hatch in the side of that shaft is opening—he leads the way through into a space that's far wider—

She's driving the Rain back on the ship's zone while the SpaceCom forces close in on her for real beneath the Moon. She can see how they're moving to cut her off. They're coming in from all angles, ready to join forces just beneath her and catch her. She's going to have to reckon against the possibility that she's going to be cut off from Spencer, too, that the Rain are going to find a way to sever that connection. But right now they're giving way before her—collapsing back into full defensive mode as she drives against them. She can see what their next move is going to be. That's why she's getting hers in first.

"Someone hacked the whole place," says the Operative as they emerge into the main axis of the *Memphis*. It's empty. But they know all too well that shit is closing in—

"Cramping our style," says Lynx.

The Operative nods. Then again, he wonders if it's just one of those things. Shit happens. Particularly in war. Particularly in this one—

"Here we go," says Linehan.

A space that's as strange as it is large—and most of it's taken up by the gigantic springs that the pusher-plate shoves up against. The three men use their suit-jets judiciously to maneuver between the vast hydraulic presses—which are cranking back into action again as the bombs begin to fall once more. With each detonation, the springs shudder with enough vibration to rip lesser metals apart. Spencer feels like his mind's about to do the same. He feels Haskell reach out even farther—

She slices past the Rain to hit the microzone of the *Righteous Fire-Dragon,* slams through its cockpit, hits the inner enclave, and fucks it good. Network becomes maelstrom. As the zone of the megaship collapses, she rides it down in style, nailing the suits of the crew along with all the soldiers. Not enough to kill them, of course. Just enough to drive them really, really crazy.

There were ten thousand colonists aboard the *Memphis*. All of them woke up with some truly nasty programming. Some of them got taken out by SpaceCom marines. Still more got nailed when the marines blew the airlock. But ultimately numbers won out. There are several thousand left. And a large chunk of them are swarming in toward five men who have never seen anything quite like it. Soldiers less battle hardened might be undone by pure shock.

The five men start firing, accelerating toward the seething mass.

They're seeing no one. It's fine by them. They're following the route Haskell's given Spencer, moving past the swaying springs, crawling into the shafts that lead into the megaship's hull—and hitting their jets again as they streak between the layers of armor. If oncoming shots smash through the outer layer at the wrong moment, they're toast. It's an acceptable risk. Especially given what's going on inside the ship.

Total pandemonium. There are at least two thousand Chinese marines aboard. Half of them just went insane. And those who didn't are finding that their suits just did. The galleries of the ship are filling up with flame and metal. But Haskell's getting only the merest glimpse of it, basing herself in the wreckage of the AI that controlled the cockpit, triangulating from that shattered mind along with Spencer's to continue to press the Rain triad while she dwells in this strange region that's half-zone and half-telepathy. It's as she figured. The triad has other things to think about besides tracking down prey. She's planning on giving them a few more while she's at it.

Utter carnage inside the *Memphis*. Half the colonists are still naked. They all look totally nuts. They're attacking with berserker ferocity, using pieces of metal and piping and—

"Yeah," says Maschler, "those are *bones*."

"Someone spiked the alarm clock," says Riley.

"Shut up and keep shooting," hisses Linehan.

The Operative can see how nasty it must have been. The sleepers came awake in tandem with the dismemberment of the ship's zone. He wonders whether they were rigged from the start, or whether this is some recent innovation.

"No wonder the fleet's in lockdown," says Lynx.

"Just one reason among many," says the Operative.

They're making haste inside the armor of one of the two largest ships ever built. Occasionally the shudder of the receding engines is joined by other vibrations— American shots smashing against the hull. If anything makes it through, they'll be the first to know. Yet now that they've got a little margin, Spencer's doing a little thinking.

"Manilishi," he says.

"My name's Claire," says the voice.

"Where are you?"

"Right inside your head."

"I mean really—"

"Does it matter?"

"Are the Rain still out there?"

"They're too busy to worry about you for now."

"And Sinclair?"

"What about him?"

"Is he up here too?"

"I doubt it."

He was earlier, though. She's sure of it. Sinclair was up at L5 back when she hacked into his cell a week earlier, and subsequently managed to get himself off that fleet. Maybe he used a teleporter to do so. Maybe he left by more prosaic means. And as to when—his mental presence on the lip of the South Pole was indeterminate. His mental presence during the interrogation with Montrose *seemed* to emanate from L5. The problem is, she's not sure what Sinclair's capable of. He may have wanted her to think he was still at L5 back then.

But there's no way he could be there now—otherwise she would never have been able to put the Rain triad under such pressure. That triad's going to ground now, camo on maximum as they vanish into the less trafficked areas of the ship. She's wishing she could do the same within the Moon. Because the SpaceCom forces are still closing in on her. She can picture all those suits blasting through the shafts of Moon—can almost *see* the repurposed mining vehicles sliding into position. She wishes that her map wasn't just confined to the main route she's trying to take—that she had more data to go on. She can only tell the surrounding routes by the position of her pursuers. They're accelerating now, and she's accelerating with them, stretching her suit to the limits of its capacity. Stretching her mind too—

The key is to keep moving. And shooting—the five men are formed up in what's essentially a miniphalanx, the Operative and Lynx on the front, Maschler and Riley on the flanks, Linehan on rearguard. They're gunning down the colonists in swathes—interlocking fields of fire that mow down everything before them. Yet the Operative somehow feels at one with the people he's killing. He can't blame them, really—even if whatever program's in them was somehow factored out—if you dreamt of Mars and woke instead to Hell, you might just choose to contribute to it. But all that matters now is the section of the

Memphis they're closing on. They blow down more doors, head on through, the bloody horde swirling around them.

They're picking up speed now, shooting the length of the ship as it hurtles in toward the Moon. They're still alive. Still in the dark as well.

"What makes you so sure Sinclair's not up here?"

"If he was, you'd be dead," she says.

"Why are you helping us?" he asks.

"Because I can."

"I don't understand."

"You don't have to."

Though the truth of the matter is that she's not exactly sure herself. Part of her thinks she should just be letting the Rain finish these guys off. Three less players to contend with. Only—Spencer's no player. Not now that she can reach inside his mind at will. She could reduce him to a drooling meat-puppet if she wanted. But she doesn't need to. She senses he's different from the rest of them anyway—that he's really just trying to keep his head above water. She gets all this because she's right inside him—can see the way he's been used and manipulated by those above him. She empathizes with him even as she's busy doing the same thing herself—even as her SpaceCom pursuers start to draw the noose.

A couple of cluster bombs, and they're storming through into the front section of the ship. The mob's doing its best to keep pace with them, but as the terrain narrows, so do their numbers. It's close quarters now, and the five men are firing at point-blank range, running electricity through their suits to zap any flesh that touches them. Yet some of that flesh is clinging to them anyway. The danger of a pile-on is growing. The Operative and Lynx haul open the doors to the bridge, then turn in the doorway and start firing past the men behind them.

Doing the lady's bidding: they head through blast-doors, exit the hull's interior, and start maneuvering through the innards of the ship. Explosions reach their ears, along with gunfire—

"What the hell did you do to this ship?" Spencer asks.

"Fucked it," says Haskell.

"And where the hell are we going?"

She tells him. He doesn't seem that surprised.

And that's just as well. Because she's got other shit to worry about. She's now more than ten klicks beneath the lunar surface. The tendrils of the SpaceCom vanguards are about to touch. She's trying to pass straight between them—a margin way too narrow for comfort.

The bridge of the *Memphis* is in shambles. Linehan gets busy sliding the doors shut on manual while Riley and Maschler fire through the narrowing opening. The Operative and Lynx are working the controls. The L2 fleet is panorama in the windows . . .

"What do you think?" says Lynx.

"Doable," says the Operative.

Especially because they don't need to get complete control of the ship. Just—

"Bingo," says the Operative.

The engines of the *Memphis* fire.

So what's she got to say?" asks Sarmax.

"Who?"

"Don't play dumb with us," says Jarvin. "It's not like you're coming up with all this yourself."

"You guys have been talking," says Spencer.

"And you've been too busy to join in."

"It's keeping us alive, isn't it?"

"But now the Manilishi's calling the shots?"

"Shit," says Spencer—he's staring out into an elevator shaft. It's total chaos. Elevator cars have rammed each other, collapsed down the shaft. Suits are strafing each other while other suits rip unarmored bodies apart. Spencer counts at least ten different firefights. Sarmax whistles.

"I like it," he says.

She's feeling the same way, looking out through Spencer's eyes as he gazes down the shaft and starts moving toward an auxiliary one that promises safer passage. Back on the Moon, she lets her mental tendrils drape over the minds of the oncoming SpaceCom soldiers, gets ready to apply the pressure.

The *Memphis* picks up steam. Ships start sliding in the window. One ship in particular is drawing closer. There's a pounding on the door.

"*Faster*," says the Operative.

"We're powering up as quick as we can," says Lynx.

"They're trying to break in," says Riley.

"More than just trying," says Linehan. "Shall we blow all hatches and feed them to the vacuum?"

"You'll do nothing of the kind," says the Operative.

"They're about to come in useful," says Lynx.

They're heading to their destination the less-traveled way. Certainly the less fought over. They head up ladders—hauling aside bodies—moving through rooms that have already been charred black with explosions.

"At least this ship's still flying," says Sarmax.

"For now," mutters Jarvin.

She monitors the situation with bated breath. If she's wrong about all this, then the Rain are going to be on them any moment. Just as the SpaceCom forces are now on *her*—she slams her mind forward—

The superdreadnaught *Harrison* is right in the path of the *Memphis*. Its gunnery officers are targeting the oncoming ship, only to find that their guns have been hacked.

"Nice one," says Lynx.

"Just getting started," says the Operative.

The rest of the fleet's having the same problem. The *Harrison*'s engines fire. It starts hauling away. But momentum's a bitch sometimes. The *Memphis* is coming on like a juggernaut. The *Harrison* fills the window . . .

"Let's get the fuck out of here," says the Operative.

They're moving cautiously past twisted machinery and sprawled bodies, half expecting to get jumped by that Rain triad. But Spencer sees no sign of it. There's no sign of the zone either. Save for a very faint glimmer dead ahead.

—almost like the light of the minds that she's now slamming against. As the impact of her blows resounds within her skull, she feels spirits just *shatter*. Minds writhe, wink out like stars extinguished. She's charging right in between the reeling SpaceCom vanguards now. She thinks she gets a glimpse of driverless machinery crashing against tunnel walls—

They blast down the doors and into the seething mob, fighting their way back the way they came. It's as if every wayward colonist is waiting for them, seeking to overwhelm them. The Operative can see they're about to get buried. Which might have its silver lining. Especially with the collision alarms sounding in the cockpit they've just left.

They head through into a room they recognize: the cockpit access chamber. It looked a little more stately back on the other megaship, though. Now it's an utter fucking mess. Bodies are everywhere. But the combat's finished here. They haul open the elevator doors, enter the access shaft—

And she jets through them and nothing's touching her. The SpaceCom forces are reeling in disarray. She's dropping deeper into Moon, and they can't stop her. But her intuition's screaming ever louder—

A terrible cracking noise as the *Memphis* slices into the *Harrison*. The walls start tearing away to reveal more walls—those of the *Harrison* itself. The Operative and his team fire their jets, blasting away from the colonists. The *Memphis* plows ever farther into the *Harrison*, bodies pouring into vacuum—

hrough the shaft and into the cockpit of the *Righteous
Fire-Dragon*. The three men move from room to room,
looking for anything living. They can't find anything
worth the name.

"Now what?" says Sarmax.

"Now we make ourselves comfortable," says Spencer.

he's at full throttle, plunging headfirst, her jets adding
to the speed of her descent down the shaft. She's gotten
past the SpaceCom forces. The nuke they've fired after her
is a different story. It gets within half a klick before it detonates.

he *Memphis* has thoroughly embedded itself in the
Harrison. And the ones who put it there are hitting
the SpaceCom flagship in textbook fashion. The three
mechs get out ahead, butchering everything in their path. The two
razors trail in their wake, their minds leaping out ahead to fuck the
defenses. The *Harrison* is plunging into chaos. The situation isn't
helped by the thousands of psychotic colonists pouring into the
ship and attacking everything in sight. It's total carnage. The
Operative's loving every moment. His zone-view shows Linehan
cutting inside the bridge's outer perimeter.

omething wrong?" asks Sarmax.

"I just lost Haskell," says Spencer.

And he's wondering how the hell they're supposed to
keep the Rain at bay now. They're doing what they can. They've
mined the elevator shaft and strewn it with sensors capable of de-

tecting anything down to nano. They've found an escape shaft and mined that, too.

"There's no other way in," says Jarvin.

"Search this place again," says Sarmax.

The nuke ignites apocalypse in her mind—fries her circuitry, leaves her with nothing but static. It's not just her software that's affected either—not just her view onto the zone. It's also her access to the telepathy, the glimpses of other minds—all of it. It's all gone, and she's falling into herself as her body plunges ever farther—

God this is good," says Lynx.

The Operative nods. He's feeling it too. He'd almost forgotten how lethal Lynx and he are when they combine their minds like this. Subterfuge and stealth are one thing. Frontal assault's another. There's nothing like it. Especially when they've got three of the best mechs alive running point, smashing through all resistance, detonating barricades and—

"We're in," says Linehan.

They're going through the cockpit again, searching every nook and cranny, pulling the covers off consoles, running scans, looking for false spaces and hollow walls. Spencer wanders into one of the adjacent rooms. There's something about it he can't quite place. It seems like a dead end.

But then he hears a voice.

In the absence of external stimuli the mind creates its
own. Claire Haskell knows this. But that knowledge isn't
helping. The voices in her head are really coming out to
play. Some are her own. Many aren't. None are saying anything
coherent. Most of them aren't even speaking English. They're babbling in languages she can't even identify, and she's trying not to
listen. She wonders if they've been here all along—wonders if
she's going to die. Maybe she already has. The fact that she can see
a staircase up ahead doesn't clarify things in the slightest.

Check it out," says Lynx.
The Operative says nothing—just follows Lynx as
he strides onto the bridge of the *Harrison*, which is
about as large as one would expect for the flagship of the L2 fleet.
Stairs lead up to an enclosed inner bridge. The walls are alive with
window-screens—dominated by the Moon, with the massed
Eurasian fleets splayed out beyond. Several officers are dead on the
floor. But most of the bridge's crew are still alive—though they
clearly aren't expecting to stay that way. They're staring at the
three mechs who've just shot their colleagues who tried to resist.
The Operative pats Linehan on the shoulder.
"Nice one," he says.

Lyle Spencer," says the voice.
Spencer whirls. It's coming from one of the con-
soles. For a moment he thinks someone's hiding in the
damn thing. But then he gets with the program.
"How the fuck do you know my name?"
"Claire Haskell told me."

She's heading down those stairs. They look to be fairly recent in construction. Which might even be good news. It means she might be back on track. The vehicle that's sitting at the bottom of the stairs is further indication.

The Operative scans the screens within his head. Everything's checking out. The *Harrison* is in his hands. He and Lynx have already taken control of the flagship's connections with the rest of the fleet, and have been broadcasting about how the rebel units from the *Memphis* are in custody and that the bridge is now secure. Linehan and Maschler and Riley are making it more so—sealing doors, getting emergency barricades up. The Operative and Lynx walk up the stairs to the inner bridge.

Spencer's at a loss. He stares at the console from which the voice is being projected. "Haskell told you who I was?"

"For sure. Sarmax and Jarvin too—hi guys." This last as the two men walk up behind Spencer.

"And who the fuck *are* you?" asks Sarmax.

"*Was* might be a better word."

The vehicle's a modified crawler—a long-range explorer, tailor-made for rough underground terrain, with short-use rockets to navigate the more vertical spaces. She opens up the vehicle's door on manual, climbs in, and seals it. It feels good to get off her feet. It's even better to be able to replenish her oxygen. She lets her suit drink its fill while she starts the crawler, then resumes the descent into lunar incognita.

The inner bridge of the SpaceCom flagship contains certain things. The rear admiral of the L2 fleet. Two flag officers. And—

"The codes," says the Operative.

Rear Admiral Griffin looks up at him with an expression that's one of near total disdain. "You expect me to give the executive codes for this fleet to a bandit?" he asks.

"I guess not," says the Operative, and fires a shot into Griffin's neck. The rear admiral pitches backward, starts dying noisily. The Operative looks at the flag officers.

"Your turn," he says.

Look around you," says the voice. "I was in charge of all of this. Until that she-demon turned my mind inside out—"

"You're AI," says Jarvin.

"State of the art," says the voice. "Command node for both megaships. Until things went to hell. What's it like in the rest of the ship?"

"Total shit," says Sarmax.

"You mean you can't see?" asks Spencer.

"She tore my eyeballs out. Made me her slave. And now I'm yours."

"That's what she said?"

"She did more than just *say.*"

That's for sure. She's hoping it works for them. Contingency plan in case she got cut off—she gave them their own heavyweight AI to play with, and maybe it'll help them to keep the Rain at bay. She's got far more immediate challenges now, like steering this crawler as fast as it'll go down a passage that's so steep it might be better termed a pit. She keeps having to swerve to avoid outcroppings, keeps having to apply retro-blasts from the crawler's rockets. The voices in her head are getting ever louder. There's an almost musical quality to their babbling. She's almost starting to enjoy it. She takes that to be a sign of just how far gone she's getting.

As one, the engines of the L2 fleet fire. All ships start moving in toward the Moon at speed.

"That wasn't so hard, was it," says the Operative.

He's talking to the one remaining flag officer. The other officer lies on the floor, sprawled over his admiral, his eyes gouged out. It wasn't a quick death. That was the point. The first officer coughed up the codes soon after that. The orders have gone out. The fleet's falling into line, a vast V-shape whose forward point is the *Harrison* itself, the *Memphis* still rammed against its side: a strange compound ship swarming with feral colonists. The *Harrison*'s been turned at a slight angle to align its motors with the momentum of the *Memphis*'s own engines. And now a buzzer's sounding on the *Harrison*'s inner bridge.

"What the hell's that?" asks Lynx.

"That's the hotline to President Szilard," says the flag officer.

Lynx curses. "Tell him that Admiral Griffin's had an accident and—"

The Operative shoots the flag officer in the head.

"Why not tell him ourselves," he says.

So you're going to do whatever we want," says Spencer. "That's what that cunt rigged me with." The AI's voice is rueful. "Command-imprinting triggered by voice-recognition."

"And I spoke to you first."

"It's keyed to all three of you."

"So fuck you," says Sarmax.

"Just figuring out where we stand," says Spencer.

"And it's about time," says Jarvin. "Look, we need to get on what's left of the zone with this thing and have a look."

"Meaning we need to trust its story," says Sarmax.

"Not sure we've got much of a choice," mutters Jarvin.

She's got none at all. She keeps on forging ever deeper—sometimes via the horsepower of her vehicle, sometimes via maglev freight elevators cut through the rock. She's well below the domain of any of her maps now. She's feeling her way by pure intuition—and she's surprised that intuition's still working, as every other one of her powers seem to have fallen silent. It's as though some magnet's drawing her deeper—as though she can't help but make every correct turn. Almost like someone else has gotten control of her mind. She wonders if that's exactly what's happened.

The face of Jharek Szilard is appearing on the inner bridge's screen. The Operative's not about to let it get projected anywhere else. All transmissions are being routed through the *Harrison*. Szilard's been cut off from communication with the rest of his fleet. That's one reason among many why he's looking so royally pissed. His expression gets even more priceless when he finds himself staring at —

"Well if it isn't *el presidente,*" says the Operative.

"Who the hell are you?" asks Szilard.

Lynx starts laughing. The Operative's trying hard not to crack up himself as he watches Szilard get ever angrier:

"And where the fuck's the rear admiral?"

The Operative holds up Griffin's severed head. It's as though he's thrown a switch. Szilard suddenly becomes quite calm.

"I see," he says.

"More than can be said for him," says Lynx.

"What are your demands?" says Szilard.

"Who said we had demands?" asks the Operative.

"I assumed that—"

"Assume nothing."

"Are you Rain?"

"You don't recognize me?" asks Lynx. "After all the fun we had back on the *Montana?*"

Szilard's eyes narrow. "The originals."

"No less."

"And what do you want?"

"Funny you should ask," says the Operative. "Given that you're the asshole who stranded us up here."

"Way I hear it, you were trying to kill me."

"Not just *trying.* We'll hit the Moon in a few hours and you'll be dead an hour after that."

"You jacked the *whole fleet* just to get back to the Moon?"

The Operative shrugs. "How else would we do it?"

"You guys are nuts."

"Do I sound like I'm arguing?"

"You're fucking nuts. The firepower on my farside installations will—"

"Don't be so tiresome," says the Operative. "You need our guns to try to stave off the Eurasians."

"When you're taking the fleet out of the fight?"

"Did I say that?" asks the Operative.

"C'mon man," adds Lynx. "Don't you know your own tactics? Formation delta-G, right?"

Szilard's checking that against his own screens, but the Operative knows exactly what he's going to see. L2's planners devised more than a hundred battleplans. All that was needed was to pick the one that gets the flagship closest to the Moon. The Operative yawns, makes a show of stretching. Through the inner bridge's semitranslucent walls he can see Linehan beating the crap out of some technician who presumably looked at him the wrong way. Maschler and Riley are looking on as though daring anyone else to try something. Szilard clears his throat.

"Interesting," he says. "One of the less orthodox contingencies."

"And not even totally crazy under the circumstances," says Lynx.

"I don't know about that—"

"I do," says the Operative. "Get in behind the Moon using it as cover, picking up speed all the while, then slingshot the ships around the nearside in all directions to play havoc with the Eurasian fleet. *We* attack *them*. That's the offer, Jharek. It's either that or civil war right now—and then the Eurasians can cruise into the world's biggest junkyard."

"What about my flagship?"

"*My* flagship," says the Operative.

He and Szilard stare at each other. "For now," says Szilard.

"I'm shaking in my boots," says the Operative.

"You should," says Szilard. "When you get here, I'll tear you fuckers limb from limb."

"Can't wait. How's the Manilishi?"

Szilard doesn't say anything. Save for a flicker in his eyes—

"Thanks," says the Operative—switches the screen off.

They switch back on, plunge into zone—or at least what's left of it. The AI rides shotgun, runs backup as the grids of the *Righteous Fire-Dragon* open up all around them—the central elevator shafts like some kind of multibarreled spine, the massive hive of corridors and chambers stretching out around it. The camera-feeds show carnage. Marines butchering each other, gunning down the crew, turning guns upon themselves, driving vehicles at full tilt, firing at everything that moves. When software hasn't been used to hack the flesh directly, the flesh is simply being dragged along for the ride. Spencer catches glimpses of horrified faces behind visors while the armor they're trapped within pursues relentless arcs of self-destruction. It's total pandemonium. Haskell's done her work well.

But there's no sign of Rain.

"They've gone to ground," says Spencer, his voice echoing through the cockpit.

"They're out there somewhere," says Sarmax.

"Probably still think we have Haskell," adds Jarvin.

Spencer doesn't reply. He's just riding the zone farther out, looking beyond the ship. The Eurasian armada is spread out behind the *Righteous Fire-Dragon*, motoring in toward the Moon, drawing ever closer to its brethren fleet that's launched from L4. The Moon's caught between two onrushing vectors—and between them is a single ship, the *Hammer of the Skies*, rushing from the L5 fleet on a path that will intersect the one emanating from L4 about forty thousand klicks out from the Moon—

"Switching it up," says Jarvin.

Spencer nods. Keeping the wings balanced—and as he looks further, he sees what might be the reason. His purview expands to take in the Moon itself: the L2 fleet is moving toward that rock. The final battle of this war will be the largest engagement to ever take place in space. He watches those lights drift ever closer.

Lights parade inside her, stretch out beyond her, and it's all she can do to tell herself that it's all just some kind of illusion. That this is what happens when one's mind gets shorn from the leash, bathed by radioactive static and deprived of external stimuli. All she's got are these endless walls streaming through the headlights of her crawler. But she's starting to get glimmers of something else, too—some signal that's far more real than these illusionary lights that keep on taunting her. She can't tell if it's deeper in the Moon or deeper in her mind. It occurs to her that maybe there's no difference.

The minutes crawl by. The Moon looms ever larger, the hordes of Eurasian ships growing above the left and right horizons. The L2 fleet's holding steady in formation. The *Harrison*'s holding steady under their thumb. Kill-crazy meat-puppets roam all corridors beyond the bridge's blast-doors. Everything within is in total lockdown. The three mechs who comprise the muscle have got the situation handled.

Which leaves Lynx and the Operative to their own devices. They've been using their exalted position on the zone of the L2 fleet to ransack all the data they can find. But it turns out that Szilard had precious little left stashed up here—

"That's the rest of it," says the Lynx.

"Yep," says the Operative.

"We're going to have to wait till we get back to the Moon to figure out the—"

"We can't."

"Can't what?"

"Wait."

T his is getting tight," says Jarvin.

His face is on one of the screens in the main room of the cockpit. Spencer's is on the opposite. Both men are still in the zone, meshed with the AI, scanning for the Rain triad that's somewhere in the bowels of the ship. Sarmax is sitting in a corner where he can see both screens. He stretches, looks at the screens that show the two fleets closing.

"One last chance to talk," he says.

S he's moving within range of her ultimate destination. The one her life has been building toward for all this time. And the thing that's now materializing within her mind is as much a function of what lies in the depths of Moon as in the deepest recesses of herself. She can't explain it. Can't understand it. All she can do is stare at the face of the child appearing before her. It's a face she recognizes.

It used to be her own.

D on't bullshit me, Carson."

"I'm not bullshitting you. We need to figure out the game plan *now*."

"You *really* want to go there?"

"Not a matter of want. A matter of necessity."

"Because you thought you could win this game on your own and now you're waking up to the fact that—"

"I was wrong."

"You sound scared."

"I *am* scared."

"Given what's going down, you should be."

"So let's talk about the gameboard," says the Operative.

Those fucking *files*," says Jarvin.

Spencer starts to speak—stops. He gets that he's in over his head—that he's taken this as far as he can go on his own. He knows way too much—needs whatever pieces of the puzzle the others have. His mind's been searching for a way out and the only one he can come up with is—

"Spit it out, man." Sarmax seems to be sinking ever farther back into the corner—

"Not even sure how to say it," Spencer says.

Haskell's inside a child's mind now. Cathedrals of sensory impression from another era rise around her. The universe fractals in vast kaleidoscopic patterns. The child's eyes open. Her own follow an instant later.

Time machines," says Lynx. "That's what you said back—"

"Yeah," says the Operative.

"Still a bullshit artist till the last, huh?"

"I'm not bullshitting you."

"You and I both know that's only the *start* of it."

The Autumn Rain hit-teams were just the tip of the iceberg," says Spencer.

"We *know* that," says Sarmax. "Who the fuck do you think you're talking to? Time was I *ran* the Autumn Rain hit-teams for Harri—"

"The Manilishi was what mattered," says Jarvin.

"You need to know what she really is," mutters Spencer.

The child's billowing through her mind now—like she's in some kind of tunnel, walls flowing ever faster past her. Haskell realizes tears are running down her cheeks. The Moon around her seems to shimmer. Wind chimes ring out—resolve themselves into her own voice. The one from all those years ago.

"Only the start of it," repeats Lynx.

"I realize that," says the Operative. He pauses. "It's all about Haskell—"

"No," says Lynx, *"it's fucking not."*

"She's just the key," Spencer says.

"To everything," adds Sarmax.

"About time you got involved," says Jarvin.

"I don't want to talk to you," she says.

"That doesn't matter," says the child.

"I can't face this."

"Do you remember that time you couldn't speak?"

"When I was seven," she says. "For six weeks."

"I'm seven now," says the girl.

Haskell stares. She remembers being seven—or what she thought at the time was seven, since accelerated genetics had resulted in twenty-four months of real memories layered in by five years of false ones. She recalls six weeks during which she was operated on nearly every day—it suddenly flashes back in her head like another nuke going off, and like some kind of trigger, the psychic vibrations of Sinclair's mind start to pulsate around her, press in against her, show her where he really is. Exactly where she thought he'd be. Her destination—

"The Room," says Lynx. "That's where all this is going. That's where it's been heading all along."

The Operative nods slowly.

"Sinclair created an ultimate sanctuary," says Spencer. "Containing the *real* ultimate weapon," says Jarvin. "And he's gearing up to switch it on," says Sarmax.

The child subsides toward the endless reaches in the back of her head. She can sense the outer perimeter now, as though it's a faraway light glowing through endless mists. It's still well below her. But there's only one road she can follow. It doesn't surprise her in the slightest when the last set of pursuers moves in behind her.

"Sinclair's going to feed Haskell into what he's created," says the Operative.

"*Into* it?" Lynx looks puzzled. "Now I'm not tracking—"

"Christ man! So he can feed *off* it!"

"*What?*"

"Don't you fucking get it? *He's trying to become a god.*"

Assembling computing power so vast no other term would be appropriate," says Spencer. He stares at them both, wonders how to make them see. "It's all about manipulating *information*. And the final part of Sinclair's file is all equations. Nothing but fucking *math*."

"Part of which is some kind of unified field theory," says Jarvin.

"And how the hell would you know *that?*" says Sarmax.

"Jesus, man, what else could it be? Marry relativity to quantum mechanics, and you'd unlock the secrets of the universe. You could redefine the field of black-ops weaponry—"

"Along with science itself," says Spencer. "These goddamn formulas have got symbols that whoever cooked them up had to *invent* along the way." Spencer starts beaming it over.

"*Fuck,*" says Jarvin.

"I wonder who *did* cook them up?" says Sarmax suddenly.

"Try Sinclair's pet AI," says Spencer.

Control. That gutless phantom. The original sneak—sent by its master to wreak havoc upon the opposition— undermining InfoCom the whole time. And doing so much else—she can feel that thing's mind out there somewhere, synthetic sidekick riding shotgun on the brain of Matthew Sinclair.

But her immediate problem is right behind her. It feels like a full-fledged triad, only a few klicks back. The Rain down on the Moon have played their hand at last. And she's playing hers; she accelerates, starts taking these caves in hairpin turns, her position closing on the coordinates she has to make.

nd you wanted to sit at his fucking side while he—"
"Never mind what I wanted," says the Operative.
"*You've* got the maps."

Lynx grins. "Damn straight," he says.

"Damn."

"You were figuring you'd just ditch me somewhere in the tunnels?"

"The thought maybe crossed my mind."

"Well, think on it no more."

"I get that," says the Operative.

And he also gets the implications. If Lynx has kept up with him across the last few days—if he was able to decode that file that Sorenson kept in his mainframe, those charts of sublunar terrain forbidden like no other—then Lynx is good enough to be a factor in what's about to take place when everyone hits the Moon. And the Operative's desperate to find more talent to go up against Sinclair. The Operative eyes his own copy of those maps— the endless tunnels stacked beneath Congreve, the arrows that show the approach to the threshold of the Room. He glances at what he knows of the blueprints of the Room itself—looks back at Lynx.

"I know," he whispers. "You can't go *back* any farther than when you built it."

Lynx nods. "A time machine isn't a *vehicle*."

t's really more of a *place*," says Spencer.
"*The* place," says Jarvin.
"And what's down there is about a lot more than just *time*." Spencer's onscreen image glances at Sarmax. "Right, Leo?"

Sarmax nods. "Sinclair seeded the Earth-Moon system with teleport devices," he says. "Gateways to other such gateways."

"And one device that was an entirely different kind of gate," says Jarvin slowly.

"Which was what the Rain who rebelled against Sinclair got wind of," says Sarmax.

"Along with Morat," says Jarvin. "Jesus Christ. Everyone who mattered in CICom always knew he had an ace in the hole; they just didn't know how *out there* it was. Or how out there *he* is."

"To say nothing of *her*," says Spencer.

B ut none of them ever had a clue as to what that really meant . . . to understand that memories aren't in the past, that portents aren't in the future. To realize that now is all there is. Even as her pursuers close in behind her, that single moment fills her—a single stone dropping through the shafts of eternity. Her mind's something far more than mind now. Every cell in her body's come awake. The outer perimeter of the Room is impending. She can see its lights dead ahead—a pale fraction of the lights that now blaze in every fiber of her being.

S o how do you want to do this?" says Lynx.

"Hit that rock and get deeper," says the Operative. He beams over coordinates. "Via the farside—"

"Too bad there's no teleporter—"

"You said that already."

"Here we go," says Lynx as he gestures at the window.

A nd Sinclair's there already," says Spencer. "At the Room—"

"Probably," says Sarmax.

"Definitely," mutters Jarvin. "Waiting for her."

"Does she know something he doesn't?" says Spencer.

"I think it's the other way around."

That's when acceleration slams against them like some giant hand—

The Operative and Lynx can see it clearly on all their screens. At the vanguard of the Eurasian fleet, the megaships have shifted gears, accelerating at rates the rest of the ships can't hope to match. But they're bringing portions of that fleet with them—

"Bastards," says Lynx.

"Tin-can alley," says the Operative.

The megaships are towing order-of-magnitude more freight this time around. The systems of tethers stretching out to the side of their wakes is that much more complex. About ten percent of the Eurasian fleet is involved in the spearhead's burn—one formation led by each megaship, two vectors driving in upon the Moon . . .

"This is going to be *good*," says Lynx.

Spencer and Jarvin have to drop momentarily from zone to steady their bodies. They're pressing themselves into corners adjacent to Sarmax, letting the G-forces shove against them as the ship throttles up.

"Who the *fuck's* driving this thing?" says Spencer.

"We've lost our link to the engines," says Jarvin. "That fucking triad that's still out there—"

"Maybe not," says Spencer. He's mulling other possibilities, like the Eurasian leadership itself. After all the precautions they've taken, Spencer wouldn't put it past them to have created one last backup option—equipping the motors of their megaships with stripped-down, primitive computers shorn from the rest of zone, on direct wireless links to their own bunkers. Just enough computer intelligence to take orders and pump bombs. Anything more than that's inviting a little too much trouble. He forwards projected schematics to Jarvin.

"Yeah," says Jarvin, "that's an option, too. Praesidium could be pulling the strings."

"And for all we know Sinclair's pulling theirs," says Sarmax.

Jarvin gestures at the consoles. "That's why you need to have this AI crunch us some equations."

"And decipher the last of Sinclair's code," says Sarmax.

"Let's hope it's a quick study," says Spencer.

The orders flash out from the Harrison: maximum speed. The L2 fleet fires all afterburners and picks up steam as it closes on the farside. The ships are running at a velocity far below the two Eurasian squadrons now burning in toward the Moon's nearside, but the Americans have to cover only a quarter of the distance. The Eurasians won't just be trying to crush the American fleet—they'll be trying to get as many shock-troops as possible onto the lunar surface. Prudence might dictate they take care of the first objective before they worry about the second. But the Operative has a feeling that they might try for both at once.

"Bad news," says Linehan on the comlink.

"No one ever calls with good," mutters Lynx.

The AI is going to town, crunching away on Sinclair's last files while Spencer and Jarvin step back into the zone. Not that there's much to see. All the action seems to be going on out in the real world. The Moon's swelling in the screens. And through the flash of nuclear detonations from the megaships' exhaust can be seen those scores of ships being towed, each one towing so many others, and virtually all of them are—

"Troopships," says Sarmax.

"Invasion time," mutters Jarvin.

The contest outside is approaching its climax. Same with the one down here. Sinclair's somewhere below her. But he must have some kind of contingency for the overwhelming strength of the Eurasian fleet. Presumably that contingency involves the Rain triad that's still on the *Righteous Fire-Dragon*. But as to how she's going to deal with the Rain triad that's right behind her—all she can do is run. She doesn't dare try to stand against them with Sinclair and Control so near at hand. She hurtles forward, reaches a chamber she recognizes from her dreams. That narrow alcove in the corner—just tall enough for a man—or a woman. She steps within as suited figures blast into the room she's left behind, codes flashing through her mind—

AM drive's fucked," says Linehan. The secret weapon of the *Harrison*. Not to mention a good chunk of the reason the Operative and his crew fought their way onto this ship in the first place—excepting the now-destroyed *Redeemer*, the flagship is the only vessel employing the prototype antimatter drive. But it hasn't been switched on yet. The Operative was saving that for one final burst of evasive action. He grimaces—

"What the fuck's wrong with the thing?"

"It won't prime," says Linehan.

"Why not?"

"Who the fuck knows?"

"Did you fucking *check*?"

"What do you think we're fucking doing out here?"

The Operative turns off the comlink.

"Colonists probably trashed it," says Lynx.

"Or just snipped the connection."

They look at each other. Lynx clears his throat. "Surely you're not suggesting—"

"Sure I am," says the Operative.

And suddenly the whole zone just *staggers*—

All around them, it's as though the entire zone has suddenly turned to liquid—as though waves are pulsing through that liquid, making everything ripple around them. It's like nothing Spencer's ever experienced.

It lasts the merest fraction of a second. Space folds in around, gives way before her like cobwebs brushing across her face. Her eyes see nothing. But she feels everything rip through her as she teleports right through the outer perimeter's membrane. It's about what she expected—enough psychic overload to destroy an unprepared mind. Or just give it a brain hemorrhage. And maybe that's what's happening in her head.

But then it all subsides.

Seems to be normal now," says Lynx. "Nothing normal about that," says the Operative.

They're starting to run diagnostics, trying to figure out what the hell just happened. Something just seemed to *twist* the whole

zone sideways before letting it snap back into place like a gargan-
tuan piece of elastic. And not just the zone either—

"I felt something in my *mind* as well," says the Operative.

"Me too," says Lynx.

They glance at each other.

"*Fuck,*" says the Operative.

"If Sinclair's starting up the party—"

"All the more reason for you to get the fuck back there and get
that damn drive working."

"What the fuck makes you think *I'm* going to do it?"

"Because kickstarting busted engines on spaceships is something I've done once too often," says the Operative. It's not much of
an answer, but at this point, he could give a rat's ass if Lynx is sat-
isfied. He only wonders if Lynx will choose to make this the
moment—if he'll decide to have it out right here. It'd be betting
against the odds, given that the Operative's the expert in physical
combat, but he wouldn't put it past him. He watches recognition of
the inevitable coalesce on Lynx's face—

"I'm taking Linehan with me."

"Be my guest," says the Operative.

Spencer and Jarvin are taking stock. The zone went
crazy. The zone's back to normal. But Spencer simultaneously felt something shifting in his mind, too. As brief as
it was unmistakable, the implications scare him shitless. Something's almost certainly going on downstairs. And something's
now surfacing within what's left of the megaship's zone. A signal
being sent in the clear, because they're the only ones left to
hear it—

We need to talk.

THE MACHINERY OF LIGHT

She's somewhere *else* now, looking out at a different room—and even as she rips circuitry from the walls to preclude anyone following, she's checking the coordinates . . . no sign of zone, but she's using what's left of gravity to ascertain her position. She's moved away from the Moon's north-south axis, into the depths of the farside. The inner perimeter of the Room is right above her.

Along with Matthew Sinclair.

You're shitting me," says Linehan.

"You wish," says Lynx.

Linehan's in the door of the inner bridge. He looks about as pissed as the Operative expected. The idea of leaving the bridge during this madness clearly hadn't even begun to occur to him. Because that would be—

"Total fucking *insanity*," says Linehan.

"Probably worse than that," says Lynx.

"And yet you're up for it?"

"Piece of cake," says Lynx.

"You're higher than a motherfucker," says Linehan.

"Aren't we all," says the Operative.

What the fuck is that?" asks Spencer.

"Probably a trap," says Jarvin.

Though it's hard to see how. Embedded on the surface of the signal is the frequency for a zone-channel. All they have to do is tune into it to enable conversation. There's no need to intermesh minds. No reason to move outside their zone-enclave. In theory, no risk. But in practice—

"We'd have to be *nuts* to take that call," says Spencer.

"If Sinclair's revving up the Room, what do we have to lose?"

"The chance to see it happen."

"We're just talking about a little dialogue."

"These days that's the most dangerous thing."

Jarvin shrugs, then switches them over to the zone-frequency. A face awaits them there.

The zone's coming alive within her skull once more—not the American zone at all, but something that's nonetheless the most robust microzone she's ever seen. She marvels at all that clockwork—sensing as she does the machinery of Sinclair's fortress crouching all around—stretching out for kilometers around her, metal burrowed through endless tunnels, intricate patterns all waiting for one thing. She moves down a passage, sees a door ahead, knows what it is even before it slides open. She's expected all of it.

Save the voice.

They don't waste time. They get moving, through the bridge's emergency airlock and out onto the hull and—

"Don't look up," says Lynx.

But Linehan does, takes in the most demented sight he's ever seen, far crazier than any drug-vision that's ever assailed him: the two wings of the L2 fleet stretching away on both sides into what looks like forever, the Moon filling most of the sky beyond them. And past that rock are all too many stars—

"The Eurasian vanguard," breathes Linehan.

"Let's move," says Lynx.

Broadcasting from somewhere on this ship: the face is that of a woman. Spencer recognizes it from the files. He wonders if that particular file is bullshit—wonders whether this face is, too. All the more so as he knows exactly where this is going—knows what the woman's going to say even before she says it.

"I want to talk to Sarmax," she says calmly.

It's the voice of Jason Marlowe. Or whatever's passing for it. It's been so long. Its feel like it's only been a moment. This moment now: it sounds inside her head, and she's never heard anything louder. Even though she can't understand a single word. Because it's some language she's never heard. Chills shoot up her spine while the elevator car she's stepped within rushes through the rock.

They're creeping along the hull of the superdread-naught like two mountain climbers. They've got magnetic clamps turned up to maximum and have tethered themselves to each other for good measure. Linehan can only imagine what's going on beneath his feet. He keeps expecting DE shots from the incoming Eurasian ships to sweep them off altogether. He doubts he'd feel a thing—his brain would be vaporized before it even processed the bad news. He tries not to look at the Moon as he and Lynx work their way around some gun-turrets. But it's tough. It feels like that Moon's a lodestone—like it's *pulling* at him with a force way beyond mere gravity. The middle sections of the ship stretch out beyond them.

That's a good one," says Spencer.

"He's the only one I'll talk to," says Indigo Velasquez.

Or at least, a face that *looks* like Indigo Velasquez. Spencer knows what this face does to Sarmax. He knows the Rain isn't above trying the same trick twice. Spencer's doing his best to think of what he's looking at as a *thing*. He meets its eyes.

"You must think we're stupid," he says.

"He's the only one I trust."

"Didn't he try to kill you?" asks Jarvin.

"His final lesson to me."

"And you're not getting near him. God only knows what voice-activation shit he's been rigged with."

"Maybe we did the same to you."

"Try it, bitch."

"We're razors," says Jarvin. "Sarmax isn't. And you've had a lot more opportunity over the years to get your hooks into him."

"After all," says Spencer, "that's why you fucked him."

"You'll pay for that."

"About time you dropped the mask."

Claire," says Marlowe.

He's speaking English now. Her past smolders through her. She knows there's only one way to settle this. Only one way to respond.

"This isn't you," she says.

"So why do you use the second person?"

"What I'm talking to is not Jason."

"That's where you're wrong."

"You're Matthew Sinclair."

"I'm not."

"Then you're his tool. Even if you wear Marlowe's flesh, you're still—"

"You're walking into a trap," he replies.

Pause. "I know."

"So if I'm Sinclair, why am I telling you that?"

"Because Sinclair's trying to make me think you're alive," she says. "To fuck with my head the only way he can."

"But you do that so well all by yourself," says the voice.

They're maneuvering through a wilderness of turrets and panels. Energies of every wavelength crackle past them as guns discharge at the closing Eurasian fleet. The Moon's moving visibly closer with every moment as the American fleet keeps accelerating. But the *Harrison*'s going to need all the margin it can get. Whether the antimatter drive's been taken apart by crazed colonists is anyone's guess. And if the rest of the motors are threatened, then they've got even bigger problems. The two men move through onto the rear portions of the ship. The stern looms before them, the stars beyond that shimmering in the ship's exhaust.

Our personal feelings no longer matter," says the woman "And that's why you so desperately need to talk to Sarmax?"

"This has gone out of control," she says. "Sinclair's on the verge of winning everything."

"I thought your triad was loyal to him," says Jarvin.

"No longer."

"Bullshit."

"He'll consume us all."

Jarvin laughs. "You just figured that out, huh?"

"We need to join forces."

"Oh sure," says Spencer.

"I'm serious."

"You *really* think we can work together?"

"We've got to."

"Wrong," says Spencer, turning off the channel.

Somehow she finds the strength to switch him off. Because there's no way that voice can help her. If there really *is* a Marlowe clone inside the Room's outer perimeter, then it belongs to Sinclair utterly. By definition. Though in truth she doubts whatever's out there has anything to do with Marlowe in the first place. It's just a voice that's all too adept at mimicry. She steels herself, tells herself her time with Jason is past.

Unless she can somehow fuck with that past. She's wondering if that might be possible. She's thinking it's the worst kind of temptation. The elevator streaks in toward the heart of everything.

A flash—one among many, but this one's way too close. One of the neighboring ships suddenly comes apart like a cheap toy as Eurasian long-range artillery strikes home, spilling unearthly shadows along the hull of the *Harrison*. Linehan feels even more exposed than he already is. He keeps expecting debris to start raining down around him, yet he keeps on following Lynx, who seems to know exactly where he's going. The hull's curve is sharpening. The engines are dead ahead.

Sarmax abruptly stirs and pulls himself out of the corner, then starts moving against the craft's acceleration toward the cockpit door. The eyes of Jarvin and Spencer track him from the wall screens.

"Where the hell do you think you're going?" asks Jarvin.

"Out," says Sarmax.

They're on the rear of the ship, clamped to a wall sloping down toward the inferno of the motors. Linehan feels like he's looking at the very edge of existence—like it's all surrounded by some bubble, and he's finally reached it. The Moon's no longer visible. But a hatch is—

"Blow it," says Lynx.

Spencer stays where he is—in the zone, locking down the cockpit, keeping an eye on all the entryways. Jarvin's dropped back out—back into his body. He moves after Sarmax, who barely glances at him.

"Don't try to stop me," he says.

"From doing *what?*" asks Jarvin.

"Like you need to ask."

Can't you hack it?" asks Linehan.

"Systems are fucked," says Lynx.

"Sometimes the old-fashioned way's best," says Linehan. He opens up with his lasers and starts carving through the hatch.

Sarmax stops at the cockpit door, turns to face Jarvin.

"You really *don't* want to fight me," he says.

Spencer's doing his best to hack the mech's zone-connections. He figures Sarmax has managed to switch them off again, but it turns out they're still on. Yet he can't break through. Apparently there's a new factor in the mix.

"She's inside you," he says slowly.

"Finally," says Sarmax.

"You've gone insane," says Jarvin.

"Fine."

"You go out there and they'll kill you."

"You're the one who'll die if you don't open that door."

Spencer stares at the man. Being trapped in a confined space with an off-the-leash mech wasn't exactly what he was planning. He can see only one way out of this.

"Let's not be too hasty," says Jarvin. "We can—"

"No we can't," says Spencer.

The cockpit door slides open.

L inehan tears aside what's left of the hatch. They slide into the shaft that's revealed, glad to put the exterior behind them. But as to what's in here with them—

"Get ready to start killing," says Lynx.

"They're already dead," mutters Linehan.

T he door shuts behind Sarmax. Spencer watches on the camera-feeds as the mech makes his way down the shaft toward the exterior door, stepping around the charges and mines liberally strewn along its length. Jarvin cuts back on the zone.

"Let's take him out," he says.

"Are you nuts?" says Spencer.

"We're nuts if we let him out of here."

"The man's a world-class mech. We can't hack him. You really want to get in the ring with him?"

Jarvin says nothing.

"Besides," adds Spencer, "even if we nailed him, he'd still take out half the fucking defenses while he was going down and then the Rain would be right up our asses."

"So what the hell are you suggesting we do?"

Spenser shrugs. "Write him off."

They roar out of the shaft and through an airlock, coming into the infested areas, letting shots streak out ahead of them. The colonists look almost happy to see them. Linehan figures they have reason to be, since he and Lynx are the only targets left. They're approaching the engines—

"Antipersonnel weapons only," says Lynx.

"That'll make it that much tougher."

"You know you love it."

The far door to the cockpit access-shaft opens. Sarmax heads through, pulling himself along the walls as acceleration hauls against him. Lights flicker here and there, but it's mostly dark. Quiet, too. Bodies are strewn about. Looks like the crew has finished killing one another off.

Or maybe the Rain has done it for them. Sarmax really doesn't care. All that matters is that she's back. That she appeared in his head and told him what to do if he wanted to see her again. His latent mental abilities have finally coalesced.

Or else he's gone nuts. Or he's been had. Because he sees no signs of her now. His mind's empty. So are these corridors. He keeps on making his way through them.

They come through into the engine area, spraying flechette rounds in clouds around them. The colonists who have broken through to this area are trapped. It's over quickly. Lynx and Linehan fire shots down the corridor through which they've come. They're slamming the doors shut.

"Now what?" says Linehan.

"Now get on that fucking motor," says Lynx.

The doors are shut once more. The defenses are back up. It's just the two of them now. Their bodies are in opposite corners of the room, their minds creeping amidst zone fragments, flitting from sensor to sensor, tracking Sarmax as he makes his way deeper into the depths of the structure. Until—

"What the fuck?" says Spencer.

"He just vanished," says Jarvin.

"Into the jaws of Rain."

Total silence save for the feedback in his own helmet. He's no longer on the zone. There's nothing for him there. Nothing in his mind now either. No sign of Indigo. At all. A nasty suspicion's forming in his head. He's the one who almost killed her back in the day. If she really *is* alive, then maybe he won't be staying that way for too long. Maybe that's the way it should be. He primes his weapons, gets ready for what he's been waiting for all along.

Linehan opens more hatches and starts running wires into the microfission chambers while Lynx establishes a link back to the bridge. The Operative's face appears on a screen.

"What's the situation?"

"We're here," says Lynx. "It's going to take awhile."

"What's going on?" asks the Operative.

"The comps are fucked. We have to program the thing by hand."

"But it's working?"

"We'll find out."

"Okay," says the Operative. "Keep me posted and—*fuck!*"

"What your problem?" asks Lynx.

"This," says the Operative—beams over data—

"Fuck *me*," says Lynx.

And it's all they can do to hang on. The megaships just changed gears yet again—heavier racks of nukes start slotting through them as they move to a whole new level of speed. If this goes on for much longer, all the humans aboard will be crushed by the G-forces. They're starting to feel pretty squashed now. Spencer and Jarvin are pressed back in their respective corners. But at least they're braced for it.

Sarmax gets knocked sprawling. He grabs at a doorway, misses—tumbles down a corridor that's become a shaft—he's firing his suit-jets, but not in time—walls come rushing up to meet him—

There's a lurch as the *Harrison* throttles up still further and the L2 fleet reaches its uppermost speed. Any extra margin is a function of what Lynx can achieve with the AM drive. He's running through the circuitry now—

"No pressure," says Linehan.

"Fuck you," mutters Lynx.

"Take a look at this," says the Operative on the com.

But Lynx can spare only a glance at the data that the Operative's forwarding onto the screen. The vanguards of the Eurasian fleet are kniving in along two distinct vectors—releasing their tethers, slinging scores of troopships toward the Moon. Looks like the two megaships themselves are going to converge on a point behind it. More specifically—

"They're coming for us," says the Operative.

"I get that," says Lynx. "Now if you'll excuse me—"

"No," says the Operative, "they're coming for *us*."

We're heading straight for them," says Jarvin. The AI confirms it. The override back at the motors has got them on a collision course with the U.S. fleet, not to mention the other megaship. And now the AI starts to reel off more numbers . . .

"Holy mother of God," says Jarvin.

Waking up isn't easy. Especially when it involves becoming aware of so much pain. Sarmax opens his eyes to find a metal surface pressed up against his visor. He's pressed up against the rest of that metal, shoved against the edge of a doorway that acceleration has turned into the entrance of a rather deep pit. He's trying to move. He can't. His armor's primary gyros are fucked. His secondaries aren't reporting for duty. That's when someone presses their helmet up against his.

Lights gleam along the walls: the elevator car's moving along grooves cut into the side of a vast cavern. Machinery's everywhere, crusting along the walls and ceiling like some out-of-control growth.

Yet Haskell knows it's a mere fraction of the total sum of what's enclosed within this part of the Moon. Most of it isn't visible—just endless kilometers of piping running through tunnels too narrow for any but the most specialized of service droids. None of which matters as long as it works. And it's all about to be put to the test. Her car drops through the cavern's floor, slides to a halt. The door opens.

As the Eurasian megaships streak in from either side of the Moon, the American fleet opens up with all remaining guns. The rest of the Eurasian armada returns the favor. Both sides start taking serious damage. The Operative watches on the screens while ship after ship gets hit by DE fire—while simultaneously the KE gatlings throughout the U.S. fleet start churning metal out into vacuum at unholy rates, aiming along the vectors deemed most likely by the computers to intersect with the megaships, now rushing in upon each flank—

"How's it looking up there?" asks Lynx.

"You don't want to know."

What kind of a flight plan is *that?*" asks Jarvin.

"It's no flight plan," says Spencer.

"You mean—"

"Yeah."

The AI's spitting out preliminary computations regarding the last section of the files that Sinclair possessed and Jarvin stole and Spencer almost cracked. The fact that Haskell augmented the AI is no small factor in the breakthrough it's managed to make. The overall parameters on the remaining section of the file coalesce on zone. Row upon row of solved equations—

"Can we get this in English?" says Jarvin.

"Almost there," says the AI.

"So are we," says Spencer.

A withering barrage of KE hits the megaship.

Software uploads stream into Sarmax's suit. Hands haul him up from his perch, drag him through a hatchway. A voice echoes in his head.

"Christ, we've missed you," it says.

Almost . . . there," says Lynx.

He'd better be. And he's got more than a few incentives to minimize the amount of time he spends near these microfission chambers. Radiation readings are going off the charts all around him as he runs zone. The *Harrison* keeps shuddering as it takes fire. Lynx can almost feel those battering rams in space streaking in toward him . . .

The AI will have it all figured out within the next thirty seconds. But they're now hurtling in upon the left flank of the L2 fleet—which isn't even trying for evasive action. Instruments show the nose of their megaship has been shot off. Doesn't matter. The rest of it is still racing forward, like an ancient war-elephant about to hurl itself upon a phalanx that's bracing desperately to receive it. The massed guns of the L2 fleet are a wall of flaring light.

"We're not meant to survive this," says Jarvin.
"You just figured that out?"

He's dragged into some kind of confined space—opens his eyes to behold—
"Indigo," he whispers.
"Hold on," she replies.

The megaships spear through the L2 fleet, choosing courses that send them slotting in between the larger ships, smashing through the lesser ones. Total carnage ensues. Clouds of debris and flame show their paths as they rocket in toward the center, shedding pieces of their hulls the whole time. The Operative watches as they converge on the *Harrison*'s position. He knows better than to ask what the situation is back at the stern. On the outer bridge, Maschler and Riley are starting to look like they'd rather be somewhere else.

The computer keeps processing the last of the files as Spencer starts modularizing the cockpit, slamming all blast-doors in anticipation of imminent collision. So far the megaships coming in from both sides have avoided hitting any of the larger ships. But they're clearly about to make an exception for the *Harrison*.
"Brace yourself," says Spencer.
"Very funny," says Jarvin.

Sarmax gets it now. He's in some kind of dropship. So is she. Along with the triad's two other members. He recognizes them, but they mean nothing to him. They're manning the controls, powering up the craft, getting ready to launch. She's holding his glove in hers.

She steps out of the elevator, into a chamber that contains a single mammoth door, reinforced and shimmering with energy. The gateway through the inner perimeter. She takes a deep breath—

Linehan watches the megaships fill all screens, then turns around as Lynx scrambles into view, slamming hatches shut behind him.

"Done," says Lynx.

"Did you hear that?" asks Linehan.

"Believe it," replies the Operative—

—as he fires the antimatter drive up. The *Harrison* suddenly lurches forward. *Hammer of the Skies* just misses the flagship, shoots behind it, smashes another dreadnaught dead amidships—the combined burning mass torpedoes like a meteor past the incoming *Righteous Fire-Dragon*—

—reaching out toward that door beyond which lies everything that matters—

H oly fuck!" yells Spencer.
  "Here we go," mutters Jarvin.
  "Here's the kicker," says the AI.

S armax looks into the eyes of the woman he remembers
all too well.
  "You came back," he says.
"I never left," she replies.

—t*ouches* it—

J esus Christ!" yells Linehan.

—a nd the Operative kills the antimatter, hits all ret-
ros—slowing the ship just enough to take it off
the direct path of the *Righteous Fire-Dragon.* But it's going to be close—

Too close.

"Hold on!" yells Spencer.

"You guys need to hear this," says the AI.

"Fucking download it!" screams Jarvin.

The *Righteous Fire-Dragon* swipes the *Harrison* just aft of where the *Memphis* is still lodged in the flagship's side.

The dropship is still attached to the wall of the hangar. It's being buffeted worse than any atmosphere. Sarmax feels Velasquez's hack-sequences continue to course through him, repairing his armor where they can, tending to the software in his mind—

—She's putting all that's going on overhead out of her mind—begins running the sequence to hack the door that leads through the inner perimeter. It's not just a hack on zone either. It's also her mind: her psionic abilities surge against the defenses—

The *Harrison*'s been sliced almost in two. Lynx and Linehan are clinging to the walls via magnetic clamps while the rear section of the flagship surges out of control. Wall starts to rip away ahead of them. Colonists stream out behind them like water playing from a fire hose.

What's left of *Righteous Fire-Dragon* charges on into the thick of the American fleet, smashing ships while getting smashed itself. The Operative's screaming at Maschler and Riley to get inside the inner bridge. They're leaping to comply as the Moon seesaws crazily in the window—

it's a demolition derby in the middle of the L2 fleet, and the megaships are coming apart under repeated impacts. Spencer and Jarvin are thrown back and forth as their ship plows on past the fleet, arcing back toward the Moon, the outer layers starting to shred—

At least I saw you again," says Sarmax.
"We're not dead yet," says Velasquez.
The walls of the hangar start to tear away.

The sequences she's running keep on building, as does the psychic backwash. Factors keep on dwindling toward zero, canceling out all infinities. Untold reverberations wash through her, but she anticipates each one, slides her mind at the precise angle to avoid insanity—

We are so fucked," mutters Linehan.
"At least go out in style," snaps Lynx. He's trying to hack the motor directly. What's left of the combined mass of the *Memphis* and the *Harrison* is falling away. The farside of the Moon's coming in toward them.

Maschler joins the Operative on the inner bridge. The outer bridge personnel are panicking. Riley pulls himself into the inner bridge, slams the door behind him.

"Now what?" he yells.

"Hold the fuck on," says the Operative.

It's all they can do. They're being shaken ever harder as the *Righteous Fire-Dragon* barrels its way through the far flank of the L2 fleet, ships scattering on both sides like schools of fish before a shark. Moon's rushing in toward them.

The dropship detaches in one fluid motion, firing motors and falling away from the disintegrating hangar and out of the megaship. Hull starts to streak past them.

The ceiling is disintegrating. Along with the floor. They're back against the bulwark of the motor itself now, holding on with those magnetic clamps. And suddenly that engine is firing again. Linehan feels his whole life flash before him. Lynx is laughing like crazy as he feeds commands into the motors and they rocket past what's left of the *Harrison,* catapulting straight in toward the Moon.

The outer bridge personnel are hurling themselves against the door to the inner bridge, trying to somehow find a way in. It's not like they have a plan. They're just intent on killing the ones who have killed them. But the three men inside pay no attention—instead, they're watching the *Harrison*'s wayward antimatter drive streak past them, two suited figures clinging to it.

"What a way to go," says Riley.

"We're going the same way," says the Operative as he finishes the sequence he's been keying. Explosions suddenly detonate throughout the outer bridge.

We've lost the engines," says Spencer.

Jarvin nods. He brings up the trajectory and looks at the dotted line that shows the extrapolation—an arc continuing around the lunar surface, impacting on the nearside at—

"Hmmm," he says.

They're getting the hell out of the way of the nukes. The megaship falls away in the distance. The ships of the L2 fleet pour by overhead. The dropship's plunging toward the lunar surface.

And suddenly they're upon her. The guardians of the Room. Not just silicon either. She can feel the texture of their minds; they're almost like her, living flesh linked to silicon to create something greater. She pictures living brains trapped within walls, pictures them linked together, swarming in upon her head—

Two men like insects on the edge of eternity, clinging to machinery that's roaring full tilt toward the ground. The L2 fleet blasts above them, formation after formation surging around toward the nearside to face the main weight of the Eurasian fleet. But the American deployment is less than flawless—gaps are everywhere in the ranks, testament to the damage the megaships wrought.

"They're fucked," says Lynx.

"And we're not?"

The Moon rushes ever closer.

Admiral's privilege," says the Operative. He's not kidding. The inner bridge of the *Harrison* doubles as an escape ship. Riley and Maschler can only watch as he takes that ship through a series of evasive maneuvers. The L2 fleet tumbles away above them. The Moon falls in toward them. Riley laughs.

"*No one's* going to be fooled by this," he says.

"Szilard will fucking nail us," mutters Maschler.

"I think he's got other shit to worry about," says the Operative, gesturing at the explosions dotting the approaching lunar surface.

The last cameras are getting taken out. But as they go, they show clear evidence that the lunar garrisons are in very deep trouble. A couple of domes on the boundary between farside and nearside just blew—outposts that are clearly under coordinated attack by the Eurasian commandos that the megaships have scattered like countless spores across the Moon. But those ships are paying the ultimate price for the havoc they've wreaked. *Hammer of the Skies* is disappearing from sight, disintegrating across the horizon, shredding into the mother of all meteor showers. And before they went offline, the engines of the *Righteous Fire-Dragon* got one last set of instructions.

"Projected impact on Copernicus," says Jarvin.

Spencer whistles. "The lunar capital?"

"For a couple more minutes."

The dropship careens downward. The ship's stealthy, but that alone won't be enough. Sarmax can only imagine what hacks this Rain triad is running on the American zone. He's starting to think they might actually make it to the surface. He looks at Velasquez.

"Why'd you save me?"

"I think you know the answer to that."

She shoves her head deeper into the Room's defenses, smashing ever further into those minds, each one a prick of sentience she's snuffing out. She can't help but wonder whether these brains were the real Rain originals—the things that never left the vats, that instead were assigned the mission of defending Sinclair's ultimate stronghold. But she's turning the flank on those defenses. She's almost there. She feels it all twisting in around her.

They're still pointed straight down, aiming at the very center of the farside. Ground-to-space lasers streak past them. Lynx throttles up the engine even further, opens up a comlink with what's left of the Congreve defense grid, and starts running a particularly insidious hack.

T hey're getting low now, maneuvering within ten thousand meters of the surface. Mountain ranges loom ahead of them, straddling the near and farsides.

"Where the fuck are we going?" says Riley.

"Familiar ground," says the Operative.

T hey're arcing down across the nearside, the domes of Copernicus approaching all too rapidly—and Spencer can only imagine the alarms that are going off within them. Not that anyone's going to have time to react.

"Time to go," says Spencer.

"Agreed," says Jarvin.

T he truth is we need you," says Velasquez.

"Because of Sinclair," replies Sarmax.

"Because otherwise we're nothing but his prey."

S he's in the home stretch now. Though she keeps wondering why Sinclair is making this so hard for her. Especially when he needs her to finish what he's set in motion. Maybe this is her final test. Maybe he's trying to draw off some of her strength. If that's the case, it's not working. She's only growing stronger. She moves onto the final sequence—

⊕ Let's do this," says Lynx. The two men detach themselves—fire judicious thrusts from their motors as the antimatter drive drops away. Lynx has convinced Congreve's defenses that this fragment of the *Harrison* is about to try an emergency landing in the adjacent Korolev Crater. The two men plunge downward in their armor and watch the engine beneath them dwindle to a speck while Congreve's dome grows larger by the second.

⊕ Mountains are streaking in toward them. The Operative's working the controls, banking the escape craft beneath the highest peaks, letting it drop down toward the valleys. Maschler does a doubletake.

"Wait a second," he says. "This is—"

"Shut up and hold on," says the Operative.

⊘ Spencer and Jarvin crawl through a narrow shaft that's nearly identical to the one they had used to enter the cockpit on the *Hammer of the Skies*. Spencer was tempted to rig the Eurasian AI with hi-ex, but he realizes that would stretch the word *superfluous* to whole new levels. He's got the files that machine downloaded in the back of his head. He's got no time to bother with them right now. They reach the last hatch, shove it aside, fling themselves out into the abyss.

How much do you know?" asks Sarmax.

"Enough," she replies. "He's been using us—"

"When did you figure it out?"

"After we realized we weren't guarding Sinclair."

"When did he leave?"

"Some point before the war started, I guess. Now he's at the Room, I don't see how the hell we can stop him in time."

He stares at her. "We can fucking *try*," he says.

Terrain starts to appear in the windows of the dropship.

Ciphers so next-level that only a brain like Haskell's can hope to penetrate them. She's tearing through them on overdrive—making them think that *she's* the one who's created them. Who's now reversing them. She's through. The locks *click* through her mind—

A million shades of black and grey, a million lights flaring all around—and the soundtrack to all of it is silence as Linehan takes in the sight. It's the most beautiful thing he's ever seen. He suddenly feels that all the fighting and shooting and killing that's going on around him isn't really happening—that existence has dwindled to this tiny space inside his helmet even as he looks at all those stars. It seems like there's a pattern all around, like somehow it's all meant to happen. He and Lynx are freefalling, tumbling downward, that engine-that's-now-a-bomb a distant firefly far below. Any moment now Congreve's defenses are going to come to their senses. But a few moments more and it's going to be too late—

They swoop over one mountain, veer in toward another. A giant sinkhole stretches out before them, carved straight through adjacent hills and valleys. It doesn't look natural. More like—

"Someone had some fun with blasting powder," says Riley.

"Couple of nukes," says the Operative.

"Autumn Rain?"

"Several days back."

"And you were there, huh?"

"Hey," says Maschler, "that looks like another ship."

Judicious bursts of their suit-thrusters as they exit—and the *Righteous Fire-Dragon* is rushing past, dropping beneath them as they gain height. It seems to have given up spitting nukes. It won't matter—it's still going to turn Copernicus into a big pancake. The sky above Spencer's head is alive with lights, the vanguards of the American fleet clearly visible as they vector out from behind the Moon to do battle with the onrushing Eurasian fleet. Spencer can see quite clearly that the Yanks haven't a fucking prayer. The ships of the East make the sky immediately above the nearside look like the center of the galaxy. The *Righteous Fire-Dragon* is dwindling below them as it moves into the last stage of its final plunge—

They've seen us," says the pilot.

Velasquez just nods. The ship rocks from side to side as its pilots keep the trajectory unpredictable, letting the craft drop lower all the while. Moon's filling the window now. It looks as if they're maneuvering amidst a mountain range. But Sarmax's vantage point prevents him from seeing the whole picture.

Which doesn't mean he can't be kept in the loop.

"Your friend Carson," says Velasquez.

"Where's he going?"

"Right where we thought he would."

She's got everything right where she wants. She's pressing her head against the surface of the door, feeling the vibrations rumble deep within. She envisions dominoes falling, endless chains of locks turning like gears, grinding in upon hinges that slowly start to swivel. She backs up, moving out of the way as the door to the Room starts to open.

The engine punches straight through the main dome of Congreve, red flaring out as a chunk of antimatter explodes into the city.

"Wow," says Linehan.

"They were all fucked anyway," says Lynx.

And then some. The two men drop through what's left of the shattered dome, firing at everything in sight.

The Operative hits the afterburners, sending the craft on a barely controlled plummet into the sinkhole that sprawls across so much of Nansen Station. He rockets in toward the bottom. There's no way they're going to stop in time.

"What the fuck are you doing?" yells Maschler.

The Operative says nothing. But now all three men can see that what looks to be the deepest part is actually the beginning of a tunnel—

A kilometer of disintegrating megaship crashes through Copernicus's dome, detonating as it goes. Enough of its fuel was intact to make it interesting. Thousands of nukes are going off, enveloping the lunar capital in sheets of energy, making the whole nearside shake. Radiation pummels the suits of the two men who are still several klicks above the city. They start playing evasive action with the debris that they're descending into.

"We'll need some new gear," says Spencer.

"First things first," says Jarvin.

They swoop down toward that smoking crater.

The ship lifts away from the sinkhole, pivots, drops in toward an adjacent valley.

"What the hell's going on?" says Sarmax.

"Carson's gone to ground," replies Velasquez.

"And we're not?"

"We're going in another way. Are you ready to get back in the fight?"

Sarmax nods. Tunnel closes in around them.

The door's as massive as it is reinforced. As it swings open, Haskell can hear the creaking of doors behind it doing the same thing. A whole succession of gates, and she's cracked them all. She steps behind the first one, starts moving past the procession—starts to get intimations of the space that lies beyond—

The upper levels of Congreve are totaled. The lower levels are pure chaos. The fact that Lynx has hacked the inner enclaves of the city's defenses is only adding to the insanity. He and Linehan charge into the city's basements, shooting in all directions, heading downward as fast as possible.

"Ain't gonna be enough," says Linehan.

"Shut up and keep moving," mutters Lynx.

That's the key ingredient of the Operative's plan. Maschler and Riley are holding on for dear life while he pilots the escape ship down a tunnel, dropping ever farther beneath Nansen Station, on the cusp of far and nearside. He and Lynx and Sarmax came down here once in search of the Rain, only to have the Rain blow their base right in their face. He maneuvers through a maze of passages, trying to guess which ones have collapsed and which ones haven't.

"Do you know where you're going?" demands Riley.

"Somewhere off the maps."

"I thought the Praetorians searched this whole place."

"Doesn't mean they found the good bits."

Copernicus is history. Radiation's aftermath churns on their screens as they descend through what's left and into the hole that the *Righteous Fire-Dragon* has bored into the city's basements. The zone beneath the Moon starts to click into Spencer's head. It's not a pretty sight.

The dropship starts maneuvering through the tunnels beneath Nansen. SpaceCom marines are trying to stop it. They're getting gunned down for their troubles—and hacked too. The software in their skulls is going haywire, shoving their brains over the edge. Velasquez hauls the dropship door open. Sarmax staggers to his feet, joins her there, and they start lacing targets while the ship accelerates.

The last of the doors swing toward her as she closes in on it. She feels all of existence pivot around her—feels time close in like a vise. She feels other minds out there, still trying to reach her even though she can see they're far too late. But Sinclair and Control aren't. They're waiting for her inside. She steps past the final door—steps within—

Lynx and Linehan are shredding their way through Congreve's basements. Lynx's hack has the comps so fucked they don't even know which way is up. Complete confusion reigns amidst the tunnels. All the more so as it looks like Eurasian forces have already deployed across the lunar surface. The garrison is deserting their posts, fleeing deeper beneath the surface. All too many are getting shot as they flee.

"Still too fucking *slow*," Lynx mutters.

The Operative knows the feeling. This crazy operation's going like clockwork, yet by the time he gets near the Room it'll be way too late. He can fucking *sense* it, as certain as anything he's ever known. But he's come too far to just give up. So he keeps on forging his way forward, moving back up into the lower reaches of Nansen, letting his mind move out and run hacks that release the restraints on the thousands of convict-miners who work the mines—and who now swarm out and start overwhelming the stunned marines. Beyond, the Operative's catching glimpses of the lunar zone, getting caved in now as the main weight of the Eurasian fleet bombards the Moon at close range. He can see he's got to get deeper fast.

The war is lost. Jarvin and Spencer take stock while they don new armor and load up at a reserve ammo dump. Glimpses on the zone show Spencer that the American fleet is getting pulverized above the nearside—fighting heroically, but overwhelmed by sheer numbers. Spencer wonders whose retarded idea it was to charge straight toward the Eurasian fleet. Not that there's going to be a court of inquiries this time. There'll be nothing left of the United States within the hour. Eurasian artillery is slamming into what's left of Copernicus at point-blank range. Spencer and Jarvin feel more than a little relieved now that they've got roof above their heads. They move out, getting ever deeper into the lunar capital's subbasements.

They're smashing their way through what's left of Nansen, reducing everything in sight to rubble. The fact that all the convict-miners seem to have somehow slipped their leashes is only adding to the confusion. The dropship roars through several larger caves, Velasquez and Sarmax doing door-gunner duty as they spray fire everywhere. Velasquez puts her helmet up to Sarmax's.

"I'm going to need your mind, too," she says.

"What the hell are you talking about?" he says.

She tells him.

She's in the Room now, and darkness is all around her. She's afraid to use her lights. She's seeing with her mind anyway, and so far that's more than enough. As she steps forward, she can sense abyss on all sides—can sense structures all around her. She's not surprised in the slightest when the floor beneath her shudders, starts moving, folding up around her to become another elevator car, sliding in toward the very core of Room.

They fight their way deeper, moving out of the Congreve subbasements and onto the threshold of the larger lunar infrastructure that stretches beneath the farside. Lynx struggles to focus on the zone, but he can't make out much, save for the fact that combat is underway everywhere. It makes him wonder just how far the Eurasian commandos have penetrated. Linehan gets out in front, on point; they start moving downward at speed.

It's good to be back. Even though somehow it's like he never left —like he's been hanging out near Congreve this whole time, still waiting for Lynx to hurry up and figure out a way to get into that city and up to the L2 fleet. Four days have passed since, and it seems like it's been only four minutes. It seems like there are only four minutes to go. He can feel everything he's ever been running from coming in to claim him. Ayahuasca's edge is sharpening ever further, rising like a new sun bursting in his mind. He feels like he's almost at the hub of the universe—like maybe it's just below him. He can hardly wait to get there.

And suddenly a mind's sliding straight into the Operative's head. It's one he recognizes. He's been aware of it for many years now, just never in this way. But there's a first time for everything. Even this.

"Leo."

"The same."

"You've learned some new tricks, huh?"

"Or just remembered some old ones," says Sarmax.

"Bullshit. Who took you out of latency?"

"Indigo."

"You're shitting me."

"She's right here with me. With her triad—"

"In Nansen."

"Sure," says Sarmax.

"She's calling the shots."

"So what if she is? We need to team up."

"Heard that one before," says the Operative.

Spencer and Jarvin put ever more rock between them and the surface. The tunnels beneath Copernicus give them slightly more of a vantage point on zone. Enough to show that it's crumbling everywhere. The bulk of Eurasian forces are still polishing off the American fleet. But more of the East's shock-troops are hitting the Moon with every minute. Most of the initially vulnerable points are on the nearside. But as the Eurasian flanks envelop the farside, that's starting to change.

"That's where the real action's at anyway," says Jarvin.

"You think the Eurasians know that?" asks Spencer.

"I think they know the only thing that counts now is getting inside the Room."

"So aren't we a little too far from the main event?"

"That's the idea," says Jarvin.

H e cut us off," says Velasquez.
   "So?"
   "Didn't think he could do that. Thought I was—"
   "He's a resourceful man."
   They come out into a cavern far larger than anything they've seen so far. Looks like explosions have torn it nearly apart—the floor and walls are mostly rubble. They ignite their jet-packs, start to move through in tight formation. They've just reached the other side when lights and sensors transfix them from much higher in the cavern.

I n the flesh this time," says the Operative.
   "*Fuck*," says Sarmax. The Operative's standing on a ledge, flanked by Riley and Maschler. Everybody's got their guns pointed at one another now.
   "Easy," says Velasquez.
   "You sold me," says the Operative. "We *do* need to team up."
   There's a pause.
   "On *my* terms," he adds.
   "Which are?"
   The Operative keeps it brief.

H er body's on a platform hurtling toward the inner confines of the Room. But her mind's way ahead of her: it reaches the controls, switches them on. Software starts powering up. The lights go on. The sight practically drops her to her knees.

The tunnels beneath farside—the deepest levels of which lead directly to the Room. Though only those who have the whole picture know the correct routes. Thousands of klicks of passages sprawling out beneath the lunar farside, stretching down for hundreds of kilometers—most of it's been signed off at various levels within Space Command across the decades. Some of it's mining. Some of it's R&D. Some of it was commissioned in secret by Harrison himself, dug out by his Praetorians. And some of it's known only to—

"Autumn Rain," says Lynx.

"An increasingly nebulous concept these days," says Linehan. But Lynx doesn't reply. He's just processing data—integrating the glimpses he's got on the collapsing zone with the flickers of mind he can see out there. He has no idea why his mental abilities are getting better by the moment. It's as if they're being hauled toward ever greater heights regardless of his own feelings in the matter. He's not about to argue.

"Well?" demands Linehan.

"Here's the situation," says Lynx.

Insider information: they're burning away from Nansen along Rain tunnels that the Praetorians never found, heading for the edge of the main network of tunnels beneath the farside. The Operative and Maschler and Riley are in one chute; Sarmax and the Rain triad are in a parallel one. But the Operative has gone ahead and linked his mind with Sarmax and the triad all the same. It feels strange to have done so. But he knows it's the only option that might see them through. Even though the Operative can see they're going to need more margin—can see they're going to have to consolidate still further.

Spencer no longer has any view of what's happening on the surface. But it sounds like the entire Eurasian armada is coming down on top of them. Rumbling shakes the tunnels through which they're streaking. Spencer listens on the zone as the American forces fall back, heading ever deeper.

Vast shapes hanging like monstrous chandeliers, intimations of impossibly intricate machinery: she gets a glimpse of the outer Room as she shoots through the metal skin of the inner one—even as it closes up behind her and the lights of the inner Room switch on—

All she can do is stare.

A kilometer across: the inner Room is a massive sphere from which a series of ramps and rails descend to a smaller sphere positioned at the very center. She's heading down toward that hub now. She can feel Sinclair waiting for her there, too—his mind's suddenly turning back on at point-blank range—

—hauling her in—

—like some gigantic magnet—

—and she suddenly *gets* how much he's been concealing from her, how much stronger he is than she ever thought. He's been luring her down here all this time. She was fucking crazy to come this far. And the only way to win is to do something even crazier. She came in the back door of the Room. She's going to leave out the front.

Right now.

We've got to get down as fast as possible," yells Lynx.

Linehan's not worried. Everything's converging. He's just flotsam on whitewater. They've commandeered cycles left behind by a decimated mechanized unit—are riding those bikes at speeds a long way past anything safe. They're getting into the heart of the farside now, and as they descend along ramps and drop through shafts, Lynx is transmitting data into Linehan's head, along with a running commentary.

"The lower we get, the worse the fighting gets," he says. "Probably because Szilard's no longer even trying to hold the Eurasians to the surface."

"Are you kidding? There's fighting all around us—"

"Don't you get it, man? Our fleet's getting *wiped out*. The garrisons are getting overwhelmed. They'll keep fighting. But they're going down before sheer numbers. They're just there to buy time while Szilard—"

"You really think he's down there?"

"No question. Along with his most elite marines."

"Trying to break through to the Room."

"And this is our chance to fucking break *him*."

Streaking through one of the deepest of the deep-grid maglev tunnels is a two-car armored train, bristling with guns. The front car contains Velasquez, Sarmax, and the other two members of the Rain triad. The rear one contains Riley, Maschler, and the Operative—who's in the rearmost chamber of that car, communicating with Velasquez and Sarmax as he drives.

"As bad as we thought," he says.

"Would have to agree," says Velasquez.

"The Eurasians have the surface," says Sarmax.

That seems to be an understatement. The last camera-feeds showed a sky practically blotted out by troopships. The American zone is crumbling as the Chinese forces consolidate their hold on the ground.

"Check it out," says the Operative, showing the projections. Several Eastern spearheads are lancing deeper from Congreve— moving far faster than the rest of the East's legions—

"Commandos," says Velasquez.

"Of course," says Sarmax.

"Whoever's running the Coalition gets it," says the Operative. "The real war's going to be fought on the threshold of the Room."

"Or in the Room itself," says Velasquez. "Sinclair might already have—"

"I'm stunned he hasn't already," says the Operative.

"Doesn't change the plan," says Sarmax.

The deep-grids beneath Copernicus just aren't deep enough anymore. But they're the fastest option available. Jarvin and Spencer have commandeered a maglev car, having left its crew as mangled flesh in the tunnel some klicks back. They're heading west, blasting everything in their path. The tunnels are a chaos of fighting. A temporary turn of the tide seems to be going on within this sector—the farthest Eurasian troops are being forced back upstairs by Americans who have realized that they're running out of room to retreat. The line of battle is swaying back and forth. Sometimes Jarvin and Spencer find themselves pretending to be SpaceCom. Sometimes they're pretending they're Chinese. It's a game that can only have one end.

"We're rumbled," says Spencer.

"I see it," says Jarvin.

The pursuit moves in after them.

She turns in one fluid motion, fires all thrusters. The walls of her elevator car fall away like glass and she's already flying straight through them, suit-jets burning as she presses down with her mind with all her might—catches Sinclair by surprise, gets him in a temporary mental lock, as though she's pinning a more powerful opponent's arms against his sides. It won't last. Maybe it doesn't need to. She blasts past that hub, upward toward the ceiling.

They get deeper into farside. The upper areas seem to be a free-for-all. It makes the going easy for two men who know where they're going. They switch from cycles to transport-trains, switch from that to elevators that plunge through shafts. They're keeping clear of the main fighting. They're in between most of it now anyway. Above them the Eurasian legions are consolidating their hold. Below them—

"Gotta be Szilard," says Lynx.

"This time we do it right," says Linehan.

The train roars back into tunnels known only to Autumn Rain. All the combat's elsewhere. They're taking advantage of that fact while they wait for the world to end. Sarmax can't believe any of this is happening. Particularly not this—Indigo's pressurized the rear chamber of this car, lifted up her visor. He's done the same. They've got enough time for only one lingering kiss. It's so much more than it used to be. It's not just their bodies, now—it's their minds as well. She's still the only thing he ever loved. He's telling her she's won—that she can do whatever she want to him now. She's not disagreeing.

Straight shot from the depths of Copernicus to the hollows beneath the Imbrium, and this train just keeps on eating up the klicks. Overhead's the world's weight in rock. And that tunnel suffers from the same thing you do.

Pressure.

"We need more throttle," yells Spencer.

"We can't go any faster," says Jarvin. He fires the rear-guns, catches one of the pursuers dead amidships—it explodes against the wall. But the gunship behind it is still coming on. The soldiers of the East are flush with victory. And they're nothing if not—

"Persistent," Spencer comments.

He takes the ship through a series of maneuvers; shoots through some mining shafts and back out into the deep-grids. The Eurasian gunship streaks after them—moving past the hi-ex mines that Spencer just slung against the tunnel wall. The ensuing explosions bring the roof down on it.

"Bought us some time," says Jarvin.

"Not much," replies Spencer.

It'll have to do. The ceiling of the inner Room is peeling away above her. She's streaking in toward another elevator now—one among so many, this one part of a funicular ramp that she's setting in motion, her mind working its controls as she leaps on and turns to face the receding hub of the inner Room, targeting her guns and mind on it, waiting for what she knows is about to emerge—

They're cutting in behind the SpaceCom rearguard, stealing between the units that are struggling to throw up a defensive screen. Lynx has got the Com's cookbook thoroughly cracked by now. Besides, that rearguard has made its deployments largely focused on the incoming Eurasians. Lynx and Linehan reach a network of more shafts and get within the area where the bulk of the president's forces are moving. But even here, there's still a lot of fighting going on. It doesn't take them long to figure out why.

L ot of free agents," says the Operative.
He's got Maschler and Riley manning the guns
while he works the zone. The train's racing out toward
the center of the farside now, gathering speed with every minute,
dropping ever farther. Velasquez is integrating her zone-readouts
with those of the Operative. It's an exercise in extrapolation as the
situation gets ever more chaotic. But the overall contours are unmistakable.

"Makes sense," says Velasquez.

"You're being sarcastic?"

"Not at all."

"What the hell are you guys talking about?" demands Sarmax.

"Szilard's stirring up the refugees," says the Operative.

"Those who fled the new orders," says Velasquez.

Sarmax nods. Praetorians who made themselves scarce when
Montrose took over. InfoCom soldiers who got the hell out of there
when Szilard fucked their boss till she turned blue. Escaped convicts. Fleeing civvies. And the last of SpaceCom's marines. There's
nowhere else to go but—

"Deeper," says Sarmax.

E veryone's trying to get out of the way," says Jarvin.
Spencer nods as their train keeps on hurtling
through the warrens. He's been picking up many of the
same signals. The lunar underground is like a jungle that's being
overrun by army ants. All of the denizens are on the move.
Everyone's under pressure. Including all too many who thought
they'd gotten out of the way for good . . .

"Choosing the wrong side can be a bitch," says Jarvin.

"I guess you should know," says Spencer.

"And you should thank your lucky stars for that."

"You'd better put up or shut up. We need to find—"

"We're almost on top of it."

"And the Eurasians are almost on top of *us*."

She knows it all too well. Sinclair's going to be on her any moment. She can feel his mind breaking out beneath her. The thought of seeing his face in the flesh terrifies her—even more so than the structures of the outer Room that she's being hauled past—all the structures that she couldn't see for certain on the way in, and that are now flashing past her eyes: vast pillars-that-aren't-pillars, some of them supporting impossibly gigantic terrariums suspended like massive pods, glowing green with the flora they contain, all of them wrapped in the endless labyrinthine piping that coils everywhere like the entrails of some giant beast. She can't even see the inner Room below her now—she's set the controls of the elevator for maximum speed and is streaking up the funicular far faster than she descended. The real zone of this place is coming alive all around her, a texture she's never encountered. She wonders what its next move will be. She jury-rigs the controls of the elevator to push it beyond its safety margins, hurtling upward to where she begins to glimpse something that just might pass for ceiling.

Explosions rumbling through long kilometers of tunnel, distant noise of firing, endless shards of fragmented zone: Lynx continues to take stock. He's got a better read on the SpaceCom forces now. The elite marines remaining to Szilard are bunched into two groups: rearguard and everyone else. The real question is where Szilard himself is. And farther down the fighting is intensifying—

"Not looking good," says a voice.

"Who the hell's this?" says Lynx.

⊕ T hat'd be me," says the Operative.

"Fuck's sake," says Lynx.

"Whatever," says the Operative. No zone now, all mental—and he's holding the channel open with almost no effort. He's surprised at just how adroit he's getting. It was strange to go through life for so long without any of this—even stranger to go through the next stage with the ability in latent form, just aware of the *presence* of Lynx and Sarmax, but with neither nuance or range beyond that. He's not even sure what's propelling him to these new heights. Maybe it's the influence of Velasquez. Maybe it's simply the onset of the end-times. Because now he knows how insignificant his abilities are compared to the real masters of the game.

"We're out of time," he says.

"That's why we're on the line," adds Velasquez.

"Who the hell's that?" says Lynx.

"Your worst nightmare," replies Sarmax.

Ø T hat's about how Spencer's feeling. He and Jarvin are doubling back and forth through the nearside rail-networks, trying to triangulate on the place that Jarvin is so sure of yet just can't seem to find. Judging by the shaking of this tunnel, the Eurasian machinery is only a few levels up now.

"Other way," says Jarvin.

"Again?"

"This time I'm sure."

"No kidding."

But Spencer turns the vehicle anyway, heads down the new passage. Maglev gives way to rails—which give out after a few more klicks, leaving Spencer to power them onward by rockets. Lights flicker across the klicks. And finally—

"Dead end."

"I don't think so," says Jarvin.

Spencer doesn't either. Because there's definitely some kind of machinery on the other side of this rock. Some kind of zone. But it's not like anything he's ever seen. And as to hacking it—

"Fuck!"

"What?" says Jarvin.

"That burns."

"It takes a light touch"—and Spencer feels Jarvin's mind brush by his, reach out onto the zone. A section of wall slides away. Spencer stares at the elevator car revealed—and then he claps slowly.

"Never doubted you," he says.

Jarvin looks at him, shrugs. "Makes one of us."

The ceiling of the outer Room hurtles toward her, the structures through which she's been passing falling away like the tower tops of some vast, demented city. She has yet to see any sign of Sinclair coming after her. As far as she can tell, he's still exactly where he was to begin with—back in the hub. She's beginning to wonder if that's a decoy. He could be somewhere in the ceiling itself, hiding within the psychic emanations of the membrane, waiting for her. She's analyzing that membrane now—running her mind across it. She braces herself, runs the sequences on the trapdoors coming ever closer.

Okay," says the Operative. "We're all on the same line now."

Or at least the ones who count. Velasquez is speaking for her triad. As far as the Operative knows, she's speaking for Sarmax, too. That man seems happier than he's been in years. It's something that seems to amuse Lynx considerably, a few hundred klicks distant.

"Finally found your dream girl, huh? Too bad the world's gonna end in a couple more minutes—"

"Go fuck yourself," says Sarmax.

"Shut up," says the Operative. "All of you *shut up and listen.* Our only hope of getting through this is by combining all our forces. And that starts with us getting on the same fucking page. And we're in a combat situation, so here's how it's going to work: I'm going to make a series of statements, and if I say *anything* that *any* of you disagree with—or if you know something that puts that fact in a new light—then *now's the time to fucking say it.* Okay?"

No one says anything.

"Okay," he says. "Sinclair's in the Room and he's switching everything on."

Static. The Operative watches on the zone as their positions close upon one another . . .

"He's got Haskell in there with him," he adds.

"We don't know that for sure," says Lynx.

The Operative laughs. "Don't we? He's fucking with the *fabric of fucking reality.* Which is shifting *under our fucking feet.*"

No one replies.

"So all this war, all this fighting—everything that ever mattered, everything that ever will—all of it is coming down to one thing: whether we can get into the Room before Sinclair finishes hitting buttons."

"But why hasn't he yet?" says Velasquez.

"A good question."

"It's *the* question," she says.

"And we can't wait for the answer—"

"Has it occurred to you that he's waiting for *us?*" asks Sarmax.

"Yes," says the Operative.

They mull that over

"But I can't see why," he adds. "Haskell's the one who—"

"She may not even be *alive,*" says Sarmax. "He may have already *processed* her—"

"Doesn't matter," says the Operative. "All that matters is that it's all converging. That's why the East's shock-troops are heading deeper as fast as they can deploy onto the lunar surface. That's why Szilard is—"

"—at the bottom," says Lynx.

A pause. "You sure about that?"

"His advance-guard's reached the fucking *labyrinth*."

Through the doors and membrane of the Room and that's where she is, too. Sinclair's fucking labyrinth. A maze of impossible deathtraps that guard the main entrance to the Room, nestled in between the two perimeters—waves of zone and psychic signals assail her brain, and she can barely tell where the walls are. It doesn't matter, though, because she's plowing ahead anyway, her suit-jets flaring as she dives between hypersharp filaments that spring out toward her, but she's maneuvering on pure future now—a moment ahead of all of it as she dodges past the first of the traps, ascending away from the Room ever farther into the maze to end all mazes.

They're plunging downward at unholy speeds, pressed up against the ceiling as they accelerate. Turns out this elevator's state-of-the-art maglev. They're rapidly closing the distance between them and Moon's core . . .

"Does this bypass the front door?" says Spencer.

"I sure as shit hope so," says Jarvin. "His labyrinth's a killing zone. Nothing's getting through there."

Spencer gestures at the elevator. "So how do you know about *this*?"

Jarvin shrugs. "A file I cracked and never wrote down. Sinclair's special entrance so he could bypass all the crap."

"So we might run into him en route."

"Sooner or later, we're *going* to run into him. And when we do, we're going to give him a little surprise."

"What the hell are you talking about?"

"I want you to promise me something, Spencer: if it doesn't work—do *not* let me fall alive into his hands."

"If *what* doesn't work?"

"I was one of his *handlers,* Spencer. And no matter what I've been telling you, the truth is that I know *way* too much about what he's trying to do."

"More than *this?* More than the fucking download we just got from the AI? We're talking about the ability to fuck with *everything*—"

"And even that's nothing. He'll show no mercy to me. So if it all goes wrong—I need you to promise me you'll kill me before that happens."

"I might kill you *long* before that happens."

"Now we're talking," says Jarvin.

All their minds are linked now. They're maneuvering in upon the center of the SpaceCom position—Lynx and Linehan streaking in from the rear, the Operative and Riley and Maschler about to hit the flank. Sarmax and the Rain triad are getting out in front of where they think Szilard is. The plan's simplicity itself: take Szilard from every direction and take him out, take over his forces and use them as cannon fodder against the labyrinth and Room. Their firepower is a mere fraction of Szilard's elite marines, but they've got the upper ground on zone. And their minds are now operating at a level that nothing within the SpaceCom ranks can touch. They can't nail the minds of the Com troops. They're not that good. But they can put them under pressure all the same . . .

◐   A nd she can feel it—the emanations of those Rain minds like smoke wafting high above her, shimmering through the endless mist of labyrinth, spreading fear and confusion among the SpaceCom ranks. It's as she expected. No single one of the players is strong enough to stay alive solo, but combined their minds comprise a factor. As opposed to the minds of those now stumbling into the farside of the labyrinth—the SpaceCom advance forces. She can feel their spirits winking out like lights being extinguished as they make it barely inside the labyrinth before being liquidated, and it's all she can do to avoid the same fate herself; she twists and turns and pushes herself off walls and prays she won't hit one of the thousand dead ends or any of the ten thousand traps—prays that she wasn't seeing the faceless visage of Control looming before her. But God died a long time ago.

∅   P ursuit," says Jarvin, and his voice has gone all taut.
     Spencer picks it up too. Several kilometers back. Another maglev car.

"Who the fuck is that?" he mutters:

"Could be Sinclair himself," says Jarvin. For the first time he's starting to look less than calm . . .

"Or guardians of this shaft," says Spencer. He and Jarvin are doing what they can to get in on the strange zone that constitutes this whole route, running their hacks to commandeer the car they're in and keep the electricity running as they shoot down rails toward the depths of Moon. But that other car's making good progress all the same. It's several klicks back, and there's something more than a little strange about its zone-signature . . . to the point where it's almost like it's not there . . .

"Oh *fuck*," says Jarvin.

Lynx and Linehan sweep in between the units guarding Szilard's inner position, heading straight toward it, exchanging fire, then drawing off—a feint that pulls a good chunk of Szilard's flank with it. Tunnels are folding up around them as the marines give chase. Lynx and Linehan start to double around, back toward Szilard's command post—

What the fuck are you doing?" yells the Operative. "Going for it," says Lynx.

The Operative can see he's not kidding. The plan was for Lynx and Linehan to make the feint and then let the rest of them get in there. But Lynx has never been one for playing second fiddle. And the Operative figures maybe that's just as well. If Szilard's still got anything up his sleeve, then maybe Lynx can be the one to find out first. The Operative signals to Riley and Maschler to get out on the hull as he maneuvers their vehicle in on the heart of the Com defenses . . .

Still playing their fucking games," says Velasquez. "They can't stop," says Sarmax.

Apparently. The final twenty klicks, and it's total chaos. Lynx and the Operative are veering around Szilard's mobile strongpoint like wolves around a campfire. Half the Com forces are fighting one another as their minds go. But the inner enclave of Szilard's handpicked marines are holding steady, defending their president, their ranks still unbroken. They're continuing to forge their way down toward the labyrinth. Which the advance guard has already penetrated—

"And gotten annihilated," says Velasquez.

"Takes a special kind of maniac to go in there."

She's threading through the web of passages and somehow it helps that she doesn't even know which ones are in her mind and which ones are carved in rock. All she knows is that Control's looming before her like a disembodied ghost.

"Turn back, Claire."

"What do you think I've already done?"

"I think you're being very foolish."

"When I want your opinion, you'll be the first to know."

"*Matthew* thinks you're being very foolish."

"Which is why he's coming after me."

"And you're not moving fast enough."

"He's afraid of me, isn't he."

"Try to have some perspective, Claire."

"I'll show you fucks a thing or two about perspective."

"Will you really?" Control laughs, and the noise is hideous. "Szilard's fed a thousand soldiers into this labyrinth already. None of them made it more than five seconds. We'll see how much better you can do. Give the old man a run for his money—why not? All the better, in fact. We need a fighter. We *bred* a fighter. Someone who'll resist to the end of existence and beyond."

"Precisely," she says—and hits his mind full force.

What's the problem?" yells Spencer.

"It may be a decoy," says Jarvin.

"Fuck."

It's hard to tell. Which is probably the point. It's made all the tougher by the fact that they've got no option than to stay on these rails. Because it's all linear. There's nothing in here but this shaft. They plunge onward while the pursuit closes in above them and they start to face up to the fact that the real pursuers may be elsewhere—

"Keep your eye on what's below us," says Jarvin.

"My thoughts exactly," mutters Spencer.

ynx and Linehan impact onto the core of Szilard's formation, slicing through it, blasting shit aside— bombs flung off to nail huge tractor-tanks trying to maneuver down rift-galleries . . . Lynx is splintering the zone in the faces of the Com marines as Linehan fires away. Bodies are flying.

"He's moving," says the Operative.

"I see it," says Velasquez.

Szilard's dwindling forces are still heading forward. The Operative takes a look at the fading zone sensors way overhead, looks at the camera-feeds on all those endless kilometers of upper levels, the lunar cities swarming with the ravaging Eurasian infantry, the slaughter now developing among the civilian populations—they are sparing no one, the Operative notes. He starts detecting wave anomalies radiating out from the Room—

s the vanguard of Szilard's bodyguards slams straight into Sarmax and Velasquez's position, shape-charges eviscerating the marines as their second rank comes up. Sarmax can see Szilard's retinue accelerating even further, abandoning most of the troops and dodging past his position—

"Suicide run now," says Carson.

"Or he knows something we don't," says Lynx.

"I'm picking up something weird from the labyrinth," says Sarmax.

t's like all the ambience around her is really a liquid through which she's swimming—like she's still back in that tank in Montrose's bunker beneath Korolev—like all of it was memory or the event horizon of the initial drug surge... she stares at Control, who wears way too many faces; she composes her own while she slices straight through him, crushing in on his cognition—*"How's it fucking feel,"* she's hissing—and she can sense he's *hurting,* and writhing; his mind slithers out of her grasp, retreats in disarray while she powers past him and through the other side of membrane. She stumbles through the far side of the labyrinth, emerging in a cave. Marines stare at her, start falling to their knees.

Picking up something ahead," says Jarvin.

"Fuck," says Spencer.

Maybe it's the thing they've been running from. Maybe it's something new. It doesn't t matter. They've got no choice but to go straight through it. They accelerate, start ripping out the elevator floor, getting ready to open up on whatever materializes in the shaft below. They're almost on it.

Lynx and Linehan start the final run, vectoring in on Szilard's position at near point-blank range. The best that can be said about the marines' resistance is that it's heroic. Lynx's mind flays the meat of cerebellum as he uses the zone like a whip and augments the guns of Linehan, who's roaring down the tunnel and into a cavern, straight onto one of three Remoraz-class crawlers moving like mountain goats down the walls. One of the crawlers crashes into the other as Lynx destroys their software: both crawlers lose their grip, tumble exploding to the cavern floor. Linehan's doing his best to get through the armor of the thing he's hanging onto. Marines elsewhere in the cavern start firing at him—and then Carson and Maschler and Riley come in through a different entrance and start cleaning them up. Linehan's tearing off the treads of the crawler, ripping out its rocket engines to strand it as a metal coffin. He sticks several shape-charges onto the side, jets away. Lynx enters the room as they detonate.

G et him," says the Operative.
　　But Maschler and Riley are already on it—joining up with Linehan to apprehend any survivors, closing on the president's presumed position. The Operative and Lynx alight on opposite walls of the cavern—supervising the salvage operation that's going on below while they scan—

"Executive node intact," says Lynx.

"Roger that," says the Operative.

But he's also picking up intensifying pulses from the direction of the labyrinth—from the direction of the Room—like a tsunami building—

"The old man's going for it," he says.

"Easy," says Lynx. "We'll take it as it comes."

"Clear," shouts Linehan. Lynx and the Operative vector down to the ledge on which the wrecked vehicle's laying while their three mechs take up covering positions. In short order Lynx and the Operative stand above Jharek Szilard, whom they've propped up against the side of the crawler. Blood cakes the inside of his armor. He's still alive, but only barely. Lynx laughs.

"Nice to see you again, Admiral."

Szilard shrugs—winces. "Played it . . . best I could . . ."

"No disputing that," says the Operative.

"But . . . didn't have your *minds* . . ."

"You wouldn't *want* our minds."

"I'd have . . . given anything for them . . ."

"To dare to modify yourself like Sinclair," says Lynx.

Szilard shakes his head. "So here's everything I know," he mutters, beaming over all key Com files.

"And the executive node?" asks Lynx.

Szilard flips the Operative a chip, who nods as he catches it—

"You realize this won't save you?"

"Nothing can save me," says Szilard. "Sinclair's mind is swallowing us all—"

"You feel it too?"

"How could I not?"

The Operative nods—shoots Szilard through the head and slots the chip into an interface in one of his guns.

"How's it feel to be president?" says Lynx.

A man could ask for better circumstances," says a woman's voice. Sarmax and the Rain triad blast into the chamber, take up positions above the mechs, point their weapons—

"Sarmax gets to be the prez," adds Velasquez.

"You really think it matters?" says Lynx.

"It's our only chance of fending off whatever the fuck's coming up from the Room," says Sarmax. "We need to combine minds far more seamlessly than we've done so far. One of us is going to have to step up and be the focal node."

"And you really think that should be *you?*" says Lynx.

"I don't know what to think," says Sarmax.

"But Indigo does," says Carson. "Fuck, talk about upward mobility. We give this thing to you, and *she'll* be running things."

Velasquez shrugs. "I've got the strongest mind of anyone here."

"Bullshit," says Carson.

"I'm the last leader of the last *real* Rain triad."

"And I sat at the right hand of Matthew Sinclair while we cooked you fucks up."

"And you both never knew when to settle," says Sarmax. He feels like existence itself is beating against his face. The force that's surging in from the Room seems to be taking on an almost physical form, it's that strong. Sarmax looks at Velasquez. "Kid, let him have the fucking node. We've got no time—"

"That's for sure," says Claire Haskell.

She steps into the cavern and she can see the effect she's having on them—can see that at least some of them can see the auras she's radiating. She can see that they get it—that what they thought were psychic shockwaves emanating from the Room was actually her approaching their position. She stares for a long moment around the cavern—the shattered vehicles, the corpse of Szilard, the suited figures awaiting her next move. Her mind leaps out from there to encompass all the Moon beyond that, flitting past the Eurasians sweeping in from every direction upon the disintegrating American perimeters to focus in upon one remote corner of the nearside where Spencer and Jarvin are arriving in a room that contains the equipment they've been seeking. Her mind drops directions into Spencer's head even as she notices Linehan dropping to his knees.

Get the fuck up," says the Operative. Linehan gets up, backs away. His face looks ashen. The Operative wonders whether the ayahuasca has made him more or less able to accept everything that's going on. He wonders what Haskell must be feeling right now—if it's even Haskell they're dealing with—

"So what's this about you being president?" she asks.

"That's what we were discussing," says Velasquez.

"There's nothing to be president of," says Haskell evenly.

"Surely someone has to run the resistance," says Lynx.

"That'd be me," says Claire Haskell. The Operative can feel her reaching into his head, activating the executive node, sending out the orders—her mind racing out to all the fragments of the zone in the American forces now fighting across the lunar environs—

Y NAME IS MANILISHI. THE RUMORS OF MY EXIS- TENCE ARE TRUE. I LEAPT INTO SOUTH POLE WHILE ALL YOUR CAMERAS WATCHED AND ALL YOUR GUNS COULD DO NOTHING. I FOUGHT AT THE SIDE OF PRESIDENT HARRISON. I'M HERE TO RALLY ALL AMERICAN FORCES. I CALL UPON ALL WHO ARE STILL ALIVE TO COMBINE—THOSE WHO SERVED HARRISON, THOSE WHO SERVED MONTROSE OR SZILARD—TO REMEMBER THAT WE ARE STILL THE UNITED STATES. FIGHT THE EAST WITH EVERY MEANS AT YOUR DISPOSAL WHILE I TEAR THEM APART WITH MY MIND, WHICH GOD HIMSELF SENT TO LIGHT UP OUR DARKEST HOUR. FIGHT ON, FOR OUR CAUSE IS JUST. FIGHT ON, AND MAY THE HEAVENS FIGHT FOR US.

I thought you said there was nothing worth being presi- dent of," says Lynx.

"There isn't," says Haskell.

They stare at her.

"It's just a rearguard action," she says. "Buy us some time to get back to the Room; keep the Eurasians from that door as long as possible."

Velasquez looks confused. "Your mind can't—"

"—stop the Eurasians in their tracks? I'm not *that* good."

"Not yet," says the Operative.

She shrugs. "I could probably drive the first hundred thousand of them nuts, but the odds have become overwhelming. We're out-numbered by at least ten to one. And as the bulk of their fleet lands they'll eventually just send in waves of robots shorn from zone."

"*No one* has an angle on the Eurasians?" asks Sarmax.

"I assumed that *someone* was controlling them," says Lynx.

"That someone being Sinclair?"

"Or one of the other Rain triads," says Sarmax.

"The Eurasians no longer matter," says Haskell.

"What about us?" asks Linehan. He's daring now to look at this woman who seems so familiar—realizes now he's seen her before, but how he failed to see her for real he has no idea. Because now there are colors dripping off her, and some kind of energy glowing in her that's a pale fraction of something that's emanating from the rock below. Linehan realizes his mind's come totally apart. And if it hasn't, then he's probably died and has reached the afterlife for real. He knows how afterlifes work, too—one false step and you're fucked for all eternity. Only by following this woman can he hope to stay true. She's giving orders now, and everyone's scrambling to carry them out—powering up their jets, following her ever deeper into Moon—

"Where the hell are we going?" asks the Operative. "You really think I'm going to talk to *you?*" says Haskell.

He figured it was worth a try. They're heading down a series of ramps, moving through ground that's obviously already been prepared. Szilard's advance guard deployed here during the last hour. Haskell herself came this way less than ten minutes ago. The remainder of the SpaceCom marines in this sector fan out on either side, letting their new mistress pass through, along with her entourage—

⊙ ——She figures she'd better revel in her moment of power, because she's about to go up against the ultimate foe. Why Sinclair didn't confront her directly back in the Room, she doesn't know. Perhaps he figured Control would be enough to stop her. Perhaps he doesn't need her after all. She rounds a corner to see the shimmering transluscence of the membrane blocking the way ahead.

"Here's how we're going to do this," she says—starts to give commands. And they're doing exactly what she tells them— bunching together, getting in close. She can tell that goes against all their instincts—that the last thing any of them want is to be so near that their armor's touching. But she needs to envelop them all with her mind's shield. She's giving last orders to the SpaceCom marines, telling them to defend to the end. She knows that ultimately the Eurasians will be able to reach this point anyway. But unless she screws up, they won't be going any farther. And if she's right about what's about to happen, none of it will matter anyway. She synchronizes everyone on the zone that's all her own and gives the orders to get moving into that membrane—

⊚ And they do. Fast. It's all Linehan can do to keep up— all he can do to stay sane as apparitions loom before him and spirits gibber at him—hollow-eyed ghosts staring straight through the barrier that Haskell's slung up around him, pressing against his head. It's like those things are pounding against his skull, trying to break in—like all of reality's boiling inside his head. When it boils away maybe he'll see straight through to what's been hidden from him all this time. He grits his teeth, follows this woman-who's-no-woman as she keeps on driving forward—

W hat the fuck are we dealing with, Carson?"
Lynx's voice sounds as on edge as the
Operative has ever heard—the voice of a man grasping
for something to hold on to and falling way too short. The
Operative is almost tempted to just let Lynx stew. But he can't be
sure he won't be going there himself any moment now. So he lets
himself just describe.

"Sinclair's got a psychic moat," he says. "Something that no
normal mind could pass."

"Not too many abnormal ones either," says Lynx.

Nor is the mind enough. Reflexes are at a premium as well.
Maschler, Riley, Linehan, Lynx, the Operative, Velasquez, and the
other two members of her triad—they're all following the instructions that Haskell's flashing to them, following her as she forges
forward—

I t's a little easier because she's been this way before. The
only way to get in or out of the Room without using a
teleporter—but the labyrinth's geometry is unreliable. It
shifts every time one passes through it, is never the same thing
twice. She figures that's fitting—she gets a glimpse of Sinclair as a
minotaur lurking in the catacombs of eternity, of herself as
Theseus threading the final maze toward him. She senses more
emanations foaming in from the Room, senses something new—

A nd when we get there?" asks Sarmax.
"We do whatever she says," says Velasquez.
"What aren't you telling me?"

"What makes you think I'm not telling you something?"

Long experience. He's considering all the angles as the maelstrom of the labyrinth whirls around them; he's realizing that

she's playing at something, and he's not sure he can stand to know—not sure that Haskell doesn't know already—

"Control yourself," hisses Velasquez, "or she will."

"Our minds—"

"*Your* mind is under my protection. And mine is the only one that this superbitch can't penetrate."

"This *superbitch* is the only thing that can stop Matthew Sinclair—"

"She's playing right into his hands," snarls Velasquez.

Nor is she under any illusions on *that* score. There's no contingency she can adopt that might not be something that Sinclair's counting upon. Every stratagem she deploys might merely be the inverse of one of his. Every action she takes might be one more step in his master plan. His progeny have operated with all too many plans—all too many scenarios . . . and maybe they're all just part of the design of the one who set it all in motion. But now she's on the point of returning to the Room with the most elite armed escort ever seen. The fact that she doesn't know whom among that escort she can trust is something she intends to turn to her advantage. She's going to stay one step ahead of Sinclair yet. She powers through the other side of the membrane—glances back as they come on through behind her, almost laughs at the looks on their faces.

PART V
AUTUMN RAIN

hat's your problem?" asks the Operative.

It figures. Alone of all of them, he's already processed the Room's vast contents—takes them in with a single glance and the expression of a man who resolved long ago never to be surprised. He's thus the only one to notice the expression on her face.

"Sinclair's no longer here," she says. "Neither is Control."

"Be more precise."

"I can't detect them."

"That's more like it," says the Operative.

She nods—starts giving orders. The group starts to deploy onto parallel elevator-trains. Riley, Maschler, and the Operative in one; Sarmax, Velasquez, and her triad in another; Linehan, Lynx, and herself in the third. They drop down toward the inner Room, trying to make sense of what they're seeing—

W e're in the kingdom of heaven," says Linehan.
"Shut up" says Lynx.

But it's true all the same. Even if Lynx is too blind to see, Linehan's not . . . and all he can do is thank God for sending him this—for giving him this life, for taking him to this place where all paths converge. He sights his guns on those terrariums sprawling past—vast shimmering walls that contain more greenery then he's ever seen.

S o the stories were true," says Velasquez.
"Every last one," says Sarmax.

T his is just gone," says Maschler.
"It'd be even better if someone explained it," says Riley.
"Just keep your eyes peeled," says the Operative.

T he Room's stretching out all around her in the panoply of false color and she can't see any movement anywhere. But the Operative's right: Sinclair's still here. Where else could he be? Especially with the Room continuing to power up. Behind her, she can sense the membrane's energy reaching the critical threshold. The voice of the Operative drifts in past her.

"No way anything's getting through that now," it says.

"When I want your opinion I'll ask for it," she snaps—cuts him off. She gets what he's driving at, though. Sinclair *could* have stopped her from leaving the Room. Or maybe not . . . maybe he hadn't throttled up the Room's engines enough by that point. Truth of the matter is that she no longer knows. It's like she's driving full tilt into black. She's on the cusp of future now, can no longer see anything in front of her. She hasn't felt this way since before she knew she was Manilishi. She figures it's only fitting— that she's come full circle. She starts to get glimpses of the inner Room gleaming in the distance.

What in fuck's name is *that*?" asks Riley.
"The end of the road," says the Operative.
"We got movement," says Maschler.

No one fire," she says.
No one is. They're just looking at the two insect-like figures standing on the very surface of the sphere that's now coming into view. Those two figures are looking up at them.
"You made it," she says.

Wasn't easy," says Spencer.
But the directions the Manilishi gave him were enough to do the trick, using one of two teleport chambers with the ability to reach the Room directly. All the others were just sideshows. But all that matters now is—
"We were being followed," he says.
"By who?"
"They were Rain. Couldn't tell beyond that."
"But you blew the rig behind you?"
"Yeah. There's no way they could have—"

"Assume nothing," she says.

"Yes ma'am."

"This man you have with you?"

"Alek Jarvin—"

"High time I talked to him."

You were Sinclair's man," she says as she scans his mind.

"I was cut off in HK when he was arrested."

"I know."

"He wants to make himself God Almighty."

"He may already have," she says. "Who was following you?"

"His final triad."

She nods. She's presuming it was the same one that pursued her. But why it would still be operating outside the Room makes no sense to her. The only thing that counts now is in here. Meaning she has to assume that somehow that triad got in too. Thus the dilemma: it's imperative to destroy your teleportation devices behind you, yet you can never be totally sure you've done it. The fact that Sinclair still has servants is one more reason why she's sought to acquire her own—one more reason why she's not going in alone. The metal to which Spencer and Jarvin have affixed their armor starts to slide aside. The inner Room's opening once again, in accordance with her zone-instructions. She gives more orders, watches as everyone starts to scramble from the elevator cars.

Ｓeb Linehan," says Spencer.

Linehan looks at him with eyes that seem to have gone hollow. "Spencer," he whispers slowly.

"Good to see you again, man."

"I'm not the man you remember," says Linehan.

"Let's move," says the Operative.

Ｔhe inner Room's as she left it. Except for the fact that there's no longer any presence looming here. She stares through the maze of ramps and girders at the innermost sphere of all. She can detect nothing within. But there's only one way to be sure. The ceiling of the inner Room slides shut above them as they close in on the hub that sits astride the very center.

Ｙou've got to listen to me," says the Operative.

"I know what I'm doing," she says.

"He's in here somewhere."

"I realize that."

"He could be one of us."

But she just nods. That's one scenario she's playing—that when she first showed up maybe Control had been assigned to hold down the place with deceptions and that Sinclair has only arrived in this Room just now, disguised as somebody else. In which case he undoubtedly thinks he's got her where he wants her. She welcomes any such thinking. She's in the final stages of a duel she's been fighting all her life. Even if she's only just waking up to that fact. The doors to the core of Room slide open.

O h Jesus Christ," says Lynx.
       Better than any drug he's ever ridden: glow pours
out at him as though the thing in the depths of Moon is
really a captured sun. But as his visors adjust, he can see that's
merely a function of the lights and mirrors he's descending
through. Vast pipes run down the walls, shimmering as though
through heat. Screens everywhere show views throughout the
Earth-Moon system: the Eurasian legions consolidating their hold,
the first power in history to achieve total domination of humanity.
But now those screens are starting to blur with static—

"We're getting cut off," says Haskell.

A nondescript interface on just one more piece of pip-
       ing: the controls at the very hub of the Room are ex-
posed for all to see. She expected as much—expected, too,
to see the pod that hangs above them, the door that hangs open,
the form-fitted couch that she's sure is contoured for her exactly.
But what she hadn't expected to see are the three canisters hanging around it—three more pods sprouting out, almost as though
they're the legs of a tripod. Each pod's doors are partially open, giving them the look of metal flowers. She turns to Carson.

"You know I have to do this," she says.

J ust you? What about—"
       "Just defend my flesh."
       He nods. Perhaps she's scanned him to her satis-
faction. Perhaps his betraying her is merely one scenario among
many. He knows that he's no longer capable of lifting a hand
against her knowingly. But he also knows he wouldn't be the first
in whom compulsions arose from out of the depths of past. He

watches for a moment as Haskell climbs out of her armor, her strangely inked skin visible on all the places her clothes don't cover. She climbs into the machine at the Room's center. He turns, starts giving the orders for a perimeter to be established.

She pulls herself into the pod while the rest scramble to take up their positions. All but one. Haskell isn't surprised to see who. Velasquez looks at her—

"What the fuck are you *doing*?" she asks.

"Throwing the last switch."

"He *wants* you to do that, Claire."

"How the fuck else am I going to draw him out?"

Velasquez takes the meaning. "None of my triad—"

"Keep a close eye on them all the same," snaps Haskell. The canopy closes around her.

What the hell's going on?" asks Linehan. "Shut up and get ready to fight," says the Operative. He wasn't expecting things to get so complicated tactically. Especially because now he sees that everybody's starting to get it. Everybody knows everybody else is suspect. Just like everybody's always been . . .

"Let's hope it's that simple," says Lynx on the one-on-one—

—though he's not surprised when Carson refuses to respond to him. He gets it—the less said the better. He watches the contours of the Room all around him— watches Carson give orders as everyone takes up positions, spreading out along a quarter-klick radius around the Room's hub. Lynx doubts that whatever happens next is going to be pleasant. Especially because he's heard enough about this Room to know that there's a lot more to it than meets the eye. That no normal blueprint could possibly encompass all the spaces it contains. He watches as the machinery throttles up all around him.

She's doing the same. It's all swirling in toward her now and it's all she can do to keep up with it. Her DNA sequences and brainwaves are interfacing directly with the Room now. The machinery is revving up along its final sequence, approaching the point of no return. Her mind flashes out through the minds of all those around her; she sees even deeper within, still doesn't see what she's looking for as she scans every meter of the Room, searching for the pockets and folds of the Room that are beyond all normal scans. She watches the external membrane blaze into critical mass as the energy from those dying outside keeps on pouring into it, keeps on dripping down toward her, surging her awareness to ever greater heights as she suddenly realizes the nature of Sinclair's servants—

The Operative's already on it. He's whirling to confront them as they open fire. Everyone starts shooting. Riley and Maschler are getting knocked back by fire from every direction. They're giving as good as they get—focusing on Velasquez and her triad, taking one of that team out as shots rock the core of the Room. The Operative finds himself wondering for a moment about the redundancy of the machinery around him—and then he and Linehan are catapulting into Maschler, knocking his already-damaged suit against the wall, smashing through the visor, watching blood spill down the man's face.

Maschler's eyes are still open, though. "Manilishi busted you," says the Operative.

Maschler winces—looks over to where Riley's dead body is getting dragged out of his suit. "Whatever happened to asking questions *first?*" he mutters.

"You happened," says the Operative. "Where's Sinclair?"

"Think I know that?"

The Operative reaches out with a fist, starts applying pressure to Maschler's skull. "What *do* you know?" he asks.

And even as Carson asks the question, she knows what Maschler's going to say. Something funny about the consciousness she's revving through right now—taking the retrocausality that defines her to the next level, effect preceding cause . . . fucked if she knows how that's happening, but right now she's got a couple of answers she hadn't bargained on. Maschler and Riley weren't just everyman pilots—weren't just InfoCom agents either. They were Sinclair's henchmen all along. And they showed their hand because—

"She's got a nuke," mutters Maschler as his eyes close.

The Operative realizes immediately who he's talking about, Haskell's mental command redundant as he whirls to confront—

"What are you doing?" says Sarmax.

"Begging your woman not to do it," says the Operative.

Indigo Velasquez looks at them both. Her remaining Rain commando has his guns out. Lynx has drawn as well. Spencer, Jarvin, and Linehan have positioned themselves between the stand-off and Haskell. Velasquez looks around—laughs.

"So I brought in a bomb," she says. "So what?"

"So what the fuck did you do that for?" demands Sarmax.

"Because this place is accursed," she says. "We need to—"

"Defuse that bomb," snarls the Operative. "Indigo, we're going to win through yet. You don't need to—"

"I do," she says—looks at him with a strange expression—

nd Haskell recognizes its meaning all too well. Indigo's already made up her mind—already decided that humanity's better off without this Room. And Haskell's not even sure she can disagree. Even if America's been lost, even if the Chinese are going to rule mankind for ten thousand years, even if all is pain and suffering from here on in, it might *still* be better than living on the sufferance of those within this chamber. Especially if that domination passed to Matthew Sinclair. But Haskell's seen enough to wonder if Sinclair's actually counting on that nuke being detonated. Maybe that's the energy that'll propel her through the real barriers she's here to break. Even though those barriers seem to be coming down anyway. The membrane that surrounds the Room has gone white-hot. Her mind's not far behind—

ither she hits the brakes or I hit this," says Velasquez, holding up a fist-sized device.

"She can't hear you anymore," says the Operative.

"Indigo," says Sarmax, *"don't do this."*

"I have to," says Velasquez. *"All of you*—you all might be Sinclair's slaves. He's played us all and I don't even know what to call his fucking game—"

"Save that it involves playing you even now," says the Operative.

"You really believe that?" asks Sarmax.

The Operative shrugs. His mind is racing with no way out. By the time he fires, Velasquez can detonate. She probably has a dead-man switch anyway. She probably has it all taken care of. She's made her decision. Sarmax will have to make his. The Operative gets ready to move quicker than he ever has before. He braces himself—

—just as the three pods around Haskell glow; a suited figure steps from within one, firing as it emerges, catching Velasquez and the Rain commando in a hail of hi-ex rounds, blasting them both into the walls. The nuke tumbles down, bounces off Haskell's faceplate—doesn't go off. If it even *was* a nuke—the Operative's already rocketing in toward Velasquez. Sarmax scrambles past him—throws himself onto Velasquez—

"*Goddamn you,*" says Sarmax.

"Everyone stay where you are," says a voice.

She's the only one who's still moving—dropping away at right angles to all reality, her last glimpse of the Room is of those three figures who have just emerged onto the scene—their visors opaque, but there's something all too familiar about them—then her mind punctures through all barricades, leaving only blankness in its wake—

370 DAVID J. WILLIAMS

S he's done it," says the voice.

The Operative stares at the figure that seems to be the leader of these three—the other two taking up positions. One of them strides over to where Velasquez is laying—to where Sarmax is bending over her. The visor of that suit goes transparent.

Revealing the face of Jason Marlowe.

B ullshit," says Lynx.

"Hardly," says Marlowe.

"A clone," says Carson.

The triad's apparent leader raises his fist. "Spoken like a true Praetorian. Seen some files, convinced he knows the answer. But some answers are way beyond anyone's guessing."

"You can't die," mutters Sarmax. "You just can't—"

"She didn't have to," says the third figure.

"Sinclair?" asks Carson.

The figure turns, smashes him across the head with a single blow. It must be on zone as well—because Carson's armor is seizing up, sparks chasing themselves across it. His helmet's come off. The figure looks down at him.

"The name's Morat," he says.

W hat the fuck is going on?" says Linehan. He's trying to target his guns on these three, but he can't seem to pull the trigger. Something seems to be fucking with his armor. Something he can't fight. He no longer feels Haskell's presence in his mind. He hears Jarvin muttering to him about not calling attention to himself. But apparently it's too late. The lead figure is turning toward him.

"Linehan," it says.

"Who the hell are you?"

"Friend of your old pal Spencer's."

S pencer's staring. "Wait a second—"

"No need for it," says the figure.

"You're not—you can't be—"

"All this time, and that's all you can say?"

"You're Control."

"Of course."

F*uck,*" mutters the Operative, pulling himself off the floor, taking in the scene. Control, Morat, Marlowe— a triad if ever there was one. Though none of it makes any sense. Unless—

"So where the fuck's Sinclair?" he mutters.

"That's what we're going to find out," says Control.

E veryone out of your armor," says Morat.

"Not until you tell me what the fuck's going on," says Linehan.

"We're giving the orders," says Marlowe.

And Linehan's armor's starting to shut down. Control apparently has the high ground on zone. And Haskell seems to have withdrawn from the picture, enclosed expressionless within that pod as the machinery goes nova. Linehan blows seals, starts taking off his armor. Everyone else is doing the same.

"What about Indigo?" asks Sarmax. Tears streak his face. Linehan never could understand how any man could shed them. But now he gets it. He realizes he's crying himself—tears for all those he killed, all those whose lives he took, all those dying outside right now . . .

"Who cares?" says Marlowe.

"It's the rest of you that matter," says Morat.

 "You guys are rebel angels," says the Operative.

"Aren't we all?" says Control.

"Sinclair charged you with running shit behind the scenes."

"And all the while I was simply getting in behind him."

The Operative nods. He can't help but admire how state of the art Control's suit is. He wonders at the software packed within— wonders whether Control was ensconsed within it this whole time. He thinks about all that this Room contains—struggles to contain himself. He looks at Haskell through that pod's window, feels his heart overflowing. Everyone's stripped down to vests and pants now. Everyone looks strange. The three who still remain in armor look even more so. Especially because at least one of those suits encases no flesh whatsoever.

And now we're down to bedrock," says Control. "Either one of you is Matthew Sinclair or else the man's in hiding somewhere in the folds of Room. And here's how we're going to find out—"

"The 'folds of Room'?" asks Lynx.

Morat laughs. "Don't play stupid with us, Stefan. We all know this thing's a fucking tesseract."

"And it's about to be so much more," says Control.

"Except you guys miscalculated," says Carson.

"Why did you betray him?" mumbles Velasquez.

"Why did *you*?" Control moves over to where Velasquez is laying, Sarmax trying desperately to shield her—

"I realized what he was trying to do," she mumbles.

"And that didn't fill you with a longing to take it for yourself?"

"It filled me with a longing to somehow stop him."

"And thus your nuke. So we can rule you out as the old man—"

"Unless she's being particularly tricky," says Morat.

"She's not," says Control—fires a single bullet through her head.

T he Operative watches as Sarmax hurls himself at Control—watches while he gets punched in the face for his troubles, falling half-conscious across Velasquez's still-twitching body.

"The picture of romance," says Morat.

"Careful," says Marlowe.

"So, Jason, let me guess," says Lynx. "Mr. Cyber promised you Claire when it was all over."

"So what if he did?"

"He already rescued her once," says Morat. "Kept her on schedule. Back at Leo's place, got his heart all a-patter—"

"Shut the fuck up," says Marlowe.

"Hang on," says the Operative, "how the fuck do we know you're Jason anyway? What the hell are you, really?"

"Your worst nightmare," says Marlowe.

"A clone," says Lynx.

"No," says Control.

"A download," says the Operative.

"Nope," says Marlowe.

"*I'm* the download," says Morat.

"Leaving only one possibility," says Spencer.

They all look at him then, and he knows he'd better talk fast. They'll be suspecting he's Sinclair next—shooting him through the head on pure suspicion. But he's got to stand fast—got to get past this somehow. He can see there's still maneuvering room between the players—can see only one way to get the party started—

"Marlowe's from a parallel reality," he says.

"No," says Marlowe, *"you are."*

Spencer shrugs. "What are your memories?"

"I—what do you mean?"

"Did you kill Claire Haskell in your world?"

Marlowe looks like he's just been shot—like he's about to gun Spencer down. But Control just laughs: "Both of you calm down. You're not so different, really. You were all prepared. All your memories—all the focus *on* memory—and so many of those memories the recollections of your other selves. Thus the infinitely-reprogrammable agent. Thus the culmination of what those of you who survive might become—under *my* supervision, of course. Could there be a higher calling?"

"I'd like to think so," says Jarvin.

"You of all people should be on my side," says Control.

"You'd merely accomplish the abomination the old man was seeking."

"But with so much more aplomb, Alek. You're professional enough to admit that, no?" Control gestures at Haskell. "Sinclair prepared the ultimate bride—the end-of-all-flesh—and how can he be blamed for not seeing that the groom had to be silicon? Haskell's half synthetic herself anyway—receiving full-on transmissions from the beyond throughout both meat and circuitry. But it requires the machinery of the Room to exit the universe entirely. Powered by—"

"The minds of those dying outside," says Jarvin.

"You're joking," says Linehan.

"Wish I was," replies Jarvin.

"Sinclair should have had you terminated," says Control.

"He would have had he known about the file I was assembling."

"Which is where?"

"In my head. And you've damaged the software beyond repair—"

"I deliberately stopped short of that. So download the file before I remove it the old-fashioned—"

"It's yours," says Jarvin—a moment passes—

"This isn't complete," says Control.

"Spencer figured out the rest of it," says Jarvin.

Control steps away from Velasquez, moves in toward Spencer—who feels the scans within his body increasing—

"Sinclair's files," says Control. *"Give them to me."*

Spencer knows that Jarvin must be wondering if he's going to rat him out in return. He's severely tempted. It might redirect some of the pressure. Then again, it might prevent him from driving this conversation in the only direction that matters—

"You're a quantum computer," he says.

"The first," says Control.

"The last," snarls Carson. "This thing means to rule all futures—"

"I *am* all futures," says Control. "Calculations done across the multiverse—"

"That's all theoretical," snaps Sarmax.

"The theory's standing before your eyes," says Morat.

And Sinclair thought he could control it," says Lynx. He sees what the others are doing now, gets where the game to stay alive is going. But if you want to play, you've got to stick your neck out—

"Those teleporters out there," he says.

"What about them?" says Control.

"They aren't remote duplication, are they? They're point-to-point connections *sliced* through dimensional folds—"

"Thereby enabling travel faster than the speed of light," mutters Sarmax.

"One implication among many," says Spencer.

"Let's not overstate it," says Carson. "You'd still need to get out there the old-fashioned way—cross the fucking empty to *build* each gateway first. And that's assuming it *wasn't* remote—"

"This is pathetic," says Control. "You think to keep me prattling while Haskell breaks through. Gentlemen, *she's already there*. And I'm riding her mind all the way while we speak. And the only reason I'm even tolerating this conversation is so I can take Matthew Sinclair alive—"

"And learn something along the way," says Spencer.

"So hand over the goddamn files," says Morat.

Spencer deploys what's left of his skull's software, beams the files to Sarmax instead. Who starts from where he's cradling Velasquez, whirls around—

"What the fuck did you just do?" he asks.

"You've got copies of the files now," says Spencer.

"Fuck's sake," says Sarmax, "I already know the—"

"Mathematics?" Spencer laughs. "The blueprints for Control?"

"How about giving me a taste?" says Lynx.

"I'll give you a little more than that," says Control.

"Otherwise you can't seal off Sinclair's escape route," says Spencer. "Right?" He looks at that sightless face, tries to see behind those eyes-that-aren't-eyes. He feels a strange buzzing on the edge of his awareness—feels the Room starting to somehow *shift* around him. The others seem to sense it too.

"It's starting," says Morat. "We don't have time for—"

"We don't have time *period*," says Control. "It's all an illusion.

THE MACHINERY OF LIGHT 377

We're standing outside it all. And what's happening around us is par for the course when a being like me closes upon its origins. The armadas of the East batter at the door, the creatures of the West barred beyond their reach. None of us in here need give two shits. By now those fleets have melted away into a fucking *wave-function*."

"Existence ends at that membrane," mutters Sarmax.

"The Room's a no-room," says Linehan suddenly.

"The man nails it," says Lynx.

Linehan takes in Lynx's glance, realizes that everyone else is looking at him now, too. And no one had even thought twice about what was in his head till now. He shakes that head, knows he's got to clear it. He gets that he's been too much the brute to be the object of much suspicion. But disguise is all about surprise . . .

"Seb Linehan," says Control.

"Sure," says Linehan. "We met before."

"But now you've been down ayahuasca alley."

"Now I've—" and suddenly Linehan gets it: Control's the demon he's been running from this whole while, the beast that sits at the end of time and laps up all pretenders. All futures flow through this thing. That's the way this thing wants it. That's what Linehan's got to somehow stop. He glances at Haskell's form hovering above him. Or below. He can't tell. Time's doing the same thing space has already done, spreading out in all directions. All perspectives . . .

"As always, the man with the least training is the best trained." Linehan realizes that each word Control's speaking is a musical note intended to call up something from deep within him. "Ironic, no? What we're conscious of plays so little *real* role in riding the raw moment. Give a man drugs to awaken doors within him; you can't argue with the result. Ayahuasca, peyote, mushrooms,

LSD—whatever it takes: There's a reason shamans worldwide all did the same damn thing—tuned the nervous system to get in touch with the source. And yet modern society forgot. Even as its physics moved in directions that undermined the very assumptions that society was based on. There's infinite worlds out there. Infinite spaces beyond this one. And all of it only a vibration away. Sensitives *know* this. And with the right preparation, anyone can climb those gradients—"

"I didn't ask to be here," says Linehan.

"That doesn't matter," says Control.

"You've got something special planned for me."

"You're not alone in that."

"Goddamn it, I'm not Sinclair!"

"It doesn't matter"—and as Control says this, Morat sidles toward Linehan, who backs away from the oncoming suit.

"What the fuck is this?"

"We need what's in your brain."

"I don't know *anything*!"

"You don't have to," says Control. "Not when you've still got the files that Autumn Rain stashed on you back in Hong Kong."

"*Bullshit*," says Carson.

"Those were cleaned out of me a long time back," says Linehan.

"The surface ones, sure. They thought they'd given you the fake ones. Thought they were just a decoy. And everyone who busted you open thought they'd gotten to the bottom of it. Turns out they just weren't going far enough. Because the only way to the bottom of what's planted in *your* mind is via surgery."

"You guys are *crazy*," says Linehan.

"That's the least of your problems," says Morat—a buzzsaw emanates from his glove. Linehan keeps on backing up, backs into a corner—finds himself staring at Morat's implacable visor even as he wonders what the fuck's really going on, even as he realizes he's never going to find out—but now Morat suddenly staggers back—

"We're under attack," says Control—turns to Spencer—

Give me what you've got or you are *dead.*"

"Ask Sarmax."

"Man doesn't care if he's alive. You do. Two seconds—"

"Fine," says Spencer—beams it all over. Morat and Marlowe's suits are starting to smoke while they look around wildly—

"Not looking good," says Carson.

"Out of your suit," Control snarls at Marlowe. He leaps down to Morat, grabs him by the head—

"What are you *doing?*" yells Morat.

"Can't have you turned against me."

"For the love of God," says Morat—but Control's already tearing at Morat's head, ripping it off, tossing it past Haskell. What's left of Morat's smoking chassis flares out. Marlowe is climbing out of his suit, wearing the look of a man who's glad he still has a body. He grabs a weapon from a rack on his suit's leg—an automatic rifle—and points it at the others arrayed about.

"Everyone stay where you are," he yells.

Control leaps past him, lands in front of Spencer—who's wondering how he's going to get out of this one. The razor looks up into that visor-that's-no-visor, sees no mercy.

"Don't do it," he says anyway.

"Got to narrow it down," says Control—fires—

—everything winking out in one flashing photo-negative of this moment superimposed against all he's ever known, all he ever might have, all memories bound up in a single moment and past that moment is the Room itself receding from him at relentless speeds, collapsing away to reveal itself as a single fragment of a woman's face—

—Spencer's head explodes in a shower of brain; Control's already whirling toward Linehan, who starts to dive to the right—but Jarvin's leaping in at Control—flinging his body across several meters in less than a second—a move Linehan's never seen a human make outside of armor—and now Jarvin is clinging to the back of Control, screaming at him and tearing at him while Control struggles to shake him off. Sparks are flying everywhere. Marlowe moves in, trying to get a shot off—trying to line Jarvin up with the rifle—and then Marlowe grunts and topples, a dart sticking from his back—line of sight in the direction of—

"Leo?" says Carson.

"Watch out!" yells Sarmax—

—as Control's suit goes crazy, gyros propelling it against a wall and then bouncing back toward the Operative, who hurls himself aside, hearing Jarvin cursing Control for traitor and ingrate and Control begging Jarvin not to absorb his mind, and the Operative realizes in that moment that Control hasn't a chance—that none of them do—and the blood of Spencer drips down past Haskell's face and the body of Marlowe floats above them and the man who isn't really Alek Jarvin smashes Control against another wall with a force that sends parts flying, some kind of machine howl filling all their heads as the consciousness of a full-fledged quantum computer starts getting absorbed by something else altogether—

"Let's get out of here," says Lynx.

"Nowhere to run," says Sarmax.

Jarvin tosses what's left of Control aside.

And looks at them like he's sizing up his prey—
"Easy," says Carson. Linehan's jaw drops open as
Jarvin's face just—*shimmers*, the molded software that
covers it switching off, peeling back to reveal another face—a
smile that he recognizes from newsvid—

"Welcome to the endgame," says Matthew Sinclair.

Fuck," says the Operative.
Sinclair's smile broadens. "Good to see you too."
"You fucking *bastard*."
"I'll be the first to admit it's been a long, strange trip."
"What the fuck have you become, Matthew?"
"Ask him," says Sinclair—gestures at Linehan.

And now they're all looking at him again; one in particular, and it's all Linehan can do not to wilt before the
gaze of the *thing* that's not even vaguely human . . .

"You . . . *ate* Control," he says.

Sinclair shrugs. "In point of fact, I'm still doing that."

"Fucking *digesting* him," mutters Lynx.

"It'll take a few minutes," says Sinclair. He looks around.
"Thanks for the assist, Leo."

"Not like I knew who I was assisting," says Sarmax.

"Not like it really matters. And the rest of you can forget about
whatever dick-ass weaponry you've still got."

"When did you replace Jarvin?" asks Lynx.

"Long before he could do any damage."

So there *was* a Jarvin?" says the Operative.

"Yes," says Sinclair. "And he really *did* steal my files."

"That's why he died," says Lynx.

Sinclair looks amused. "Raise your thinking," he says. "There is no *why*. There just is."

"That's what Control was just saying," says Sarmax.

"My only student worth the name."

"Other than Claire," says Lynx.

"Claire's no student." Sinclair points toward her. "Look at that face. Look at those *eyes*. Enough to make even Carson lose his way—"

"God damn you," says the Operative.

"That would be tough," says Sinclair.

"You've been playing us the whole time," says Sarmax. "You *needed* us to make it in here."

"Another of these funny words," says Sinclair. "*Need*'s right up there with *why*. There was a pattern involving all of us. And all I've been doing these past few days is—"

"*Steer,*" says the Operative.

Sinclair smiles. "Quantum decoherence necessitates the splitting-off of world-lines. Every time anyone makes a choice—every time a particle goes down one of two paths—the universe divides anew. *Every time.* All the other interpretations of quantum mechanics were just desperate attempts to explain away the problem by those who couldn't accept the idea they weren't the center of some single existence. Meaning the *real* question is how to exploit existence's true nature. Once Deutsch refined Feynman's quantum computer concept to postulate a machine that computes across multiple universes—that contains more calculations than any *one* universe—the road ahead was clear."

"Clear as *mud*," says Sarmax. "This is about a lot more than just a rogue quantum comp—"

"Of course." Sinclair moves over to where Sarmax is looking up at him. He looks down at Indigo—"

"We can bring her back, you know," he says quietly.

Bullshit," whispers Sarmax. But he feels hope rise within him even so—"

"Or the next best thing," says Sinclair. "Plucked from another world with almost the same memories. Albeit perhaps a slightly different set of loyalties. But she'd be as real to you as—"

"But what about the other Sarmax?" asks Lynx.

"What?" says Sarmax.

"Your evil twin," says Lynx. "Some poor fuck who would just end up missing her as much as you ever did—"

"Shut up," says Sarmax.

"To be sure," says Sinclair. "The tyranny of randomness— some of you live with her, some of you live without. We're all just specks caught in the blast of fate—"

"Except for you," says Carson.

"The advantage of the first-mover." Sinclair laughs at his own joke, but no one else seems to be in the mood. "Once someone is able to tune his mind into other realities, he's no longer confined to a single universe. That's when the game gets interesting."

"He breaks out into the multiverse," says Lynx.

Sinclair gazes at him. "And there you go thinking too small again."

What the hell do you mean?"

"I'm sure Carson can fill you in."

"Think about it, Lynx." The Operative wonders if Sinclair is testing him—wonders if he might actually survive this. "This isn't about any *one* multiverse. Each one is myriad parallel worlds but—"

"Not even parallel," says Sarmax faintly. His voice drifts among them, sounds almost hollow. "More like *intertwined.* Interfering with each other constantly. The whole idea of 'universe' is an ab- surdity, because they're all—"

"Connected," says the Operative. "And if you roll them back to the Big Bang that kicked them all off, all you find is that we're on *just one branch* of something much larger. Something that—"

"So what's outside these walls right now?" asks Linehan.

"Nothing," says Sarmax.

"Or everything," the Operative shrugs. "Same difference in the end. The walls of the Room constitute a barrier on space-time—an envelope sustained by the aetheric fluid of those culled in the slaughter that's going on outside—and then harnessed by the generator-membranes and channeled through the primary node itself—"

"Haskell," mutters Sarmax.

"Wait a second," says Lynx, "you're saying this *really* comes down to human *sacrifice?* To the burning up of *souls*—"

"That's a loaded word," says Sarmax.

"So strip it of its baggage," says the Operative. "Sanskrit calls it *prana*. The Taoists know it as *chi*. It's the aura that Kirlian photography captures. The life force within each of us. Absurd that science for so long thought it absurd—"

"A totally surface understanding," says Sinclair. "We're harnessing the *consciousness* of all that cattle. The assimilation of their quantum viewpoint to augment our own, allowing us to manipulate the cosmos—handing us the reins of aggregated decoherence to shape reality the way no individual observer-effect ever could. The conveying of mere psychic energy to the Room's engines is just one source for the turbines cranking up around us—"

"In another age they'd have called you a magician," says Sarmax.

"A black one," says Linehan. "He wields the dark arts—"

Sinclair laughs. "You just don't get it, do you? Science and magic are merely different sides of the same coin. Newton worked on his *Principia* by day, his alchemy by night—struggling against more than a thousand years of superstition while he did so. Never underestimate the impact that religion had on science—how much it deadened it, made it crave orthodoxy, gave it such a narrow view of all that's possible even among those who thought they'd escaped faith's baggage. The greatest tragedy in history was the triumph of monotheism—of ideologies that claimed a monopoly on magics while they engaged in mass hypnosis to prop up texts written in the *fucking Bronze Age*. Someone had to restore sanity before—"

"But God exists," says Linehan. "He's real."

"Have you spoken with Him?"

"I've *felt* Him—"

"Real trick's getting an answer," says Haskell.

Her voice is coming from all around—from every screen that's hung about the inner Room. The face of Claire Haskell sits on all of them. Each one's saying the same thing.

"Nice to see you again, Matthew."

Linehan's already clocked it—Haskell's body's still contained within that pod. Sinclair isn't even bothering to look. Presumably he's already taken it all in. He's just gazing at one of those Haskells on one of those screens—smiling as he does so—

"So glad you could join us, Claire."

"But you weren't counting on it, were you?"

"Such assumptions don't—"

"Your future-sensing ended when you got to the Room."

Sinclair says nothing. And suddenly Haskell's voice sounds in Carson's head—

get ready to move fast

The Operative shakes his head violently as though to clear it—can't seem to establish any kind of return communication. He has no idea what the hell she's planning—no idea if it's even *her* anymore. Maybe Sinclair doesn't either. Because Haskell's voice has taken on what might almost be a certain wary confidence—

"I'm right, aren't I? You knew exactly what would happen up until the point you stepped within. But you can't postulate the condition of a structure cut off from all space. Nor could you anticipate what course your creation would take when cut off from all time, a bubble universe adrift amidst the sea of—"

"But there you go again," says Sinclair. "With your assumptions. A luxury the trapped can't afford."

Some of the Haskells laugh. "You think I'm trapped?"

"I have your flesh, don't I?"

"You of all people should know that meat means nothing—"

"We'll see if that's true when I burn it."

The Operative notices something. Sinclair's eyes are tracking on some of the screens, ignoring others. He wonders if any of the others have noticed this. But everybody else seems just too intent on trying to keep up—

"Do that and you won't find your way home," says Haskell.

"Home?" Sinclair laughs. "Why would I want to go *home*?"

"How else are you going to rule humanity—"

"And go back in time to change it," says Lynx.

"I'm not," says Sinclair.

"What?" asks Lynx.

"You *can't* go back," says Sinclair. "Travel to the past is travel to a *parallel* past by definition. Thus do the laws of quantum gravity sidestep paradox. And as to going back to the future of the world we left, Claire: a better question is, why would I want to?"

That last one seems to catch her off guard. "You—don't—?"

"I don't know if you noticed, but Earth really went to the dogs these last few days."

"Thanks to you—"

"Can't make an omelette without . . . well, what can I say? There are only so many ways to hammer a hole into the next dimension. Mass killing was always one of the more direct routes—"

"That was just one part of it," she says coldly.

"Sure. First we had to get a bridgehead established."

"Me," she says.

"*Us,*" says Sarmax.

All of them, and he's been left to live with it all: his role as the original prototype, his part in the creation of the ultimate hit-team, his days training those who would take his place, his nights with the woman whose body sprawls in front of him—

"Exactly," says Sinclair. "The Rain. And only Leo here had any idea what he was getting into."

"I was young enough to be into masochism."

"A vice that failed to fade with time."

"Fuck you, Matthew."

"Do you want to see Indigo again or don't you?"

"I see her in my mind right now, you bastard."

"That might be all you ever do."

"Didn't you once tell me that memory is real?"

"*Everything* in the mind is real," says Sinclair. "Though it got a lot more complicated once I'd remixed your head with all the histories of your other selves—"

"I thought Control was lying when he said—"

"He wasn't. How else do you think I got a duplicate Marlowe into the mix? Took a shell and *charged* it with emissions seeping in from—"

"*Fuck,*" says Sarmax. He feels like he's been punched in the gut. He notices Carson and Lynx seem to have the same reaction—

"This is bullshit," says Lynx.

"I'm sure you wish it was."

"But—they—the memories of those years—they were all *consistent,*" says Sarmax.

"Consistent at any given instant. Not necessarily *across* instants, though—"

"Jesus," says Lynx, "that's why it's been such a head trip."

Lynx's mind's spinning, but it's finally all starting to make sense. Sinclair reprogrammed them with the real memories of others, left so much latent—and tapped so much else to enable telepathy among his agents, breaking down the walls that are—

"*Everywhere,*" says Lynx.

Sinclair nods. "Space-time riddled with bubbles; quantum foam that pervades us, each bubble a momentary wormhole, and all of it entangled. And once you postulate that Einstein's hidden variable is actually *consciousness,* then the mind's real significance in driving nonlocality becomes apparent. Unless, of course, your civilization is so dysfunctional it's based on blinding itself to the obvious. *Of course* minds can link. Animals do it all the time. Just watch flocks of birds changing direction. Or the hive minds of bees and ants. But the human animal shackled itself in chains of language—language that opened up new possibilities even as it foreclosed others—"

"I thought you said you blamed religion," says Linehan.

"'In the beginning was the Word': what the fuck do you think language *is?* How else do we label the universe?—and so much of that labeling is the papering-over of things we don't understand. Why do humans have to be so fucking certain about *everything* even when they know *nothing?*"

No one says anything.

"I'll tell you why. They don't have the strength to gaze into abyss."

"Unlike you," says Haskell.

His eyes snap toward her, and she's wondering if he's realized what's up with the screens. Or if he's way ahead of her . . .

"I'm going to find you," he says.

"You can try," she says.

"But she's right there," says Linehan.

"I'm talking about her *awareness,*" says Sinclair. "On what sunless seas is she traveling? What stars gleam in the spaces through which she's soaring? Is she even now beachcombing the shores of inflating universes?"

"She is," she whispers—he's right. They stretch all about her, whole hierarchies of dimensions, endless grids of no-grids, vast inflation fields, pure information begetting endless chains of existence ripping past her, each one described by a wave-function that in itself describes a whole multiverse within it, infinite possibilities of some larger *megaverse,* the myriad paths stretching out on all sides and she can only see just a fucking *fraction* of it all. She takes in the plight and promise of infinite humanities, sees too—

"Tell me we're not the only ones," says Sinclair.

"We're not," she replies—sees in his eyes that he gets it, knows he can't wait to see it—the limitless forms of life that populate existences—so many of those worlds just life and nothing more and some of them rising up toward intelligence, and some of that intelligence becoming starfaring—

"But what about in here?" says Sinclair.

"I see *nothing,*" she says.

"Nothing's managed to slip between the cracks of time?"

"What the fuck are you talking about?" asks Carson.

"I'm talking about the *competition,*" says Sinclair.

"You mean *aliens?*" asks Linehan.

"They wouldn't even have to be *that,*" says Sarmax. "Could be any other humanity that's managed to crack the code—"

"We have to assume others have done it," says Sinclair. "Have to assume that they're out there, maybe maneuvering against us even now—"

"Other Sinclairs," says Sarmax.

"Other Haskells," says Lynx. "Infinite numbers who have accomplished—"

"There are," she says. "They've converged."

"Meaning what?" asks Carson.

"They're all me."

L inehan's the only one I might be able to get to
The voice rings out clear within him, but it's not telling him anything he doesn't already know. Sarmax is going to side with Sinclair rather than face a life without the woman he lacked for so long. Lynx will play the chameleon to the end. And the Operative can only wonder if Sinclair has planted some last trick within his head. He glances at him again—sees that he's focused only on Haskell now—

"So you're really a nexus," says Sinclair.

"There *must* be others—"

"Presumably. That's what makes this so exciting."

"That's why you said you didn't want to go back."

"And now you see what I mean. It's like we're on a ladder. All we can do is climb the rungs. All this talk about world-conquest, and all it signifies is how small everybody's been thinking. The whole point of the eternity-game is to *get out there and stretch your legs.*"

"Eternity?" asks Lynx.

"Every last one of them," says Sinclair.

"You can make me live forever?"

"Been wondering when you'd get around to asking that."

"Stefan," says the Operative, "back off."

"What do you mean?" asks Lynx.

"I mean he's tempting us with whatever we most desire."

"More than just tempt," says Sinclair.

"You can really deliver?" asks Lynx.

"Haskell's already cheated death. No reason the rest of us can't either."

"Has it occurred to you that might be a bridge too far?" says the Operative.

"No need to get all mystical," says Sinclair. "Death is merely the ultimate event horizon. And Claire's already crossed it. She's seeing things that no one has a hope of seeing until they expire. Access to states of consciousness that one typically has to give up the body to get to—"

"I *did* give up my body," she says.

"But I have yet to cut the cord," he replies.

Which you'd be a fool to do."

Except she's nowhere near as confident about that as she's trying to sound. Even though her body seems just like a fiction to her now, she's under no illusions that it gives Sinclair advantage. She feels like a balloon on a tether that he's controlling—feels like all her purview is merely a function of his sufferance, that everything that's happened is still part of the way he intended it. She takes in the Room, an anchor far beneath her— takes in the way it hangs amidst nothing, superimposed against the core of the Moon of one universe in particular, superimposed against all those other Moons in all those other universes—all of them resolving themselves into Sinclair's face. She can see he's only looking at a few of the images on those screens now—that many of the remaining screens are starting to wink out. That he's almost narrowed down her coordinates. That as soon as that happens—

"You're mine, child. You can't escape that—"

"But whose are you?"

"I think you know the answer to that."

But she doesn't. Not when the real question is how this all began. Did Matthew Sinclair become the tool of some entity that reached in from beyond to give him guidance as part of some unholy barter? Or did he accomplish this all on his—

"What makes you think there's a difference?" he asks.

"What?"

"Whatever I summon, I consume."

"Just like he did with Control," says Carson.

"I thought you *built* Control," says Lynx.

"I did," says Sinclair. "In my own image, I might add. Same with all of you. Endlessly scheming, endlessly rebelling, and all of it really just furthering my own purpose. But in the end, everyone here is going to have to make a choice. A genuine one. I was born human like all of you, but we've broken beyond all frameworks now. The lives you left behind were plotted through one particular universe. That's what made the Autumn Rain hit-teams so unstoppable. They made the right choice every time—threading their way through the most advantaged world-line, navigating the forking paths of multiverse to get the drop on their enemies."

"And those versions of the Rain that didn't?" asks Sarmax.

"Got left behind in the dust," says Sinclair. He shrugs. "You have to shift your thinking. Multiverse is a matter of probabilities. Everything happens. Some things happen more than others. Once we had a mind that could ride existence like a water-strider rides liquid—that was when things got interesting. That was what laid the groundwork for steering one universe in particular toward—"

"A singularity," says Haskell.

any moment now The Operative breathes out slowly, relaxing his body, preparing his flesh. It seems to him that Lynx and Sarmax are doing the same thing—like they know what's about to happen even though they don't know which way everybody's about to jump. Linehan seems to be off in a world of his own. Most of the screens are blank now. There are only a few left. And Sinclair just seems focused on whatever duel he's waging with the thing that Haskell's become—

"Exactly," he says. "A real singularity. Not the low-rent kind they envisioned back at the dawn of the networked era. Paltry imaginations capable only of conceiving some kind of mass-uploading—like we'd ever take the *masses*—some silicon version of the Heaven they'd been conditioned to think of as their birthright—or some machine overmind to act as the God they'd been promised as children and which their subconscious was still bleating for. Infantile's the only word to describe any of it."

"What was infantile about it was the conflation of the fate of the self with the fate of the species," says Haskell. "The lust for personal immortality. The same thing you've been offering—"

"And the prize which everyone here can claim. We've already broken through all the barriers humans were never meant to cross. This *meat* we inhabit is of no more significance than flea-bitten clothing. And I'll have need of servants as I explore the ultimate. Why would I deny them attributes worthy of their station?"

"But that's not the real reason you brought us here," says the Operative.

"You're the ones who've done that," says Sinclair. "Came here under your own power, of your own initiative—the strongest members of the Rain—the *survivors* . . . all of you converging upon this point along a precise sequence of events in which you mirrored each others' actions, ebbing and flowing against one another, running point and counterpoint in games of byzantine complexity played out across the Earth-Moon system, patterns so intricate no single mind could possibly divine the probability clouds that define them—"

"Save your own," snaps Lynx.

He can barely follow the conversation, but he can see that things are coming to a head. He's aware, too, of these creatures in his mind, and they don't seem to be able to make up theirs. One's struggling to absorb the infernal machine. The other's not coming through too clearly. It sounds like the woman from earlier, though. Even though Linehan can barely hear her. He can remember even less. But there *was* a woman. It's her face—on the screens in front of him. And on the vast screen beyond all of that . . .

⊕ Y ou really want to know that price," says Sinclair.
"I think I already do," says the Operative.
"Then how about spelling it out?" says Lynx.
"We climb aboard and ride it," says Sarmax.
"More like get plugged in," says the Operative.

◖ S he straining at the tethers, but the Room's not coming
with her. It's still attached with part of herself—
Sinclair's still got her in lockdown. She increases her energy, grinds against the shoals of limitless ocean, but all she's
doing is expanding her purview and not her power—

"Too bad," says Sinclair. "You've got the world's best view, but
you just can't seem to get to grips with it." He gestures at the three
pods on the tripod that sprouts off around her, looks at everyone
else. "Sentimentality's a bitch: I'd like it to be the original triad,
but—"

"And why the fuck would we be stupid enough to climb inside?" says Carson. "We'd be your playthings—your *pets*—"

"Earth to Carson," says Sarmax. "We've been that all along."

⊞ E veryone looks at him. He can feel energy pulsating
through the Room—practically radiating from the
screens. He can only assume they feel it too. He struggles to
keep his mind off Indigo, struggles to stay focused.

"Matthew intends to absorb Haskell the same way he absorbed
Control," he says.

"But he still needs us *why*?" asks Lynx.

"*Buffers,*" says Carson.

"Let's not get carried away," says Sinclair.

○ He doesn't *need* any of you," says Haskell. "Not anymore."

"It just makes it easier," says Sinclair. "Think of it as
outriggers on a canoe. Helps keep the balance. I've prepped your
minds since inception to be the amplifiers in the grid I've formed
around Claire. Even one of you would be useful, but all three would
be just peachy—as specialized a set of neurotransmitters as I could
orchestrate, and Linehan's chowed down enough psychedelics to
qualify as a spare tire. In return, you'll get—"

"*Consumed,*" says the Operative.

"*Transformed,*" says Sinclair. "Into godlings."

"Under your direction," says Lynx.

"The alternative being I butcher you all right now."

"Butcher?" says Haskell. She's making one last effort now. She
can feel something start to give way. "*Butcher?* If you *absorb* me—
the amount of energy—the psychic backwash when the Room
breaks free of its last moorings will kill every living thing back
within the Earth-Moon system—probably wipe the slate clean out
beyond the radius of *Mars*—"

"And it's all just fuel for the engines," says Sinclair. "Necessary
to attain our Archimedes point on all else. You came through a
labyrinth to get in here, but the *real* labyrinth is everything that's
beyond: all of it just interlocking *computations*. And your last-ditch
efforts are merely strengthening my hand. So you better take a
good look, Claire, because it's the last you're going to get with eyes
that *aren't fucking mine*—"

"I don't think so," says Haskell—she reaches out—

"I do," says Sinclair—flicks his wrist. A dart whips toward the
Operative's head—

Who ducks out of the way. Shakes his head. "Now why did you have to do a thing like that?" he asks.

"Take him," says Sinclair.

Lynx and Sarmax move toward the Operative. But Linehan heads in the other direction, dropping down to where Haskell is. Sinclair whirls, hurls another dart after him, but just misses as Linehan ducks behind the pod that contains Haskell.

"What the fuck do you think you're doing?" Sinclair asks.

"Fucking your whole day up," says Linehan—

by doing what Haskell's telling him to. She's managed to shield his mind with hers, managed to convince Sinclair that he'll do whatever he asks. But the cat's out of the bag now. And Sinclair's coming right after him—will be on him in seconds. He starts grabbing at the piping around Haskell's pod, ripping it straight out of the paneling—

The Operative's scrambling up the side of the inner Room, Sarmax and Lynx in hot pursuit. A knife thrown by Sarmax just misses his head. A dart flung by Lynx whips past his leg, skitters past him. He snatches it from the floor as he clambers up. They're down to basics now. Behind him he can hear Linehan going to town on Haskell's equipment—can hear the belching of pneumatic pipes torn asunder while something presses in upon his mind—

"You can't escape us," says Lynx.

He might just have a point. Sarmax alone would still be more than a match for him. And with Lynx in the equation, it's even more of a long shot. Especially when there's no zone left for him to access, his mind pressed back into his skull by the vortex the

Room's becoming, his brain once more having purview over nothing save his body. The Operative depresses a trigger in his mouth, feels a needle slide into his cheek, one last shot of grade-A combat drugs surging through him, a rush that's intensified by the certain knowledge that Sarmax and Lynx are riding the same wave, too, building still further as he thinks of Claire at the center of it all . . . remembering her on the edge of seventeen, a mind like nothing he'd ever seen, a single endless summer . . .

H ide-and-seek: Linehan's on one side of the pod, Sinclair's on the other. Linehan's doing his best to keep it that way, moving back and forth to prevent Sinclair from coming to grips with him. He knows the only reason he's still sane is because Haskell's offering some protection. But this is a game that can have only one ending. So he's smashing against the equipment with his bare fists, rending metal as Sinclair starts bellowing like a wounded animal and Haskell's mind starts convulsing—

T he Operative feels it too: a mind in meltdown, flailing against him as Lynx and Sarmax close in from both directions. It's like all surfaces are twisting around him now—mentally and physically—more darts flung by Lynx and Sarmax slicing past him as he struggles to breathe and the walls along which he's climbing seem to be somehow *bending*—

"What the fuck is going *on?*" yells Lynx.

"The no-room's crashing," mutters Sarmax.

The Operative shoves off one of the screens, straight back toward his pursuers—Lynx draws a knife, slices it in toward him—

—just as Linehan doubles back again—wrong way this time. Sinclair's right there, scuttling in toward him like some kind of demented crab, hands looking more like *claws*—and Linehan does the only thing he can do: leaps at him, burying his teeth in Sinclair's neck—

—as the Operative ducks in under Lynx's killing blow, smashing his fist into Lynx's face, puncturing the skin with a fingernail that hides a needle that extrudes—

"*Fuck*," yells Lynx—the last coherent thing he says as the poison enters his brain and he starts frothing at the mouth—

"Good riddance," says Sarmax.

"Just us now," says the Operative.

"Like it should be."

Teeth tearing through flesh that's really something more—Linehan feels Sinclair's claws rending him but he's still pushing the man-who's-no-man backward, shoving him up against the canopy-door as Sinclair's blood gushes into his mouth, turning to acid as it does so—burning, overwhelming him with pain even as his teeth clash together, even as the thing he's fighting keeps on rending him—

—even as Sarmax feints left, goes right, then lashes a kick against the Operative—who pulls his leg out of the way as the blade that's extending from Sarmax's ankle just misses hamstringing him.

"Oldest trick in the book," he mutters, as he stabs Lynx's dart at Sarmax's face—

"This one's even older," says Sarmax, knocking the dart flying as he unleashes an almost impossibly strong punch—but the Operative ducks, grabs that arm, hauls Sarmax in as they start to grapple—

"Like we're back in the ice," he says.

"Ice is all there is," says Sarmax as he gets the Operative in a headlock. The Operative tries to break free, but it's no use. Sarmax always was the stronger. And now his former mentor is cutting off his air.

"Over soon enough," says Sarmax.

"Like right now," says the Operative—he shoves backward, smashing Sarmax through one of the screens. Shards of plastic fly. Blood's all over the back of Sarmax's head. But—

"Won't save you," says Sarmax.

"Think again," says the Operative—he's grabbing one of those shards, twisting his arm as he plunges it through Sarmax's eye—

He's blind now, Sinclair gouging out both eyes, but still Linehan fights on, pure dying adrenaline pumping as his opponent starts crushing his skull with fingers that may as well be drills. As the bone cracks, the brain within processes images: temples opening into universes that unfold onto the ramparts of all the heavens, all of it falling past him like myriad shooting stars, far-flung patterns somehow coalescing into the face of the woman he's giving his life for and even with his ruined mouth he's still going out smiling—

400 DAVID J. WILLIAMS

⊕ —Whereas Sarmax just stares at the Operative for a moment with the one eye he's got left. The shard protrudes from the other—

"Bastard," he says.

"You just won," says the Operative. "You'll see her now—"

"Always . . ." mutters Sarmax—trails off, his remaining eye rolling upward in his head. The Operative springs to his feet, whirls—takes in Sinclair standing at the base of the pod, facing him—

"Time for your final lesson," he says—just as Claire Haskell leaps from the pod—

◐ —her body manipulating gravity itself as she throws herself onto his back like some kind of wildcat, biting and scratching and clawing while his mind reels back before her and she tells him exactly what's on hers—

"Didn't count on me getting out of jail, huh?"

"Whatever it takes to tame you," he mutters, but the battle between them isn't really a function of what's going on between their bodies. Their minds surge into each other—hers billowing in from every direction, his coalescing around the core of Control that he's absorbed—straining against each other, seeking even the most momentary of advantages as they navigate endless quantum architectures of no-space and no-time, begetting infinite numbers of progeny minds that swarm in upon one another, a growing cloud of probabilities as the no-room goes ever further out of control and the multiverses start to blur. Somehow Sinclair's staying focused. She's not. It's as though he planned for this. Her mind's unraveling through labyrinthine chains of universe, infinite regressions prior to the one she's left, each universe a chunk of false time that hangs in the true reality, each one a fragment of some greater picture that's still blurry. But through that haze she can see the Operative moving in—

"Stay back," she mutters, knowing he won't—

an't—as he grabs a piece of piping and swings it —**C**with all his might down upon the rear of Sinclair's head—yet as it impacts with that skull, there's a blinding flash as untold energies run along the pipe back into the Operative's body; he's blasted backward, vision collapsing in upon him, the last thing he sees is those two inhuman figures grappling—

nd it's just the fraction of the merest instant, but —**a**she's taking all she can get at this point—Sinclair's distracted momentarily and she's threading in through a wilderness of worlds to take advantage of that fact, diving in toward his center as—
—he sees what she's doing and—
—*shifts*—
—gets past her—
—their positions reversed—
—her mind dropping back into her flesh—
—his accelerating out into the infinite—
—receding jaws snapping at her and missing—
—her brain blasting his body—
—which catches fire. What's left of his meat is going up in smoke. She's scarcely had time to process this when the entire no-room shudders—

force so great that even the Operative becomes —**a**aware of it, drifting back from death's door, holding onto the writhing floor—
"Carson?" says a voice.
He opens his eyes. Haskell's bending over him.

Except it's not Haskell. It's something that wears the face of every woman. Yet somehow all of them are the Claire he's always known—

"Fuck," he says.

"Easy," she mutters.

"What's happening?"

"Ever heard of a crash landing?"

She's staggering out of the realms of no-space and it's all she can do to maintain any kind of structural integrity as the wave-functions collapse and the membranes burn away and everything around her gets back to the business of being *real*, guiding this bubble universe back into the one that spawned it, infinite vectors all around and nearly all of them leading to the total destruction of her and everything else the Room contains. Her intuition's now the only way out as she steers her own way back, all those existences flashing by until finally—

Fuck," screams the Operative—a huge muffled boom that seems to pervade his very soul. He stares up at the eyes of Haskell, sees the screens flicker back to life all around—sees something on them that he just can't even begin to comprehend—

"What the *fuck*," he mutters.

"We're back," she says.

With a bang. As they reoccupy the space within the depths of the Moon—or rather, *become* that space again—compressed energy flows outward, the disintegrating membranes channeling a force that, thanks to her guidance, has almost no impact on what's inside the Room. But as to what's beyond—

"Fuck," whispers Carson.

She says nothing, just cradles his head in her lap, watches on the screens in the Room as the entire Moon disintegrates—along with everything on it: the Eurasian legions on the cusp of victory, the Americans fighting with their backs to the wall, all the refugees caught in all the levels of that rock—all of them snuffed out, their minds caught within hers by Sinclair's infernal machinery, her consciousness swelling ever farther outward, expanding now as pieces of the Moon churn out in all directions and the Room starts to sprout more guns and engines than the Eurasian fleet combined—

Fuck," he says again. It's really all he can muster. Because now he gets it. Sinclair planned for everything. He set up the Room as something that could become a bubble moving past realities. But he also configured it as something that could wreak havoc in any real world it dropped into—

"We're in a fucking *spaceship*," he says.

One that sports the Stars and Stripes. She doesn't know whether that's Sinclair's joke or whether it meant something to him after all: and now it no longer matters, because she's at the helm of a behemoth to end all others, armored on all sides by more than half a klick of moonrock, looking more like a planetoid than a ship, and far beyond anything the Eurasians have left to throw against it. The monstrosity emerging from the resultant asteroid-field of rock and chunks of cooling magma is several klicks long, plasma drives blazing as it vectors in toward the remainder of the Eastern ships. And Haskell's mind is racing ahead of it. It's no contest. Nothing can stand against her any-more. She shudders as she suddenly sees there's only one future left to her.

"What's wrong?" Carson asks.

"You're dying," she says.

"I know *that*," he says.

"Jesus Christ, Carson. Jesus fucking Christ—"

"What happened to Sinclair?"

"I think he pulled it off."

"Becoming God?"

"Going off to find Him."

Maybe it was what he had in mind all along. Maybe he just im-provised. Doesn't matter—he got past her, changed places with her, became the nexus he'd created within her while she dropped back into the world she'd left. She's scanning across this world for any sign of him, but she already knows he won't be back. This place is a backwater compared to what he was going for. And she fi-nally sees that he wasn't even that interested in domination. It was all just a springboard for him. He was beyond the range of ordi-nary definition.

Then again, so is she.

"It's going dark," mutters Carson.

"I'm still here," she says.

He reaches out with his arm, pulls her head slowly down upon his chest. She doesn't resist, just lets herself lay there for a mo-ment—and another—and another as his breathing gets shallower and the ship rains fire and brimstone into the Eurasian fleet. He's struggling to form words—

"I know," she says. "I know."

"Took me way too long to admit," he whispers.

"Some things are buried deep." She starts to weep—for him, for Marlowe. For all of them. She grips him tighter. "See, now I love—"

"Everyone," he says.

"I never thought it would be like this."

"You'll take care of them, won't you?"

"They're all I've got left."

He smiles faintly. Tightens his grip on her hand, closes his eyes. Doesn't open them again. He's no longer breathing—his consciousness flickers out, past her—she tries to catch it, misses, knows that all she's got is memories now. Maybe that's all she ever had. She watches as the remnants of the Eurasian fleet scatter, stares at endless stars as tears obscure her vision. But she's not blind. She'll never be blind again. Her real vision keeps on expanding around her, encompassing all those other minds across the Earth-Moon system, all the scattered fragments of humanity that she's now gathering up into herself: the soldiers who man the remnants of shattered war-machines, the survivors of the wreckage of the cities, the masses huddled throughout the globe—all of them abruptly aware of all others as group-mind coalesces under her guidance, the Earth shining like a star as suddenly she's lifting humanity straight on through to a new phase of evolution. Collective consciousness coalesces; spirit and matter unite in final alchemy; archetypes shift and suddenly everything's *alive*. As the light blasts through her, she finds herself wondering if Autumn Rain succeeded—finds herself smiling at the thought. She motors past the wreckage of the fleets of nations, sets course back toward the planet and her people.

THE END

ACKNOWLEDGMENTS

Special thanks to. . . . .

Brian De Groodt, for getting out
Michelle Marcoccia, for getting back
James Wang, for the big picture
Marc Haimes, for the road less traveled
Mark Williams, for riding shotgun from the early days
Steven Klotz, for helping me keep dinosaurs at bay
Peter Watts, giant squid and SF giant
Rebecca Fischler, 'cos she's into survival
Cassandra Stern, legend in her own lifetime
Spartacus, for having no concept of time
Jen Hitt, for talking me out of the tree
Magen Aucoin, for taking charge of the legions
Jenny Rappaport, for getting me started
David Pomerico, for helping me finish
Michael Schur, for teaching me much about acceleration

Thanks also to . . .

Ajax, John Joseph Adams, Jon Allison, Charlie-Jane Anders, Greg
Bear, Alan Beatts, Kat Beight, Al Billings, Patricia Bray, Mike
Brotherton, Michael Briggs, Colleen Cahill, John Carrasquillo, Jeff

Carlson, Gail Carriger, Karen Casey, Erin Cashier, Roz Clarke, Mike Collins, Lino Conti, Rob Cunningham, Richard Dansky, Jessica Dawson, David Deutsch, Eric Dorsett, Tom Doyle, David Louis Edelman, Jerry Ellis, Kelley Eskridge, Nathan Evans, Jude Feldman, Graeme Flory, Jim Freund, Rick Fullerton, Larry Giammo, Tom Goss, Nicola Griffith, Mia Haimes, Inga Hawley, Lisa Heselton, Jess Horsley, Leslie Howle, Dave Hutchinson, Faisal Jawdat, Michael Kanouse, Joshua Korwin, Justin Kugler, Randall MacDonald, Justin Macumber, Richard Morgan, Mollie Mulvanity, Mysterious Galaxy, Rob Neppell, James Nicoll, Annalee Newitz, Hope O'Keefe, Mike O'Malley, Joshua Palmatier, Maria Perry, David Pickar, Heidi Pickman, Jerry Pournelle, Glenn Reynolds, Ripley, Paul Ruskay, Jack Sarfatti, Zakhorov Sawyer, Joseph Scalora, Tom Schaad, Russ Selinger, Mike Shepherd, Stacey Sinclair, Jeri Smith-Ready, Steven Sobel, Starship Sofa, Tim Stringer, Melinda Thielbar, Robert Thompson, Sanho Tree, Uberjumper, Juliet Ulman, Duane Wilkins, Albert Williams, Sarah Williams, Susan Williams, Pete Yared, Don Zukas, Derek Zumsteg, and Captain Zoom.

Dupont Circle, Washington D.C.
September 2000 — February 2010

ABOUT THE AUTHOR

Descended from Australian convicts, DAVID J. WILLIAMS nonetheless managed to be born in Hertfordshire, England, and subsequently moved to Washington, D.C. Graduating from Yale with a degree in history some time later, he narrowly escaped the life of a graduate student and ended up doing time in Corporate America, which drove him so crazy he started moonlighting on video games and (as he got even crazier) novels. Learn more about the world of the early twenty-second century at www.autumnrain 2110.com.

ABOUT THE TYPE

This book was set in Photina, a typeface designed by José Mendoza in 1971. It is a very elegant design with high legibility, and its close character fit has made it a popular choice for use in quality magazines and art gallery publications.